Law

1a

THE LAMENT OF
THE LINNET

Anna Maria Ortese

THE LAMENT
OF THE LINNET

*Translated from the Italian
by Patrick Creagh*

THE HARVILL PRESS
LONDON

First published in Italy with the title *Il Cardillo Addolorato*
by Adelphi, Milan, 1993

First published in Great Britain in 1997
by The Harvill Press
84 Thornhill Road
London N1 1RD

1 3 5 7 9 8 6 4 2

A CIP catalogue record for this book
is available from the British Library

This work was translated with the financial support
of the European Commission

ISBN 1 86046 206 5

Designed and typeset in Fournier at
Libanus Press, Marlborough, Wiltshire

Printed and bound in Great Britain by Butler & Tanner Ltd
at Selwood Printing, Burgess Hill

CONTENTS

I

Joyous Excursion of Bellerophon and his Friends to the Sun

II

Brief Tale of Baba (La Joie)

III

The Second Proposal of Marriage

IV

The Sad Tale of Sasà (The Paummella)

V

Prince and Elf

VI

The Dead

VII

Mutter Helma

THE LAMENT OF
THE LINNET

I

Joyous Excursion of Bellerophon and his Friends to the Sun

The three friends

Towards the end of the eighteenth century, or Age of Enlightenment, three young gentlemen, the Prince de Neville, the sculptor Dupré, and the wealthy merchant Nodier, all of them citizens of Liège, where they were universally known and esteemed, one for his wit, another for his elegance, and all three for the fashionable and exceedingly costly way of life they led, resolved to undertake a journey to Naples, for a reason which could scarcely be taxed as reprehensible. Alphonse Nodier intended to stock his chain of luxury haberdashers with gloves purchased abroad, and there was at that time no city which produced such fine gloves, and enjoyed such fame for it, as did Naples; and in Naples there was no manufacturer of this sort of accessories to equal Don Mariano Civile, *Monsieur* Civile, as he was affectionately dubbed by Nodier. Half the world over he was adjudged to be the king of glovers. His late father, connected (it was said) with the Court, had in his time supplied gloves to both London and Paris – as was asserted, with a touch of gratification perhaps superfluous, by Alphonse Nodier. In reality Don Mariano, whom Nodier had met fleetingly a few years earlier during a trip to Rome, was of interest to him principally as a man, partly on account of his extraordinary character, grave and taciturn; of his dedication to his work, and, moreover, the splendid results of the latter; but above all because he had, in his heyday, married one of his father's employees, a certain Brigitta Helm, of obscure birth but famed for her beauty, who had borne him twelve children, many of whom were already abroad in the world manufacturing gloves or trading in hides; and all, it was said, of imposing stature, with blond hair and blue eyes, and by nature aloof and taciturn. At home, in the "divine" neighbourhood of Santa Lucia, Nodier was of the opinion that there remained only two or three daughters, equally tall, unbending, beautiful, and insufferably *silent*.

Yes, it was this *silence* of the girls, as of their mother before them, to judge by a few hints dropped by Don Mariano, himself a man to be reckoned with in point of holding his tongue: it was this *silence*, or inability to express, even in the simplest terms, their own girlish sentiments, assuming they had any, that spellbound (I use the word advisedly) rather than interested the scatter-brained Nodier whenever he thought of those haughty and alluring sisters. For a talker – and he was a talker born – it was something he could not accept.

As for de Neville and Dupré, they were merely amused – and de Neville not a little disdainful – at hearing these tales of humdrum domestic virtues, then much in vogue. It was for quite other reasons that they fell in with this proposal for a journey to Naples. De Neville, being a poet in his way, though little known as such, had hopes that by wandering those mythical regions formerly visited and lauded by illustrious travellers, he might refresh that poetic vein which the years (the prince was approaching thirty, in that epoch the threshold of drear maturity) and the excesses permitted, if not justified, by wealth and youth, had sapped and rendered querulous. He was, besides, intrigued by the reputation for opulence and fast living enjoyed by Naples – now reinstated as capital of a kingdom – as also by its dark and sanguinary past; and furthermore by those vague, remote, engaging tales of Sybils, of Sirens, of females communing with the Lower Regions . . . Such, at least, were the daydreams of the decadent de Neville, not a man of real virtue, and though already ageing still endowed with extraordinary attractiveness; for the tawny hair, the eyes of a deep green, slightly deep-set, the whiteness of his skin, the magnificent brow and tall, elegant presence inherited, it was said, from his mother, one Leopoldine of Brabant, together with his lofty and supercilious mode of address, had not yet deteriorated. But perhaps we have erred in calling him not a man of real virtue, for de Neville was capable of being purely and simply vindictive. For the rest, his feelings were much like those of a host of men: the ever-deluded dream of a woman who would satisfy his *genius* – we dare not say his *taste* – and the need to travel to forget, or to stupefy, a certain void of which, to tell the truth, he was not yet to any great extent aware.

For Albert Dupré (Albert was the artist's first name, though nothing to do with the French sculptor, our young man's talents being limited, so that his reputation never extended beyond the end of the century or the borders of his homeland) this trip was simply a question of merriment and living it up. He was possessed of beauty, a thing which to our ears, in view of the way we have been schooled to reckon beauty, could well mean nothing. But a rare and indefinable quality of spirit, namely *ardour*, enlarged and amplified it, rendering that youthful visage similar now to a sun, now to a moonlit night; while at almost every moment he radiated the light and the bedrowsing sweetness of an Ionian seashore in the month of May. He could also be likened to woodlands in April, when the snows are melting and the birch-tree boughs hang down like slender arms, silvery girl-child arms. (For good reason we have employed these rhetorical expressions; for without rhetoric nothing serious and truthful can be said, in the absence of that degree of *falsehood* which is the measure or mainstay of the truth. At least, this is our own opinion). Albert, in short, with his great blue eyes and long, wavy hair the colour of sunlight, his well-knit physique, a brow as pure as polished marble, the beauty of his features and the sad little smile that from time to time visited his rosy lips, as if to say *"but why . . . why all this"*, Albert was the glory of the sun chariot bearing those three young travellers, the very Bellerophon of the triad; and when that chariot set out, hoisted aloft by the fiery Pegasus of European Romanticism, to traverse a France no longer pullulating with Jacobins, and then the blue Alps, and joyfully to glide the azure length of Italy; and when lastly, having almost in a single bound surpassed the roseate blaze of the first Mediterranean dawn, it touched the lovely soil of Naples, we may suppose that numerous sea-nymphs (if we are to credit the classical recollections of de Neville), and various denizens of the springtime air, emerged from behind the rocks, or opened the green doors of hovels bordering the crystalline sea near which rose the house of Don Mariano Civile, to spy on that arrival with laughing eyes . . .

For there, as everyone knew, lived Don Mariano; and in the colourful, innocent Fisherman's Village, all nets and fishing-boats, there stood, like a dream or an incongruity, the splendid Doric-columned palace which had seen the budding of his youth, his fame, his children, and the amazing wealth and affluence fabled in Naples and far beyond . . . All strictly verified? We shall soon see how much of the questionable, or adventitious, there was in the legend. For our own part, having rendered homage to the gilded and dream-rapt youth of Europe, and to the charms of Naples, we shall leave aside both rhetoric and literature. In Naples, as in all the world, wherever the authority of princes and of beautiful women reign supreme, and money trickles in rivulets from the palaces to be lost in the excrement of the streets (literally excrement, at least in those days, it being a time not of electrical conveyances but impetuous horse-drawn carriages, or clumsy carts also dragged by luckless beasts;

a time when flocks of sheep would scamper bleating across the elegant thoroughfares). In Naples rhetoric and Grub Street literature were entirely a question of fashion, they glittered in the vapid and coquettish ways of the great Ladies, they sparkled in the reception-rooms, in the opulent churches, in the naves of the Cathedral decked with purple and gold for a sombre and grandiose Novena. Rhetoric and Grub Street literature are but carved and gilded doors wrought by the artificers of dreams. But, once they are opened, nothing stirs but life, dark and cold, like a trickle of water at the foot of the doorsteps. You too, curious reader, as you follow this story, will see that they open onto nothing. And nothing will you hear, there below, but a pathetic *gurgle-gurgle*.

The Glover's daughter

The three travellers, aglow with a gaiety, an exhilaration, a pride justified by their youth, the occasion, and the means at the disposal of all (even if the artist was almost devoid of means, this was of no concern to him, shielded as he was by his own insouciance, as also by the munificence, as supreme as it was secret, of the prince, who was also his guardian and besotted over him), gave orders for the carriages, their own and that of their retinue, to draw up before the Hat of Gold, perhaps the best hostelry in the whole city, and of which Nodier, through an exchange of letters with his representatives, could vouch for the orderliness, cleanliness, and freedom from pickpockets. Jumping down from the depths of a blue coach, they could scarcely repress a cry of wonder and admiration at the harmonious ensemble of the scene which lay before them. An airy and tranquil piazza, bordered to their left by the light blue line of the sea and the four great towers of a mighty, dove-coloured castle. Upon that sea rested the last rays of the setting sun, as if languished by some amorous recollection. To the right a low hill, almost domestic so to speak, being so close at hand they could all but touch it, was covered with pale verdure and topped with a castle. Yet another castle, more weathered and ancient, rose opposite. And on the hill stood tall and slender pine-trees of a vivid green (today they are greyed by Progress), between them glimpses of a sky of the rarest azure; though all the clouds were pink. And here we call a halt. We cannot re-evoke the landscapes of the past, we might even say that God forbids it; for there is in them some remnant of an Eden vouchsafed to man but once: he cannot re-enter it. But in short, it was seven o'clock of a May evening, and there were roses in the air, the scent of roses, and plump garden roses here on terra firma. Nor was there any lack of flower-girls, very placid and beautiful.

The three friends were at once convinced they had arrived in a place of enchantment, and would perhaps have preferred not to make a stop at the Hostelry, had it not been that they were obliged to change their clothes, but to proceed at once to the Jib-Sail district to call on Monsieur Civile, who was expecting them between eight and ten o'clock some evening, if not that particular one, in his celebrated mansion near the seafront called, after the name of the quarter in which it stood, *Jib-Sail House*. They were soon ready, and a flower-bedecked equipage belonging to the Hostelry bore them to the rendezvous.

The master of the house, unattended by servants (at that hour certainly still awake, but the Glover was an unassuming man), was awaiting them at the top of a flight of fine marble steps, giving access to a vast, deserted entrance-hall. On every side were mirrors in gilded frames, gilded console table, French clock, lamps, Sèvres porcelain and Bohemian crystal; then further mirrors, silk-tasselled curtains, and tall, standing, flame-tipped chandeliers. Not one picture, however, or carpet, or book, so that the atmosphere of the place was cold.

Sedately, but with a benevolent smile, Don Mariano embraced Nodier, having an affectionate memory of his rosy features (Nodier was a fat, jolly soul), and bowed to the other two. He then led them into a drawing-room (a liveried servant had at last appeared, and ceremoniously opened the white doors embellished with pastoral scenes) where, after the usual enquiries as to health and the discomforts of the journey, he informed Nodier that his wife, who had been very ill for some time, was in the country, and that living with him were only his youngest daughters, Teresa, eleven years of age, and "dear Elmina", of sixteen; the other ten, young men and *demoiselles*, having been for some time out of the nest and plying their trade in the world. Sad to say, *le temps passe*, he murmured as if to himself, lowering his chin onto his chest with an air of dejection which caused Nodier a little shudder (the others were too taken up to notice it), and induced him to cast his eyes around with renewed wonderment at that house which was, thus devoid of youth, the clean contrary of what he had always imagined, and almost gave the impression of being uninhabited. At that very same moment the sound of a spinet was heard coming from the floor above, in a dainty and melancholy French air then in vogue, accompanying a young boy's voice, dulcet and blithe. "Elmina," said Don Mariano, with gratification. He added that he did not know if his daughters would come downstairs to meet the guests; for them the hour was already very late. Nevertheless, shortly afterwards, in the silence which had succeeded that distant music, and which seemed to immerse the house in a dreamlike calm, in they came. And the attention of the visitors was all for them.

In saying "attention" we are endeavouring to describe something both more and less than an abrupt resumption of interest, because in that instantaneous, lightning "attention", especially on the part of Dupré and de Neville, and especially towards Elmina, there was something which those gentlemen were unaware of, a sort of bewilderment of the very soul. The fact is, they held their breath.

Elmina's beauty was great indeed, and that of Teresa, though she was still a child, did not fall short of it. Despite their difference in age they were of almost the same stature; and we do not presume to say whether Elmina it was who, for courtesy's sake, had curbed her growth, or Teresa who in impatience for life had hastened hers on. Full-fledged figures, though lacking nothing in delicacy; stupendous arms snow-white from dimpled elbow to slender rosy fingers; their garments a matching pink, with camisoles of pink silk trimmed with ivory-coloured frills; lace collars, pale green or ivory, sustained the lovely blossoms of their faces, their delicate golden eyebrows and pupils also golden (though in Elmina, at certain moments, green), as cups still damp with dew will ever and anon harbour a rose. Both sisters wore their blond hair short and in tight curls, though gathered at the nape, in Elmina's case, with a brown satin bow and amber comb, in Teresa's with ribbons. Their brows were touched with perspiration, for the evening was warm; their smiles were in Teresa artless, in Elmina reserved and grave. Moreover, perhaps because she was the elder, in Elmina, who wore on her breast a gold cross surmounted by a small black bar, there was something further. A coldness, it seemed to de Neville, that might be overcome; to Dupré a distance, *an abyss* impossible to cross.

While he was gazing at her, as men are sometimes apt to gaze at a woman, with a touch of humility and despair that eludes even their own awareness, she went and sat down beside her father; and tender as was her smile, it was superficial, so that Dupré found himself thinking that her thoughts, behind that small and shapely brow, were far from the room, her father, her own self. He was sure of it. She loved no one; or not as loving is generally understood. She loved not even herself, albeit she was so gaily decked out and attired. She seemed to be nursing a secret. What this might be was the question which, as he watched her, gave a sober turn to the artist's thoughts.

But let us not forget the proprieties, and that we are in a splendid drawing-room in Naples, in the presence of strangers. The same servant, now more friendly, served them delicious refreshments; there were exchanges of compliments, news, information concerning art, and commerce, and society – though this last, out of sheer good manners, was barely touched on. They spoke of other countries, of travels, of theatres, of lofty personages or those more modest but of interest. Don Mariano twice named, as among his numerous acquaintance in Naples, a certain "Scribblerus", who must have been among these last, but whom he accounted "a good sort". They went on to speak of princes and of politics, and Elmina, the while, remained smiling and *silent* (a word that recurred obsessively in Dupré's memory, being the burden of what his merchant friend had told him); inwardly silent, as if she were not a young woman of great charms and sweetness, but a stone. And from this image of her, banal as it is, and so often to be met with in novels with regard to women of reserved demeanour, it came naturally to Dupré, so versed in statuary and ruins, to revisit in his mind the sacred places of Antiquity, those prodigies of melancholy glimpsed in the narratives of travellers returning from Egypt or Greece or Asia Minor; the dark stone ramps outstretched towards a cloudless sky, or those stone tablets of awesome height, like broad-bladed daggers of giants, piercing the cobalt aether as if to cleave it, and at the same time deep-rooted in the earth, or rather in the golden desert sands, as if seeking escape or destruction in their depths. Beneath those monuments, in deathly spirals of shadows, silent and secret, run dim-lit crypts and tunnels where the gold-clad mummies of Queens, of Priests, of Kings arise and walk; and where sublime and terrible mysteries are conserved. And he thought furthermore – for he now, on behalf of them all, was Pegasus himself, was indeed that bold Bellerophon – he thought that she, Elmina, was the triform Monster (goat, lion and eagle) that he must vanquish; that she was the wondrous Chimaera.

While these things, both ardent and melancholy, in the intervals between a hot chocolate served in a flowered Dutch cup and a gilded sweetmeat from a celebrated confectioner's, were passing through the mind of our handsome Dupré – whose blue satin dress-coat trimmed with silver, flaunted on his twenty-year-old person like the banner of night herself, attracted even the far-from-happy gaze of Don Mariano, and could hardly remain a matter of indifference to the two young ladies – the younger of the sisters, still, as we have said, a child, burst out laughing for no apparent reason; and, affectionately questioned by her father as to the cause of this mirth, gave no reply but to raise to her mouth, to silence it, one small hand. So she at least was not actually dumb. The cause of this laugh was shortly afterwards revealed to be one of those candid, irreverent and infantile thoughts that occasionally cross the minds of young girls, and make them burst out laughing so rudely as often to cause some embarrassment among those present. This was not here the case, the company being extremely courteous and well-disposed.

Signor Dupré, or rather "Monsieur Albert", she eventually told her father, with an ingenuousness that charmed by its very audacity, was "*come lu cardillo*"; that is, he made her altogether think of "their old *cardillo*".

"What," asked that dreamer eagerly, "is a *cardillo*?"

At which, with severity tempered by leniency, Elmina intervened, and placing her hand on the scatter-brained girl's impulsive head, pronounced the French name of the bird. And she added (who could not have believed her?) that their pet bird, a linnet, had died that very day. They had forgotten, both she and Teresa, to change its water and refurnish it with millet-seed for two whole days, and there it was: dead. They found it in the morning, belly upwards, near the wicket-gate, and immediately offered it to the gardener's cat, which however (solidarity between animals, they said) had refused it.

This last detail horrified Albert, and for several minutes he spoke not a word; while his friends, Nodier in particular, seemed to have heard nothing, and were laughing over some slur or other, unknown to us, cast on some Prussian general and reported by Monsieur de Neville.

Elmina had not failed to notice, though with apparent unconcern, the discomfiture of the youngest of the travellers at the sadness and cruelty of the episode. She therefore, by offering him a porcelain dish laden with fresh delicacies, from which Teresa did not scruple to grab a titbit in passing, found occasion to whisper to him with reference to what Teresa had said about the linnet, that Monsieur Albert resembled it, and as if taking it for granted that he was upset exclusively by the comparison between himself and the bird:

"She's always being silly. *Un rien l'amuse.* Be so good, Monsieur Dupré, as to excuse her. I assure you that she meant no offence by saying you were like the linnet. She's a good child at heart."

Albert, not thinking of himself in the least, but solely and with genuine distress of the bird, barely restrained his tears. At the same time he felt strangely consoled by her voice, in which he failed to perceive what de Neville, who had heard all, took to be amusement and connivance at an act of downright nastiness.

Albert therefore gave her a look of gratitude; but at that look Elmina, though remaining the soul of courtesy, did not in the least unfreeze, or even smile.

For the following day, as the evening drew to a close, they were all invited to dinner by Don Mariano. This dinner was at five in the afternoon, in accordance with the Neapolitan custom of the period. He begged them not to forget, and further urged them to be punctual, not least because (and here he smiled), "in this world nothing ever is."

The proposal of marriage

De Neville had conceived a sentiment of genuine hostility towards the elder of the sisters. There was in reality no justification, even colourable, for this; because Adelmine (the girl's name in German) had behaved towards the three guests neither more nor less politely than would have any other young lady of wealthy family, even if not particularly well educated (which Elmina was not), in Liège or Paris or London. She was a true daughter of a prosperous, and perhaps unpolished, merchant. A little music, a smattering of French but no more; manners short of the exquisite but not openly reproachable. And yet de Neville (Ingmar was his Christian name, but for some unknown reason he was slightly ashamed of it) felt the urge to reproach her. To attack her, would be an apter term for the far from refined nature of his animosity towards her; and the first of his reasons – if we may so call them – lay perhaps in a feeling of mild exasperation which the girl's unresponsive and clearly commonplace character – for such it appeared to him – produced upon the highly sensitive prince: a woman insufferably satisfied with herself and her little domestic realm; while the second was perhaps at the root of everything: his having discerned Albert's mingled *enthusiasm* and dejection throughout the evening to be a sure effect of her spell, and consequent power over his heart and mind. De Neville possessed strange powers of divination; he sensed things hidden; he had even been witness to *inexplicable* psychic events and phenomena chiefly consisting, unless checked by his better judgement, in his seeing (or simply understanding?) what was happening in the heart of another, or even in another room; and he had perceived that evening, with all the strength of his jealous devotion to his friend, that Albert, having entered serene and carefree into the glovemaker's house, was now leaving it disquieted and inwardly trembling with an emotion that he, de Neville, considered both strange and dangerous.

Of all this our merchant friend Nodier had noticed next to nothing.

Returning towards midnight to the Hat of Gold, followed at a short distance by their armed servants (the empty carriage was going on ahead, as they had chosen to walk); returning at that lonely hour, beneath a sky of velvety blue, such as they had never seen in all Europe, and embroidered with a filigree of golden stars, not only de Neville but also his friends were strangely immersed in thought; and hearing their voices, whenever they chanced to speak, resounding softly on the air, they imagined they heard all round them, like an echo, the haughty, self-satisfied snigger of the Glover's elder daughter (to the younger, the mere child, they naturally gave no thought). Until at a certain moment, realizing from their own silence that they all had one and the same person in mind, they came out with a laugh, albeit forced, in which Albert joined little, and with little warmth; so that Nodier, by far the simplest and best-natured of the three, all of a sudden enquired:

"Why so thoughtful, Albert? Did the lovely Miss Elmina not take your fancy?"

"On the contrary, very much indeed," returned the artist, touched by his attentiveness.

"But you are sad," persisted his friend. "Or else I cannot see you well by starlight."

"Yes, it is true," admitted the poor young man, with a look of gratitude, while his eyes glistened with some timorous impulse. "And I am sad – would you believe it? – on account of that business of the linnet."

"That and something else, I imagine," hazarded de Neville with an enigmatic little laugh, bouncing the tip of his exquisite walking-stick on the flagstones.

"Not all young ladies, it is true," added Nodier, "would have passed the matter off like that. However, it was not out of cruelty, but rather from indifference."

"Indifference! What sort of thing is *indifference*? Can one be *indifferent* to the suffering and death of a little creature of the air?" Dupré almost shouted. "And as for the rest of the story . . . !" (he was thinking of the cold body thrown into the yard, the rejected offer to one of the tabby kind). "No, I feel that these girls have not been properly brought up . . ."

"For what, though? Not 'properly' for what state and condition in life, if there is no place in it – you must excuse me, Albert! – for a little cruelty, for a certain willingness, in short, to see life as it really is?" Thus, with an uncharitable smile, the prince.

"Cruelty! You see life as cruelty! Ingmar, you must have gone mad!

Upon my soul the two of you seem to me mad this evening," cried the artist, on the verge of tears.

At this point it was perfectly clear that Dupré's emotions, under the impact of the lovely Elmina, had reached such a pitch of intensity that everything, even a trifling incident, if you wish, such as the death of the linnet; everything, I say, if ascribed to *her*, was therefore a pointer to, almost a proof of, her moral being (or its opposite), and became a Truth, a sworn statement, a solemn, unforgettable testimony of the soul.

"Poor young thing! At her age one speaks without thinking most of the time. You ought to know that," was what the merchant found to say, shaken by such evident distress, but careful at the same time to safeguard the reputation of the family he thought of as his friends. "It's a naïve time of life . . . simple . . . very simple."

"But *not her*! She oughtn't to be, not with that face. With those piteous eyes! Yes, those golden eyes of hers express – didn't you notice it? – an infinite compassion, I'd say almost majestic!"

They had now reached the hotel. The three friends said nothing further, but hurried up to their rooms. Here only the artist, after sitting for some time, as in a dream, at a mahogany table on which was the wherewithal for writing (and having, it seems, indeed written something), went to bed; which is to say he lay down fully dressed on it and, owing to his mental prostration, fell asleep at once.

Not so the other two. Both Nodier and de Neville remained a long time awake, each on the white wrought-iron balcony of his own room – deep, silent balconies separated by a massive column in the façade of the building, which concealed the two friends from one another, so that although very close they could neither see each other nor converse, but were severally immersed in a curious solitude. Nodier (at whose sentiments we will glance for a moment) was sufficiently contented, thinking of the people he was going to meet on the morrow, and also of the Glover's magnificent house, which he compared with houses in Liège and Brussels, and which had on him, all in all, the same effect as a church; for with its mirrors, knick-knacks and gilded clocks, its vast profusion of marbles, its tall windows, the two girls, and the enchanted stillness of that dwelling at ten o'clock at night, it all seemed to him divine. He was saddened only by the solitude in which Don Mariano now lived, his beloved wife being ill and absent.

And if his elder daughter were to marry? How would he then be able to manage?

As for de Neville, he was simply wondering what means he could employ to dissuade Albert Dupré from delivering on the morrow, to Monsieur Civile, the letter in which he implored him to vouchsafe Elmina's hand. An instant proposal of marriage had been written. There was no doubt of it. He, de Neville, without making the least effort to acquire the knowledge, as if the doors of the hearts and the rooms of those dear to him stood open before the eyes of his mind, as if he had never even left the artist at the white door of his room, had already seen what Albert had resolved and acted on in the pain and ardour of his dream. He, the mediumistic de Neville, now saw before him, superimposed upon the darkened seashore of Naples, Albert's open writing-desk. On its surface was a letter. And the letter, inscribed in large flowing characters, and left unsealed with the consummate liberality of youth (or of lovers), thus began:

> To the Most Excellent Don Mariano Civile
> Jib-Sail House, Naples
>
> Sir!
>
> At the mercy of a sentiment which I am unable to define, let alone describe, and which places me in your power, and in that of your most innocent Daughter – though it is mightier than any I have ever in my life experienced, even *la Gloire* itself . . . (and so on).

A little further down (the letter consisted of but a few shattering lines), appeared, as in a cloud of tears, the name of Elmina.

"He," thought de Neville who, having run his eye over those first lines (the rest were unnecessary), went on to perceive, somewhat further away, Albert himself stretched on the white bed, still fully dressed in his midnight-blue suit, his superb blond locks afloat above a faintly sweat-moistened brow, tranquil as a dead hero; "he, Bellerophon, knows not that he has come, be he never so beloved of the Gods, above all in grace and innocence, to the place where vengeance has awaited him all the days of his life; and I did not foresee it. Oh, to save him! Is it still possible to save him?"

At that point, from a nearby tavern, came the din of a scuffle between pickpockets and armed constables; which did not, however, distract him.

"Take heart, Ingmar," he admonished himself, having cast a last glance at a glimmer that filtered, between column and wall, from the neighbouring balcony, a sign that Nodier also was wakeful, "take heart! There is perhaps another way to save him from this desperate fate. You will tell Don Mariano, early tomorrow, that Albert possesses nothing in his own right, nothing that he can add to the fortune of his wife. You will not hesitate, though you ought to be ashamed of it, to confess that you have always maintained him yourself, in secret, for reasons of poetic zeal, and that the young god does not know this. It's an abomination, but strictly necessary."

This abomination, unfortunately (or fortunately, with regard to setting the prince's conscience at rest), corresponded precisely to the truth.

Ever since his birth, in which he had lost his mother (and immediately afterwards, in a duel, his father, an impoverished and unimportant baron), Albert, in blessed unawareness of his poverty, had been the protégé of the prince's family, and subsequently of the heir, Monsieur de Neville himself.

Thus relieved of anxiety, even our noble friend went to sleep; and towards dawn, and thereafter during the splendid sunrise, which in those parts, nearly two centuries ago, was exceedingly pure and silent, not one of the foreign guests was yet awake. They slumbered serenely in their spacious chambers with white plasterwork, and cherubs, and pink-striped curtains at the windows, while the landlord below was already preparing great jugfuls of coffee and mountains of rosy brioches dripping with honey, and the upstairs servants, emerging like gnomes from all directions, were busy outside the doorways with immense red brushes, polishing a great number of indolent, elegant boots, in readiness to be once again donned and admired.

The proposal purloined to save Dupré.
The false apparition

Bellerophon awoke suddenly from a wondrous dream. Elmina was in his arms, her face suffused with ineffable emotion and wifely humility. Tears as expressive as love-letters entendered her golden eyes, the promise of a radiant future. Behind her stood waiting the child Teresa, holding a wickerwork birdcage. In the cage was a bird, the linnet that had died the previous day. Alive it was, risen from the dead, and lo! the cruelty of life – that alone was a dream. Putting her beautiful face to the cage, while her glad eyes shot glances at the two lovers, Teresa pursed her lips in a kiss and the linnet hopped cheerily towards her.

"It's alive! The cruelty isn't true! Death is a liar and Elmina loves me!" cried the artist in a rapture of joy. And he saw, beyond the cage, a great red light. It was the rising sun! And indeed the sun, rising at that moment, and streaming in at the windows flung wide towards the sea, awakened him.

Albert, as he woke with as much joy in his heart as in his dream, gave a cheerful glance at the letter lying open on the table, it too illuminated by the first rays of the sun. He decided to deliver it to the Glovemaker's house at once, without even rereading it.

In almost no time he had changed his clothes and was ready to leave; and, having requested a saddle-horse (from the hostelry to the Glover's mansion was but a step, but he intended to prolong his excursion), he set out. As in a dream he traversed a fair part of a strange town, rich and poor at once with dawn-pale colours and, at least at that hour, without a sound. Or, more precisely, sleeping. All things around and within him were a dream; all things were sleeping, and as they slept they laughed . . . But was it only laughter? He reached the mansion, crossed a spacious fore-court leading to an inner courtyard, divided from the first by a low gateway. Beside it was the porter's lodge. He dismounted and called out. A very old man, still only half dressed, came out to meet him. Albert handed him the letter (*"Pour Monsieur Civile, vite!"*), together with a gold coin which left the recipient open-mouthed. Then, back in the saddle, he galloped blissfully along the beach, to his left the broad, turquoise expanse of the sea, to his right a further vivid expanse of gardens, a marvel of sweet disorder . . . The name of that quarter was Chiaia, and it straggled off until almost lost at the foot of another gentle eminence, lovely in its patterned greens and greys, the name of which our lover did not know (he was later to learn that it was called Posillipo). From that spot, where he himself resembled a sunbeam, weightless and radiant as the beams themselves, the prince's ward, after pausing a moment to admire the scene (a pause such as occurs even in the greatest happiness, like a truce in a battle or swoon at the height of a rapture), and probably also recollecting his friends and the further joyous engagements that awaited him, turned back. He plunged once more amongst the unpretentious houses with pinky-yellow fronts, the modest villas either pink or white, standing like rows of children and immersed in violet-shadowed gardens under the gilded tufts of palm-trees. He strayed for a while through dark alleys and a paradise of lanes, once more traversed the "Riviera" flanked by smart shops now opening for the day, amidst the millings and bleatings and curious stares of flocks of sheep and goats driven by shepherds and milk-maids supplying the local families; with which bleating of sheep and cheery cries of shepherds there gradually mingled the voices of others, of fishmongers, greengrocers, florists, water-carriers – in a word, the full diapason of life in that easy-going, savage city tenebrous and beatific, famed throughout Europe for its gaiety, though astir at times with a sorrow as outlandish as it was senseless, and explicable (we can only imagine) by a political situation equally strange and precarious – it being the capital of a kingdom with no basis in rhyme or reason, lost in the realms of fantasy.

In a short while our wingèd youth drew rein at the Happy Hostelry, as we are fain to call it; and here, having kicked off his stirrups and handed the horse to a groom, he rushed headlong (there's no other word for it) into the lobby, impatient, like a child after a brief separation from its mother, to see the faces of his friends, who in his case represented that mother. But a surprise was in store for him. The two gentlemen, already fully dressed, and strangely silent, were awaiting him in the still deserted breakfast-room, their cups almost untouched before them. They regarded him with consternation.

"*Eh bien?*" queried the radiant youth.

They replied, heedless of his aura of joy and the yearning for more of it, that during his absence, which they supposed due to his wish for a salutary early ride (only de Neville, by avoiding his rapturous gaze, seemed to know the true motive), a message had arrived from Monsieur Civile. The invitation to dinner must be considered as postponed. In the course of the night Signora Brigitta's condition had much worsened, and her husband and daughters had hastened to a place called Casoria, where the unfortunate was being cared for by two aunts. From the tenor of the message Don Mariano in person had left at the Hostelry some hours earlier, when he was already in the carriage bound for Casoria, Nodier surmised that there were few hopes of the invalid being restored to the bosom of her family; the sudden aggravation of the malady aroused fears that only a few days, and perhaps even hours, remained to her. Signora Helm (called by this name even by her husband) was on her deathbed, maybe she had already breathed her last, and Don Mariano would, for the time being, certainly be unable to return to Naples.

"Ah! So this was the message I received! This was the joy foretold in my dream!" blurted out our sculptor, too upset to mind his tongue. And since his friends had heard, and were nonplussed, he at once recounted the dream he had had at dawn, omitting only Elmina and their embrace. The picture he drew of the linnet restored to life, the wickerwork bird-cage, and Teresa's delight as she attracted the little songster with a kiss, all this touched the other two, who after a pause went on to say:

"Yes, dreams sometimes play us false. They predict the opposite of what is going to happen. Real life is, luckily, more ordinary, and I venture to say . . ." (this from the good Nodier) "without these surprises of . . . what one might call the imagination."

They turned to a discussion of what was best to do. The first thing was to send a message to Don Mariano at Casoria (which was only a few miles out of Naples) assuring him of their sympathy for his adversities, as also the staunch devotion of his friends from Liège, who asked nothing better than to receive a command for some service or favour, to obey it forthwith.

This was done, and a messenger dispatched.

They then began to discuss the possibilities of joining their merchant friend in the whereabouts of his sufferings, Casoria, to follow the course of the illness in person and to repeat their offers of friendship, with a view to having some favour requested of them, as already somewhat pompously expressed in their message. They soon agreed that for this purpose one person only should be appointed, and that this could not be other than the oldest friend of the family, that is, Nodier. He might be accompanied, presumably, by de Neville.

"Why not Albert?" queried de Neville at once, not being too disposed to meet Elmina, who according to the message must already be with her father and Teresa beside the sickbed. However, seeing signs of distress come into Albert's face, and being almost certain of the rash act committed by the youngster, he swiftly resolved to help him out by offering to take his place as a visitor to Casoria. He would himself accompany Alphonse; he was ready and willing.

Albert gave him a look of infinite gratitude.

"It's done!" thought the prince. "He has taken the letter to Jib-Sail House. His proposal of marriage now waits only to be read by the widower on his return." And there instantly entered his mind an inspiration ideally calculated to relieve him of his anxieties. He would be the one to remain in Naples and, during the absence of his friends, and that of Don Mariano and his daughters from Jib-Sail House, would call at the latter on behalf of Dupré, and by giving some excuse would abstract the letter. The imprudent petition never having been received, silence would fall on the proposal which had inspired it, and with the mourning of the Civile family, and a prompt departure on their own part, there would be no ghost of a chance that Dupré would repeat his request for the hand of Elmina: a request he would certainly assume to have been refused.

At this point it was not difficult for the audacious de Neville to find some justification for his sudden second thoughts about his offer to stand in for Albert on the visit to Casoria. He was feeling a little tired; he was after all the eldest of the three, he said, and the least suited to console a family sorrow. Besides, he found Albert somewhat out of sorts, and (quite overlooking the grievous nature of the occasion) said he would be glad for him to enjoy some small diversion.

This change of programme upset Dupré. In it he discerned an excuse, the prince's antipathy towards Elmina. But for no reason on earth, so incapable was he of causing any annoyance, or refusing any favour, to the friend he adored as the best of brothers, would he have disputed any preference or desire of de Neville's. He obeyed without a word.

Thus, shortly afterwards, while his friends were galloping towards

Casoria, Ingmar (wishing to run no risk of detection) ordered a carriage to convey him to the mansion where, by hinting at a request from the sender, who wished to recopy the message, he had no difficulty in retrieving Albert's letter, still lying with others on a shelf, waiting to be collected by the servants with the rest of the day's post.

As he was starting back, gazing with curiosity around the vast, flower-filled courtyard which Albert had crossed before him, and was peering into the second court, onto which gave a number of internal windows and balconies, he espied, at a window near ground level in this inner court, a face watching him intently. He received a jolt. It was nothing less that the face, alert and set, of Elmina. He had the feeling that the girl, with a slight movement of those eyes which he had supposed to be of stone, was regarding him with reproach and, worse still, *staring* at the sculptor's letter in his hand. He felt, so to speak, at a loss; he felt faint. No, not physically.

He remembered at once that Elmina had left early in the morning, with her father and Teresa, to be at her dying mother's bedside. He then slackened his pace, overcome, if not positively choked, by another thought: that the sorrowful, misty face behind the window-pane was not a real face, but only an image that had come to him through the blue aether, projected by Elmina's thoughts of her home in Naples (since her heart, if she had one, must be there). Ingmar was initiated into these mysteries of the psyche, be they realities or illusions, and from this fact he derived a certain pride and sombre comfort; but this time he was mistaken.

He retraced a few steps (the face had vanished) and asked the porter – as if by some oversight he had not done so before – when Signorina Elmina would be returning from Casoria, and was told that the young lady had not yet left Naples, on account of certain duties entrusted to her by her father; but that she would certainly depart in the course of the morning, about midday at the latest.

So it was really her! And so meek and unassuming, as if stripped of all her youthful glory; like a servant, or a poor relation, whom they had not thought it necessary to introduce to him the previous evening; and now waiting, perhaps for news, at that lonely window. Ingmar could not believe it! Discarding at this point the improbable idea, which had none the less occurred to him, of a relative, or even of another sister, habitually in hiding, who lived in the house and whom he had mistaken for Elmina, he returned to his first impression: that the young woman was indeed Elmina, but mysteriously solitary and indifferent. And this certainty, of having been seen and made the object of her scrutiny, however indifferent, while he was removing the letter (it was still in his hand), struck him as appalling. Unacceptable, to say the least. Sooner or later, the porter being party to it, it would be learnt that he, de Neville, had of his own initiative removed the letter addressed to the Glovemaker by the enraptured Albert, and this with a view to thwarting the proposal of marriage. He would therefore be condemned as all that he found most intolerable: intriguing, petty and jealous. Justifications had he none – or else each appeared more shameful than the last. In his confusion he therefore made an instant decision to maintain, if questioned, that the letter recovered by him was a letter of his own, but imprudently delivered by Albert. Yes, he, Ingmar, would be the one to mention the letter, even if there was no call for it, as his own personal proposal of marriage to Elmina, later withdrawn as a consequence of more mature reflection. He did not (he would assert) have the means to fulfil so great an obligation as the maintenance of the Glovemaker's daughter in the state to which she was accustomed. He was far from wealthy. He would not go into details, but the fact was, such a rash act was out of the question for him. He would thereupon confess everything, candidly and in every particular, to Albert. But Albert would have to undertake not to bring up the matter again, or reveal the truth about the prince's unlimited financial resources, under pain of the revelation of another truth, one concerning Albert himself; and this is, that he possessed nothing of his own, and therefore could not address proposals of marriage to young ladies of high social rank without being thoroughly ashamed of himself.

Thus, having really given the matter very little thought, our prince, who of the principles expected of a nobleman seemed to have learnt precious little, returned much cheered to the Hat of Gold. Here he ordered luncheon – partridges followed by strawberries from Sorrento – and tranquilly consumed the same while leafing through a back number of *The Monitor*; after which he went out for a walk, indulging in a few minor purchases, including a miniature silver sword for Albert and a walking-stick for Alphonse, who adored such things. On his return, towards evening, he received a grief-stricken message from Nodier. Donna Brigitta Helm had departed this life. He, Alphonse, was staying on at Casoria with Dupré to be comfort to their friend "who, however, has borne his misfortune bravely", and to be present at the doleful but inevitable ceremonies. *"Au revoir, mon cher*, Alphonse."

He replied to the message, and thinking that he had two or three entirely free days to look forward to, made plans to enjoy them by visiting some of the sights in the vicinity of Naples, and also calling on a number of entertaining Gentlemen of the Realm to whom he had letters of introduction.

The month of May. The frolicsome fountains of Vanvitelli and a rather indiscreet Duke

His choice luckily fell (so he later congratulated himself) on a duke of whom he had not previously thought, and who did not reside in Naples but at Caserta, the birthplace of the deceased Donna Helm; and to be exact on Benjamin von Ruskaja, a Pole, who had been, among other things, a very dear friend of the Princess Leopoldine, our hero's mother. It is true that he did not enjoy great repute as a person of flawless propriety, in his habit of first dreaming up and then judging the goings-on of the *beau monde* (nor in drawing permissible inferences as to the conduct of others); but to the ever gloomy and world-weary Ingmar, as indeed to his worthy *maman* during her lifetime, these supplements to true fact were not too displeasing. From him he would request information, to be subsequently filtered through reflection and further enquiries, upon the vastly important matter of the extent of Don Mariano's estate. This would serve him as one reason, among others less fathomable, for his intervention in an affair of the heart; or rather, in the question of a marriage that ought to have been the exclusive concern of his beloved friend but instead, as his guardian, and even more on account of his own passionate heart, concerned him as well. The Glovemaker's worldly assets were not, should he become the artist's father-in-law, the first of such reasons, as Ingmar well knew simply from feeling such aversion for Elmina; but the matter was, in those times when Life was synonymous with infinite worldly pleasure, and therefore money, a perfectly valid reason for hostility or, on the contrary, benevolence, in all those situations likely to be permanent (as was a marriage) within the circle of one's closest friends.

Having thus dispelled all scruples regarding his own actions, let alone any thought of solidarity in distress, which he did not feel, with his absent friends, our amiable prince set off the next morning at dawn, very cheerful about the happy hours awaiting him; and we see him, after a dashing ride, entering the famous city of Charles III of Naples, graced with one of the finest royal palaces in the world.

He decided to begin by viewing this marvel at close quarters.

That day in Caserta the month of May shone forth in all its glory. Nowhere in Europe, in the previous ten years of his life of gaiety, did the prince remember seeing a sky like that: an immense dome of purest and most lucent blue in every iota of its vault, such as to bring to mind – a hackneyed image, but at this moment no other occurs to us – the surface of a freshly washed glass set down on a cool, bright leaf. It was as if the whole world brimming with springtime were reflected, upside down, in that sky, like a mirage in the desert. Everywhere, therefore, whether he raised his eyes or lowered them, he seemed to see palaces, fountains and gardens. It was extremely hot.

The prospect of the Royal Palace of Caserta, which he had hastened to approach, wrought to its uttermost his emotion at living in a world, such as that in which we too are immersed, replete with wonders. He felt, in short, that he was treading on air.

Very soon, having ample time for his visit, he found himself strolling beside the Gardens of that famous Palace; a truly wonderful complex of buildings, lately brought to completion, and fruit of the imagination and untrammelled mastery of the sublime Vanvitelli; a work, it seemed to him, almost prodigious in its serenity, the sight of which moved him to the thought of what life and human reason might be, if truly developed and cultivated. Which they were not. Even more was he stirred by the spectacle of the Gardens, and exalted by that of the fountains, and he bestowed unconditional admiration on the artist of Netherlands descent who had conceived that inspired ensemble. Indeed that marvel of waters that seemed – if perchance we may dream a little – to be so many maidens summoned to a merry-making, instilled in him we know not what mystery of life; a mystery that resided (he felt) in the very freshness and fluidity, the flow and the fall, the incessant vanishing and resurgence of its infinite variety of forms. For those brief instants, genuinely transported, he forgot his practice of, or at least his passion and propensity for, the magic arts, and that curiosity, that impulse towards unwholesome dominion over lives and events, which at other times possessed him. His heart did homage to God! Alas, only for a moment! The next, he was once again the subtle, irresponsible and none too benevolent investigator and juggler of the secrets and destinies of others.

* * *

As a seagull rises from a rock on which it was sleeping, to swoop upon a darting fish on the broad surface of the sea, so his mind, emerging from its brief contemplation, threw itself with a silent cry on his recent thoughts concerning the safeguarding of assets, snapping up in its beak the foremost of them: the investigation into Elmina. A moment later his elegant, radiant, though none the less somewhat sombre figure was following that image in its flight; in the sense that Ingmar found himself riding, swift and intent as thought itself, towards the house of Duke Benjamin, which lay in the old quarter of the city.

He made his way through a garden, skirted a white colonnade all wreathed with roses, saw fountains playing, heard the singing and fluttering of many birds in the depths of a rose-bush, while there assailed him the pungent, debilitating odour of magnificent scarlet blooms; and, in the midst of this sort of debauch of nature (a soft warm breeze was wafting over all), he glimpsed the cheery figure of the Polish nobleman whom he purposed to visit.

Benjamin, who, perhaps informed by a servant, was standing waiting for him beside a bamboo pergola entirely interwoven with blue bell-flowers, a positive little birdcage, looked to him for all the world like a fantastical white cloud come down to bid him sprightly welcome to that fairy garden.

Well into his nineties, but erect and ruddy as a youngster, his poll as white as polar snows, his blue eyes shrewd and mischievous, he was regarding the prince as if he had followed his steps not from the gate, but throughout his journey, ever since his stroll before the Royal Palace (if not, we may hazard, for some hours previous to his departure from Naples).

Their conversation took place in German and French, but the host did not omit – a pleasing touch – certain typical Neapolitan expressions, perfectly understood, as if through divination, by his much diverted foreign visitor.

"My dear *pazzariello*," began Duke Ruskaja in Neapolitan, though passing at once into his native German, which we shall endeavour to translate as best we may, "do not be surprised, but I saw you as early as yesterday – woe is me, I forget the hour, perhaps ten o'clock, when I did not yet know you were in Naples – while you were making your way in some anxiety to the home of Signorina Elmina . . . Is it not so? Am I mistaken?"

"No, you are not mistaken." (This after a moment of confusion, for the old man's skill, his sheer *technique* as it were, quite took him aback in spite of himself, causing him a pang of professional jealousy, together with some dismay at finding that he, who had intended to bring powers to bear, was himself in the sway of the other). "No, you are not in the least mistaken . . . It was indeed yesterday, but I was not anxious . . . that would have been too foolish."

The old man here started to laugh, we do not know whether to mask a lie on the part of his young friend, or to make light of his own merits.

"Quite so . . . A simple reading of the mind, or rather the emotions, of a young man – so much and no more was granted me to understand; and then only because it was clearly written on your brow, while you were on your way to Jib-Sail House. But how was I to know, my son, that you had hastened to the mansion to rectify an act of imprudence on the part of your friend and ward? This I learn from your agitation at the present moment."

Into whether or not there was any coherence in this (or even sincerity, or untruth) we will not enquire for the time being, having no wish to interfere. The fact is that five minutes later, seated in the rose-garden in front of the arbour, and served with coffee and ice-cream by an impeccable footman in yellow livery, the two men threw themselves into the liveliest conversation. The truth was that they were, in spite of all, of an age: the old man, in frivolity of heart, was young; the young man, in curiosity and will to power over things human, was old. Equals, therefore! And over the heads of these two sorcerer's apprentices gaily fluttered the birds.

Granted that the interest of Leopoldine's son lay purely in safeguarding the interests of the sculptor Dupré, his ward (as Ruskaja well knew), and implied no ill-feeling towards Signorina Elmina, who had done him no harm (which was perfectly true, though while the prince was making this assertion his host's eyes took on a very deep shade of blue, as though he was loath to believe these declarations); granted this, then, Ingmar admitted that he was interested in ascertaining the young lady's character, as also the financial standing of the Civile family, now that Signora Helm, as the Duke was certainly aware (the Duke, however, denied that he had been informed), had departed this life, and Don Mariano had therefore to allocate the entire patrimony in favour of his sons and daughters. Was there a Will? How much did it all come to? The estate would be divided up: what share of it would fall to Elmina?

"At this very moment," explained the prince, lowering his eyes, "before she has even put on mourning, Signorina Elmina has received, or has at her disposal, as many as two proposals of marriage. The one from Dupré (and this proposal is in my possession), and another, which as yet she knows nothing of, from myself, should she, in giving Dupré his freedom, demand reparation. It is indeed my intention to take the risk of sacrificing myself, for the sake of rescuing Dupré. He is altogether too dear to me."

The magician had not the slightest doubt about this, or even the rest of it. De Neville had told him the plain truth in every detail, and for psychic reasons, the fruit of his mediumistic gifts, he was in a position to verify it immediately. The prince had only lied about, or at least withheld, the reasons for his instinctive aversion to Elmina. And to these Benjamin, who was very religious, did not, since matters of the soul were in question, wish to enter. Therefore, though suspecting some intriguing motive far removed from property matters, he did not cross the threshold of the discretion proper to friendship. But he could imagine, without too much self-reproach, that the profound religiosity of *maman* was now, twenty-four years after her death, influencing the tacit judgement (for antipathy, they say, is an *a priori* judgement) of young Ingmar with regard to the rustic Elmina. But he wished to proceed gently, and not fall into the trespass of backbiting.

"To my knowledge," he therefore began, having helped himself to another spoonful of ice-cream, of which he was inordinately fond, "to my knowledge Don Mariano's assets – let us speak first of those – in houses and lands in his own right, and in workshops and emporiums as far afield as Rome, largely on the side of the late Brigitta, are very ample. Perhaps grandiose, or even incommensurate, would be more appropriate terms. Many years ago, by means of this strange marriage with one of his father's ex-dependants, he became as rich (his family was not so) as is a 'real' prince (not, I mean to say, my boy, as one of the crowd of titled *pazzarielli* you see going round Naples in carriages, paying visits all day long). Yes, a girl who hankered for the splendours and pleasures of the world could not wish, even supposing her to be more beautiful than Elmina, which I cannot imagine, for more than will now fall as a dowry to that girl; even deducting – and it is not little – whatever may be due under the Will to her ten brothers and sisters (Teresa excluded, she being Don Mariano's natural daughter); all of whom are at present established in distant parts of the world, busying themselves in commerce and trading in hides. The girl, therefore, is exceedingly wealthy, and your ward could not do better for himself than setting up house with her" (this was the expression he used, rather than "taking wife", the more Neapolitan phrase which even the Duke was wont to employ). "There remains one point of doubt, however, regarding the propriety and perfection of this marriage, a point upon which I cannot and must not dwell. It is not my business, and perhaps not even her confessor's . . . or maybe that – yes . . . One would first have to know if she has one . . . and who it is . . ."

"What do you mean, Duke?" queried Ingmar, full of curiosity.

" . . . Mind you, there is one thing I take for granted, indeed I am certain of: that she is truly religious, well brought-up, and a woman of honour. There are no stains on her character. She has grown up with Don Mariano, who is most intensely jealous of her. Your Albert, by marrying her, would not forfeit his soul. But there is in her . . . I don't *see* it, mind you – it is only a matter of intuition (whereas everyone in Naples declares they know, perhaps out of pure spite, who can say?) – but there is in her a secret regarding her relationship with her mother . . . with her now *late* mother. As you told me yourself, she did not hasten at once to visit her . . ."

"She was unable to," put in Ingmar quickly, already hoping for some revelation to Elmina's discredit (as for Donna Brigitta, he obviously had nothing to tax her with), but thinking it improper to solicit it.

"She *did not wish to*, my boy. I am aware that her father had entrusted her with a number of tasks, but that was not a valid excuse, given the circumstances. The truth is that she hates her mother, or did, at least, hate her. Everyone here knows that. And that is why she did not hasten to see her yesterday morning."

"You mean . . . they know about her even in Caserta?" exclaimed Ingmar.

"About the mother? About Donna Brigitta? All there is to know!"

By "her" the prince had meant Elmina, but he had no wish to make his meaning clear. He had reason to suspect the Duke of erring on the side of inventiveness, and already a lesser degree of trust, if not downright vexation, was creeping over him. A sardonic glint came to his eyes.

"For goodness' sake, my dear Duke," demanded the prince despite himself, though burning with curiosity, "what grounds did this Brigitta give for the whole town, as well as her daughter, to detest her?"

This the Duke had not said, but Ingmar felt sure of it.

"She was illegitimate. Not the daughter of a Prussian officer, as has been maintained – Helm is merely a name made up as a blind for another – but of a lofty personage at Court . . . exceedingly lofty, indeed perhaps none loftier . . . who at one time led a dissolute life, and of a cook (just imagine), perhaps even a skivvy, of equally questionable principles. Such are the origins, not a little common after all, of Donna Brigitta, raised from childhood in the disorder and luxury of an ambiguous situation in life. Eventually, having met Don Mariano, she broke free of it. She was only fifteen years old . . . She obtained employment as an artisan. No, do not smile, because the affluence deriving from her royal connection had at that point ceased – her mother had died in mysterious circumstances . . . The wealth came later. Don Mariano's sentiments were therefore of the purest, and soon thereafter rewarded by the news of an enormous legacy. That is how it all began. The couple had a great number of children, their life prospered and was covered with glory. Their last daughter was Elmina, and curiously enough it was because of Elmina that things changed . . ."

"Changed in what sense?"

"I have told you (have I not?) that Donna Brigitta was an illegitimate child. A very different kettle of fish from the story told to Elmina, that her grandfather was a Prussian general, highly respectable, and devoted to his highly respectable wife. A wretch of a maid, who was later dismissed, a certain Ferrante, or Ferranta, had informed the little girl down to the smallest details. Illegitimate! For her, full of airs as she was, it was more than enough, and she prevailed upon that most loving of fathers (which Don Mariano still is, towards her) to turn Donna Brigitta out of the house. For ever! The unhappy woman withdrew to Casoria, where she owned a country house, and where nothing further came to gladden her days, all her children having grown up and left their Neapolitan homeland. Jib-Sail House itself fell silent, just as you found it. Thus the poor woman entered upon a nine-year exile, which came to a sad end the day before yesterday."

Ingmar was aghast. Between indignation and astonishment at this family tragedy brought about by the despotic authority conceded to a child – on whom however, since the cause lay in a traumatic blow to the family honour, he could lay no blame – he was all but bereft of words, and had the momentary impression that the Duke was taking advantage of his ingenuousness; but this suspicion was swiftly dispelled.

"Illegitimate!" he exclaimed. "And Don Mariano was willing to marry her all the same? How could this be?" He was beside himself with astonishment, and the Duke's subsequent assertions (Brigitta's exile, the silence of the house in Naples, all too sadly true) almost entirely escaped his attention, all of which was concentrated on the gravity of that first revelation.

"And do you not ask yourself how could your Albert . . . ? No? It is perfectly possible, my young friend. Great beauty, an uncommon allurement . . . but in Don Mariano's case there was something more. A Christian man, compassionate and just, he wished to remedy the evil committed by another (the lofty Personage I spoke of), and he bestowed on Donna Brigitta a tranquillity and happiness she had never known, and an honoured name, and added to her own assets – inherited later from the *cook*, and a considerable legacy it was – a new and incontrovertible fortune. And she, for at least twenty-seven years, was a happy wife. Until, as I say, Elmina was of a certain age. Because at six or seven years old – her mother was already approaching fifty – having learnt the truth from this Ferranta, and having forced her father, who adores her to this day, to confess to her mother's true origins, she had Donna Brigitta relegated to a distance – to Casoria, in fact. But really she must never have been able to tolerate her. A cold-hearted girl."

"To chase her mother out of house and home! To manage to do it! As a mere child!" Ingmar almost shouted in stupefaction, not to say horror, having finally grasped the whole story. "I refuse to believe it!"

Even with this shout on his lips he well knew that he did believe it, that it was true, though perhaps with some extenuating circumstances which did not at that moment interest him.

"She," added the Duke, "the woman you fear, has a further motive for her inhuman conduct, though an extremely feeble one, especially in one so young. I do not know your own thoughts on the matter, but she abhors, and has always abhorred, the Bourbon monarchy, and therefore her own unfortunate lineage and the person to whom she owes it. Do not mention this to Don Mariano, for he is of a mind with her, and it is my belief that he secretly shares her anti-royalist sentiments. Hard words, but true: both of them today are placing their hopes in the rising star in France, and openly sighing for the '93."

These words, as also the allusion to the still obscure Buonaparte, were of as much indifference to our Belgian man of the world as if they had been village gossip. He was convinced that the sole object of the fair Elmina's hatred was her own lowly and dubious origin, while her detestation of her mother was due simply to her own overweening pride. Had her mother been born legitimately at Court, she would have forgiven her. She was contemptuous of all that fell short of opulence and grandeur. Hers was that hard and vulgar heart which he had divined in her. *Bien!* If that was the case, neither Madame Dupré nor Princesse de Neville for her! Never! A few hours later, with a heart full of relief, and a touch of regret, for after all the prince was only human, de Neville took his leave of the smiling sorcerer, and mounted on a fine white horse, and accompanied by a servant of the Duke's, rode thoughtfully towards Naples. He did not dally to visit Pompeii, or make the tour of Vesuvius, but none the less it was late in the evening when he reached the city, beneath a sky teeming with stars.

And these, to his eyes, from every part of the blue vault seemed to be pointing the way back to the Low Countries, or to express his thought more precisely, back to Europe (for that Naples also was a part of Europe did not, very unjustly, occur to him); and of this signpost, without a shadow of doubt, he was heartily glad.

The proposal accepted and the happy bridegroom.
A friendship put to the test

The prince, having retrieved his peace of mind and friendly feelings, since he was now sure of having his protégé's destiny in his hands, intended to set off early the following morning, if a boat were available, for Capri; or if this were not possible – an even more cherished prospect – for the Phlegraean Fields, because (due to the revival of classical culture) everyone was even then singing the praises of the magical shadows emanating from one or another of their countless Grottoes. His choice depended partly on the weather. For Capri it had to be dead calm and windless, since de Neville fell a ready victim to seasickness.

But neither the one thing nor the other came to pass, for an astonishing event was about to be revealed, of which the prince (probably due to the winds rising from the east-north-east and resisting the passage of the psychic waves arriving from Casoria, which lay to the south) had no premonition; indeed it had already occurred, and was merely on the point of being revealed to him.

This was nothing less than the return to the Hostelry, only a minute or two after that of the prince himself, of an Albert Dupré beside himself with joy, the betrothed (and in the very house which had witnessed the death of Brigitta and where, like great gowned shades looming behind the relatives and servants in their black mourning, there thronged the unspoken questions as to how many changes there might or might not be in the Will, and how much would fall to this person or that); the betrothed, I say, of an Elmina miraculously disposed to bestow her hand on him, without having even received the proposal in writing, and therefore, clearly enough, without a moment's hesitation.

This news was announced at ten o'clock at night, like a rumble of thunder heralding the birth of spring, to a de Neville then fatuously intent, together with his valet, on reviewing the shirts which he was most inclined to wear for his excursion on the morrow.

"Open up, Ingmar!" cried the voice of his young protégé, elated and almost exhausted with joy. "Open up! Most wonderful news!"

And when de Neville, paling slightly, opened the door to him, Albert – laughing, out of breath and in his seventh heaven – threw himself into his arms.

"Elmina is going to marry me!"

De Neville had schooled himself since boyhood not to respond at once to terrible announcements – and such this was. Therefore, though paling still further, he said nothing, but merely returned to the bed, on the embroidered counterpane of which his shirts were laid out, and ordered his valet to put them away again (he would make his choice later) and to hold himself in readiness for a departure for Capri or Cumae first thing in the morning.

Albert did not even hear him. On the servant's exit he went to the window and threw it wide.

"She's going to marry me! She's accepted me! She's marrying *me*!" he repeated like a madman, in a voice from which pride and, strangely enough, a trace of sad humility, were not absent.

Here that savagery which was, in the prince's refined disposition, fortunately always of short duration, turned to calm, as he continued to busy himself with the shirts:

"Close the window, Albert, if you would be so good." (There was in fact a rather chill draught, the possible prelude to a break in the weather, such as happens in the changeable and ever-capricious climate of Naples). After which: "So, she has accepted you. Very good. You have of course told her how much money you have."

"Nodier told her."

"And none the less she accepted you?"

Albert turned towards him a face barely recognizable, one of a super-human sweetness and profound tranquillity, but also of great gravity:

"Yes, none the less she accepted me. It's something quite different from what you think."

"Try to make yourself clear. I am listening with the best will in the world, but I do not understand you. In what way, different?"

"In this: that she, Elmina, did not *choose* me. She did not, in my belief, intend to marry. But she wishes to obey her father. And she has promised her father, who wishes it, to marry me, and to make every effort to be a good wife. That is all there is to it. Alphonse explained my financial situation to Don Mariano, that I am not rich, and have nothing but a modest legacy from *maman* and the house in Liège. She accepts me all the same."

De Neville forced himself to repress the host of questions, and also the anger, aroused in him by this incredible account; above all the mystery of a Don Mariano Civile, a merchant of vast wealth, whose name was known and honoured in all the capitals of Europe, asking an impoverished foreign artist to do him the favour of accepting his beloved daughter in wedlock.

"To me it seems strange that Don Mariano has chosen you as a husband – and a penniless husband at that – for his beautiful and much sought-after daughter; and that when seeing you for only the second time, and in such distressing circumstances. It seems to me curious . . . Does it not seem so to you?"

"No . . . Why should it?" But Albert's face at once grew pensive. "Yes . . . I wondered about it myself," he admitted, seating himself on the bed. And, ridding himself of his cloak and a boot that was pinching him, he stretched out one blue-clad leg on the embroidered counterpane. "But please let me go back to that wonderful moment, when I saw her approaching me (we were in her father's study, Don Mariano was close behind her, and seemed to be begging a favour *from me*, just imagine) to tell me graciously, looking me in the face: 'I accept my destiny on account of the obedience I owe my father, *mon cher Albert*. I did not desire any marriage, but rather to live with him for ever. That cannot be. Let it be forgotten.'"

"That is what she said?"

"Yes, those very words. I suppose that until now she has nourished some propensity for the religious life. I seem to have gathered that she grew up with the nuns."

This conflicted with what de Neville had learned from the Duke concerning her true character ever since childhood, her pitiless conduct towards her mother, and the fact that she had been a martinet in the house. He had no compunction in suggesting calmly:

"Perhaps she loves another, but . . . one can scarcely know."

"Perhaps," agreed Albert without fully understanding. "She has such a profound, such a wonderful soul . . ." And, so saying, he appeared to fall into a reverie.

De Neville was scarcely able to restrain his rage. Further questions, of the most trenchant nature, were on the tip of his tongue; further incognita urged themselves upon him; and above all Albert's blindness, the utter stupidity into which he had fallen, was a torture to him. He saw nothing! He saw nothing of the mystery that lay behind that reciprocal compassion, hers for him, his for her, which the artist called love. Perhaps the girl was expecting a baby by some unpresentable suitor, maybe even a scullion, as once – though at that time the suitor was unattainable merely because of his regal status – had happened to her maternal grandmother. Or perhaps, another hypothesis that came to mind, thinking of the Christian motive which all those years ago had induced the Glovemaker to marry his humble employee, a similar intention, that of performing an act of charity, now prompted him to gladden the life of an unknown foreign artist. Perhaps a second vow . . . But why? He marvelled at himself for not having yet questioned his friend as to the manner of that extraordinary scene, the order of events. Had Don Mariano already known of Albert's love at first sight for his daughter? And from whom had he found this out?

"Oh, yes," replied Albert carelessly. "He knew. He had been told, but without making much of the matter, by Nodier."

"And this . . . But how could that have been enough to make him suppose that you . . that she . . . I mean that both you and she could have a serious reciprocal attachment, such as to arrive at the notion of marriage? Is it not surprising? And how can Elmina have imagined . . . ?"

He wanted to say "that you admired her?", but Albert interrupted him.

"She did not *imagine*, believe me! She simply *saw* you the other morning, from a window in Don Mariano's study, while you were going to retrieve a letter . . . She realized that it was a letter from me . . . a letter to Don Mariano, that is; and this was because the door-keeper, who had gone upstairs for this very purpose, had told her that I had delivered it, adding that you had for some reason come and taken it back. She asked me to tell her if I knew anything about it (her mother had then barely breathed her last), and I told her the truth: that it was a proposal of marriage from me, and that you, probably, were against it, and that is why you hastened to retrieve it."

"You told her that?"

"Yes."

"And you believe it?"

Albert gave a rueful smile.

"A fine scene I must say," commented the prince with some despondency. "The deathbed . . . the mourners in tears . . . And you and her behind a curtain exchanging such *honourable* confidences!"

"It wasn't there . . . nor at that moment. It was afterwards, in a little sitting-room next door."

After a long pause, "So then, she will hate me," said the prince, meditative and seeming chagrined.

"She doesn't hate you. She thinks you are jealous of my affection . . . of me . . . that you don't want me to leave you . . . that this is what distresses you."

This was so very true that the prince, then and there, did not bestir himself either to deny or to justify it. The plain fact was, it was a disaster.

"It will no doubt enter her mind that I did that, that I purloined your letter, because I am in love with her myself. And she is marrying you because she is at war with me."

"Oh, now you are out to hurt me . . . to make me repent . . . But you won't succeed! Never!" burst out the young man, laughing and suddenly himself again. And jumping down from the bed he ran again to the window and threw it open. In rushed a gust of cool air, perhaps the herald of a storm, and at once, over the sea, appeared great white clouds edged with silver, as they are at night in Naples, coursing westwards in a sky traversed by a pallid moon that likewise seemed in flight.

"Oh, I would never have thought," exclaimed Dupré once more, as he looked up at the clouds, at that magic sky all fleeting and hidden lights, "I would never have thought that it could be so wonderful to be alive! And alive *in Naples*, what is more. Ingmar, I'm staying on, you know? It is decided. I am staying in this city of joy." He turned and faced his friend, in his great blue eyes a visionary gleam. "I'll set up a studio here . . . I'll work, I'll love, I shall be loved. The years will pass, I shall grow old – here! And these memories of infinite joy, I believe, will sweeten my life, if I live, to the very end . . . to the very end." Thus he concluded, almost in a shout, but meekly.

Ingmar at this point generously turned his back on all his violent hostility towards Elmina, on the contempt he had harboured for her in his heart, and also on all inauspicious forebodings – fuelled perhaps by prejudice born of her cruelty to the linnet – and resolved to second the happiness of his protégé to the very best of his ability.

Of the heart of the girl, of the fear he had of it, and also of many things that appeared to him obscure and clear by turns, but always secret and fugitive like those lunar clouds in the sky of Naples, he did not for the present wish to think.

Certain discussions.
The child in the locket

The three absentees, Don Mariano and his daughters, followed faithfully, or rather preceded by some hours, by their friend Nodier, whose solicitude amazed even the refined prodigality of the prince (he contrived, among other things, for a birdcage containing six white doves to be placed on Elmina's window-sill, this by arrangement with the door-keeper, who at this point, of the three giddy young gentlemen, scarcely knew which to prefer, since at every slightest service came the flash of a gold coin; the birdcage moreover, at the mere opening of the window by a certain small enchanted hand, would open also, and at once the six inno-cent creatures would rise in a flight of salutation); the three absentees, therefore, returned to Naples. And the presence of Nodier, with his cheerful devotion to the family of which all were now guests, and the extraordinary promptness and ability he showed in every least situation that required the application of a practical mind; this same presence became increasingly precious in the eyes of Don Mariano, not a little down-cast in spirit, and also in those of his friends, who were vaguely intimidated by encountering such a vast number of novelties as those which soon offered themselves to the youthful curiosity of our foreign visitors. Who had scarcely moved from the Hat of Gold to the Glovemaker's (on this point Don Mariano had refused to be thwarted of the pleasure of hospital-ity, for the house was large, and a small suite had been put at the disposal of each of them, provided with every convenience including a valet), than the whole of Jib-Sail House was thrown open to them as to the closest and most cherished friends of the family. There were visits, of mourning and of congratulation, a strange but inevitable contrast on those occasions when joy and sadness are conjoined, and the tidings of a twofold event spread everywhere on the wing – visits from the whole Nobility and Commercial World of Naples. The Nobility, lamenting her loss and lauding her merits, took the part of Baroness Helm (the name by which, strangely enough, she was known, on account of some tie of blood never fully ascertained, though accorded no importance), while Commerce, in prayer and thanksgiving for the marriage, clustered about the father of the bride-to-be. Nor was there a shortage of Nobodies, who arrived in streams of carriages from both the elegant quarters and the gay purlieus dotted with villas; for Don Mariano was extremely open-handed and had friends everywhere. They came to partake, in his splendid reception rooms, of rosolio and coffee, sweetmeats and ice-cream, or the delicious hot chocolate then in fashion, served in the finest porcelain cups adorned with scenes of dances and rustic merry-making; and meanwhile, with divers little cries of astonishment and insincere bowing and scraping, to meet and size up the "French" guests, distinguished as such simply because of the language they spoke (though nothing more was laid to their charge, since one of them, the eldest, was connected with no less than the House of Brabant). The confusion of names and countries, seeing that in Naples so little was known of the Low Countries, was understandable. Not least because the one dearest to heir Neapolitan hearts, the most *on show* (if we may so put it without outraging the depth and delicacy of the sentiments involved) was on every occasion Alphonse Nodier, who almost miraculously, seeing the short time he had spent in Naples, spoke a mixture of French and Neapolitan. Even Elmina, or Adelmine, although now officially affianced to Dupré, showed an indisputable and affectionate predilection for the tubby, warm-hearted merchant. It was Alphonse here, Alphonse there, Alphonse Alphonse everywhere. De Neville missed nothing in those gatherings marked by a certain gravity (though a greater degree of gravity would not have come amiss, he thought, in view of the recent bereavement), and by a more than justified excitement at this "artistic" marriage, as they called it; and he did not fail to notice, with a pang at heart, how Dupré seemed to be treated like a well-mannered, very sweet child, but nothing more. The real hero of the occasion was, for everyone, Nodier.

On the seventh day following that betrothal, problematical to put it mildly, when the weather had turned indubitably cold and rainy, which did nothing to encourage the legitimate happiness of all concerned, de Neville, taking advantage of the fact that Dupré had accompanied his fiancée and father-in-law to Posillipo to visit a small house which an aunt had intended to leave to them, found himself with Nodier in the latter's suite in a wing of the mansion, where only in the last few days had the tiresome crowds of visitors begun to thin out. Indeed, that morning there was no one in at all, and they were alone. The prince was glumly silent. The seawind was blowing over Naples (for the sea was there, close at hand), and the rain was beating steadily on the windows. On the mantelpiece stood the portrait in miniature of a creature of divine beauty, fresher than a rose, more poetic than a bird, a girl of perhaps six or seven, with huge eyes and smooth golden hair, reading in a little golden book that lay open on her lap. Her lightweight pale-coloured gown was not long enough to cover her ankles, and indeed one could see two slender pink-and-white feet, quite bare. Her eyes were wide open and very beautiful, of a clear grey, but they were not following the text. She seemed to be looking, with the sadness of resignation, into herself.

"What a lovely creature! But I haven't seen her before this morning: yesterday evening this portrait wasn't there," exclaimed de Neville, taking it up in his hands as if it had been a creature of the air, almost the very one by which, like poor Dupré, he himself was most unfortunately subjugated.

"No, it wasn't there," said Nodier simply. "I think it is a gift which Don Mariano intends to give to each of us. I believe both you and Albert will receive one like it, as a mark of the close spiritual relationship that has been established between us all."

At any other moment de Neville might have reacted vigorously to that assertion; he was not in agreement on the "spiritual" quality of their relationship; which was, rather, the product of his protégé's folly, as well as of circumstances which had so fallen out, as if from spite, as to encourage that disastrous folly; but at that moment he was greatly, almost painfully absorbed in the angelic image of the little girl of the miniature, enclosed in a locket.

"I would like to know who the girl in the picture is," he said. "Perhaps another of Don Mariano's daughters, who died in infancy."

"I know nothing about it. I can't tell you anything. It may be as you say. However, from the colouring it seems to me pretty old. Probably a family heirloom."

Dropping this fortuitous theme, they went on to speak of other things, and soon enough (since the matter was dear to the prince's heart) of the secret and mystery of Elmina's immediate assent, given purely in obedience, to her father's choice of a marriage to the sculptor, whose real financial status was still unknown to them; and above all the brainstorm which appeared to have come over the Glovemaker in planning such a thing. Of Albert, at that time, he knew next to nothing, and the prince therefore saw in that decision some great anxiety to get his daughter off his hands as soon as possible, or perhaps to ensure her safety. However, even the first of these hypotheses, given the adoration in which he held her, did not seem very likely. De Neville thus plainly showed that his mind, and above all his sense of logic, was incapable of grasping, indeed of accepting as at all explicable, that decision of Don Mariano's to entrust his daughter to an infatuated foreigner.

"Yes," said the merchant almost resignedly, without disputing the foregoing objection, "I admit that I too was very much struck . . . A real surprise it was, my dear fellow. But then I said to myself . . . Well, I looked about that big house, with the old wife dying, and realized that Don Mariano was not only oppressed by his wealth, but also by countless disappointments which he never betrays. Did you notice that of his children, ten in all besides Teresa and Elmina, and all away and well set-up in life, not a single one put in an appearance, or made his presence felt by the least little message of affection? And yet they had certainly known of their mother's illness for some time. And even stranger: no one mentioned them, or alluded in any way to their absence. As if those young people were far from expected, or did not exist at all. In my opinion there is a not inconsiderable rift between Don Mariano and his children, perhaps on account of the separation, however formal, between him and his wife. He does not count on them for any support for their sisters, and hence his anxiety to make a quick match at least for the elder, to whose care he can then entrust the younger."

"And who was to blame for that separation?" asked the prince, ever spiteful and fault-finding, though under his breath as if to prevent Nodier from hearing. In which he succeeded, and Nodier continued:

"There is between those two, father and daughter, a relationship such as has rarely been seen between two kinsfolk of different generations. No order of hierarchy, as you will have noted, but an almost religious mutual devotion. They reciprocate with the silent precision of the two hands of a clock. On her side, she wishes nothing better than to obey her father; for him there is no greater happiness than in devising Elmina's welfare . . ."

"The other sister, the flighty Teresa, is Don Mariano's natural daughter, I hear," threw in de Neville nonchalantly.

"So I imagine . . . No harm in that, after all," replied the merchant with the suggestion of a smile, slightly troubled and embarrassed. "They tell me," he added, "that Naples does not excel in matters of morals . . . But these, my dear fellow, are mere baubles. Life in general is pretty disordered wherever you are . . . assuming that morality is to be identified with a certain order of things . . ."

De Neville did not bat an eyelid at this: his own life had always been plagued by the lack of any real order, other than social, and it was not his place to lay down the law. He therefore confined himself to listening to what Nodier, ever disposed by temperament to see things in the best light, did not hesitate to add:

"Don Mariano dotes on this creature of his; he trembles for her. This is an explanation, if such were needed, of his behaviour; apart from the fact that Albert is the angel we both know him to be, and there is scarcely need for us to sing his praises: he inspires confidence and joy in all and sundry. As for Elmina, her beauty and goodness are there for all to see. With regard to her obedience as a daughter (and what better guarantee of her perfect fitness as a wife?) one cannot sufficiently stress the Christian virtue of it. Her father, to her, is everything; she worships him above all things . . . or rather, very nearly so, the highest place being reserved for His Majesty the King."

". . . His Majesty?" quavered de Neville, staggered. "But do they by any chance frequent the Court? Have they sometimes been at Caserta?"

"No, not even the unhappy Brigitta, although her lineage, as perhaps you know – though it remains a confidence – would have justified it. But she never went there in her life. And let us not speak of Elmina, proud and reserved as ever. But, despite some disappointment with her mother (so they tell me), she has always been and still is a legitimist at heart. The authority of the King has for her all the power of the sun itself . . . First the King, then her father . . . and lastly marriage. Alas, my dear de Neville, you are too worldly to understand these things."

De Neville, on the contrary, had indeed understood, and he restrained himself no longer:

"You are too naïve, Nodier!" he almost shrieked. "Marriage cannot come last. It is a trumpery which I see you lend yourself to. As regards legitimism or – as my information goes – its opposite, it is quite irrelevant because that too is trumpery. Can you not see that our beloved Albert's betrothed is, for all her wistful smiles, as uncouth and ignorant as a nanny-goat? In this house there is not a book, except the one, as it happens, depicted in that miniature of the dead girl; there is not a single picture, and no indication that the thoughts of mankind or the mysteries of nature have ever been remotely perceived or held in the least esteem. And you speak to me of legitimism! Village-green legitimism, if you ask me. According to you they detest the Revolution, and probably Buonaparte, though I have heard it asserted to the contrary. But in any case, what do they know about that young man Buonaparte except that he married – and before that lived in sin with – a negress? Money and prejudice is their only morality. I am sorry for Don Mariano, for whom, I confess, I feel a great liking, but do not talk to me about Elmina and her so-called political leanings! You are not by any chance going to tell me she's a Girondiste . . . I can't help laughing!"

De Neville, as we see, always spoke at random when angry, and at that "Girondiste", applied to the girl who had thrown the linnet to the cat, the overgrown child Nodier opened his eyes wide and replied as follows:

"Ingmar, for goodness' sake do not speak so loudly, or the servants will hear you. This is a friendly house, of little or no culture, I grant you, but of sweet-natured and irreprehensible people. You have seen how they have accepted Albert without so much as ascertaining whether he had money, and with what dignity they have borne the sorrow that has afflicted them . . . their bereavement, I mean; and every day you see with your own eyes how hospitable and kind they are, and how they love each other. It cuts me to the quick to hear you, who are always so just and noble, expressing yourself in such terms . . ."

De Neville now grew ashamed of his outburst (not unaware of what wound, or maybe disappointment, had caused it), but not of his indignation, which remained, though softened by a sense of inevitability, and also by involuntary acceptance of what was affectionate in his own nature, and the goodness that flowed ever in the depths of things. He ought not to have spoken that way, this he acknowledged. At the same time it weighed on him not to have told Nodier the worst. He would have liked to have openly discussed all he had learnt from the Duke, the base Court origins (not real noble lineage) of Brigitta Helm, and therefore the consequent vulgarity and petty ambition of the whole female side of the family. And could one then except Elmina, with all her stuck-uppishness and ignorance? But he stopped himself finally, or at least in time, by meditating Nodier's remonstrances, and remembering not only that he was the guest of these people whose behaviour he disapproved of, but that he had come into possession of the secrets of the house, deplorable as they were, by a means of investigation that suddenly appeared to his eyes as highly questionable; and he now, at the mere memory, felt a discomfort very akin to shame. He therefore abruptly changed the subject.

"Have you gone so far as to promise any . . . support to our Albert?" he enquired, expecting an affirmative answer.

"None whatever," replied the merchant with the utmost promptness (and we are tempted to add, candour, and maybe even freedom from responsibility, though we are reluctant to judge). "In fact I have been meaning to tell you, but never got a chance to: they positively prefer it this way. Elmina, as you know – and Albert, fortunately, is indifferent to the situation – is rich enough to take your breath away. She would be the envy of not a few of our leading titled families at home. She could buy the whole of Flanders. But this appears to cause her such displeasure as to lead one to think, that had she not known you to be a wealthy man, in obedience to her father she would have accepted *even you.*"

De Neville thought his heart had stopped.

Only after a moment did he grasp the purport of what Nodier had said regarding the attitude of those two, and particularly Elmina, towards wealth. But he remained sceptical. He felt certain that not only Don Mariano, but the girl also, were intensely interested in money. This was evident from the fact that they never mentioned it (for the really rich it is taboo). On this point he was immovable, as ever, and to some extent undiscerning with regard to himself. But it is also true that he behaved, where money was concerned, as the night to its stars, or an apple-orchard to its apples: his fingers dripped with fairy lights, but at bottom de Neville was extraneous to it. (We shall see in due course whether this was a fault, or an exceptional case of immaturity.)

A pause ensued, during which the rain was to be heard pelting against the windows as if in grief.

The prince, in thoughtful silence, fell to wondering whether a woman who marries a man for money, or else – a simply untenable hypothesis – out of *hatred* of it, and in any case invariably conducts herself according to the wishes and despotic designs of her parent, is a real woman at all, and not a slave.

Truly, Elmina did not find grace in the eyes of Monsieur de Neville.

And inwardly he came to the conclusion that he would not care to be in Albert's shoes. On no account. Ever.

De Neville departs, but without making peace.
Elmina in a swoon. Further mention of the Linnet

The departure of De Neville and Nodier, which was to take place immediately after the wedding, arranged for the 31st of May, was brought forward some days, at least in the prince's case, on account of a dispatch which he received, as he claimed, from Liège. "An affair of State," he explained sarcastically. Nor was he too far from the truth, or at least from some possibility of truth, in making this claim, there being no secret concerning the relations obtaining (of highest and most friendly trust, almost of humble submission, on the part of the lofty personage who had sought and solicited them, and whom it is better not to name) between this certain personage and the brilliant and imperious son of Princess Leopoldine; relations consolidated, one might say, at every moment, due to the shortcomings of the "personage" and the (we venture to say) *moral* worth of the other; moral inasmuch as it had been arranged that the latter should not receive, in return for his devotion, favours of any kind, other than the enhancement of his reputation as a highly astute diplomatist, and also as a sincere friend to those who placed their reliance on him, and one devoted to the cause of justice and the welfare of Flanders.

De Neville had therefore received, or at least gave it to be understood that he had received, a message from *high places* urgently recalling him to his homeland; and without further ado, off he went. But it was a departure neither cheerful nor, strangely enough, truly wished; for Elmina's enemy would have preferred to drain the last bitter dregs of his defeat, and of the victory gained by the young Nanny-Goat, as he now dubbed that lovely maiden, to the detriment of the dearest of all his friends, Dupré the weak and scatter-brained artist. He would have liked to be there (the appointed day, a Saturday, was not far off) in the poetic church of Santa Lucia, where the ceremony was to take place, and there, mingling with the enraptured crowd, in a jubilation of lights, of hymns, of the perfume of lilies and roses, and also of jasmine, to attend those detested nuptials which for him seemed to prefigure the funeral of his own cherished youth, together with that of his beloved Albert. Over for ever was the gay life of travel, of enthusiasms, of ravishments, of riding-parties, of courtships! Above all he would have liked to have brought it home to Elmina that he had seen and judged her, as far as anyone (in view of her being still almost in girlhood, and endowed with such graces) would have considered possible. And that, together with a few feats of skill from a jeweller in Chiaia to whom, despite his hostility, he had paid a visit, would have been his real wedding present – reproach and farewell – to that unscrupulous couple: for this was how the poor prince saw the matter, in the bitterness of his heart at being betrayed by them both. But, as we have said, he left before taking his revenge, and without being able to witness it. But was his warfare really over? (Knowing the prince's ill nature we doubt it.)

Nodier stayed on to help the bridegroom and keep him company, promising to remain at his side for as long as necessary, that is, until the newlyweds had removed to the little house at Posillipo which Don Mariano had been to visit in advance, for the specific purpose of planning any expedient alterations.

And here it may be useful to undertake a brief consideration of the loss of memory which happiness ofttimes brings about even in the best of men.

The frenzied joy of our artist was not in the least degree dimmed by the departure of the friend he so loved (not to say, until recently, revered), and to whom, with the exception of his good looks, he owed all that he had in this world. Not a word of regret, not a whisper of "What a pity, he could have been with us on the day" etc. No, nothing of all that. Perhaps the young lover did not even realize that de Neville had flown. And he did not realize it partly because Nodier, in a true fatherly spirit, for all his mere four and twenty years, and also on account of the imaginary old friendship for Don Mariano which he liked to attribute to himself, had assumed, in all and everything, the role of godfather and destined administrator which should have been that of the prince. And it is only fitting, in our belief, to report on the manner of dealing with all the practical matters, that is, the discussions, if we may so term them, and not affectionate conversations, between Don Mariano and Nodier (Albert was always left out, as if they were things ill-suited to his childlike sensibility), concerning the part that "Belgium" (an obvious circumlocution to allude to the munificent prince) was to play in augmenting the patrimony of the family in Naples. It is only proper to relate the whole, although there were few surprises with respect to the admissions already made. That is, on Albert's side, Nodier reconfirmed the modesty of his birth (the title of baron did not count for much) and the scantiness of his resources – the small legacy from his mother and the four-roomed apartment in Liège previously mentioned –, adding only one thing, which did not displease Don Mariano Civile, nor yet particularly move him to enthusiasm, given his somewhat depressed state of mind after the death of his wife. However, the addition was this: that Albert had recently obtained the "protection" of a second lofty personage (of the first, devoted to de Neville, we have already spoken), who, within the scope of those powers still bestowed by history – through sheer inadvertence! – on the modest Olympus of Belgium, and this Olympus being still possessed of secret hopes and grandeurs (such were Nodier's words), had reserved for the Arts the first place, or one of the first, in the project known by the name of *Avenir*. In brief, that palpable treasures and proud intellectual passions had gained a place therein and therefrom received impetus. And even more briefly he said that young talent had thereby been much fostered. For Albert Dupré and his artistic merits, he concluded, disposition had been made, and approval obtained, for an annuity which the artist could enjoy even when abroad and for the term of his natural life; an annuity, should he predecease his consort, transferable to the same and to his children, if any. And seeing that the expression "artistic merits" brought a woebegone smile to the lips of Don Mariano, who did not appreciate the worth of such things, Nodier went on to speak of a commission already received and executed by the artist, for ten busts of Belgian bishops for the Royal Park in Brussels, and the same number of small heads of children and women of unknown identity for the English Cemetery in Rome. He said further that he and de Neville, who during those days in Naples had drafted and drawn up the greater part of these arrangements (and this was no less than the truth, for the prince, following his conversation with Nodier, had been ashamed of having so foolishly neglected the practical duties long assumed by him towards his ward); he said, therefore, that he and de Neville, at the beginning of each year, would personally see to the dispatch from Liège of the agreed sums of money, drawn on the Royal Banks, to Naples; and this as long as Albert was alive, transferring them thereafter (though, it was to be hoped, at some far future date) into the name of Elmina. And he went on to guarantee the first of these letters of credit which the prince had addressed to his Neapolitan bankers, and of which he presented a copy, with his own honoured signature as a Belgian merchant, a thing which would never have crossed his mind outside Neapolitan territory, but which, in that land of muddles and mirages, appeared to him absolutely indispensable. And to confirm and reinforce those preliminary declarations in the most unequivocal manner he drew from a locked cabinet (the conversation was taking place in the merchant's own room, where Don Mariano had come to call on him) a small sack of coarse jute, stuffed to bursting with gold coins, together with a bundle of lingots of the purest gold, all of which ought, he said, comfortably to advance the equivalent of ten annuities, thus creating a fund at the artist's disposal now and for several years to come; and he placed it – he was not a little agitated – on the mantelpiece, so arranged that the contents gleamed through the loose weave of the sack before the eyes of the indifferent Glover. And it was at this point, while Nodier was wondering what, on the face of the planet, could conceivably reanimate and gladden that good old man, for whom he nurtured the kindliest feelings, that he noticed that the miniature of the barefoot girl, which both he and the prince had received as a much-admired gift, was no longer there, but had been replaced by another, depicting a horseman in the act of fleeing astride a black horse, outlined against a sky heavy with stormclouds.

Into his blue eye came a flash of uncertainty, of bewilderment, because he immediately thought that de Neville, jealous of the miniature, which he wanted to keep entirely for himself (for jealousy, often extreme, was an ugly component of his character), had purloined it from him.

At this there came into the golden eye of Don Mariano, along with a slight start – as if he had instantly understood what had astonished Nodier, and what was missing from the mantelpiece, and why – a deeply rooted melancholy; which showed that such singular occurrences were, in the atmosphere obtaining in his house, a thing he had long been aware of, and far from happy about.

"Yes," said he, by way of useless and paltry explanation, "Elmina often complains of the all-too-frequent disappearance, in this house, of certain objects, albeit of no intrinsic value, and of how they are then rediscovered by chance in other rooms. She is convinced, as indeed am I myself, that this is the work of a maid whom we have for some time wished to dismiss; but we fear that she would suffer a great deal from dismissal, and also wonder whether her partiality for glittering objects (perfectly understandable in any human breast) is not due, rather than to a mischievous whim or less innocent greed for money, to the little shadows which haunt a sick mind; seeing that such shadows are known only to God. However, *mon ami*, for the loss of the miniature you will, both you and de Neville, who may possibly have had the same experience, be compensated with an identical miniature, or one even more beautiful."

Nodier, a man, as we have seen, of benevolent disposition and ever inclined to excuse the imperfections and curiosities of this world (maybe simply in order to have one worry the less, rather than more; and this contributed to his flourishing state of health), assured the master of the house that he need not be in the least put out by the (perhaps only momentary) disappearance of the object in question, and brought the conversation back to the point at which they had left it, that is, Albert's marriage portion, not only demonstrating, so to speak, the valuables before their eyes, by weighing them in his hands and lauding them in none too subtle terms, but providing further confirmation as to how, and at what intervals, the agreed monies would, through the established channels, arrive in Naples. And perceiving such an incomprehensible lack of interest in the master of the house, when confronted with so much of monetary value, he ventured to suggest that it would be advisable first to deposit it in a bank, but subsequently to invest it in the purchase of houses and lands, with an eye to building up a conspicuous dowry for any daughter with whom God saw fit to bless the spouses.

"Daughter? Let us hope not," said Don Mariano with a smile, though a swift look of pain passed over his face, leaving the good Nodier perplexed. He hastened to add, "In any case, as you know, Elmina's dowry will be sufficient to meet the needs of any additions to the family . . . It is considerable . . . No, to speak frankly, money is not the family worry . . ." And he concluded, as if regretting having begun, "If one can speak of worries, and not rather the heartache of living . . ."

Nodier was on the point of asking, God knows with what promptness and eagerness, "What is the worry, then?", but he stopped himself in time, prevented by the good manners instilled by his upbringing and also the suspicion that there was, in that house, some intricate mystery that weighed upon them all, and into which it was best not to enquire.

Nevertheless, cheerful and easy-going as was Nodier's mind, that "Daughter? Let us hope not", so totally unexpected, refused to quit it.

* * *

If the jealous de Neville had taken due consideration of the following axiom, true in nearly all situations in which there is some point impenetrable to, or impossible to resolve by, the light of logic, but which may be sensed in a certain unhappiness pervading such situations; something which had until now eluded Nodier and was even more likely to elude the prince, who felt neither interest in nor affection for those unfortunates; if, therefore, de Neville had even faintly reflected on the fact that curiosity is not always a good thing – indeed, if bereft of compassion, is the worst thing possible; and if he had questioned himself as to the scant expedience of his intrusions, or even his mere insistence on learning the truth about the Glover's family, he might perhaps have decided, like most men of good sense, that it is better to steer clear of the afflictions of others, rather than batter at barricaded doors; because if they are the afflictions of friends our battering can do nothing but harm, while in the case of an enemy, which Elmina was for him, it is simply an exercise of cruelty.

But he was incapable of steering clear of anything. Although apparently so detached, our prince was passion and indignation personified – instant, blind and absolute – at the least intimation of being got the better of, and it therefore seemed to him not so much his right as a veritable duty, after a *revelation* that in reality he had himself sought out and provoked, to take action against that detested wedding, in this way reopening hostilities that had seemed at an end, and breaking the truce which, from the latest events as he had assessed them, he now construed as a positive snub to justice.

Not two days had passed since his departure for Liège, as he had announced, and thereafter for Brussels, and hence only two more days remained until the ill-fated wedding, before he reappeared on the scene with the plain intent of rendering that wedding impossible, or much embittered, with the terrifying message to be found below, addressed to Nodier. This message had only apparently come from the Low Countries, evidently entrusted (for the ingenuous) to the swiftest messengers of the Realm, or to the wings of some fantastic windstorm. From what we shall learn, and as some persons later surmised, Caserta was the sole place of origin, and one servant alone – a servant devoted to Ruskaja, recognized as such by his features, principally his Mr Punch-like nose, but also by his yellow livery (a description given by the jeweller, to whom the unhappy Glover rushed at once on recognizing the English name of the firm) – this servant alone was the bearer of the infernal injunction. This servant (to call him a booby would be the last word in courtesy), arriving in Naples towards midday, and taking delivery from Brothers & Co. in Chiaia of an extraordinary article of jewellery, commissioned beforehand by de Neville for Elmina, and intending, according to the rude lights of Casertan youth, to simplify his mission, made his way at once to Jib-Sail House, where instead of dividing his burden between the respective addressees, he insisted on delivering the lot – the letter and the coffer containing the gift – to a single one of them; and even then not to Nodier, as he had been specifically instructed, but to the unfortunate Elmina. The gift was enchanting, and precious in every way. The letter, addressed to Nodier, was otherwise, to put it mildly. Neither enchanting nor civil, at one stunning blow it annulled all the excellence of the gift with insinuations and unjust (if not infamous) slanders on the person of poor Elmina. Indeed, with regard to the Stone Maiden, or Nanny-Goat of the Gulf, as he chose to dub her, the prince, like a complete madman, expressed himself in these terms:

Liège, May

My dear Alphonse,

Cost what it may – and obviously I will take responsibility for all conceivable damages – remove our Albert immediately from Jib-Sail House. From a source above suspicion, clearer than crystal and, believe me, in the *loftiest spheres*, I can assure you that mortal danger threatens not only his body, but his very soul. He is lost unless you, with the speed of light, do something to save him. You are at liberty to disobey me; but know that I shall curse you to all eternity if you do not rescue him from his cruel fate. You may count, for the entire business, and the requisite compensation for moral damages (though, given the persons involved, I think only material ones), on my entire patrimony. In confidence: the Basket enclosed herewith should be given to the Nanny-Goat. There let her browse on her *true* fodder.

de Neville

As, understanding nothing, she read these words, and then reread them, Elmina, who was in the drawing-room with the dressmaker, trying on her wedding-dress, and though perhaps not radiant with joy, at least innocently contented and suffused with a faint tint of happiness and well-being (at the same time attempting to ward off the overexcited Teresina and two very young maids who were going into ecstasies over the silver lace decorations which enhanced the wonderful veil), grew woefully pale. She had barely time to hold out the letter – and to thrust aside the jewel, while with her other hand she covered her eyes – to the enamoured Albert, entering at that moment bearing a delicious bouquet of pink rosebuds interspersed with pale hawthorn blossoms, before she slumped into the arms of the eldest of all the maidservants, the faithful Ferrantina (known as "Carlo's Ferrantina" to distinguish her from two other Ferrantinas who had also been in service in the Glover's house since time immemorial); this maid, with the trace of a leer on her features, having entered the room shortly before Albert.

"O Holy Mother of God," she was heard to exclaim, according to the dressmaker's (presumably faithful) account, "and Merciful Patron of the Birdcage, how bitterly am I now paying for my harsh treatment of the Linnet!"

This exclamation was the most touching demonstration of her innocence of heart, as also of certain small flaws in the same, and furthermore of less-than-happy circumstances in her infancy at Jib-Sail House. Manoeuvred by some creature hostile to her, these now turned her youth and her very future against her (always supposing that Albert Dupré beyond any shadow of doubt – an undemonstrable assertion – represented the future of that most upright young lady).

Oh, if the spiteful Monsieur de Neville had been present! Would he have been ashamed of himself, or felt only triumph? So unfathomable, so devoid of perspicacity, is the human heart, as soon as the roaring Passions gain the whip-hand! (But in any case, he was *not* present).

Behind the message, a prince's grief revealed,
and we are present at an unlawful enquiry
into a remote childhood episode

If the benevolent and peradventure puzzled reader of these pages expects from us an accurate and substantiated representation of the scene which ensued after the delivery of the message at Jib-Sail House, we are bound to disappoint him. On the other hand, as perhaps he will see in due course, that scene was to fall into perspective by itself. It is, however, incumbent upon a scrupulous narrator to pick up the thread of events at the place where it became tangled, in its proper place, which we do not wish to describe as malicious, but as irresponsible, certainly. And this place was nothing less than the heart of the *sorcerer-prince* of Liège.

As had immediately been supposed by those who found it strange, that so few days after that nobleman's departure a message should have been delivered from far-distant Liège, he had not, on departing, directed his steps towards his cultured, austere and verdant homeland, though in truth it was thither that his wounded and wrathful spirit longed to return, but rather to Caserta, to the house of his late mother's friend Benjamin Ruskaja, Polish exile of ancient (and sorcerer of more recent) date. Here he had no need to give any detailed recapitulation of the whole affair, which so many happy days before, under the bluest of skies, he had with plain misgiving foretold to his friend; Benjamin was already up to date on everything, both on account of the friendships he enjoyed in Naples (which had many listening ears even in the kitchens of Jib-Sail House), and owing to his well-known gifts as seer and magician. Therefore, seeing de Neville enter altogether pale, only in part due to the wind into which he had been riding for several hours (having chosen to arrive on horseback in advance of his suite), he said:

"My son, the deed is done! It now behoves you to set your heart at rest."

This expression, which gave rise to the supposition that he, de Neville, was in reality lovesick for Elmina, and suffering the pangs of hell at seeing his place in her heart usurped by another, albeit Albert, caused our noble friend, who was in any case taking no oath as to the secret depths of his soul, to quake with indignation and at once reply:

"I admit to not having been entirely insusceptible to her charms, dear Duke; but now the question is quite another. We are concerned solely with Albert. The girl . . . the girl he is to marry, the sweet and gentle Elmina, is a . . . is one of us, my friend. There lies the secret."

"*One of us!* What do you mean?"

"That she practises the magic arts, all of them, you understand, even the most dangerous; and as a shield to this end uses holy religion itself."

Benjamin laughed.

"Have you proofs of this? Can you give me even one?"

"*This* is one . . . the least and most superficial," said de Neville, implying that there were plenty of others, which there were not, thus shamelessly paltering with the truth while extracting from the blue morocco wallet in his breast pocket the miniature of the Horseman, which he too had found, though without breathing a word about it to Nodier. And the moment he saw it his face, pallid enough already from the wind, paled still further. The figure in the miniature was no longer the Horseman, but once again the lovely barefoot child.

"The image which was there before!" observed the Duke simply.

"Yes . . . and this is terrible. That this picture which, I concede, enchanted me at first sight, should change all on its own into another! Because when it was exchanged in my room in Naples, this could have been done by any servant jealous of the family's possessions; but during my journey this morning – and after Ponticelli I took it out and looked at it, and the child was not there – it can only have been by some inexplicable power that sees and holds dominion over all, including my life and actions. And I can attribute it only to *her*!"

"Does it not occur to you," proceeded the good Duke, very calmly, "that it is your own wonder-struck psyche that has restored it? And that you are the sorcerer, Ingmar, and not poor Elmina?"

"As to my . . . my powers . . . I do not deny knowledge of them," admitted the prince, not a little embarrassed and nervous, "but we are here concerned with something else entirely. This image represents . . . shall we say a shadow, a mystery of *that house*, a house where I sense something far from good, far from clear. And a sorcerer," he almost shouted, "is not necessarily a man of less heart and intellect than one who has not the same gift . . . I deny it. Although endowed with certain powers I feel myself to be a man, and a sinner, like anyone else, and I pray to Heaven that at the end of our experience on earth my soul may be saved . . . And having said that I have said all. I do not believe the same of Elmina."

He then threw himself into a velvet-covered armchair patterned with green leaves and white flowers, situated conveniently near the fire (for outside, at intervals, the mournful east wind was heard to sough), and thus continued:

"No, there is no clarity in the spirit of Elmina. This it is which terrifies me, in entrusting Albert to her. And these are fears I can no longer suppress. I do not reject the notion that there is in me, together with this horror, an inextinguishable sadness, because I feel the fundamental *virtue* of Elmina, respect her as a woman of strong character, but she is not *wholesome* in the sight of God, I say: a mystery far from healthy lies at the roots of her heart, a heart one would wish to think entirely innocent."

To his great surprise, instead of the rebuke which the prince in trepidation expected in reply to his shockingly obvious slander (for such we may call an assertion based on nothing but the prince's antipathy for that young woman, or Nanny-Goat), Ruskaja, who, seated opposite him in a larger and very plush pink velvet *bergère*, was turning the exquisite miniature over and over in his fingers, said as if to himself,

"You are evidently alluding to a fault, if not to a downright sin. And what might this be, according to you, my dear fellow? She is certainly not wicked."

"No, no," stammered de Neville, "I don't think that."

"Then look into your own heart, my young friend," said Ruskaja, fixing him with a stare. "We are generally led to believe," he went on, "that the hearts of children, or of very young people, are immune from at least one sin. But look into your own. Ever since you were a boy, and still today, do you not suffer agonies over another person's wonderful happiness, rather than misgiving, as you suppose, regarding his future?"

"Yes . . . maybe . . . I don't know . . . Oh, who can say what is in his heart?" Ingmar practically shouted. "I . . . I cannot!" he concluded almost with a wail.

Benjamin threw him a glance full of compassion.

"This small creature," he said quickly, we assume to change the subject, "this little girl . . . now I see it quite clearly . . . Be so good as to hand me that lens." And the majestic old man indicated a large magnifying-glass with a milky lens, set like an eye in a velvet case resting on the low table; and this lens seemed (an illusion, for sure) to be peering warily about it. Ingmar, his heart in tumult, obeyed on the instant, and at once the following words greeted his ears:

"Ingmar, there is no aura of life around this creature's little blond head. And this lens, among the dearest treasures bequeathed me by my mother, has never deceived me. She – the little girl – is no longer of this world, but only for a few years has this been the case. And I am able to tell you . . . wait while I look more closely . . . that she died purely and simply of grief, eight or nine years ago, and Jib-Sail House was witness to that grief, and sees and remembers it to this day. She was the youngest of all the daughters of Donna Brigitta (by a first husband, the late Colonel Helm – on this point my previous information was faulty), and was the gentlest creature in the world, the jewel of the household, loved for her grace and good nature by her brothers and sisters and the servants, and by her second father perfectly adored. But not by Elmina, who was then eight or nine. Why was this? The Lord alone can tell, because Elmina, though different from Florì, was no less beautiful, or gay, or beloved. But this mystery, of the horrible suffering in a soul on account of something *more* it imagines it discerns in another – what a lacerating mystery of the human heart, at the root, maybe, of every drama in the world – this mystery no one and nothing, except religion, in those who possess it, will ever succeed in illuminating. Poor Elmina, you ought to commiserate her. Florì had a linnet . . ."

Ingmar, his eyes wide, was hanging, as they say, and none too rhetorically either, on the old man's lips.

"Duke, did you say *Florì?* Did you say *a linnet?*"

"Yes, my boy. Her name, the little girl's name, was Floridia, and the children of the air were her religion; even though, in her innocence, she used also to go to church. But she worshipped only birds. She fell sick, though, of the languor, a malady very frequent, as you know, amongst our poor young girls; and her new father (Don Mariano, whose profound unhappiness has already struck you, and we now see a cause for it) did nothing but move her from place to place, from villa to villa, from garden to garden, from Portici to Sorrento, all the best-known health-resorts – but Florì did not recover her health. She was therefore with-drawn to Jib-Sail House, to a room which no one was permitted to enter except Donna Brigitta and the Glover – Teresa was still with the wet-nurse – and occasionally Elmina, though this would not have been strictly necessary; a room overlooking an internal garden; and there she lived out her last remaining days, growing paler and paler, in the company of a few birds. And among these, master not only of the wickerwork bird-cage but also of the little girl's gilded chamber, was Dodò, her beloved linnet, a present from her father . . . Ah, here I can see the whole scene . . . things of which people have spoken, but aggrandized or aggravated in their own minds . . . But this lens, which brings the past to life, does not err . . . it has never erred . . . It was made in Cracow, the work of a craftsman of genius such as are no longer to be found . . . (Let me breathe on it, it seems slightly clouded). There! Do you see nothing now?"

Apprehensive (for, untroubled by magic, he was troubled by the things of the heart), Ingmar gazed into the lens and saw, or thought he saw, as in our television screens when we turn them off for the night, a point of light in the blackness; but a point which expanded instead of diminishing, and in its centre revealed a simple, touching scene: Floridia asleep in her little silken bed. The Linnet, on the pillow near its mistress's face, was billing and kissing her hair, as if she were but another bird like him, only a little bigger . . . and this very tenderly and playfully.

"And see . . ." (for here the Duke's voice intervened in the magic scene from the past, to explain and perhaps bring it to life with a learned commentary), "see, the door now opens . . . In comes Elmina . . . Some nine years old, so just a little older than Florì, she enters the room, haughty and vain, maybe in order to close the window now standing open to the spring night (a duty taken on herself, with her usual bossiness). She immediately sees the bird, and observes the exquisite tenderness of this creature for her sister. At once her features harden. She steps swiftly to the bed. The innocent bird looks at her in surprise. 'Go away, go away, you naughty thing!' she seems to be shouting. The bird flees. She chases it, without a sound, grabs it, squeezes it with unbelievable cruelty in her little hands. She opens her fingers . . . The loving little wonder is no more: a pathetic little corpse slips from her fingers, falls to the floor, a lifeless object. Elmina hurries from the room. At that moment Florì wakes up, opens the pearls of her eyes, seeks her loved one there beside her face. But Dodò is on the floor, and dead, and does not answer."

"And then?" shrieked Ingmar.

"Calm yourself, dear boy . . . Do not weep . . ." (Ingmar was in fact in floods of tears). "Such things are not rare in children . . . jealousy is by no means rare in those little angels. And then," (letting go of the lens, suspended on an elegant ribbon), "I now remember what was said of her by the Marchesa Durante (my very good friend, so if you return to Naples do pay her a visit and give her my regards, if she is not already in the country)."

". . . What was said of her?"

". . . that the angelic Florì was not entirely blameless. That morning she had provoked Elmina by using a harsh word . . . almost a swearword, in a child . . ."

"What . . . was it?"

"It began with the letter *u* . . . (and was, I imagine, *ugly*), and it referred (I fear) to one of the lineaments of some poor servant whom Elmina (you know what little girls are) had then taken it into her head to stick up for. Unfortunately that is all I know."

"An act of iniquity none the less. Whatever the poor child might have said, *she*" (meaning Elmina) "had no right to punish the poor Linnet. But tell me," continued the indignant prince, "tell me at least this: was she sorry? What excuses did she make for her spiteful deed, if she could find any?"

"How can I tell? Who can know after so many years, my son? Alas, that same night Florì herself (having after a faint cry given no further sign of consciousness, but lying calm and trance-bound in her bed, her eyes open on her last vision of her little friend), that selfsame night Floridia died. Elmina, according to the account I heard, threw the Linnet out of the window, presumably to eliminate any proof of her guilt. And it is said, and mark you, it is merely *said*, that during the night the creature, suddenly awakened from its slumber (perhaps the effect of the mild air), spread its wings and fluttered . . . and fluttered towards the stars that bestrewed the whole dark vault of the Gulf of Naples."

By this picture of events even our dread de Neville was reduced to sobs, thus showing himself to be a worthy friend to Albert; while his tears at least to some degree assuaged his hatred for the Glover's daughter. And here there was one further revelation: poor Brigitta had herself, of her own free will, left the house in Naples to take refuge in the country at Casoria. She wished nevermore to set eyes on the elder daughter. This was the true motive for her leaving the house, not Elmina's discovery of, and heartless reaction to, the lowly (and also partly Bourbon) origins of that worthy woman who was her mother.

Without even having noticed, in the old wizard's tale, at least this contradiction between one rumour and another, with respect to his previous account of the facts – that it was Elmina who had exiled her mother at Casoria to punish her for her relations with the Bourbon Court (but we know how fickle and fluctuating is truth, especially when entrusted to the tongues of malevolent relatives and senile retainers) – the prince, quite worn out, accepted the Duke's hospitality for the night. But – if we may so speak of a fearless gentleman and a diplomatist skilled in all the vices and deceits of the most celebrated Courts in Europe, with regard to what is, after all, a story of spiteful children and enamoured Linnets – his was a heart destroyed.

First thing next morning he dispatched a manservant of the Duke's to Naples with the message we know of, a message which ended up in the hands of Elmina, while the gift for Elmina, the golden Basket encrusted with rubies collected in Chiaia from Brothers & Co. and refused by the unfortunate girl (as we have seen) with unutterable anguish, was – by the same befuddled young boor still lingering in the room – thereupon delivered with a bow to the dumbfounded Nodier. And for the remainder of these stormy events, O sensitive reader, we now pass to the Glovemaker's house.

The desperation of Elmina. Albert (verbally)
challenges the imprudent prince to a duel.
But nothing comes of it

In Albert's heart there passed not a moment between the perusal of the sheet bearing the message (with a number of roses, as was then the fashion, embroidered along the serrated edge of the paper, this being the only thing suitable for a letter to be found in the Duke's secretaire, a relic of his distant infancy and the pains his *maman* went to over his birthday); not a moment passed, therefore, before that candid heart was devastated by the most unimaginable indignation. The unfortunate Ferrantina ("di Carlo") who was, as we know, one of the most elderly maids in the house, and had in fifty years of faithful service seen and heard everything under the sun, her ears being particularly attentive, still declared almost twenty years later – to a nephew who was nursing her through an illness (from which she luckily recovered) and was indiscriminately collecting her delightful *mémoires* on behalf of a French journalistic hack employed during Republican times to testify to the hatred the people bore towards the Bourbon yoke – that from Vesuvius itself, that mountain of fear and of fable, no one on that occasion, or since the days of Pliny himself, could have expected better, or rather worse, than the avalanche, and fury, and lava-flow of abuse that spouted from the mouth of Bellerophon when confronted with his friend's vile act. Rage, indignation and desperation on account of the state to which he saw his beloved reduced, and, in addition to that, shame – shame for the whole of Flanders, in the eyes of her father. And it appears from the pages of the frivolous reporter that he expressed himself, not a little absurdly, thus:

"Oh! Oh! Oh! Did you ever hear of such a fiend? My sweet Elmina, take heart, take heart or I shall die of it! And you, Nodier, upon my soul as you see me and understand me: judge, therefore, whether for a single moment I deserve to be thus assaulted by the best and most faithful of friends, and yet not ask myself if the Universe itself has not disintegrated and turned upside down, and whether by some calamity Satan himself does not reign in the place of Our Lord Jesus Christ! O Elmina, my innocent one, take heart, revive, or I am done for. I shall certainly kill him, and at once! Madame Ferrantina, the smelling-salts! *Mademoiselle Thérèse! Mademoiselle Louisette!* fetch water! You, Nodier, waste no time! Fetch my sword — it must be in my cravatte drawer, at the bottom of the wardrobe — and polish it up. I cannot think you will refuse to act as my second. The other will be found. As for this Ruffian, where is he? Let him be sought out and informed. A priest must be present — we are not yet under the Jacobins, thank Heaven! Kindly see to all that, Monsieur Civile: that distressing side of the matter is your province!" Meanwhile Adelmine, chalk-white and silent, reopening those golden eyes which had rendered the artist, not without pangs and for ever, her slave, feebly reached out to him one bloodless hand, and almost leaning upon his shoulder, whispered faintly,

"*Vuie pazziate, Albert, mon ami*" (one of the few French expressions she used in the course of their betrothal), "you . . . are not yourself . . . And your friend . . . he too . . . he is not in his right mind . . ."

At this point Nodier, the plump and well-beloved purveyor of the peace and well-being of his companions-in-revelry from their first youth up, was visited by a blessed vision of deliverance: an anchor proffered by Heaven itself, or by friendly spirits, he perceived and readily grasped in his firm hands, and under his guidance the vessel of the Belgo-Neapolitan marriage sailed clear of the sandbanks of obliteration. He, arranging his every lineament in an expression of infinite placidity (the which, save for stony hearts, to witness was to understand), and even of amused and tolerant compassion, pronounced as follows:

"Such a true friendship had to end like this, in a fit of jealous rage!"

The word "jealous", together with that gentle regret which attributed the prince's slander to "a fit of rage", were not lost on those present, who seized on them at once, including the bewildered Glovemaker's daughter.

"Then . . . what exactly do you mean, Monsieur Nodier?" asked the poor Glover himself, who had only just entered, but had grasped the whole situation.

"I didn't wish . . . I hesitated to . . . it seemed very terrible . . ." stammered the merchant, dramatically wringing his hands, "but now, alas, I see the fruits of my discretion . . ."

"What d'you mean, Nodier? What's this all about?" cried Dupré himself, leaping to his feet. "Did you know something of it? The reason for this hatred was known to you?"

"Not hatred! Love! Don Mariano . . ." He turned to the Glovemaker standing crushed and almost petrified beside his daughter, "Don Mariano, you must forgive the *mademoiselle*: it is no fault of hers. Our friend de Neville . . . he has lost his head over your daughter . . . therefore, though he is the best of friends to all of us . . ."

"Are you telling me, Nodier . . . that he wished to marry my Elmina himself, and that these slanderous accusations arise from his distress . . . Is this what you mean?"

"Precisely," said Alphonse Nodier with an air of gravity.

"Apart from all that," put in one of the dressmakers present, who had caught a glimpse of the letter as it lay on the floor, "our young mistress is not a Nanny-Goat."

The observation passed without comment.

"My love . . ." Thus began Albert, who had retrieved a desperate calm, and disposed himself once more on his knees before the yellow satin chaise-longue where Elmina, semi-conscious, was reclining. "My love, I believe in you most absolutely, I believe that your heart is entirely mine. But tell me, *ma reine* . . . have you not by any chance given him some reason for hope? That horrible present of his . . ." (here alluding to the controversial but none the less admirable so-called Basket). "What did he expect from you? Did he not, perhaps, have hopes?"

To this the fair Elmina (whose aversion to the prince we have already shown, and whom such questions could therefore only still further distress and exasperate; but of this the incautious lover could scarcely be aware) made no reply. A brawling as of a myriad birds in a wood, as of wrathful Linnets, roared in her head.

"These accusations . . . On what grounds could His Highness possibly base such accusations . . ." the unhappy father was muttering, as it were to himself. And all of a sudden he started to sob, as if he not only disbelieved those accusations, but also thought that in the whole affair he was afflicted not so much by the hypothetical blameworthy sentiments of the prince, as by something beyond these, something *other*; by a *real* fault on the part of his beloved daughter, that had barely been touched on, and that he could not, *must* not, reveal to a living soul.

It was at this point that His Highness's unfortunate young friend recalled the exclamation, so piteous and strange, that fell from the lips of Elmina on reading the dispatch: "Holy Mother of God and Merciful Virgin of the Birdcage, how I am paying now for my harshness to the Linnet!"

Covering her hands with kisses, he begged for an explanation.

This he received, with great promptitude; and whether it was sincere, or else dictated by some childish terror of punishment, it was as follows.

The real Linnet in the story (even if Albert remembered hearing of a second Linnet, that mild evening of stars and silence on which they met) was not the one which had died a few hours before their arrival, due to being left without water in its dish, but another, which had belonged to a sister of Elmina and Teresa's who had died in childhood: Dina, or Dinuccia, also known as "Ratlet", unfortunately not a pretty child, as implied by her nickname, but much beloved for all that. However she was not good-natured, Elmina was sad to say. She had two things which she held very dear, as often happens with little children who are not quite right in the head (and here Don Mariano gave sorrowful assent), to wit a small picture of the Madonna of the Birdcage – who is venerated in the Capella delle Grazie, and under whose protection Donna Brigitta had placed her at birth, observing her to be so singularly unendowed – and a little bird, a linnet, identical to the one which died the day of their arrival.

"*Eh bien?*" burst out the passionate Albert, his eyes aflame with hope in the absolute innocence and virtue of his loved one.

"Well then," she resumed with effort, but with great firmness and candour, "I was severe towards Nadina, and this was a fault, indeed a real sin, I now believe. It always displeased papa, but I wished to be of guidance to her, I wanted her to grow up sincere and good; which I am bound to say she was not. And she died, not more than six or seven years ago, by throwing herself out of her bedroom window because she had found the Linnet dead; and shortly before, complaining of this to a maidservant who reported it to me (Ferrantina will bear me witness), had accused me, saying it was I who had killed the Linnet. In this way she was siding with *maman*, who idolized her and at the same time had no great liking for me. She threw herself from the window believing – she was so naïve – that she would come back to life at once . . . It was intended as a joke, but it came to a bad end. *Maman* really never forgave me. And this" (here she burst into tears again) "is the background, Albert dear. I was accused of having hated the Linnet out of sheer spite, and my sister also, and of having myself driven her to despair. And over this *maman* left the house!

Luckily papa did not believe the story. Papa," here she passionately addressed herself to Don Mariano, "is it true that you believe your Elmina? That my sister Nadina told a lie?"

"Yes . . . yes . . ." muttered Don Mariano, forcing his poor chin up and down.

"And I believe you too, dear heart," declared Albert, with mingled tears and laughter. "All things considered, it seems just a nursery tale, and I cannot understand this intrusiveness on the part of de Neville, or what is in his mind, or can have prompted him to slander you so vilely with an allusion, it seems clear enough," and he cast a glance at the letter now lying on a chair, "to some story of enchantments, of powers hostile to the soul . . . It is really extraordinary . . ."

"That's because you don't know what people are like!" interposed the dressmaker, Signora Olinda Benincasa, with great bitterness and removing two pins from her mouth for the purpose. "But Naples, alas, is made that way. We tear each other to pieces because we don't think of the consequences. In fact, because we never think of anything at all."

"And it's mostly the innocent who go to the wall," added one little seamstress with almost excessive indignation.

Albert sighed, entirely won over.

"But you have never told me," said he lovingly to Elmina, holding out to her the roses with a sprinkling of snow on top, which someone had carefully picked up and deposited on a marble table, "you have never told me, my adored Elmina, whether you are really and truly religious . . . whether you believe in God and the Blessed Virgin."

"In God, the Virgin, and all the Angels," came the answer, frank and forthright.

"This is a great relief to me, believe me. And . . . to what else do you turn for guidance? Have you – forgive me for asking – some *philosophie*?"

The poor thing did not understand the French (or Latin?) word *philosophie*, but replied in tones as prompt as they were woebegone:

"I believe in the Spirit of Evil."

And once again, grave and serious, her father nodded, and all the women round them nodded too: yes, yes, Evil – Spirit or Majesty as it may be – really exists, and the signs of its passing are there for all to see.

"And what would it be . . . in what does it consist, *ma reine*, this *Esprit du Mal*?" gently enquired young Albert, leaning a little forward over that beloved face, already forgetting his sorrow and expecting to hear such words as "Pride . . . falsehood . . . betrayal . . . slander . . . envy", all the defects of the prince, in fact, and the same of which the poor girl stood accused. But instead, with the calm of resignation, she replied:

"Happiness is evil, Albert. Loving other creatures is evil. One must love only God and the King. The rest is sinful."

"The King? The King? *Est-ce donc le Roi qui a fait les créatures, ma petite Elmina?*" tenderly and with heartfelt and good-humoured courtesy enquired the impassioned lover, who had quite forgotten the stumbling block in friendships and betrothals between persons of different nationalities. "Is the King God himself? *Vous aimez Ferdinand, est-ce bien cela que vous voulez me dire?*"

"*Oui, Monsieur Albert.* God made all creatures and their sorrow. All creatures live in sorrow, and only sorrow must we love, only those who are lost must we serve .. even His Majesty obeys . . ." declared the Glovemaker's daughter with a sort of saintly grandeur; repeating, as in a sad refrain, not in truth perceptible to the ears of all (except *one*, and for now we will not say who): "Only life is evil, only joy is evil!"

And purest tears (we are tempted to say "of otherwhereness", or even of dementia) at least as copious as those of her Belgian wooer, as she so spoke – or raved – coursed down the face of the fair Elmina, tracing who knows what obscure incomprehensible word upon that radiant soul of only sixteen summers; not darkening it, but infusing it with light, as the dawn sometimes sheds lustre, even before arising with roseate tremor, on the darksome gardens of the world.

Dupré did not hear, or understand, all the Neapolitan-cum-French she spoke, at times something more than childish, but his fervour for his spouse-to-be, the lightning sensation that she was, simply, one of those few sublime spirits who from time to time alight upon this earth, still trembling from their headlong flight, sent a shock through his being. An enormous gratitude swept over him, almost petrified him with astonishment, at finding himself the one beside whom, and for whom, she would spend the days of such a hallowed life, conferring also on her husband that superhuman beauty of which she alone, mysteriously, seemed to enjoy the privilege, and which Albert, unlike the cynical de Neville, too proudly perhaps, but also profoundly, honoured.

Once more, in silence, and prey to the most lofty emotion, he bowed his head in adoration to kiss that hand.

The effects of Elmina's sublime "explanation" and its beneficent results at Caserta

From his refuge and stronghold in the Duke's house at Caserta de Neville had (or thought he had, which is almost as good) witnessed the entire scene, in part through the magic lens, which the Duke aimed like a telescope, pointing it south-west, and in part relying on his highly inflamed imagination (in which, honestly, he believed rather less, and he was right); but above all he was informed of the concluding events by some gossip which arrived the next morning from Naples (thus supplementing his information in retrospect) through the dressmaker, Signora Benincasa, who had been at Jib-Sail House at that tragic moment for the fitting of the wedding-dress, and who was also dressmaker to the Marchesa Durante. She (Olinda Benincasa) had that very same evening recounted all to the marchesa, who passed on the information to the most trusty of her lovers, Cavaliere Del Giorno, who in turn discussed the matter with a certain Bartolomeo Percoco of the mail service, equally trusty, but who also had useful acquaintances amongst the Duke's retinue. De Neville was apprised of it in great detail – his host, as is only right, had been informed earlier – and by ten o'clock the following morning he had the story in every particular, together with the brioches and honey, the coffee and the local *Monitor*, which was of little interest to him.

Then fell, as falls a mighty wind, no sooner had he heard so many at least apparent contradictions and nonsenses (the ugliness of Florì, assuming it was the same sister, or else the invention of a nasty, spiteful "Ratlet", and the whole of the piteous tale concerning both the Linnet and the mysterious infant); then fell, I repeat, all the wrath of that great Sir into a kind of stupefied vexation; and the disdain that ensued in some degree tempered his malevolent sentiments towards Elmina, whom he declared to the Duke to be, in his opinion, not only a Legitimist and a Nobody but the most incredible bigot in all Naples, quite apart from her prodigious talents as a liar. What!! "Happiness is evil. Loving created things is evil. Only affliction must we love. The rest is sinful." If this was the case, what would she do to Dupré? But ah, of course, the man was lost! The only difference it made, in de Neville's mind, was in his attitude towards this foreseen catastrophe: well deserved! Albert had asked for it! De Neville all but agreed with Elmina: one must not love created beings. All too dearly had he loved Albert! He had no further wish to interfere.

The Duke listened to all this with a smile.

"Dear boy," said he, "that is not exactly your way of thinking. Let me speak, and tell you how I view the matter. You are despondent, upset, disillusioned. You still love that poor girl; and also, though a little less, on account of his good fortune, Albert Dupré. Well, you are mistaken. I do not want to tell you more because I admit that I do not know more, and perhaps have no wish to. God, in granting me the gifts known also to you, did not permit me, as he does not permit you, to raise the veil of the future. He only allowed me for brief moments to witness the actions, and hear snatches of conversations at present in progress or already past, not to discern their true and inner causes or fearsome interconnections; he did not grant it to me, or to you, to encounter the terrible Days to Come and look them in the face. And therein sleeps the secret, there lies the ultimate truth, for only in its consummation is preserved the truth of any life, and in that alone, whatever its beginnings may have been, is its Destiny revealed. And I thank that same God for it, at least in this case, because every time I say, *Dupré! Albert Dupré!* I experience a sensation I cannot define, one of mortal chill and melancholy . . . or is it of joy? For two days now I have felt this. To these two young people I wish good fortune, although I do not know them personally, as I would to any pair of innocent creatures . . . yes, supremely innocent, even if confused and frequently overweening, as Elmina is. They are rising as in flight, as do we all, radiant and content in the first light of day; as yet they do not see the burdens they will have to bear . . . But do not make me speak."

"Oh, if it comes to that," replied de Neville none too benevolently, "we all carry the same burdens."

"In my view," continued the Duke, "you, dear boy, would do well at this point to forget your minor chagrin over this affair" – with a smile at the word minor – "and as you did in a manner of which I wholly approved, some days ago,* you should act with propriety and benevolence . . ."

"But . . . how?" stammered Ingmar.

* Not true, as we have seen, but praise was part of the Duke's method of moral instruction.

"I don't really know . . . I should not like to interfere. But, if you feel up to it, go back to Naples – Saturday the 31st is the wedding, so you have a whole day and more – and send another message, a sincere, repentant one, to Don Mariano's, a worthy and affectionate thought that cancels out the first, and assures them that you are at peace with them and wish them all the luck in the world. In addition . . ."

"In addition . . . ?"

"It is merely a thought, mind, not a piece of advice. Pay a visit, if you can, to the main cemetery in Naples. There are in fact two, adjoining each other. The lower, and larger, is the cemetery of the poor; above this, fewer in number (as in life), the gentry are laid to rest. I suggest that you halt at the dividing line, marked by a short flight of steps between the two levels – and also two final estates. In the upper cemetery, order, light and beauty; in the other . . . That dividing line (do not look below you) is the place I exort you to visit. Go there, as soon as you arrive, with Attorney Liborio Apparente (Don Liborio is a friend of mine, I will give you a letter to him), and seek out the Old Chapel, or Family Vault of Monsieur Civile. The first you come to, on the right of the avenue. It is very small and unassuming, so do not be surprised. There is another larger, the work of an outstanding artist, specially built some years ago and registered by him in the name of Donna Brigitta, his one and only love. It is of less interest. There, at the first, you (and you alone) will, if you watch carefully as you read the inscriptions, receive more information than you could glean from the entire nobility of Naples and all their servants put together. Another piece of advice, but this, my boy, is for your ears only: spare a charitable thought for Don Mariano. He, the poor Glovemaker, is the most stricken person in this whole story. More I cannot tell you."

And sure enough the Duke added not another word.

No more, for that matter, did de Neville. His features overcast, and with no passing cloud, but as if winter with its pale though unbroken greyness had filled his whole soul, he was by this time cold and indifferent towards all these tales of wives and sweethearts, of children's spite and the adversities of Linnets, and blamed only his levity in abandoning Liège, in the company of his beloved friends, a month ago, before the coming of May.

Oh that he had never left his home, and the tedious fashionable life of that wealthy, frigid, sensible, and highly respectable society into which he was born!

A touch of dejection and
the prince's meeting with the "Scribblerus"

The prince, this time in but a few melancholy hours, made arrangements for his departure for Liège, planning only one stop, or rather
a deviation, though whether for a matter of minutes or for one or more
days he did not know, to the capital of the Realm.

Here he arrived on the Friday, at about midday, alighting once more
at the now cheerless Hat of Gold, where he was warmly and tiresomely
fawned on by all and sundry as the noblest and best-loved of clients, the
most liberal, the most affable etc.; and this, in our belief, not solely on
account of the generous gratuities he had left. The fact is there was no
one, with the exception of Elmina, who did not see that magical traveller
through rose-tinted spectacles.

Unable, at any rate, to endure the style and manner of these adulations,
and feeling almost on the verge of tears at the inevitable contrast between
the light-heartedness, the gaiety, the unalloyed happiness of his arrival a
few weeks earlier, with all that sunshine, that blue and rosy light on the
Castle and the sailing-vessels in the harbour, and the present greyness
reigning in his heart and in the landscape, he at once changed his clothes
and betook himself to the address of this Attorney Liborio Apparente,
whom the Duke had counselled him to seek out. He did not find him. He
remembered, however, that he had a duty to perform, and set off accord-
ingly to wander through the fashionable centre of Naples, dodging his way
among the carriages and flocks of goats, in search of a new gift for the
spouses, one that he hoped would bring peace at least to his own troubled
mind. With this end in view he paid a further visit to a number of jewellers.
At one of these, Smith Bros., he selected a gift which ought, in his opinion,
greatly to rile and at the same time delight the Nanny-Goat, if only on
account of its costliness; and this was a birdcage of pure gold, its bars
encrusted with sapphires, in the centre of which, on a hinged perch that
swung back and forth, was set the most beautiful linnet fashioned in
coloured enamel – its plumage grey as smoke or mist, its head gaily tilted

upwards, and on that head, and on its grey breast as well, a red disk bright as the sun. But the original feature, compared with other such birds that had taken his fancy, consisted in this: that with a turn of a golden key in its back (no danger of its escaping, secured as it was by a golden chain to three rings on the top of the cage) the bird *sang*; that is, it nodded its guileless head and emitted through its beak, which opened for the purpose, a few melodious notes resembling a boatman's call on a moonlit night, a simple:

O-hoh! O-hoh! O-hoh!

or more simply still:

Ohhh! Ohhh! Ohhh!

which seemed at times, to one of fine discernment, to contain a sob; and this sob, the prince thought in his impetuous heart, would surely recall to Elmina how remissly she had wrought upon the hearts of others; and to Dupré how he had betrayed, and how mightily!, the heart of a friend. De Neville was perfectly foolhardy in making this violent appeal to his loved ones to remember him, and in so doing to pity him . . . and to address a tender thought to their "poor Ingmar"!

We are not much in agreement over that "poor", or indeed the rest of it. But thus, dear Reader, is the stormy unhappy heart of man when suddenly shaken by the fitful winds of youth.

In the early afternoon (he had meanwhile asked the jeweller to be so good as to deliver the propitiatory gift to Jib-Sail House) the prince, having ascertained that Notary Liborio (a notary, not an attorney as the Duke had stated) was impossible to locate until someone informed him that in Naples the Notary's real name counted for far less than the generic nickname which for him, as for all lettered men at that time, was Scribblerus; and having told him of his friendship with the Duke, and the brief time at his disposal to see Naples (this he said out of pure politeness, for he had indeed already seen too much of it), and also of his intention of going, on the Duke's behalf, to pay his respects to the forebears of Don Mariano, entreated the Notary to be so kind as to accompany him in a carriage to the place where had lain for many a year, destined to wax ever more numerous, an entire population which had danced and wept, had been happy or woeful there in Naples, since the earliest days of the House of Aragon; people of palace and hovel alike, of the Court, the market-place, the theatres, the churches; people who were no more.

This Notary Liborio, a man of some fifty years, with a mole-like and afflicted air (though probably not that way at all), very courteously agreed. De Neville, who had already procured some flowers, stated that he had a particular wish to pay homage to, and say a prayer at, the tomb of the late Brigitta Civile, wife of the Glover; to which, without turning a hair, though with a slight start and a pause on hearing that lady's name he had fallen silent, the Scribblerus assented, saying "*Très bien*, Monsù, as long as we manage to find that chapel."

"What!" barked the prince. "Manage to *find* it?" (The carriage was at this time turning out of a colourful little sidestreet into the broader and more airy Via Costantinopoli). "What do you mean, Monsieur? Have you never been there? You do, however, know where it is?"

"Forgive me, forgive me . . . It's just that . . . You see, Monsieur, there are two chapels, not one, belonging to the . . . umm . . . Civile family. One of these is his, Don Mariano's, in which lie all the glovemakers of the family, obscure and worthy persons who bequeathed him his trade and his good heart (Don Mariano is a man of great good nature and generosity of soul, in his modest way, and loved for that alone). The other . . ."

"The other?" asked de Neville eagerly.

"The other is at some distance off, very costly, very beautiful. It is that of his second wife, who was not in fact his wife, though she might have been: I refer to Brigitta Helm, whom everyone in Naples knew as Brigitta Civile. This chapel, though very grand, has never attracted me . . . and that is why I said 'if we find it' . . . I've never been there . . . although I know where it is."

"So Monsieur Civile has been twice married? That I did not know," said the prince, surprised and shocked, as flocks of silent thoughts alighted in his mind. "Strange that I have not been told," he added almost under his breath. "And how was it he never wished to regularize this second liaison?"

"It is not that he did not wish to, monsieur; let us say that he was prevented. In truth, Donna Brigitta herself was so prevented, in that the Will of the deceased Colonel Helm, the real father of her ten children, laid it down that she was at liberty after his death to lead as free a life as she cared to choose; but not to remarry, under pain of losing the usufruct of the entire patrimony (Donna Brigitta's personal property had passed automatically, on her marriage, to her husband), a patrimony highly beneficial to her, and in consequence (for the Colonel was aware of her sentiments) to Don Mariano. And this, for our Glovemaker, was a great grief . . . Indeed, it *is* a great grief," proceeded the Notary pensively. "He fell ill over it. Because there was an element of illegality involved, although merely superficial, and for this it was only the youngest two daughters who were destined to pay the consequences . . ."

"The more I hear the less I understand," said de Neville. "But if in all this there is something that ought not to be communicated to outsiders, do not spare my feelings, *mon ami*, I have no wish to hear it."

The Notary, for a while, spoke not a word, while the carriage had already entered the splendours of Via Foria, flanked by fine houses.

Whereupon, "Look there," said Don Liborio, pointing to a red mansion quite detached from the neighbouring buildings, surrounded as it was by a high red wall covered with green creepers. "The house you see, all shuttered up, was the town-house of Donna Brigitta Helm. But she, after the death of her last daughter by her first husband, the little Floridia Helm, never wished to set foot there again, and withdrew to Casoria, leaving Don Mariano to take care of Elmina and Teresella (the latter not a sister by blood, but an orphan procured from a convent, to keep the desolate Elmina company). And her exile from Naples, in a certain sense voluntary, lasted until the unhappy woman departed this life. A month ago, to the best of my knowledge."

De Neville, being still in a bad mood, and in his heart of hearts increasingly ill-disposed towards the Glover's family, had followed the whole of this account, lengthy and tortuous as it was, with scant attention, not to say frank disinterest. But of a sudden he was struck by all the enormities he had heard (if he was to believe this Scribblerus), which seemed to shed a faint light, as of sporadic oil-lamps, on that chequered history which was beginning to emerge as a picture of perfectly unimaginable ruin.

"Excuse me," he said, "but I didn't quite follow you. That is where Madame Helm lived?"

"*Oui, Monsieur*. It was the house where she had lived for twenty years with her husband, the late Colonel Helm, whom — even when she met the worthy Glover and later, when left a widow at the age of thirty-eight, and therefore free, reciprocated his warm affection — she never wished, or was able, to forget. We might say that she always remained Signora Helm."

"And the reason?"

"Ten children, my dear sir, as I have mentioned; ten upstanding youngsters, and all bound, by law and inclination, to the Colonel, and therefore interested – as is only natural – in their father's property, which was, and still is, very considerable. It stretches almost to Caserta . . . woodlands, houses, vineyards . . . Don Mariano, even then, possessed nothing; only unflagging industry and universal esteem . . . nothing more. In Jib-Sail House, one of Donna Brigitta's many properties, she having been as rich in her own right as the Colonel (they say she was related to the Queen), at the time of their meeting, which occurred on account of this very tenancy, he at first occupied only a modest apartment. But this, due to his good nature, presented no problem. A man of frugal ways and as temperate as can be. In any case, because of her children, who would one day become owners of everything (as the Colonel had laid down), Donna Brigitta was unable to alienate any property whatever, or even remarry – at least publicly – without coming into conflict with the harsh terms of the Will. But pretend to be remarried, that much she could. Therefore . . . – driver, turn that way please – therefore, after the requisite time had passed, she played, in the eyes of all Naples, the role of second wife, with a second wedding celebrated before the Pope in person . . . in the year . . . It was not the truth, dear sir, but it brought Don Mariano enormous credit . . . and with it enormous affluence. His business, which had been rather at a standstill, prospered and multiplied . . . at least, so they say. Because it is still uncertain how he later lost all his assets: maybe by misguided speculations, maybe in donations (possibly to his beloved Brigitta) and maybe to previous binding commitments. The fact remains that he now has nothing. Donna Brigitta, in the meanwhile, never shared his life at Jib-Sail House, she simply visited. There was truly implacable hostility between the two little girls, Floridia and Elmina, and this was known all over Naples. Her absence was viewed in the light of this."

"But what sort of hostility, pray?" (The prince did not consider he was being indiscreet, seeing that this hostility had existed between the two children.)

"Adelmine, the fair Elmina, the daughter neither of the Colonel nor of the Glover, but of a distant relative of the former (they say that her mother ran off with an obscure minstrel from Cologne, thus permanently blotting the family escutcheon, but this is not a story to pass on – both parents came to a bad end); Adelmine and Donna Brigitta's youngest, and perfectly legitimate daughter, the angelic Floridia Helm . . . did not see eye to eye."

Better and better! And besides, there was no mention of any Nadina, or "Ratlet", and the prince, ever more sullen and ill-disposed, was confirmed in the suspicion that the very existence of that hideous child was an invention, fruit of some evil instinct on the part of Elmina.

"I was told about this Floridia . . . She was some nine years of age . . ."

"Yes, sir, when she died. Our lovely Elmina was then about twelve . . ."

The dates, in this long chorus for many voices, or conflicting voices, did not coincide; but nothing, on close scrutiny, coincided in the aggregate of these accounts or versions of a family memory bordering so closely on mere hearsay, so anomalous when it came to concrete facts, a sure sign of a basic falsehood in it, and of many things added by common gossip to a nucleus perhaps in itself insignificant. Better so, concluded the heartsick Ingmar.

"Little Floridia died of languishment, I was told," said he, more out of courtesy than any real curiosity.

"Of languishment, yes. She was too good for this world . . . A universal malady, as you know . . . Even though, in my opinion, she would not have fallen ill but for . . . but for an unpleasant incident which occurred some years earlier, which was blamed on the lack of vigilance, to say the least, of Elmina. The two children were at Jib-Sail House, and Donna Helm – it was a Saturday, Saturday in Easter Week – was visiting the Glover's family. Floridia, then about four or five years old, was waiting at the window . . . She saw her mother coming, leant out with open arms to greet her . . . Elmina, who was at her side, did not restrain her. She fell. She was not killed, for she landed on a basket of laundry, but she was badly shaken . . . It was then that her malady began."

"Elmina was at her side, you say?"

"Yes, sir, that was unfortunately so . . . and she too was shaken, for various reasons . . . she was accused, in short, of negligence, if not of lack of charity. You understand, do you not?"

Suddenly all the incongruities of those versions of the accident and the illness, heard here and there, converged in a single intuition, and the prince saw clearly, though with great sadness, and absolving all concerned (poor Elmina in particular), how things had gone. He understood that thenceforth the despairing mother had given up, her love for Don Mariano, never more than lukewarm, had come to an end, although with great sense of solidarity and friendship she had kept faith with her social commitment. For people at large she had always remained an excellent wife to him . . .

In reality only a good and faithful friend who for his sake had borne, with Christian fortitude, the probable hostility and mistrust of her numerous children, as well as the inevitable animosity of Elmina and, worst of all, the loss of Floridia. And this last was the girl of the Linnet, so there was no question of a third luckless child called Nadina or Dinuccia, nicknamed "Ratlet".

"Was Don Mariano very much distressed by this misfortune?"

"My dear sir, as distressed as it is possible to be. He adored both the girls (Teresa, though well loved, had not yet been taken to the bosom of the family), and as for Elmina, he would have given his eyes for her: she was sun, moon and stars to him. But this Florì had a special grace about her, *vous savez*: she was a voice of pure delight. My wife, who saw her, said she was like a little linnet."

So once again that bird cropped up in the story! No longer understanding at this point whether there had been, in the little girl's life, a single linnet, or two, and whether the spiteful Elmina had twice maltreated the bird, he, Ingmar, the Benefactor, felt only a pang of shame at his most recent misdeed: his second wedding present to Elmina. That bird was a tragic bird, not a memory to summon back into the lives of the young couple. What an impudent churl he had been! What he wouldn't give to retrieve it!

But then, in a flash, as he sat in the carriage and they were already in sight of tranquil slopes on which the cemetery lay, he was struck by a thought of stupefying clarity, a thought that threw into confusion, as an earthquake might devastate a garden, the whole of his previous assessment of the situation, arrived at half in jest and half in earnest; a thought that destroyed the peace of any (already questionable) union between the two young people, the one, though bewitching, very obstinate and slightly daft, the other totally out of his mind with love: and this thought was that Elmina, the lovely Elmina Civile, almost certainly no longer had a penny to her name. With the death of Brigitta Helm the whole of her grandiose patrimonial situation had collapsed. The ten legitimate heirs of the Colonel would spring forward like knights armed for the fray.

And Albert knew nothing about it!

"The youngest, the twelfth (let us say) 'daughter' of Don Mariano (like Elmina, she was never properly adopted, and is extraneous to the two families), that is Teresa, will not be affected by this upheaval." The Notary cleared his throat. "The Baroness, at the entreaty of Don Mariano, who had obtained her from a convent on this condition, settled a small dowry on her. Only Elmina inherits nothing. This was a specific disposition of the Colonel's, before his death: that the offspring of an obscure organist in Cologne (worse than a child of sin, the product of a fall in *class*) should be totally excluded from the estate. Yes, Elmina possesses nothing except the infinite devotion of her counterfeit father."

A perfect example, this story of Jib-Sail House, of the chaos reigning in Bourbon families, and in view of the fate of Elmina, truly appalling.

For Albert – if the prince had not made provisions, as he had in fact done, though he did not dream of telling the Notary so – it would have meant penury.

De Neville, like an automaton, addressed one last question to Don Liborio, and to judge from his tone of voice as indifferent as it was mechanical:

"Where will they go and live?"

"There is an understanding that, for the sake of appearances, Don Mariano and his two 'daughters' will stay on for a certain time at Jib-Sail House, if he so wishes; the heirs have not yet come forward, and it is not impossible that the poor things may instruct a lawyer to contest the Will, though in their position as mere beneficiaries, indeed simply friends, of Donna Helm's, they have no legal right to so much as a chair to sit in.

"As regards Elmina, who is to be married tomorrow, Don Mariano is providing for her with the gift of a cottage – nothing special, in fact rather dilapidated – above Sant'Antonio at Posillipo, which Brigitta let him have on very favourable terms at the beginning of their acquaintanceship. That is where they will live, and she will have to do without servants . . . Everything is changing. She will take with her only old Ferrantina, who practically brought up Don Mariano and knows the whole sad story . . . She has, of course, some valuables: necklaces, brooches and so on; and there is a small fancy-goods shop of Don Mariano's – unmortgaged – of which she will divide the profits, if there are any, which I doubt, with Teresina. But we are nearly at our destination . . . Driver, turn in here!"

The unhappy Glover. Names, on a tomb,
that appear and vanish again, including that of
a certain Hieronymus Käppchen (Caplet).
De Neville recovers his peace of mind

De Neville was persuaded he must be dreaming, and for the remainder of the journey he said not a word, pretending to be absorbed in the colourless landscape. He was wondering whether this man, so well informed, had not lied or intentionally slandered the unfortunate Glover's family for some disreputable reason, such as an old grudge or some professional rancour of his own – he was plainly not the notary appointed by the Helms. The prince was more than ever torn between amazement and a sort of doleful compassion. There returned to mind the words of Benjamin: "He, the poor Glover himself, is the worst stricken person in this whole story . . ." And something akin to total bewilderment, due not only to the overwhelming financial revelations, but to human folly, on his own part and Albert's, and finally even on that of Benjamin, who with his lens had seen everything except the utter lack of assets and the moral catastrophe of the family at Jib-Sail House, led him to feel that he had been made fun of, and was therefore unworthy of himself and of his own esteem. And he saw, he was convinced of it, that Ruskaja's advice, far from being attributable to the work of magic or divination, was nothing but the fruit of continuous and atrocious gossip between Caserta and Naples. There, what with the gentry and their servants, the hostelries, the mansions and the post-houses, everything was known . . . only the underlying truths remained unknown. And in what base contempt were held the fixed canons of loyalty and correctness, in human relations as in those of commerce!

How would Albert react if now, at this moment, someone were to inform him? Would he be free to leave, to return – in safety – to his native Belgium?

And as he dwelt on these things, and pronounced to himself the word "safety", he was again overcome with shame. He saw that Elmina was innocent; or, at least, unaware of the gravity of the disaster, as also, in a muddled way, was her father; and that if there had been a measure of calculation in him, it was not due to money (after all, he had been told that Albert possessed nothing in his own right); if, therefore, there had been some calculation involved in desiring that marriage, this was not due to greed for money, but to some mysterious reason known only to the terror-struck Don Mariano himself. A reason concerned with the salvation of Elmina, and founded on her removal from that house of silence by means of marriage; and also on the possibility of drawing a veil over the unhappy obscurity of her birth: rejected by her "official" father, and entrusted to another who was unable even to adopt her! And to this end, that of reassuring a Don Mariano who was utterly lost and humiliated, she had consented – though not really loving Dupré, and indeed having no inclination to marriage, or to loving anyone at all – she had consented to marry the artist. Simply to leave that house, now that an end had been put to the deception of Brigitta as an exemplary wife and mother, she had given her consent. Or it may be that her father persuaded her to this, so that he no longer, in thinking of her and of her future, felt death clutch at his heart.

Meanwhile the carriage was proceeding apace, and before long it drew up before a great open gateway.

The two men walked the length of a broad avenue, the prince still silent, and then a narrower way which described the letter S. Thence they arrived at a field – there is no other word for that treeless area – which led in turn to a modest garden. De Neville was so gloomy and oppressed in spirit that few things on earth could have increased his gloom and depression. Everything was still, calm, stagnant, and of inexpressible melancholy. He cast his eyes about him and saw only this same wasteland, and a few steps ahead of him the Notary, walking a little bent, as if dawdling, as loafing boys do, looking down at the ground and with his hands clasped behind his back. And not a soul in sight. Then, at the far end of the little field, they heard footsteps, and we may imagine their surprise on observing the tall figure of the Glover. He too, bearing flowers, had entered from a cross-path and was certainly on his way to pay homage to the recent grave of his wife. But first, finding himself in the vicinity, he was passing by to bring a greeting to the Old Chapel, where so many of his best-loved relatives were laid to rest.

Catching sight of him, Ingmar and his companion exchanged a brief, silent glance.

"I imagine . . . I can only imagine that Monsieur Civile has no wish to share his emotions . . . or simply his feelings," Ingmar corrected himself in time, "with anyone else. But I make so bold as to ask you, my friend, how should we best conduct ourselves?" And as he spoke he himself was a-tremble with too many conflicting emotions.

"As simply as possible," replied that common-sense mole.

"Yes . . . that will be best . . . you are right." And a moment later, striding ahead down the pathway through another garden, adjacent to the first, and almost (and on purpose) bumping into Elmina's father, the prince swept off his hat.

Not a word, but a smile of great finesse and delicacy . . . Courageous also, in the circumstances. Don Mariano looked at him as if not immediately recognizing him, his thoughts being elsewhere, but then, in a kind of agony:

"Ah! Prince! . . . My dear friend!"

They stopped, shook hands, both of them rigid and distant. Then, suddenly, they embraced.

"Forgive me my follies," burst out the prince impetuously.

"Oh, they are mere nothings . . ." returned the Glover after a slight pause, his eyes shining with tears. "Indeed, I would venture to say that your message had a beneficent effect."

They then realized that they had a stranger in their midst, to whom some explanation was due; but the prince, in his rage for sincerity, destroyed that tacit understanding at birth, so to speak, by informing Monsieur Civile that he was there to satisfy a curiosity which he now regretted, feeling that it was not only useless but above all reprehensible:

"I wished to know, *mon ami*, about your relations with . . . with this cold world . . . with your loved ones who are no more. To read your wife's name clearly . . . "

"My wife – but maybe you already know it, Monsieur de Neville – lies elsewhere, some way off, in a place less humble than this. And she does not bear my name, and never did: life, and circumstances, forbade it. She did not even bear her father's name, but solely that of her first husband, the Colonel-Baron. A respectable name, I must add, however much that respectability came to weigh upon me. She is therefore still called Brigitta Helm, and under that name she now stands in the sight of God . . . I hope."

"Does that change anything for you, for all of you?"

"For us, for me, no . . . (a great friendship, you realize . . . absolute respect . . . always . . .); and I hope not for my son-in-law either . . . When he comes to know, not now."

"I would beg you to invite me home with you . . . if I were not afraid of putting you to trouble . . . and disturbing the preparations for the wedding, which they tell me is imminent. I would have liked to have a word with you alone."

The Glover, reading into these words something terrible affecting the poor spouses, instantly paled.

"No, don't be anxious, it is not what you think" said the prince kindly. "It would have been . . . I should say, only to reassure you . . . and as amply as possible."

For these words the Glover, as long as he lived, retained such enormous gratitude as to induce him to forgive in advance any conceivable grief, or mere displeasure, which Dupré's friend might see fit to cause him; but at the same time they were hammered like nails into his mind. He realized that his whole life was an open book; he became aware, like a lamentation within him, of the sound of deep waters.

"Your gift arrived, my dear prince, shortly before I left the house, and my children are now in a thoroughly animated and jocular state of mind . . . I wished to thank you for that as soon as I saw you . . . But then, when I *did* see you, I perceived that you knew of my misfortune . . . my guilt . . . my whole situation."

"Of that, Monsieur, let us speak no more. Or, if we do, only to your advantage. But tell me at once," begged the agitated prince, "was the gift of the Birdcage not taken in ill part by your daughter? Did it please Miss Elmina? . . . It was but a little while ago that I realized I did wrong in sending her the linnet."

Seeing that the Notary, either from tact or from boredom, was walking some way ahead of them, until he disappeared behind a small building surmounted by a cross, the two friends looked with true sincerity into each other's eyes, the one with infinite benevolence, the other with supreme devotion. Finally the Glover said:

"I wish that with these words of yours I could assuage the sadness that is in my heart. And so it would be, if this world were a little simpler . . . such is your benevolence, my dear and noble sir. But there is . . . there is in this world *un noeud*, something we shall never be given to understand; and this weighs upon my daughter's life . . . and in consequence on mine also. More than that I will not tell you for now, and perhaps never, as long as you may live, which I trust will be long indeed; while I, alas, feel that I shall not accompany you. The road I travel is shorter by far than yours."

"Come now!" exclaimed de Neville, his irritation tempered by affection (for this heavy-heartedness he attributed to the secret of Elmina's humble birth, otherwise he would not have found it easy to reply). "Come now! You speak as a man with a great sorrow, to be sure, and I am aware that you are still mourning your wife. But think, the rose-tree continues to flourish," said he with a smile worthy of a child. "You still have your two daughters. Why despair?"

"Perhaps you did not hear what I said: there is a *knot*."

"No, to tell the truth I did not grasp the meaning of this word."

"Rather haphazard French, mine is! Please forgive me. Perhaps I wished to say something else. But better so" (this with a touch of bitterness), "better so, my dear sir."

"Something we shall never be given to understand!" repeated de Neville to himself. "And indeed . . ." he pronounced ceremoniously, "I take you to refer to the heart of a woman?" (And he had in mind the uncouth heart of Elmina.)

"No, sir. The heart of a woman is, after all, a fairly simple matter. I refer to the heart of Nature herself, Monsieur."

These words had a disagreeable effect on de Neville, who saw in them a kind of affectation; as if, in speaking of his daughter, the Glover presumptuously called into account the whole of that Nature which had engendered her; a gross error, since Monsieur Civile threw him a side-long glance, withdrawn and unassuming, and said no more, as if fearful of interpretations that might cause him embarrassment and a more serious discourse which it was as well not to embark on. Our prince therefore confined himself to saying, as he pushed at a stone with his foot:

"Yes, the heart of Nature is a deep heart indeed, sir. But how very distant from us!"

"Not always, or at least not as distant as we would wish . . . at any rate at certain times," replied the Glover, as if speaking to himself.

They had now reached the Civile family chapel, which together with that of Signora Helm was the object of their journey, and here they found the Notary, perhaps simply to busy himself, and therefore for motives of tact, attempting to read some of the names inscribed in gilded letters in double columns on a blind window of the said chapel, which dated back to the early seventeenth century and recorded many of them. And having found some, even quite recent, somewhat obscured or worn by the mud and rains of the previous winter, he scratched at certain letters with a fingernail and read, or more precisely spelt out, in a sufficiently audible voice:

"Nadina Civile aged 3, 1788.
"Hieronymus Käppchen (Caplet) aged 300, 1805.
"Albert Dupré (Babà) aged 2, 1798."

Monsieur de Neville, two paces distant from the inscriptions, gave a start; then he too craned forward and read, or seemed to read, with terror and stupefaction, not only the first and second names but the third; all names of children of two or three years old, though in the case of the second, by some error, the number 3 was followed by two noughts. They remained now inscribed, perfectly visibly, in black letters, all but the third, which glittered for a moment in tiny letters of gold; but when, in anguish, he read for a second time, it faded and, along with the others, vanished altogether; while though he was still petrified with terror an enormous surge of relief filled his mind with joy. And in any case the ages, and the dates of the deaths of those infants, made the whole thing absurd. Albert Dupré a child, indeed, when Albert was already over two years old before the Revolution!

Peer as he might, he saw nothing more.

It did not escape the prince that those names had been read, before him, by the Notary; but seeing that worthy's face as blank and expressionless as before, he realized that even the Notary's spelling out the names and dates was something that he, Ingmar, had dreamed.

Lastly he discerned that his own heart was sick with melancholy. Reading *Baba*, as if his young friend were really only two years old (and between ourselves it was not far short of the truth), and Nadina Civile (*Ratlet*) instead of Floridia Helm (two names for one and the same child, as he had deduced from Elmina's impassioned account on the day of the "message"), convinced him clearly of his own mistaken reading, due to an excess of imagination and to melancholia. Not to mention that insane Hieronymus Käppchen, swiftly replaced by a mere scratch. The names of those poor children, real or imaginary as they might be, had danced on the marble like elfin sprites, and akin to such (excepting, possibly, the real name of Nadina) they had immediately vanished. Now to be read in their place were various Neapolitan names of the latter years of the century, Gaetano, Gasparo and others, of no interest to de Neville. From which the prince deduced that his heart was obsessed with shadows and presentiments (or maybe memories of unhappy events?) that it was inadvisable to harbour; and it was only of these memories that he would have to cure himself.

From his troubled state of mind, pallid and grave, he was roused by the sincere and kindly tones of Don Mariano.

"Having paid our homage," said he, as if he had witnessed nothing, "let us leave this place, let us move into the open air, dear sir. We may visit Signora Helm on another occasion, or else I myself will convey your respects to her. Let us get away from here. It is not a place to linger in, even though I perceive you are devoted to the life that once was. Let us return, if you have nothing to the contrary, and see how the spouses have received that most kindly of airy creatures, your Linnet; yes, that most charming of gifts, the good auspice of your Linnet."

The Little House. Further dispositions in favour of
the spouses. Rain falls on Naples and also in the heart
of the prince. "Do not so soon forget me, O my friend!"

The names which Ingmar had read, or thought he had read, on the marble of the chapel were to be impressed on his mind for life, but not in the sense, which the Reader may be led to suppose, of childish superstition, but as a clear sign of that malady of the mind which for years over and over again he had resolved to turn his back on, with his travels, his friendships, his much-flaunted dissipation, and even with an *ars poetica* not sufficiently noteworthy, alas, as to exceed the boundaries of a narrow circle of admirers. Enterprises of no avail, for Melancholy is ineradicable from the heart in which it is born, just as is the yearning for the most ardent and abundant life. Yes, ineradicable! The prince had for some time been aware that his malady was of this nature, but never so much as in Naples, in that fated circumstance of his youth – a marriage in which face to face, in mutual distress, were set the two prime sentiments in his heart, and the most painful: his love for Albert Dupré, and that (which he dared not confess to himself) for the young man's bride, the fair Elmina.

But we do not wish to, or perhaps dare not, lose ourselves in subtle descriptions of the human heart, least of all in a matter dating back to just before the penultimate century of modern Europe, an epoch sufficiently remote; particularly since we are concerned with things so very transient as money and the money-troubles of merchants, the choices and destinies of unblemished spouses, and also childhood quarrels, and tales of spiteful little girls too tender, albeit, to undergo this life.

Therefore, dear Reader, let us come back to the complex and ridiculous events which weave the starry web of our splendid human passions.

Returning to the Hat of Gold, with the intention of being present the following morning at the wedding ceremony of Elmina and Albert (an intention, as he had already informed the Glover before their parting, perfectly easy of accomplishment), and after giving instructions to his valet to brush up the blue costume chosen for the function in church, de Neville (it was already ten o'clock of a fine spring night) felt his atrocious melancholy of the afternoon growing on him apace, accompanied by an impulse both cruel and selfish: that of fleeing Naples at once, leaving for Rome, and thence for Civitavecchia, there to embark without delay for some northern port. He had no further wish even to see the Alps, which had so jocundly greeted the descent of the Chariot of Pegasus towards the mysterious rose-blue light of the Mediterranean.

"Farewell and for ever, dearest Bellerophon!" cried he with tears in his eyes, as he walked up and down the spacious room in the Hat of Gold, the same as on his first evening in Naples, before the window which he had shuttered up so as not to see the blue of the night illuminated by the red torch of the Volcano and the ample piazza stretching down to the quayside. "And farewell also to you, cruel Elmina!"

But soon enough, in his mind, where no thought ever really tarried for its just repose, or conversely, by good fortune, disheartened him for any length of time, three actions and modes of conduct began to take shape, with which the generous prince might honourably conclude that dolorous episode in his young life. First of all he must write Nodier a long and detailed letter, telling him of the revelation he had had of *some measure of difficulty*, as he would put it, in which Monsieur Civile found himself, entreating him to keep any allusion to this revelation jealously to himself, and also to comport himself, in consequence, as if such allusions (his own and those of others there in Naples) could not possibly have reached his ears due to the obvious difficulties of language; and also to adhere scrupulously to the instructions and dispositions agreed on together before the *incident* (which incident the prince intended to be a matter for inference). Now more than ever the latter must be rigorously respected, and by their means most generous and discreet assistance must be furnished to the unfortunate couple and to the Glover the moment the need should arise; assistance for which he begged him to render the most meticulous account in letters dispatched, in the diplomatic bag, to Liège. He went on to confirm that he, Ingmar, should needless to say be informed at lightning speed of the least difficulty or emergency; and that at lightning speed he would make provision.

This done, the prince informed Nodier of his decision to leave the very next day for Rome and Civitavecchia, without attending the wedding, on account of having remembered some pressing commitments to a certain minister. Finally he charged him to give instructions for the immediate renovation and repainting (preferably in its original shade of pink) of the house at Sant'Antonio, which he would go and inspect before his departure on the morrow, with a view to obtaining an estimate, if necessary, for the *works to be put in hand* (such were his words).

And if these actions most certainly appeared quite fantastical and unthinkable in the light of any normal sense of proportion, imprudent even *then* for the scant sense of the ridiculous which a great man of the world thus betrayed by behaving like a daydreaming child; if, etc. . . . we are truly at a loss as to how to present them *today*, in times such as ours, so completely alien to friendship and generosity and delicacy of mind. But to make some mention of them, even blushingly, seems to us advisable, while excusing such sins of liberality on the part of the poor prince on the grounds that the Revolution had, at that time, taken only the first steps in terms of the cult of economy and decent moderation (or limitation) in questions of aid and comfort, inapplicable in any case to our hero, since "poor Ingmar" was born a couple of decades before the events of '93, too early, alas, to be brought up in accordance with the principles of Reason or, if your prefer, tightfistedness. We are also pleased to point out that at that time – exception made for the Illuminati – dreams and superstitions due to the frailty of the human heart, and fears and tears occasioned by the intrusiveness of some unknown and foolish Linnet, still dominated everyday modes of conduct. Not only *l'argent*, dear Reader, glittered like a sunbeam in the flowery woods of a springtime of the heart that was, in those days, most wonderful; but also loves and friendships and fair damsels . . . while dreams and *jeux d'esprit* and the refinements of life were still coveted aims in the life-style of the lordly. Therefore, no outrage, or smiles, or pitying winks, but only sincere thanks to Heaven that our times, and perfect democratic upbringing, have exempted us for ever from such intemperances of joy and grandeur, and insane confusion between the youth of the body and genuine, wonderful purity.

Then our Ingmar at once wrote a few lines (in blue ink) to his well-beloved Albert; lines into which he put his heart and soul; and while he prayed Heaven to illuminate and protect his life and happiness with a thousand blessings, he seemed to have his beloved friend there by his side, and to see nearby, beneath the painted arch of a doorway, the fair Elmina, vexed yet tender, gazing at him and interrogating his attentive, benevolent eyes: "Why, why, Monsieur de Neville, do you do us so much ill?"

"But I wish you no ill, dearest Elmina," replied the enraptured friend of Albert and Nodier, "I wish only your good! This is the very reason for my departure! And I am bequeathing to you the being closest to my heart, my beloved Albert. Oh, it is I who must beg of you to do him no ill . . . as you have done (ah, but only a trifle!) to me . . . Because you, dearest Elmina, nurture a secret in your bosom."

And it seemed to him that at these words he saw the girl turn aside towards a little serving-maid, or it may have been her sister Teresa, who was waiting two steps away, holding a wickerwork birdcage in her hands; and that she cried through her tears:

"Then bring on the Linnet! Let the Linnet come forth! And let my secret be known, and pardoned by the Angels that are in Heaven!"

And as she spoke these words (the prince seemed to see her, clearly, in the little pink frock of that first evening at Jib-Sail House), so she vanished, and de Neville turned his tear-filled eyes around, seeking his friends and all those whom (save for Nodier) he feared he would never set eyes on again.

Having written his letters he closed them, sealed them and entrusted them to a servant who was ever in attendance, with instructions to deliver them first thing in the morning to the residence of Monsieur Civile. This servant he also ordered to put away the blue ceremonial costume. He would no longer be attending Dupré's wedding.

The grandfather clock in the passage had therefore already struck eleven before he, calmer albeit, but in no light spirits, prepared for rest, in view of the exertions of the morrow; rest that did not come easily. Indeed, he was long in going to sleep and late in waking. The sky was overcast and at last it had started to rain; Naples, even from the white balcony of his room, looked a different city.

At about nine o'clock a carriage conveyed him at a leisurely pace, as perhaps was his wish, to Posillipo, where the prince laid eyes that morning on a hillside both awesome and humble, very bare. The rock had taken on an almost violet hue. The vegetation on that side was sparse. And on the crest of a spur, accessible by a narrow flight of steps between the rocks, but which the carriage reached by way of a more gentle road skirting the hillside, were a number of cottages of shabby and abandoned aspect. One of these, which the prince noted at once, since it was isolated from the rest, appeared (mistakenly, for the ground floor was all but invisible from below) to consist of a single storey of perhaps five or six rooms, topped by a kind of shed on the roof. That at least was the first impression, because on closer viewing it was a ramshackle turret, with one or two narrow openings fitted with broken iron gratings, from one of which projected a stick, raised like a halberd towards the gloomy sky. On the stick a few rags (were they a child's flags?) had been hung to dry.

Round the house ran a narrow, untidy strip of garden, more than a stony terrace, with a few plum- and cherry-trees that the wind, beating ceaselessly, had deformed for ever.

This was to be the home of the young couple.

The blue shutters were closed, like weary eyes, but the garden gate — almost as if the house were of no value, merely a scrap of paper or a stone, and anyone who wanted could walk in — was open.

"But how is my Albert to manage?" wondered Ingmar, distressed and all but terrified. "How is he to struggle down from this hilltop every time he goes in to Naples, if not by carriage? And what about Donna Elmina?" (he already gave her the title of *donna*, which in Naples was bestowed on married women, countesses and concierges alike, as a token of proper respect). "And what about his studio? Quite impossible here. Where would he put the statues?"

And wondering thus, in an anxious interrogation addressed to himself, he entered the little garden and, through a misted-up window-pane on the ground floor of the house, descried a large room which appeared to contradict his misgivings, and looked in every way suited to become a sculptor's studio, so vast it was, with a floor of beaten earth, and full of blocks of marble lined up in perfect order and surrounded by the equipment needed for sculpting. So it seemed that the Glover, or Albert himself, had already seen to everything, and that the big room was now ready for the long days of solitary work. Further away, against the end wall, a large curtain appeared to have collapsed, or perhaps a big blind, such as are used to protect delicate eyes from the summer light, and silhouetted against the bare panes a tall woman, her back to the prince, was busy straightening it out and putting it back in place. He supposed it must be Ferrantina (but not "Carlo's Ferrantina"), the most elderly of the three maids at Jib-Sail House who bore this name, but (he then thought) at this hour the old woman must certainly be in church, amid lights and draperies and the overpowering scent of roses. This must be another servant, perhaps a housekeeper.

The prince was far from well. Indeed, we are to suppose that he had reached, since the previous evening, the depths of his fanatical melancholy. He was therefore not surprised – convinced as he was of his "malady", or, as he hoped, the mere indisposition of too errant a spirit – when he saw the old woman turn towards a figure hidden in the shadow of a long block of marble, herself appearing now of somewhat lesser stature than before, though with a face still refined and comely, as she calmly said,

"Do not act that way, Albert. Yours is a veritable obsession. Tell me, rather, if the curtain is now to your liking. Or would you prefer another *morsel* of light?"

The figure in shadow, whom we must suppose to be ill, or in distress, or simply lethargic, stretched upon a rickety chaise-longue, made no reply; and after a certain void in which silence reigned, the woman, the window, the curtain, and everything else, vanished.

"I must see a doctor when I get to Liège!" And then, at once: "I must tell Nodier to take particular care over this garden. To make it cheerful! To have roses everywhere, and especially yellow carnations!" muttered the prince, almost on the verge of tears, but consoling himself with the thought that in sunlight, and not, as now, in the rain, that humble dwelling would be *divine*. And later, when there were children in it, better still. After all, Nodier would be staying on in Naples for a while and, at his urging, would put Albert in touch with famous artists, both native and foreign, in whom Naples abounded. Imagine the evenings they would spend in that studio! And besides, should the house prove too gloomy and unconducive to happiness, the young couple could move to a large apartment in Chiaia, such as the prince had thought of more than once. Nodier ought to see to this, he thought impetuously, instead of wasting time on this hovel. But he would soon enough make the necessary arrangements.

It occurred to him at this point that the ceremony he so feared was surely even then taking place, and maybe nearing its end. He envisioned all the gilded and spurious splendour of the church of Santa Lucia, saw the fine dresses of the fine ladies; there reached his ears the swell of the hymns, he witnessed the emotion of those present, heard the doleful serenity of the bells. He forgot the woman and the shadowy studio, and remembered only the unhappy Glover, and everything that he, Ingmar, had promised to do to help the old merchant. Better to depart without delay, therefore. When he got home he would re-examine the whole situation, and see to the appropriate remedies on better appraisal and with more freedom of choice.

Back in the carriage, the hood lowered, he was better able to appreciate, as he gazed from the window, the agreeable vista of the hillside, descending with its subdued colours and light touches of grey and yellow towards the violet gardens and pretty yellow houses of the Riviera of Chiaia. And here the cabby at last gave a long sigh and, swishing his whiplash over the skeletal back of the poor horse:

"Young gentleman," said he to de Neville, taken in by the aetherial and strangely youthful appearance of a man of nearly thirty, and so rich the stars in the sky were just pieces of tin to him, "young gentleman, I didn't like that there house! But if I was to tell you why, I couldn't do it. Would you oblige me with a spot of fire?"

His thoughts far away – yes, far away indeed from the flame, the smoke, the glow of the cigar – de Neville obliged him.

And lo, in the flame, in the bluish glare that lit the cabby's cigar, and while both cabby and carriage vanished away, approaching through the drizzle came the smiling face of his cherished Albert; and now he was running, and whether smiling or weeping was no longer certain; and he cried out:

"Wait, wait, dear Ingmar! Oh, do not flee!"

And then, halting and breathless, and raising one hand towards the prince:

"Remember me! Do not so soon forget me, O my friend!"

The rain came on more heavily now, and thus they were riven apart, by that thin wall of water, by that grey road.

"I shall not forget you, Albert!" replied, or cried, passionately but without a sound, the pallor-struck de Neville.

The end of the joyous excursion. De Neville returns to his palace in Liège. "Should a Linnet enquire for me, show him in."

W e shall not be numbered among those authors who calmly abandon their characters, in the squares and streets of a foreign city perhaps, just when they are threatened with the most appalling adversities, such as no father, even the most uncaring, would care to witness. No, we shall not altogether, or not for ever, abandon Albert Dupré, his lovely bride, and Monsieur Civile; while at least the first of the three is bereft of the ingenuousness of youth and the bliss of ignorance and while the classical façade of Jib-Sail House, or House of the Linnet, also fades, with a dancing cadence heart-rending to all who see it, receding into the distance. But before returning (alas, not at once) to those hills, those crystalline waters, to the hostelries such as the Hat of Gold, to return once more to scenes of erstwhile children now young ladies, and hidden Linnets, and the reticent hearts of men and women grown (perhaps) the wiser, we shall let our minds follow our munificent prince, accompany him on his road home, through the lesser Alps, which he skirts this time by choosing the route through Nice, and alight with him from the carriage before his splendid house in Liège ... Alone! Neither the artist nor Alphonse Nodier are now, and perhaps never again will be, at his side.

Flanked by two short ranks of footmen in glittering liveries, the prince steps through the gilded gates of the Garden, ascends the short flight of steps to the Palace, crosses the grandiose and silent vestibule. He enters his study, the place dearest to his heart.

Hush ... The prince seats himself, his features affable and we might say, at first glance, radiant and serene, at his desk for Personal Correspondence, topped with red and green leather and inlaid with ivory (it cost a king's ransom at an auction in England); the lamps are burning, the Servants are arrayed about him in silent deference. Through a window open onto the Garden, between the light swirl of the curtains ruffled by the evening breeze (even here, in the Low Countries, it still seems to be

Maytime), a bird, perhaps a nightingale, pours its impassioned, jocund, limpid refrain . . .

"My friends, did any post arrive for me during my absence?"

But he waits for no answer! Of one heart alone – or is it two? – would he care to have tidings, and the dearest of names, why, he knows not whether it begins with an A or an E.

No one, obviously, replies.

"I shall retire early this evening; I shall therefore not receive. But should a Linnet enquire for me, *bien* . . . show him in."

Gravely and fatuously they answer with a nod.

Left alone in the austere chamber, he inclines his proud head over the table as if in weariness, and, as his thoughts dwell on the Linnet, buries his lean features in his exquisite hands.

II

Brief Tale of Baba
(La Joie)

The young couple restored to wealth

Those friends of the prince's who, remaining in Naples, bustled around the young couple, as invariably happens, to lighten the load of their happiness, were very soon successful, not only by dwelling at wearisome length upon the "gifts" announced or delivered to his wards by order of de Neville subsequent to his departure (there was talk of a villa in Calabria, and also of jewels for Elmina that *sang*, as the common people had it, to wit, a diadem belonging to the late Leopoldine, set with a pair of sapphires which had only to be lightly touched to emit enchanting sounds) – all of which reports were without any foundation whatever; but also by malicious insistence on certain of these items which revealed, or were supposed to reveal, in his intentions, a conspicuous favouritism on de Neville's part now for one and now for another of the lovers. And this, in our opinion (if the Reader will forgive us our indiscreet intrusion into the narrative), was no mean falsehood, not to say iniquity, insomuch as that fiery heart, born straight from the clouds, lightning and (we imagine) flowers of the land where Europe ends at the feet of the North Sea, was of a kind more subtle, unfathomable and therefore inconceivable to mediocre persons and the hall-porters of dreams; in that de Neville was divided equally between the two elusive aspects of life: the vast enthusiasm and the infinite coldness of being. Needless to say his enthusiasm – on which he set most store – was all for his tender Albert, while to his tortured heart Elmina appeared as the custodian of all the chill of a midwinter's night, though rendered precious none the less by that secret hinted at in the prince's imaginings and his speculations during the abortive visit to the tomb of Brigitta Helm. But on this point we will not insist. Such high degrees of purity are not accessible to all, we are bound to say, and understand them who may; others are at liberty to continue to think as they please.

As a matter of fact from Liège, by many channels and over a long period of time, arrived such gifts as wonderfully to improve the financial situation of the Civile-Dupré family, quite apart from the great security offered by the annuity; thus annulling all the consequences of the Glover's disastrous decline in fortune, just as long as the three of them made reasonable use of the money. Albert (*not* Elmina) was endowed with a so-called "garden" in Calabria, in the vicinity of Tropea; a lovely spot, with a small country house attached; and the whole representing a value far more substantial than the "Villa" dreamt up by the gossip-mongers. It was, moreover, accompanied by a revenue worthy, for those times, of a Royal House. This was to meet all the expenses of maintaining the peasant family that would care for it and render it profitable.

For Elmina (through the good offices of Ruskaja, who had particularly trustworthy couriers, supervised as they were by the famous "Lens"!) arrived a constant stream of fabrics bearing the trademarks of the most accredited Flemish manufacturers: silks and velvets, damasks and lace of incomparable beauty, but also fanciful gifts such as porcelain saucepans of floral design and pairs of bellows wrought in iridescent feathers, all objects entirely unsuitable for any practical use. In addition, through Notary Liborio and other members of the Neapolitan acquaintance of the spouses, there arrived sumptuous gifts for the Glover himself, including the title deeds, together with the keys, of a new residence on the Riviera of Chiaia, opposite the recently constructed "Villa", which should, in the intentions of the donor, be numbered among the assets to be bequeathed in due time to the spouses and their heirs. And this latter fact revealed the motive, which was in reality nothing but affection. It was not long, therefore, before the whole of Naples knew that the Civile-Duprés were once again wealthy, very wealthy indeed, to a degree that the Colonel and his consort, who had by Will despoiled them of everything, could never (even with the greatest of displeasure) have imagined. And of the late Baroness Helm and her ten surviving children, predators of the highest order, with the exception of poor little Floridia who had for some years been out of the running, no one any longer spoke except in tones of contempt and mockery. They ceased to be of interest! After a while, however, people began to talk once more, and with compassion, of Don Mariano and the young couple, between whom there was no lack of disagreement and conflict; not, to be sure, on account of the "gifts", but equally not entirely unrelated to the prince's evident benevolence now towards the one, now towards the other. It was said, among other things, that the prince had had by Elmina, who was not the young maiden she seemed to be, but already some thirty-five or forty years old, a baby boy dead in infancy, nicknamed the Linnet, a child of incredible beauty and sweetness . . . And there were other slanders of the kind. And here it may not be superfluous, in the interests of that deeper understanding of the human heart which the narrator of histories must always strive to attain, to dwell for a moment on the true state of mind of the young couple and the Glover at that time, and specifically with regard to that wondrous good fortune which once again, thanks to the prince's munificence, had presented itself on their doorstep and was kneeling, so to speak, awaiting their orders.

Such state of mind – the reply, in short, which they showed themselves able to confer on such a deal of beauty, marvel and goodness on the part of their distant benefactor – may be swiftly summed up, apart from a few utterances such as "Oh, look how lovely! De Neville really shouldn't have put himself out!", or "You tell him so, Albert!", as a species of far from radiant indifference. It appeared that those persons had none of them ever taxed their minds with even the smallest computation of monetary values. And if it might be astonishing that a man of business, a merchant, a manu-facturer as we would say today, such as Monsieur Civile undoubtedly was, should greet with a melancholy smile the title deeds and finely chased silver key of a grandiose apartment on the Riviera of Chiaia, no less surprising was the total indifference of Elmina at the sight of those rolls of silk and velvet which she hastened (so that they wouldn't spoil, she said) to shut away in an old wardrobe situated in a passageway behind the kitchen. Shut away, moreover, only in a manner of speaking, inasmuch as anyone – for at least in the early days there was no shortage of maids and other girls employed to assist Ferrantina – anyone at all was at liberty to rummage in that cupboard and remove any length of silk they took a fancy to, or a roll of precious lace, or a Flanders tablecloth. And so with every-thing from cooking pots to necklaces! Everything lay strewn about, in still other cupboards or on some upper shelf in the passage or in the kitchen itself, simply covered with a cloth to protect those marvels from the dust and the smoke from the fire. Of Albert Dupré, at this point, this need not be wondered at, since even before the wedding he had ignored the advan-tages of revenues, annuities and other privileges of the sort. As for the "garden" in Calabria, he had never even been to visit it, confining himself to asking Alphonse, if he ever had a moment to spare, to go and look it over. From the very first day of their marriage (they had moved from Jib-Sail House to Sant'Antonio immediately after the ceremony) he had set to work with enormous, almost sullen energy to sculpt small marble heads, working in the same dim-lit room that had depressed the prince on his visit to the Little House. He had eyes for nothing else. What with neo-classical statues, which had been commissioned from him to adorn villas and public buildings in Naples, and these small heads, there was scarcely a minute in his day to spare for Elmina; who in fact made no complaint, and indeed seemed perfectly untroubled. Untroubled also by the fact that instead of using her, his wife, as a model for these famous heads, Dupré continuously sculpted *one* head, always the same: that of a little boy, of great beauty, but which Elmina could not bear the sight of, though mani-festing her disapproval, or indifference, entirely tacitly. It was that of a curly-headed child bearing no resemblance to any of the sculptor's friends or acquaintances, and certainly not to de Neville (as he might have been in some imagined infancy), but who, everyone said, reminded them of *something* barely glimpsed and lost at once, but loved for ever. The face was beautiful, very beautiful, of dreamlike charm, but in that face (which the artist intended to entitle *La Joie*) the most striking quality was not the beauty, so much as an expression of desperate expectancy, or else a vision of some benison too great for human senses to bear, at which those eyes were gazing; but which none the less was invisible to the observer, as might be a beam of light received from on high, or a mother's kiss, or who can tell what else. Of this *Joie* Albert had already carved, since the day of his wedding (which he spent working), at least seventy "variants", but he was constantly tormented by the thought of not having yet *expressed all*.

"But what more do you want to express, Albert?" Elmina would ask placidly. "The *creature* is beautiful, that's plain to see. Isn't that enough?"

"Oh, for that matter we can see he's in good health and eats everything that's put in front of him," the artist replied on one occasion, giving her a strange look. "For goodness' sake, Elmina, don't make me lose my temper." Thus irritably did our loving husband conclude the argument.

Loving to what extent? And to what extent was she in love with him?

Concerning that marriage no one could have uttered a word of criti-cism, but it is equally true that they could have uttered many. Albert was fond of Elmina, and Elmina accepted this fondness without fuss; and between them there were also tempestuous, or particularly tender, days. But days and nights always, always *alike* – that is, of no importance – insomuch as, quite clearly, for both the one and the other the be-all and end-all of living was no longer, or perhaps never had been, married life.

The latter was by now, more than anything else, merely incidental.

*The decline of Don Mariano and his attachment to
a cardboard box. Ingmar receives letters from Naples
signed by the Nanny-Goat and her sister Teresa*

For some time everything went, or appeared to go, reasonably well, but it came about that at a certain moment the health, or perhaps the balance of Don Mariano's morale – a place of darkness which had none the less withstood many shocks – began to falter. Health troubles and the infirmities of age, but above all a state of deep depression, had obliged him to sell off his last shop, for all that it was Teresina's dowry (though the receipts were scrupulously put aside for her, for when she came of age). We should add that he, who had never brought himself to occupy the apartment on the Riviera of Chiaia, the gift of the prince, finding one infantile excuse after another to postpone the move, in the end was forced to do so; his workshop at Jib-Sail House, a mere couple of rooms of which the temporary use had been granted him by a letter from Brigitta Helm to her lawyer, was reft from him overnight by a Court Order; and this was the work of Pasqualino Helm, the youngest son of Donna Brigitta, a little scoundrel who had sunk to joining the Bourbon Police, and the only one of the tribe who had presented himself in person to claim his share of the estate (the others, presumably taken up with trading and profitable ventures in Africa, had placed their affairs in the hands of lawyers). For Don Mariano this sudden and irreversible separation from the house he loved, and which he had not left even for an hour since the departure of Elmina, was a terrible blow. And he left it, to move to his new apartments, in the dead of night, or shortly before dawn, taking with him on a two-wheeled cart, and covered with a tarpaulin, only a few personal possessions, amongst which a cardboard box which might perhaps have contained a puff of wind, so featherweight it was. Seated beside that box he wept throughout the journey, and then, on arriving at his destination, he babbled a few words – addressed perhaps to the horse, or to some invisible friend – which bore witness to his prostration and great turmoil of mind. Thus began his new and, alas, brief life.

Much censure was forthcoming on this occasion (indeed who could refrain from it?) regarding the unwonted loneliness of Don Mariano and the *selfishness* of the young couple. But that was not how things really stood. It was Don Mariano (and this was known and much regretted by his most intimate friends) who absolutely refused to follow his daughter and son-in-law to the house at Sant'Antonio, in spite of Elmina's having long since prepared him two pleasant little rooms on the upper floor, containing a number of articles of gilded furniture from Jib-Sail (in this respect the Notary had erred, for some things had remained to him), and had in addition given him the run of the turret and the terrace for his days of wool-gathering. But Don Mariano, prior to receiving the keys of Chiaia, and, as we have seen, even afterwards, had never resigned himself, other than with heartbreak, to moving house. It seemed as if his very soul was there in the old house, and had been ever since his meeting with Donna Helm. In the end he was forced to submit, by night, in tears, and only then to an injunction of the Court, but taking with him the precious box (tied with coarse string and full of holes) of what were readily supposed, so light was the burden, to be the few "love-letters" he had ever received from Donna Helm. Things, in our opinion, which may be even more readily pardoned. And from those "letters", and from those rooms, the gift of the prince, he never again departed, not even to visit his "children". He sat all day long in the entrance hall, while in the splendid drawing-room, amongst mirrors and gilded consoles, he had had a small bed set up; on a chair nearby were a pitcher for water and a plate for the food which the concierge went to fetch once a day – O extremity of wretchedness! – from a cook-house down in the street. The box, as a rule, was kept at the bedside, and on occasions, the concierge told a friend, the string had evidently been tampered with. A sign that the precious letters came out in the night-time, for a hazy perusal of memories by the light of a candle, or of the moon that gleamed upon the sea.

We do not wish, and may not need, to add more about the torment of those last years, or the decline of the amiability and intelligence, the benevolence and charm of that outstanding gentleman and craftsman, in consequence of the death of the woman whom he considered, rightly or wrongly, to have been his beloved wife.

We should mention that even his love of his daughter was tarnished by this, and in fact he never failed to respond, in answer to her gentle

"How are we today, father?" each time she came to visit him, with a weary "I would be better off dead, my child."

"Papa, don't say such things!" And the poor soul trembled.

And with a sigh: "And you, my child, will you promise me before Almighty God to do your duty when I am no longer here?"

"Papa!" (with feeling), "You'll live to be a hundred!"

"And you, Elmina, will you promise me that at the end of that hundred years you will still do your duty? Will you promise me, child?"

"Papa, I would die rather than not do my duty. Only the Angels could prevent me, but they will not," was the reply, as sorrowful as it was sibylline.

This said, she would at times approach the cardboard box, brushing it with the precious hand which had so driven the prince's wits astray, and lingering in a caress full of devoted and deep-felt dejection.

That the "letters" should be safeguarded after his death from the heartless curiosity of heirs, or of mere acquaintances, appeared to be the single despairing obsession of Don Mariano. And the reason why he did not make the resolve to destroy them, thus saving them, while he still had the chance, from whatever of better or worse the future might bring, may be perfectly understood by all those who live on memories, or for whom memories are the sole source of survival.

For those "letters" – for the time being we cannot but describe them as such – were the very breath of his being.

But clearly Don Mariano's mind was already disordered, and his daughter was not blest (even were she to think only of herself) with any chance of disregarding him. For we should not forget that her father was also God to her.

In view of this it may perhaps be understood why there was no real happiness, even under the favourable influence of lofty Flemish constellations, in the lives of the two young spouses. For Albert, obviously enough, the impediment lay purely in those limitations which, at times with genuine despair, he saw in his genius, in his inability to achieve a perfect head (*La Joie*). In Elmina, indifference towards these heads, with all their sublime beauty, and the tantrums of art, mingled with that unfathomed love, devout and simple-hearted, which she had vowed to her father. And now the object of that love was paling, fading . . . The iron had entered the young soul of Elmina, but living away from her father, and worse, watching him vanish among the eternal sunsets of the world, wrenched molten tears from deep within her, which never once did she reveal to Albert. He was outside the poor girl's magic circle, and in any case, even had he wished to behave differently, he would not have understood her. Little by little Elmina had come close to despair, and to repenting that marriage which had sundered the old man from the young people, hastening the decline of the former, and not, to be sure, at the desire of the latter, but through the inevitable falling out of circumstances, which turn upon the ages and characters of the protagonists. In a certain sense she no longer loved Albert (if indeed she had ever loved him, her woman's heart being in thrall to grave compassion for her own father). The consequence was a degree of departure, with respect to her own life, from the thoughts, if not truly happy then certainly tranquil, of the early days; a departure which unfortunately escaped Albert, and this displeased her a little, for it seemed a neglect of her.

"You work, work, work at your *Joie*," she observed one day with some bitterness, "and that is enough for you. Of all the rest you never notice anything."

"And what, pray, should I notice?"

"Well, my father is very ill, indeed he is dying, just to mention one thing. Had it escaped your attention?"

These words, and this truth (which, however, he considered "exaggerated"), affected Albert deeply, and with genuine sorrow, forasmuch as between him and the old Glover there existed an instinctive and spontaneous friendship, founded on their common disinterest in outward values, and also on some secret passion that neither of the two ever really revealed (perhaps a *memory*, or an idea or ideas about the celestial nature of the world), and this, far more than ties of family or of property, formed a bond between them, as was not the case between Albert and Elmina; so much so that the bride, on occasions, without feeling jealous, her own father being in question, was perhaps a trifle upset.

"We all know he is a friend of yours, but it does not seem that until now you have been much concerned about him," said she to mortify her husband.

For several days Dupré, relinquishing his chisels and marbles and variants of *La Joie*, virtually established himself, in the sense that he spent many hours in Chiaia, with the Glover. From which sojourn, in a moment of genuine anguish, of strange unbearable ravings and regrets, ensued what appears to be the only letter addressed by him to Ingmar.

It was couched in the following terms.

Sant'Antonio, Naples, brumaire*

My dear Ingmar,

I am suffering in a way you will be hard put to imagine. I have scarcely thanked you for all your gifts (lost as I have been in the novelty of my new studio and the work I am doing), but I am bound to say that I would willingly exchange them all for two things: to have you here, at once, beside me, and even more than this to see our beloved Don Mariano return to health, and to a happy life again. Do you know that he is very ill?

He no longer leaves the house, never goes for a walk, does no work.

Formerly he at least used to get dressed and go out.

No, living (or, at any rate, understanding) is too difficult, and in consequence I do not know if I shall be able to go on working on my *Joie*.

What a shame! It was almost finished.

Come soon, if you wish, dear friend, dear star or stormcloud of my heart.

(Love from Elmina!)

Albert

On receipt of this letter, marked, among other things, by the grey, disfiguring blotches of tears, de Neville, torn between elation and concern at being still loved by his friends, even in such painful circumstances, at once gave his private secretary orders to prepare for a second journey towards the Sun, or Lower Mediterranean. He counted on being in Naples, travelling this time by sea, in a fortnight's time, but an accident intervened to bring this scheme to nothing. This was simply a fall from a horse, but travel he could not, and there ensued two terrible months, immobilized by a broken foot. When he had further news from Olympus it was over the signature of Elmina. His heart leapt into his mouth but thereafter, for other reasons, gave a lurch. Finally his blood ran cold on observing that the (laboured) signature was indeed hers, as was the dictation, but that the whole sheet had been written by Teresina.

---

* For young Dupré, immersed, as the young always are, in the language of his day, the Revolutionary changes in the calendar at that time were calmly accepted, like the cut of clothes and other frivolities of fashion.

In any case the poor Nanny-Goat could not, without help, have addressed a real letter to the Benefactor from Liège (and we may add that the fact had not troubled her). The purport of letter was as follows:

Sant'Antonio, Naples

Most Illustrious Monsieur de Neville,

My husband, Albert, has instructed me to write to you, as he is at present prevented by his work on his statues, as well as a pain in one eye. He charges me with informing you, and I am sorry on your account, that my father, Don Mariano, is now with Our Lord. A Mass will be said for him in the church of Santa Lucia on the Tenth of the current month, at nine in the morning. We ask you (it is Teresina writing) to join your thoughts with ours.

I got the dolly. Very, very beautiful.*

My husband (this is Elmina talking) tells you that he is expecting a son, and will call him after you. It is the least you deserve. For my own part, I do not mind. I would have preferred my father's name, but it is no matter.

On my father's behalf I send you this chain.

Papa said to wear it always.

A thousand blessings from Heaven. (Elmina)

I am doing well at school now. (This is Teresina)

The medal has to be polished. The two horns come separate (against the evil eye). On the medal are the Vatican Church and Mounts Somma and Vesuvius.

Your friend would be very pleased to see you.

Teresina and Elmina (the sisters)

Over this letter de Neville laughed and cried, while into his mind crept an awareness of the passing of time, which until then had all but escaped him. Olympus had collapsed into the sea. With Don Mariano dead, and Dupré distrait and perhaps in despair with that damaged eye, the Nanny-Goat had learnt to talk, and had sent him that missive with the help of her waggish little sister, or perchance of the latter's doll.

Yes indeed, in the midst of many other thoughts, Ingmar dwelt at length on the passing of time. And it seemed to be borne in on him that more

---

* A brief reference to a gift to Teresa, apparently memorable. But no more is known about it.

time still – much more! – would pass, with mysteries ever so simple, freshness ever so painful. And deep within himself he suddenly heard the voice of the mechanical bird, with its "O-hoh! O-hoh! O-hoh!" and "Ohhh! Ohhh! Ohhh!" as if it were crying out, but there was no way of understanding (and he at least, Ingmar, was desperately sure that this was because there was nothing to be understood) what the cry could mean.

"O happiness!" he burst out. "O wondrous, blessèd happiness! And thou, O youth! But tell me, O sisters, happiness and youth, who are you? Why, why do you deceive us? Oh, if I could but see you again, Albert, Don Mariano, Elmina! But even now I know that such a day is not numbered, or not in the manner I would wish, among the days of my future or of yours."

Birth of Baba. Rejoicing in the Little House
and further minor mysteries of the heart of Elmina.
(From a letter of Nodier's)

From other letters, both Nodier's and Teresa's, we learn as follows. The baby boy was born in April of the year following all these many events (for Albert, on the 18th of germinal), and was the occasion of immense rejoicing for the family at Sant'Antonio at Posillipo, and among their friends, who, having in recent times somewhat neglected the Duprés, now hastened to make up for lost time. One great cause of excitement was the extraordinary charm of the child, who in the end was not called after the prince, as had been promised, nor yet after Don Mariano or Albert, but was given the fanciful name of Ali Baba, which brought to mind nothing remotely domestic or "family", but merely a Middle Eastern fairy-tale. The decision to dispense with honoured and beloved names, and to plump for one so absurd, was taken on the initiative of Elmina, seeing that Albert was not thinking of the prince at all, but solely of his father-in-law, and in his opinion Mariano was the only name to give the boy. Strange, and contradictory with regard to what she had previously maintained, was Elmina's objection to her husband's preference: "He is your son. You are the father. Mariano would be gratuitous." By which she meant an exaggerated devotion, more than he had any right to claim. To be happy about it was another matter, and in fact superfluous, but Albert could not but note the great poise, and indeed the serene detachment, that lay deep in his wife's heart. She doubtless distinguished between her various degrees of love, and for her the sacred name of her father could be lent to no one else, not even a Dupré. And perhaps he asked himself, "Has this woman ever really loved anyone?" And then, ruefully and tenderly, he was obliged to recognize that she had truly loved, passionately and almost religiously loved, her father, the improvident Don Mariano who had made a collection of other people's children; and by such an act, by declaring that name to be non-transferable, by reckoning its worth as superior to anyone whatever, set apart in this from the Duprés and from all others, she kept that name more truly and entirely his, in the church or silent temple of her heart. Such, at least, were the deductions arrived at by our artist.

Ingmar, on the other hand, when he learnt of the new choice of name, did not suffer the least sense of betrayal – for the matter did not greatly interest him – but rather of uneasiness, that in forgetting him Albert was at best in the grip of a sort of obsession, which was making its presence felt in his new nature (as the shadow rises on a building hitherto exposed to the sunlight when little by little other buildings rise silently around it), and was severing him from the erstwhile enthusiasms of his youth. And finally there was another reason why that choice did not please him: for it seemed to him that if it bore his name, and was called Ingmar, the child would have been placed, so to speak, under his jurisdiction, and that he, Ingmar, would have had some recognized right to preside over his future happiness; while as things stood he could not do so, or it would not be the same thing. In a word, he was uneasy, and (despot as he was) he went so far as to plan to undertake at this stage, and with real reason, that second journey to Naples which he had desired so much, but which his accident had unfortunately prevented. Once there (clearly this was his heart casting around for solid reasons), he would take the opportunity of having the already registered name of Ali Baba cancelled, and to bestow a third, perhaps double-barrelled, in which the two forgotten names, of Don Mariano and Ingmar, would find their appointed place. Thereafter this Baba could become a second name, for some such trifling whimsicality might be acceptable. He immediately wrote to the sculptor with this proposal, but received no answer. He had the impression that the spouses had been visited by some other and unforeseen cause of unhappiness; and, while making arrangements for a first, fantastic christening present for the baby (a medallion, the work of a master goldsmith in Liège, bearing on one side a cross in sapphires, and on the other the Great Bear and the Chariot of Pegasus, with the Chimaera in the background, all in tiny diamonds), a gift which he requested Nodier to deliver to the child's parents, he asked his friend whether there were by chance any reasons for anxiety in Naples, seeing that it was some time since he had received news from there. Nodier's answer arrived, and justified the young couple's silence, and that of Teresina as well, with news – which indeed was scarcely news, but simply confirmation – of the most radiant, extraordinary and irrepressible happiness, which was the reason for their silence and indifference towards their distant friend. Little Albert, for Albert had been accepted as a second name, though everyone continued to call him by the barbarous but legal name of Ali Baba; Ali Baba-Albert, then, was increasing in health, in charm and in every blessing, and was the joy of the household. To say his father was mad about him would be gross understatement. During that period he had carved his finest busts, even though he had not yet succeeded in expressing, as he said, "'my idea, you understand, Alphonse, of a thing transcending human comprehension, a thing for which there is no explanation, and therefore akin to a lamenting cry in a beauteous heaven as blue as it is total, gladsome, inexplicable'. This then, my dear Ingmar, is his freakish (but how sensitive!) response to fatherhood."

Reading this, Ingmar, who had grown pensive (the name of Albert, coming after Baba, now seemed to him incongruous), began to wonder whether his friend really felt that Elmina loved him; and he was inclined to think not, inasmuch as he well knew from experience how a love, even the least reciprocated, if it is authentic, leaves no room and no thoughts to spare for other dream-figures. In any case he considered it prudent to disengage himself for the time being from his passionate involvement with the Neapolitan Olympus, partly because he had certain political wrangles to sort out, and also because he had for some time been planning a visit to Germany, on account of a marriage which he intended to arrange between two neighbouring petty states. And for this reason also he thought that a holiday from his old thoughts would not come amiss, and indeed was just what he needed. On this he acted, and on a series of journeys which took him as far afield as Turkey he spent the best part of a year, amid bold and lofty projects, alternating with delightful amusements, before returning once again to Liège, where he was able to read with joy, soon overshadowed by a displeasing surprise, two letters which had arrived on different dates, the one from Nodier, the other from Ruskaja, both of whom simultaneously pressed him (though by chance, since the two were unacquainted) to put in an appearance in Naples, were it only for a single day, "to learn of strange things and happenings, my dear Ingmar, which would I think much enrich your experience. Benjamin."

The letter from Nodier, which he opened immediately afterwards, later to return with trembling hand to that of Ruskaja, began with news of the business transactions on which he had embarked in Naples, and which were proceeding pretty well, while the city itself, however many pleasures and entertainments it had to offer, had ceased to be so very congenial to him; and he was thinking of leaving it and returning for some time at least to "our dear Liège, which is never absent from my thoughts".

One cause of Nodier's disappointment lay, indeed, in their mutual friends, who at the outset had been the primary reason for his enthusiastic decision to reside in Naples. As regarded the baby, he declared, great joy; but for the rest of it more than one darkening shadow. "No real or profound discord, certainly, but rather a temperamental antipathy, *something infinitely subtle, dear prince*, divides those two. Obviously, the upbringing of Baba is at the root of everything, but part is also due to the increasingly manifest aversion of Donna Elmina to her husband's art, which she never criticizes (such a fine upbringing, amounting to an education, did she receive from her father!). But she could not state more plainly what she thinks of it, than she does by simply detaching her gaze from his work, should it chance to fall on the nose or a shoulder of one of those busts. That she does not approve of art is now abundantly clear to me, or of culture in general (and in that she is *divinely* Bourbon!); only of the family and domestic virtues. And returning to what I said above, she is a perfect mother, but for her own little creature, my dear Ingmar, how little *interest* she displays! I had not seen them for several months, and just yesterday, going to pay a short visit to the Little House at Sant'Antonio (very light and airy, I have to say, though strangely enough, for the house of two young lovers, of positively Spartan bareness); returning, as I said, to visit them, I became aware of something that thitherto had always escaped my notice, and this something perturbed me. It was evening, or better, it was sunset. The house was all lit up in rosy colours by the dying sun, and Ferrantina (you remember the old housekeeper who managed Don Mariano's mansion at Jib-Sail, and who as soon as she could flitted off like a bat into the kitchen? I was never able to tolerate her, and never will); Ferrantina, then, entered the room with a lamp, to announce that supper was served. Now – and here follow me carefully – during this announcement from the old maidservant, nurse to the children at one time, if not, as her age has sometimes led me to believe, to Don Mariano himself (though now her hair is almost blond); while Ferrantina, I repeat, was making this announcement, Madame Dupré, who has been somewhat paler of late, and was wearing the same pink dress as on that delightful evening of our arrival at Jib-Sail House, was seated near the window, sewing a little jacket for Baba. On hearing the words she rose at once to her feet, and cast a tender but stern glance at Albert who, sitting beside the cot, was playing with the "urchin" (the term jestingly applied, in Naples, even to children of a year old). Baba, standing up in his cot and leaning over the edge of the big basket as on a window-sill, was stretching out his arms towards the linnet-cage, that wonderful gift you sent, if you remember, as a sign of reconciliation to the marriage you had opposed. Well, while with one hand the young father was clasping the little silken hand of Baba, with the other he was dancing that coveted object up and down before his son's eyes. And the game consisted in this: lowering the cage to the level of the boy's nose, and his expectant face (needless to say the bird inside seemed dead, for the sound-mechanism was broken), the father rapidly chanted the following words:

> *Flutter, flutter, flutter, fly little Linnet!*
> *Flutter, flutter, flutter, Oh! Oh! Oh!* *

then swiftly snatching away the cage from Baba's hands, with a motion so rapid that the babe pulled a great face, between laughter and tears; at which Albert lowered it again, dangling it in front of his face and chanting the cry you are familiar with:

> *O-hoh! O-hoh! O-hoh!*
> *Ohhh! Ohhh! Ohhh!*

"And it was this refrain, uttered rather hoarsely, almost emotionally, that made Baba laugh until he cried and, in raptures of delight, repeat together with his father:

> *Dalinnet! Dalinnet! Dalinnet!*

and then:

> *Aha! Aha! Aha!*

thus varying, as you see, only the refrain of this mournful barcarolle.

"You see how it was, my friend, they were laughing till the tears streamed down their faces, the tears that were there in the refrain! (As you now know that lovely toy is broken, and the bird emits not a sound on its own account, and can do no more than make to lower its head onto the

---

* This *Linnet's Song*, which we here give as known since the eighteenth century, dates historically from the first decades of this century. The shift from one century to another is not due to lack of regard for the history of the song, but to the power of some songs, or street cries, to fix themselves in the memories of men, when heard in childhood, free of temporal barriers, as profoundly *natural* things.

red flush on its breast; but those two, father and son, have learnt the song.) In a word, it was a strange moment, a moment of pure joy, and I imagine that nobody, not even the King himself, would have interrupted them, but stood enchanted by that scene of filial and fatherly love. But she, Elmina, having calmly observed them for some time (she had already called Albert by name without receiving a reply), went up to the cot and politely, but extremely firmly, removed the broken birdcage from her husband's hands, saying:

"'How many times do I have to tell you, Albert, that this cage is broken enough as it is, and you must leave it where you found it, on top of my chest-of-drawers. The key has snapped.'

"'Begging your pardon,' returned Albert promptly. 'It was in the hatbox, not on your chest-of-drawers.'

"'I am not in the habit of telling lies. It was not in the hatbox.'

"Whether Albert had lied, from mere childishness (though I do not remember his ever lying as a boy, he's so darling and sincere), or she was lying out of animosity towards her husband, I have no means of knowing. Unfortunately, the baby started to yell like a mad thing (and believe me, Ingmar, I have never heard such a frenzied, heartbroken voice, but the little thing adores his father, whereas for him Elmina is something of an enemy), and to struggle and writhe about. Wriggling free and trembling, he bawled in his ridiculous infantile rage: 'Gibbaba Dalinnet! Gibbaba Dalinnet!', growing hoarser every moment as his voice was consumed by the fire in his heart (but do not be anxious, Ingmar, for all tots of that age are the same when they are coldly thwarted).

"Without a glance at his wife, Albert seized the child in his arms with such vehemence and compassion that it sent a frisson right through me, and I trembled for Elmina. But she, as if confronted merely with two squabbling children, rather than her noble and handsome husband and tender babe, tore the latter from his father's arms, calmly consigned him to Ferrantina (and the very name of this allegedly devoted servant is an indication of how *ferrous*, or compounded of iron, is her character!), took the candlestick from the maid's hand and as cool as you please, on her way to the staircase, said: 'And I hopes that's a lesson to you.' Without, as you will have observed, minding her grammar.

"Shortly afterwards we went to table, and we could still hear Baba bawling in an upstairs room, and the raucous voice of the old woman attempting to soothe him. I can tell you that my eyes filled with tears, and I received the impression that those two, Father and Son, were like God the Father and the Infant Jesus, a single Good, sole, indivisible, inseparable – and not to be shared with others. But Elmina, of the trio, is certainly not the Holy Ghost.

"She is, I now realize, an obdurate, sullen creature."

The Duke is of one opinion with the merchant. The effects of a lens skilfully repaired. The decline of Ali Baba, and what the lens saw in the garden at Sant'Antonio

To tell the truth this meddling by Nodier (for so it appeared in the state of mind in which Ingmar found himself after his travels), this meddling on the part of the merchant in a minor disagreement between the spouses, perhaps the first, concerning the infant's upbringing, did not much please the prince; in it he glimpsed an act of spite entirely detrimental to Donna Elmina, whom many in the city, at least according to Nodier, already considered to be an inappropriate wife for the artist, and above all not the woman to understand his art. Indeed she was becoming the object of opprobrious epithets, such as "Hun" and "Witch", though sometimes also "Jacobin", oddly enough; the common people being, in their passion for justice, family dramas and capital punishment, always willing and indeed eager to exaggerate their suspicions and verdicts. And the Neapolitans were no exception. They took to speaking well again of *poor Donna Helm*, as Elmina's victim, and did not forget the fate, still wrapped in mystery, of little Floridia; and so on and so forth. And they commiserated, as occasion arose, now with the grandmother, now with the grandson. The fact was that in Naples Albert Dupré was not reaping much success, either in his art or in his personal relationships, on account of something about him — Nodier could not quite put his finger on it — that was excessive; or maybe, to the prince's way of thinking, that was *lacking* in him, for he was well enough aware of the penchant of the inhabitants of the Kingdom of Naples for anything, whether in a person's character or way of living, that tended to the light-hearted and superficial, which had at first seemed to be one of Albert's attributes, whereas in the course of his residence in Naples his nature had completely changed; for that gay young charmer, rightly at one time styled Bellerophon, had become — especially after the loss of his father-in-law, and except for the brief period of enthusiasm which had marked the birth of Ali Baba — had become, I say, a solitary, often melancholy, changeful in his moods, and above all haughty and sarcastic in his strictures on other artists; and furthermore ever less in love with his wife. This displeased his friends and the city at large. Everyone at this point, having initially sympathized with the husband, now openly commiserated with the wife for the indigent and isolated way of life she led, which they doubted not was the result of lack of interest on Albert's part. True or false as this judgement may have been – shedding light, as it did, on the origin of that unhappiness in *her* undeniable coldness – it was displeasing to Ingmar, who saw in it, as we have said, a pretty undisguised antipathy towards Donna Elmina. But what he went on to read, on taking up the letter from Ruskaja, was calculated to worry him still more.

It began thus:

You would be astonished, dear Ingmar, if you could take a look, after this long lapse of time, at your protégés in Naples. Not having made use of my lens (the reason being, as you may remember, a little screw that had fallen out of the handle again, and my not knowing who to go to for discreet repairs, but also – don't laugh – because I had promised our good Father Alexander, who has for some time been all the rage in Naples with his sermons against the Devil, sermons preached in San Domenico, where the whole nobility swarm to hear him), I applied for news of them to my dear friend the Marchesa Durante (the mother, not the daughter, who is no friend to Elmina), and you will be amazed to hear what she told me. What she said was, in essence, as follows: Donna Elmina has disposed of nearly the whole of her new fortune (they therefore knew that the first had come to an end with the death of Donna Brigitta), including the "garden" (that is, the farm in Calabria), and the apartment in Chiaia, selling them without Albert's knowledge and plainly in an underhand manner. The author, or accomplice in the matter (such, be warned!, are the friends of Donna Elmina), was Don Liborio Apparente, that same Notary Liborio better known as the Scribblerus, a profession in bad odour with His Majesty; and for this very reason we must be indulgent towards him, and do nothing to encourage the rumours circulating about the part he played in the business. But alas, the thing is already done, even if illegally, and it's no use crying over spilt milk. To Albert the whole matter was presented as stringent necessity in the face of further debts and catastrophes recently come to light in his father-in-law's affairs. (In parenthesis, this looks to me not a little improbable, since the debts were not all that many, and were paid off without undue effort following Don Mariano's death.) So resign yourself to it, all your benefactions have thus been disposed of, and all your gifts have disappeared with the exception, I am told, of a tiny cage containing a canary or some other bird, all in solid gold, given to Albert at the time of his betrothal. I may be wrong about the details, but the substance is this. Do you deny it, or are you also informed about it? There is, however, one thing that you certainly do not know, my poor Ingmar, and which might be of consolation to you, by confirming the great purity of spirit of your protégés (or perhaps of Donna Elmina alone): it is that not one penny of that extraordinary fortune was retained by Donna Elmina for herself or her family, but once the supposed debts had been honoured, the entire proceeds of all those sales and transfers, down to the last farthing, she donated to a charitable institution famous in Naples, the Artigianelli (just imagine!) and other hospices or institutions for the care of the needy, especially orphans and the aged. Another strange thing is that Albert, on learning what had become of his own fortune, displayed complete indifference, as if it caused him not so much anxiety as relief . . . And they tell me that the income is suffering the same fate . . . All your benefactions, my poor Ingmar, going to the poor! the orphans! the lowest of the low! to all the lost (and forgotten) souls of this sorrowing city . . . What is the reason – many people in Naples are now asking themselves – for such unnatural, if not downright monstrous, generosity on the part of a young and beautiful woman, well married, with a child of her own, and who is by no means a nun, and not even given to acts of piety – indeed far from it; what is at the bottom of it, if not some monstrous and ineradicable guilt, the weight of which she is unable to bear except by renouncing, as soon as possible, all her personal welfare and happiness? Her mad husband – and such I may truly call him – has not for a moment noticed the strangeness, and I may say the inhumanity of it, seeing that they have a son! Here – I do not wish to say it, but after all why not? – here there is *talk*, and the least infamous libel is that she is protecting, or under protection, or in short has obligations, or secret relationships which have ensnared her life in their meshes . . . and this ever since she was a child. Could it be on account of the death of her sister Floridia, for which she was blamed? Who can say? But she is *not free* — that is how it appears to an old nosy-parker like your Benjamin. The fact is that those two now live solely on Albert's small legacy from his mother and on Elmina's *work*. She is, if you will believe me, a shirtmaker, and though never showing fatigue she works as hard as any man, and for an increasingly extensive clientele, procured for her by the old Marchesa Durante among her friends and those of her daughter (recently married to an officer in the Royal Horse Guards). In that house, therefore (I paid a visit with the old marchesa, with a view to commissioning Albert to make a statue of Hermes for my garden), there is now nothing to be seen but shirts, and lengths and lengths of silk, cotton, linen or whatever else you need to make perfect shirts for men and boys. The marchesa declares that Elmina's skill in this field approaches the sublime, and so does her capacity for hard work. She has taken on, as her only concession to luxury, four girls to do the trimmings. Teresa deals with that side . . . As for Baba, he is now in the sole care of Ferrantina, since even Albert seems so distracted these days.

So what do you think of all this, dear boy? I dare not think anything. I do know that, justifiably in my opinion, poor Baba bursts into tears at the sight of his mother; he has a real terror of her, although she, they tell me, has never scolded him. His great love is still his father, and when he sees him he laughs for joy, and although he now talks fairly well in Franco-Neapolitan he keeps repeating, as if spellbound, a certain refrain which ends with *O-hob! O-hoh! O-hoh!* or *A-haaa! A-haaa! A-haaa!* (a sort of sob, therefore), and which is called, it seems, the *Barcarolle* or *Linnet's Lament*.

In the house there is certainly no suggestion of poverty, but of austerity very much so. Albert has rented a studio outside the "shop" (as he calls the house), a grubby little room not far from Sant'Antonio, and when people meet him he sometimes laughs and sometimes cries, he talks to himself, smiles beatific smiles and has outbursts of rage that set his interlocutors trembling. He also has long periods of absolute calm, of desert-like silences, in which it seems his soul has left his body. He talks without making much sense, and I imagine that the cause of it all is the inability of that born artist to achieve perfection in the work dearest to his heart, *La Joie*, which has now reached the considerable total of two hundred versions, all of them busts of Baba, or "The Linnet", as he calls his son.

The boy is now two years old, and after a period of extra-ordinarily flourishing health now looks to me rather on the peaky side. I have gone back – did I tell you? – to using my lens (poor Father Alexander!), and can therefore positively state, at variance with the optimistic opinion of the marchesa, who is ever ready to excuse her friend Elmina, that he is not the boy he was. His mother (if she mentions the matter) says that he has "the worms", while others generally hold that these "worms" are the result of the irrational fear which his mother inspires in him. Yet Elmina remains ever beautiful and sweet-natured. Some days ago (and I will not say *by chance*) I once more directed my lens at Naples, and seeing that it was functioning to perfection I could not over-come my inquisitiveness: turning it somewhat south-south-east I arrived at the garden at Sant'Antonio, and there I was surprised by the unusual coming and going of people, and by the absence of the child and the governess.

Following the word "governess" was an asterisk referring to a note at the foot of the page, a digression unusual in the limpid and flowing style of the Duke, and which the prince interpreted as a confirmation of the gossipy spirit which had laid hold on that noble mind, due to its traffickings with Naples. We report it purely as a matter of curiosity:

I have never told you that the fact of having entrusted this serving-maid, naturally of obscure birth, with almost the entire responsibility for the child seems to me one of the greatest acts of imprudence on the part of Elmina . . . and of Albert, I should add, were your protégé not in the condition he is . . . I need only say that she, Ferrantina, never leaves the child for a single instant. Even when sweeping the floors, or working in the kitchen, she has him in her arms . . . Not jealous, perhaps, but frightened they will take him away, or for some other reason that bodes no good. The other day, while I am on the subject, the marchesa told me that on leaving the house after a visit to the Shirtmaker she had raised her eyes, and in so doing had espied the old woman on the roof, looking down, as if she were expecting someone. At that very moment Albert came in through the garden gate, and instantly the woman (who also, now, seems to have become blond and beautiful) withdrew as if in fear of being detected. She was therefore watching for the sculptor's return. What can I say? The infant Dupré now seems to me like a sick bird: he clasps his arms round the old woman's neck, hiding his face, and there is no more sound of voices and songs and laughter. My opinion is that she, Ferrantina, is waiting for something ... And that this is no less than the total collapse of the family at Sant'Antonio. *Your* money, in my opinion, has been alienated by *her*, taking advantage of her power over Elmina. For what reason? Ask me another ... This world is indecipherable, Ingmar. All I can say is, woe unto godless families – especially Jacobins.

I shifted the lens. I was frightened. Two days later I learnt from the marchesa that the child had had an attack of *convulsions*. He recovered, thank goodness.

Benjamin's letter continued with other news and still further conjectures. De Neville, as he read it, entered upon an indescribable state of mind: he shook with terror, but ultimately with indignation at the fact that they had not called a doctor. And in his anxiety for Albert, and even more for Baba, he cast off fear and weariness so that, albeit he had scarcely returned from the lengthy travels we know of, he gave orders for the carriages to be put into immediate readiness for the journey to Marseilles, whence he intended to embark without delay for Naples. Perhaps by paying several times the cost of the journey impossibility itself could be rendered possible.

But our wingèd hero was destined to be constantly thwarted in those plans designed to draw him back to the fateful Gulf of Naples, to see to the safety of his treasured ones. He gave no thought at all to Ferrantina, but only to Albert seriously ill and the child run-down in health, and beloved Elmina so apparently abstracted. Baba, he told himself, he would at once remove from that accursèd house (and what house, inhabited by Elmina, was *not* accursèd?), perhaps by simulating a kidnapping with the complicity of Nodier; about poor Elmina he did not wish to think – after all, she had her friend the marchesa, and her shirts, and certainly the good

Teresa . . . But alas! the first carriage was already on its way, it had left ten minutes ago, and the spirited horses – flanked by hedgerows and pervaded by the stunning sweet odour of spring – were filling the road and the air with the clatter of hoofs, when a courier from the prince's palace reached them with a message, just received. It was from Nodier. Baba had died the day before, while in the garden with his father, who was feeding him. The "worms", or rather the *convulsion*s, had done their work. Having attempted to reanimate him with kisses, entreaties, slaps on the cheeks and other pathetic efforts (even frantic massage with sage-leaves), realizing that little Baba did not stir, Albert burst into uncontrollable weeping and outcry, and when Elmina came running out, all unknowing, fell upon her with a dagger . . . Luckily they were separated, and he thereafter had no memory of the occurrence; indeed, though without always recognizing her, he accepted at her hands the sedatives which she prepared for him.

"So this is how things stand," concluded the good Nodier, in a postscript added at an uncertain date, but obviously later. "That lovely family and its happiness have come to an end in a briefer span of time than even the greatest pessimist in the world would have been pleased to imagine. We must at this stage congratulate Elmina on her obstinate insistence in taking on the reponsibilities of working for a living. She has resumed her tasks as a shirtmaker, grief-stricken, they say, but supremely calm. And she pays every care and attention to her husband, whom she never leaves on his own. Her sister Teresina, who is now living with them, has in this crisis shown herself a young lady of great humanity. She looks after Albert in every possible way, and when, after the girl has been chattering away for a while, one nonsense after another, he turns his head and sees her there, his woeful and grateful look, full of heartbreak, is harrowing to see. In that heart of his there is a light, and a lament, that will never leave it, so beloved was poor Baba – and he was but two years old."

Into the prince's mind at this point flooded all that happy past, up until the time of his visit with Notary Liborio to the Glover's family vault, and that sad inscription on the marble with the name "Dupré" (the other two he had forgotten).

How true it had been! Who would have said at the time that he hadn't dreamt it? Or perhaps, yes, he had been dreaming, but the inscription was no less true for all that: "Albert Dupré (Baba), age 2". If only he had insisted on the name of Don Mariano, or his own, thought the superstitious prince, little Albert would have eluded his destiny. But instead, the scrupulous priest had inserted the Christian name of Albert in the *first* place in the baptismal register, and it was due only to Elmina's displeasure that it was followed by the beloved name of Baba. But the question of one name or another was no longer of importance. Solitude and a horror of shadows, solitude but above all cruelty, the prince was certain, had, after so much throbbing and expectancy, stilled the little heart of the poor *Linnet*.

Unexpected return of serenity to Sant'Antonio.
De Neville sets his mind at rest and after other adventures
forgets Naples and the days of his youth

In the heart of de Neville the violent emotions of that time were succeeded by an enormous weariness. He could no longer bear, even in thought, the name of Elmina, so severely had it been wrought upon not only by events themselves, but by spiteful tongues and her own indecipherable conduct. Nevertheless the Nanny-Goat, as with bitter irony he continued to dub her in his own mind, now roused in him a compassion which went hand in hand with the compassion he felt for Albert.

The idea of going back, of revisiting the regions of the Sun, for the first time had no appeal for our magnanimous Ingmar. It seemed to him that he had dreamt every bit of it, the enchantment and enthusiasm no less than the ruin and death, and he had no further wish to set eyes on the places where he had brought and kindled the radiant torch of youth, to blaze but for a moment and to perish, with all the dreams of a European nobleman. He was loath to accept the fact that the end had come.

There none the less ensued two months of incessant correspondence with Naples, during which he learnt from Teresina (who revealed herself, perhaps because of the unforgotten gift of the "dolly", as the most darling of girls and most practical mind in all Naples) increasingly reassuring family news about his friends. Albert's condition was improving, and His Majesty, informed by Captain Argante (Marchese Durante's son-in-law) of the great misfortune of the Duprés, in a fit of benevolence typical of that somewhat boorish individual, had given him a commission for three statues of Minerva for the Royal Gardens. The whole of Naples, whether following that lofty example or from natural compassion, was now bolstering up the sculptor with encouragement, not unmindful either of the great integrity of Elmina and her works of charity. A certain Polish prince was enthusiastic about the busts, especially the latest but one, which as usual portrayed Ali Baba. The artist had at last succeeded, it was said, owing perhaps to his great sufferings, in rendering all the sweetness of that face, and the startled look in the eyes that appeared to be following the aerial flutterings of a dove invisible to others. Indeed Albert had entitled the work *La paloma* (while nothing less than a dove, by no means a butterfly, sitting on the child's shoulder, appeared to have created all that peace and heartsease).

The very latest bust, which had deeply affected everyone, masters and servants alike (which should never be the case with a statue, but at that time Romanticism held sway), surpassed all limits of human expressivity. It was practically worth all the pains of existence (it was thought of Albert) simply to achieve it. It depicted a sleeping boy, tired out it seemed (it was still Baba, but with something new, something *more*), with reclining head and a hand raised to his brow, as if to shield him from the harsh light of day; and on the lips a faint smile. But the brow – if the visitor stepped round and peered beneath the little hand – revealed a dreamlike immobility, an absolute serenity and peace, as if dreams themselves had been surpassed; it revealed, in a certain sense, less Baba than Albert himself, perhaps in childhood. Which in fact in his inmost soul he still was. ("You would have liked to see it, but His Majesty has bought it for his antechamber. It is a great honour. Yours, Teresina.")

"In short, things are better," Teresa went on. "As regards Elmina, she is much changed, more silent than ever she was; she does nothing but pray for the infant's soul, though I do not think there is any need. He had no sins on his head. How everyone will remember Baba for his wonderful gaiety!"

"Gaiety my foot!" thought the prince. "What with a mad father and a frigid mother, he died of solitude. He was killed by his fears. Perhaps by another Linnet there in the house . . ." he thought sarcastically.

And as soon as he thought these things, or said them to himself, he repented. They seemed to him womanish superstitions of the kind which Naples childishly lapped up without even believing them. But for Naples, which he dreamt about often, by day and by night, he now felt an unspeakable horror, equal to the sentiment left in the heart of a worthy and ingenuous man by the memory of a girl he has adored, but in whose nature he has chanced to discover something horrible. But what was there, in fact, so cruel and horrible in Naples, that did not abound everywhere beneath the veneer of religion or upbringing, that was not the common heritage of all men (and women!) in all the cities of the world, of all those who busy themselves without pause or purpose on the blue surface of the globe that gave them birth?

"Poor Elmina," he thought, "tender Chimaera! And you, luckless Bellerophon! Of the three of us, it seems to me, only Alphonse has emerged unscathed. But then," he concluded none too charitably, "merchants always do. They have no fear of dreams, they don't even dream them. *Ils sont vraiment chanceux*."

He also had good news from Ruskaja, if good is the word for it, concerning the conduct of Ferrantina, who had been not the least cause of his worries. Sorrow had aged the poor woman, who – said Ruskaja, repenting his slanderous allusions or perhaps mere flights of fancy – had never been blond and beautiful. Now she could no longer tolerate Albert ("you know, like when a mother-in-law gets old . . ."), but she helped, despite her old bones, yes, she helped Elmina in every way. Furthermore she had taken to her room ("in the turret on the terrace, you remember?") the Glover's few belongings, principally the box of "letters", ". . . in which from time to time, when it is shifted, a faint sound is heard, as of bells – I refer to the cardboard box over which Don Mariano shed so many tears. Poor woman, and poor Don Mariano! Remember them in your prayers, my son. Benjamin."

De Neville did not, for the moment, send any more gifts down to Naples, nor did he spend many words in writing to his friends, being sufficiently reassured to learn that they enjoyed new patronage in high places; though without telling a soul he entailed on Albert and any future heirs one tenth of his fortune, which was in any case virtually limitless, and for this reason sometimes weighed upon his mind.

There then occurred what frequently does occur in many lives which appear irresponsible and frivolous (and such de Neville's had always been, or appeared to be), and which suddenly, on account of a chance meeting, become serious matters and change their entire course. He met, and married, a girl of august and austere family, an act which rather increased than diminished his affluence, and for some time even made him happy and satisfied with his life. In her company he travelled much, enlarging his already vast acquaintance; and this rendered him more level-headed and benevolent. They had no children, and he was glad of it. But in about the seventh year of his marriage, the last five of which were spent almost entirely at St Petersburg, charged with engrossing assignments which made him unmindful of all other cities and parts of the world whatever, his wife, whose name was Geraldine, began to fail in health. As once did the girl of the Linnet, she fell ill of the languishment, and no riches on earth availed to save her.

De Neville was then about thirty-seven years of age, and the fever in the blood was tamed. He suffered, and was perhaps improved by this misfortune, without being shattered by it. He had returned to Belgium, and was living once more in Liège. His life became less hectic and intense, though remaining rich in political and humanitarian interests. He was still a man of gracious ways, with a strikingly warm smile, and a manner of melancholy kindliness, even when conversing with strangers.

III

The Second Proposal of Marriage

Mother and daughter.
The dolorous "Scalinatella"

There were places in Naples perhaps lacking in extensive views, but endowed with a loveliness all of their own, which the passing of centuries, not to speak of the countless virtually supernatural events of history, seemed incapable of erasing, at least from memory. For example, until seventy or eighty years ago, you might have heard persons of great age and gentle sentiments, not far removed by birth from the much lauded and lamented Age of Enlightenment (which is of no present interest), speak of the path, or ramp, known as the "Scalinatella", but in later days by the more modest appellation of "Sant'Antonio a Posillipo", the by no means provisional scene of our story. We imagine it to have lain on the seaward side of the hill, though it might also have been on the slope facing the fearful, sulphur-belching Phlegraean Fields. However that may have been, accurately remembered or otherwise, or even completely imaginary, the location we have assigned to the dwelling of Elmina, Albert and Ali Baba, and where we have followed their ingenuous goings-on, is that place and no other; and whether it existed in reality or unreality and to what extent it entered the one or the other hemisphere of our being, we dare not enquire.

This, then, was the place. And leading to it, apart from the aforementioned lane which provided access to a carriage, and running parallel to it, were at least a thousand steep steps (though the exact number cannot, of course, be verified). These steps were cut into the living rock beside the lane, and from neither of them, as one clambered upwards, was anything to be discerned but green or greyish terraces flecked here and there with lilac, or the gay tops of flourishing gardens, with their rosebushes and white clouds of washing all tangled up in clotheslines strung from branch to branch. But in all those gardens there was not a soul to be seen, as if the hill were uninhabited. And one of these little houses, silent, faded, its faint flush of pink half hidden in a garden green from rain as gentle as it was endless, was the very one which Don Mariano had purchased, though never finished paying for, from the woman he loved, and bestowed as a dowry on his daughter and son-in-law, and which thereafter, on becoming the rude place of refuge for the family of Elmina Dupré, had seen its original character much transformed. Into how it had been transformed, and on account of what further melancholy events, we do not for the moment wish to delve. But changed it was, as also of necessity were the habits, the conduct and the very appearance of the formerly haughty daughter of our Glover.

More or less at the same time as Monsieur de Neville, in Liège, was forced into the realization that society life and continual amusements had – with so little fuss that he had scarcely noticed the fact – given place to calmer and more thoughtful pursuits, the reading of good books and the cultivation of old friendships, so that his grief over the death of Geraldine did not strike him directly, but no more than obliquely, and then only by night as a kind of philosophical sigh; more or less at that time, or rather just a little later, one November evening when it was raining as it does certain autumns in Naples, a city strangely renowned for its clear, shining skies, at about ten o'clock – so late was the hour – one November evening of steady, interminable rain there climbed the dark, deserted steps, sturdily and showing no signs of discomfort, the figure of a woman for which one could find no better description, judging solely by her mode of attire, than that of "antiquated". A term already cheerless in those early years of the nineteenth century, but for us today decidedly gloomy. Her skirt was long but by no means ample, and showed signs of having in the past been of a fine bottle-green, now faded. Her jacket and short cloak were furbished with three rows of blue beads, as was her bonnet, which was bordered with dark velvet from beneath which strayed a number of golden ringlets. In her right hand (the slender wrist emerged from a puffed sleeve) she held an open umbrella as frail and frayed as a straw roof; a roof scored, what is more, by two or three rents (or perhaps gaping holes is more the word) which afforded glimpses of that watery firmament; while her left hand held that of another woman, but one so small as scarcely to reach to her knee: or maybe a small girl entirely *dressed* as a woman. This small creature was little Alessandrina Dupré, known as Sasà, three years of age. Her father had been dead for two of these, after many winters of mental derangement, and Elmina, now the widow Dupré, was walking home with her as she had every evening for some years, after leaving the mansion of

Donna Violante, at Chiaia, a house to which she repaired every afternoon to work at sewing and mending for the vast household (composed almost entirely of servants) of the old marchesa (the young marchesa being forever lost in a round of balls and parties); and this work, together with a few humbler tasks whenever the servants shirked them, was the only means that enabled the widow, who had renounced all other sources of security, to keep the wolf from the door. She unfailingly took along with her her second child by Albert, because Ferrantina, now practically blind, was unable to look after it, and it was not every day that Teresa, who had made herself indispensable to the abbess of a nearby convent, was able to visit her and to some extent alleviate the widow's terrible weariness.

Of the dazzling, proud young lady whom, that May evening at Jib-Sail House, our Gentlemen from Liège met in the Glover's house, there seemed to have survived but the vaguest likeness. It was her and yet not her. No less beautiful, in the manner of certain works of art in which the underlying aura remains, yet deprived of almost all the intensity of its colours, the yellow, the rose, the turquoise; no less tender but at the same time colder; dark yet still dazzling; still the same flush on the cheeks, the crisp golden curls, the short, bold nose, those eyelids touched with pink and gilded eyebrows arched over sunsets of green . . . But something had departed and gone: that enthusiastic confidence of manner, that self-assurance, that winning arrogance. And a veil as of a cloud-hidden sun or a moon in autumn had descended upon that fair young form of a girl and all the triumph of her sweet sixteen. At this time she was twenty-five, and a woman who had been stricken: not in her pride, for that was indomitable, but in her awareness of the world, in the passing away of persons and of certainties once before her eyes, and now no more. In a scant ten years she had lost three of her immediate family; with the exception of Teresina she had all but entirely alienated Don Mariano's relatives, and Jib-Sail House had become a doleful dream. Her bustle and energy, almost unnatural – or at least surprising in a woman related (as was still thought) to personages at Court – and her work as a shirtmaker that had formerly procured her both satisfaction and financial security, had been demolished by the trials she had undergone: the death of her son, her husband's long illness (whether madness or not was by now a conundrum to everyone) and finally her penurious widowhood. Her life, especially in the first years after the death of Baba, had been truly terrible, with Albert almost constantly in a state of breakdown, so that her shirtmaking business gradually became impossible. After which all her savings melted away. Without a watchful eye on them her girls took to pilfering, and Ferrantina was no longer able to keep them in check. They were dismissed, therefore, and on her own she could do nothing. And then there was her little daughter, no small worry. Elmina would willingly have entrusted her to a sounder and more financially secure family than hers was now, consisting as it did of herself, Sasà and old Ferrantina. But a certain scruple, or something less, or something more, always held her back on the threshold of this thought. Baba's sister had none of that early-morning splendour of Albert's firstborn. She was titchy, tongue-tied, not very intelligent, and to her mother (though affectionately and patiently on the lookout for anything good about her) she also seemed rather plain. Worst of all, she never either spoke or laughed, and Elmina began to think her daughter did not love her.

This was her fate, thought Elmina, to be soon forgotten or despised even by those she held dear, or had held dear. And thinking thus, that evening like every other since Albert had died, quite out of his mind and mockingly exorting her to remarry at once (with contempt, she felt, and affronting her wifely fidelity), she looked around her, at the trees dripping moonlight in the monotonous patter of the rain, at a few distant lights . . . and she felt afraid. Her daughter beside her was walking like a tiny ghost, barely touching her hand with small, cold fingers on one of which, Elmina knew, was an iron ring bearing a blue stone, a gift from Ferrantina which the little girl never took off. So there you are – thought the widow Dupré – the things of this world appear and disappear, it starts to rain, it stops raining, a feast-day comes and goes, and there is someone there beyond, unseen, who moves all things. It is the Angels!

A ghost!

To reach the door of the Little House there still remained a hundred and fifty steps, half broken and slippery, and she had to take care how she trod on them, especially with that infant holding her hand. The widow went clasping her bulky satchel to her side: it contained a few small coins to give Ferrantina to buy the bread in the morning – the baker's boy delivered every Friday, and one loaf lasted the whole week – and a humble copper coin for the Rosary, the bequest and behest of Don Mariano (for Elmina was little given to prayer). She remembered the latter because she was afraid. For some days there had been ugly rumours abroad at Posillipo. There were several thieves at work in the neighbourhood, but that was of no consequence, for thieves do not harm a widow and her infant daughter with only a pittance to feed them both. The trouble was, alas – and she had never had such notions, but now they haunted her dreams – there was talk of apparitions, of the ghosts of executed men. These had lived at Sant'Antonio, and no sooner had they recovered from their great bewilderment than they returned: men such as the lawyer Giuliano Feroce (more ferocious in name than in nature), who passed on to a better life for having spoken ill of the King. He had already been seen in the neighbourhood, and had even called, begging for a crust of bread, at the convent where Teresa lived; and the Reverend Mother, alert as ever, had slammed the door in his face. Between the shade of this Giuliano (and many another), and apprehension as to the robbers who, albeit without harming her, might deprive her of her few coins, our seamstress scarcely knew which she feared the more. And instinctively, with her heart in her mouth, she started to pray for the souls of the dead, and especially those who had come to a violent end, who certainly were the most aware of what it means to leave this world. She was sure that a kindly light would somewhere or other appear, to illuminate the dolorous steps for her.

And just as she had begged in her prayer, humbly, in the depths of her soul, the still and silent soul of the young girl of yore, so the light appeared.

But it did not come from one side or the other of the interminable steps. Strangely enough it came from above, from the topmost point of the winding dark flight she still had to climb; and as soon as she saw it shine out and approach her she realized that it came from the very house she and Sasà were making for, and where Ferrantina was awaiting them.

But Ferrantina was certainly already asleep, and what is more she could see nothing or next to nothing, and could never have made her way to the steps to brandish that light. She had never done such a thing.

Who could it be then?

The widow Dupré halted, and her face was pale and drawn. She backed against the wall to one side of the steps, thinking, should the light descend still further, to let it pass her by. In her black satin bag she had also her principal working tool (in common with all the seamstresses of her time she was never without it), namely an enormous burnished pair of scissors. Having closed the umbrella and tucked it under her arm, she slipped her hand into the bag, extracted the scissors and swiftly placed them on top of it. The movement was automatic, not aggressive, but she had to take her precautions. The next moment she found herself thinking:

"It's a ghost!"

An instant later the light had gone out (perhaps turned in the opposite direction), but the tall, jaunty figure which had been bearing it had continued to approach her in the darkness, and a shaft of moonlight through the now sparse, silvery rain illumined it. It was none other than the most extraordinary and atrocious person in the world, that de Neville who had come to Naples with Dupré and Nodier, with all their baggage of happiness and misadventure. Maybe he had died, and this was his ghost.

She heard a call: "Madame Dupré!"

"I thought you were dead," replied that lady as faintly as could be.

She was so pale and still she might have been turned to stone, or one of those carvings which had for so long taken over the ground-floor room of the Little House, and in setting eyes on her now the prince was overcome by a strange feeling of uncertainty, of being confronted by a nameless majesty, like an unattainable country, sorrowful and yet a wonderland.

That mild, white face (for so it appeared), now bereft of youth, but still possessed of so much delicacy, was the face of Elmina Dupré!

Sasà at her side, as if the meeting were nothing to do with her, sat quietly on the low wall, where there was a recess at the point where her mother had stopped. Her long skirts, dark and ugly and identical to those of her mother, were trailing on the ground. The hair beneath her bonnet was smooth and drawn back, ending in two small pigtails casually tied together at the nape with a black ribbon. Her face was ashen with cold, perhaps also weariness. In her joyless eyes a black light, deep and unwavering – like water at the bottom of a well – watched her mother's admirer with a wary but indifferent expression. Her small hands, almost unnoticeable, were placed one upon the other as she had been taught, and the blue stone in the ring was uppermost. Feeling strange eyes upon her she turned her head away in embarrassment, like a grown-up.

To the widow's response de Neville replied promptly, in German: "As you see, I am not dead;" and at once added in French, with lively interest: "And is this Mademoiselle Dupré?"

"Yes, it is."

Sasà too looked round and about to espy the young lady referred to.

"*Nun'a parlate*. Don't talk to her, she won't answer. She's not very bright," proceeded Elmina with infinite weariness. By this time she was almost in tears, but she struggled to be polite and asked de Neville whether he had come from the studio.

Yes, indeed he had come from there, after waiting a good half-hour; he had arrived with Nodier. Growing worried on account of the rain, he had come down with a lamp to meet her.

"And your friend is up there?"

"Yes, he stayed with Ferrantina."

"Has Ferrantina told you *everything*?"

"She has. But Nodier had already informed me. A month ago he wrote to me in great detail about . . . your further bereavement."

"I am left with this daughter," said the artist's widow after a while, with a touch of bitterness but of tenderness also. "I cannot say 'unfortunately', but neither can I claim the reverse."

The little orphan listened in, all ears, as rejected children will, sensing that they were discussing her, and mention was being made, to this stranger, of her "misfortune" in having taken the place that was Baba's when that house was a happy one. As a result of that (thus had Ferrantina reckoned the years for her) her father had left the house.

De Neville, on hearing this, suddenly and without a second thought, exactly as Albert would have done, sat down on the wall and drew Alessandrina to him, though without taking his eyes off her mother.

He was not really thinking straight, as he watched that calm face; but whether the cause was joy or indignation he could not have said. He had some extraordinary news to impart to her, but this was not the time and place. He was afraid she might be indifferent, that she might say "You are wrong, I am not even thinking of it, Monsieur de Neville". Everything was possible, with Donna Elmina. He must not forget that when still a child she had slaughtered a Linnet and distressed her gentle sister; not to mention having despised her mother (though the latter was only adoptive, and had a certain guilt on her side). He felt that coldness and pride, in Elmina, had survived the passing of time, and were part and parcel with her magnetism. And it took a friend to acquit her of the accusation of wickedness. Coldness and pride, in her, were like two old tumbledown doorways with no house beyond them. Beyond those ruined portals there lived and breathed only an enormous forest.

Now came another voice, shrill and childlike, from the top of the steps; and another lamp, another cloak. Somewhat strident with anxiety, the voice was Nodier's. And his was the cloak.

"Ingmar, is that you down there? Is that you, Donna Elmina?"

"Your servant," replied the latter without the least trace of good cheer – unimaginable anyway – but with calm and courtesy. "We are nearly there."

She drew Sasà towards her without really seeing the girl, and addressed de Neville:

"Will you be staying?"

"Yes, I should be glad to," replied he, almost on the verge of tears. "I have been Nodier's guest in Chiaia since yesterday, but we should both be only too willing to stay overnight with you, if there is room. Alphonse," he called, "hold the lamp a little higher." Then, without a trace of irony, though understandable in the circumstances, he at once added: "Donna Elmina is *grateful* for your solicitude."

At which he gave the young widow a keen glance, but her face remained mild and impassive.

Thus they continued up the laboursome steps. On the last stretch Donna Elmina had gathered up Sasà into her arms, and the child's head lolled over her shoulder. As the prince was following a little way behind, her small eyes, at the same time alert and asleep, never left him. Such a sad creature de Neville had never seen. "Perhaps because she can't talk," he thought. She also looked feeble, almost weightless and without any strength or faculty whatever, even that of closing her eyes. And thinking of the great joy coming to him shortly he gave her a saucy look which Sasà – after a while, still in that posture as of an abandoned doll or forgotten piece of rag – avoided with great seriousness, turning away those tiny eyes immersed in a dreamlike light.

In the meanwhile they had reached their destination.

The house door was open and Nodier, who had timidly retreated up the few topmost steps, was now waiting outside it, in the light drizzle, with Ferrantina beside him.

They were all there now, on the narrow terrace which rain and grass and darkness enclosed and embraced on every side, like an enormous living creature. Ferrantina made to take Sasà in her arms, but Donna Elmina would not allow it, saying that she must not overtax herself: Sasà was not tired. She should go back to her room. As to the sheets and blankets, Donna Elmina would see to them herself.

"We have put you to a lot of trouble," apologized Nodier in a mixture of French and Neapolitan and lowering his eyes the while.

"No trouble at all. My husband's friends" (she expressed herself thus, as if Albert were still alive) "are always welcome in this house." This was said with some effort, but also with a smile.

As they entered, Nodier had eyes only for her, while Sasà, who had already climbed up onto her brother's high chair, had eyes only for de Neville. In the depths of her stupidity, as her mother was wont to put it, every detail of that meeting was transformed in her imagination into a story of elves and policemen; that is, she was convinced that "Signor di Nevì" was the policeman whose duty it was to force the elfin sprite (her mother) to repay the "debt" (this from a hint of Ferrantina's) undertaken on her behalf. But that debt could never ever be repaid!

Immersed in these thoughts the little girl held her breath, while being subjected to the scrutiny of this "Nevì".

Oh, if only her father would come back home!

Without even changing her dress, but showing no particular signs of weariness, Elmina Dupré (who had simply removed her cloak and propped up her umbrella to drip in a corner) went to the dresser – they invariably ate, evidently, in the same dark, badly-furnished room – from which she fetched out two plates, with silverware of the finest quality (the plates were hand-painted porcelain, the spoons and forks of solid silver): but only for the guests. For herself and her daughter she laid two cheap metal bowls and cutlery to match. On the table she placed some rather stale bread cut in doorsteps, and for the gentlemen two help-ings of potatoes and onions, stone cold. For herself and her daughter, a few boiled greens. And in so doing she seemed (albeit secretly) pleased at the vague uneasiness that such conduct might perhaps have aroused in her guests. Guests who, one might well think, were not truly welcome, for the simple reason that no one at all should any longer set foot in that house, and if anyone did so it was at their own risk and peril. To suggest that in the breast of de Neville, as he followed all the movements and even the thoughts of his beloved Elmina, indignation and distress arose clam-ouring from the happy past to sadden and disconcert him, would pose us psychological problems of a complexity that for the moment we do not wish to face. We shall confine ourselves to saying (and great was his agita-tion of mind on this account) that he began to doubt the success of the present enterprise. And in his own mind he put the blame on Nodier, with his enthusiastic confidence that the project would come off. But now he was seized by a profound and sombre sense of awe for that young woman.

As if divining the prince's thoughts, and perhaps deep down feeling pity for him, Elmina became more affable, and beside the plate of either guest she placed a snow-white napkin, finely embroidered, relics of the days of Jib-Sail House. This done, she asked leave to withdraw and change Sasà's shoes and her own, returning a moment later, shamelessly, with a pair of man's shoes for herself and of old crone's slippers (they were in fact Ferrantina's) for her daughter.

Sasà began to cough, and Donna Elmina, neither paying her attention nor making her move, hauled the high chair up to the table beside her. Nodier and his noble friend, who having been invited to take their places had already done so, thus found themselves, once seated, exactly face to face with the mother and daughter. The table, luckily, was a large one, so little discomfort was caused by their respective proximity.

"If something displeases you," the expression of Albert's widow seemed to say, as her glance passed with unruffled hauteur from one to the other of her guests, "well, you gentlemen have to blame it on your taste for surprise visits. Here in the house of Donna Elmina there is neither time nor place for the things of this world."

De Neville was by this time neither angry nor frightened. Little by little he had regained control of himself, or rather of his emotions; not, as yet, of his thoughts. He was not confused, but simply perplexed. The proposal which he had undertaken to present to Donna Elmina on behalf of his friend, a proposal which, for obvious reasons, the two friends had talked over for a whole day (the prince had been in Naples for two days, but only on the second had Nodier confided in him, placing his life – the word is quite in order, so mad was he over Elmina – in the hands of de Neville and trusting in his tact and gifts of diplomacy), now seemed to him like a road impossible to travel, a dream road up a phantom mountain, thick with thorns and broken branches, and purposely leading nowhere; such was his task, to tread a road of risk, of misunderstanding and offence, above all of dream and offence. All of a sudden he *saw* into the woman's soul, as ten years earlier he had partly seen into her as a girl, when he was opposing Albert's wedding: she loved no one, and he was doing her no favour in proposing marriage, even to a respectable, rich young man of good character, and an old friend of the family, as was Nodier. For this, indeed, was the reason for his visit, tactfully to propose to Elmina a second and more sensible marriage, this time to Nodier, whom she had now known for ten years; and by means of this marriage, with none of the glamour of nobility or art, but only good sense and practicality, to provide a thorough cure for all her troubles, not excluding responsibility for the little girl. If she wished to go on working, or rather begin again, since she had long since ceased to do any shirtmaking, then well and good. Nodier would open a real workshop in Chiaia, entirely for her; they had already found the premises. She would once more be a free and independent woman, her old customers would come back to her. And this was the least of it, for Sasà would have a father again.

And just as he was thinking of the orphan and the way she was sitting there beside her mother like a little animal lost and prostrated, he realized (or seemed to realize), with a sort of dolorous wonder mingled with rage, that Sasà mattered little or nothing to Elmina. Nor was she to blame for it. In her spirit, often so tender and gay, a mother's worries simply did not exist. He looked intently at her and seemed (so he thought) to surprise a totally unconscious question in those golden eyes, though it was at once snuffed out as she said politely:

"I see that you wish to tell me something."

"Maybe yes, maybe no. It depends on what the Linnet has told you."

This answer, or quip, was too subtle for Elmina. She blushed on account of an allusion she thought she had caught in the prince's words. The Linnet, she thought, might stand for love, that whimsical thing that was banished from that house, whereas even de Neville, if the truth be told, did not know what meaning he had attempted to convey: the words had tumbled out of him as if it were some kind of boyish tease (for such was his nature). Then he remembered the unkindness Elmina had done to Floridia when she was ill (which practically amounted to murder), and the sadness of Albert's voice as he bounced the mechanical linnet's cage up and down before Baba's eyes, intoning,

> *"Flutter, flutter, flutter, fly little Linnet,*
> *Flutter, flutter, flutter . . . Oh! Oh! Oh!*

ending on a strange note of lament, so that for her, Elmina, "the Linnet" could well mean Remorse.

"And anyway I don't know what this Linnet means," said Elmina after a pause to dab at her beautiful lips, for she had taken a sip of water. Her voice quavered ever so little. "Here, as you see," she continued, "there are no Linnets."

And seeing that Sasà, on hearing the word "Linnet", was straining her ears keenly, unhappily, she muttered extremely grumpily:

"*This one*, in any case, hears everything."

This One, caught in the act, became a mere crumb of a girl, and immersed her whole face in the plate before her.

It needed not a word more to confuse the prince still further concerning the true nature of the relationship between mother and daughter, and the far from happy atmosphere that weighed upon that house, an atmosphere that he (though it erased nothing of his affection for Albert's former bride) felt frankly to be one – perfectly intentional – of punishment and castigation, of mortification and a refusal of normal life and the breath of life. As if she, Elmina, had decided, and at no recent date, and perhaps not of her own free will, to punish, frighten or at least do harm to something or someone – maybe by weakening that person's confidence, or maybe simply by a series of deliberate omissions. It had already happened with Albert. In the present case, seeing how hard Elmina was on herself and her daughter, and how much mortification for both was the most immediate result of the damage she was determined to provoke, which was mortification and fear, the prince once again felt all but certain that remorse – long-seated, indestructible remorse – was at the bottom of such harsh conduct, and might in a word be called Donna Elmina's malady; so the much-discussed and all but flaunted proposal of marriage which he intended to present on behalf of the retiring Nodier, and the words which he had planned to employ for this purpose, soon died on his lips together with his smile. He cast a glance at Nodier: and that poor wretch was smiling.

Nodier accepted

It is the custom of many narrators of stories intended to amuse complaisant readers with the doings of grown-ups, it is the facile custom, in referring to scenes, dialogues and possible thoughts passing between them, to touch on the presence, in such scenes, of a small child, as if it were something absolutely without interest, if not altogether fortuitous. But the custom is not always justified, as it is not in this case, since it is by no means always that the children present at such scenes absorb their details (often turbulent to the point of madness) with that happy indifference which a whole convention concerning the health and happiness of children imposes on these writers. Neither healthy nor happy, in our judgement, are the greater number of children; nor are they shielded by naïve feelings. All eyes and ears they spy, from atop their high chairs, or even from under the table, on the unfolding scenes of this great world. And they have no little influence on its mysteries and on the passions of the leading protagonists of these mysteries. We here refer to the damsel whom de Neville himself, though highly sensitive towards creatures weak and speechless, had in all his exchanges with her mother quite ignored: in short, to Sasà.

Without going too far back in time, or leaving those four poor walls, the abode of anxieties and justified suspicions, we shall say that a fifth Personage, totally hidden and invisible, was present that evening at the frugal repast of our friends, and that this Personage stood for and represented all the sad and mournful thoughts of the little girl. The Linnet, no more and no less, that bird that was not a bird but a sort of destiny, which her mother, but also Teresa and Ferrantina, often spoke of as being the origin of all the family woes and the melancholy master of their lives; the Linnet, which ever since the gentlemen had sat down to table had been fluttering here and there beating its golden wings against the ceiling, uttering its piteous cry. It was a Spirit! In this respect Sasà thought exactly as her mother did, as far as was possible in her state of practically bottomless melancholy. It was a dead person who wished mischief to her mother, as it had to her artist-father and their happy child, and it wished mischief now to her, Alessandrina; and ever since it had appeared in that house, ever so many years ago, everyone had been sad. The statues were the Linnet's eggs! All those statues, which every so often Sasà went to touch and finger, were the eggs of the Linnet, which could never know peace because it had been forced to leave them. And this was why Donna Elmina hated the Linnet and the statues, and would say to Ferrantina (Sasà heard all):

"Would that the Linnet had never entered this house, would that I had never believed it! But I meant no harm! It was my father's wish!"

And Ferrantina, gazing with pity at the little girl, would often sigh and add: "God save you, my child, from ever meeting the Linnet!"

(In their house, as Sasà well knew, they used to hide even the bread-crumbs, so as to leave nothing for the Linnet to eat; but even with no food the bird lived on at its own sweet will, and had a fine time.)

"You may be sure it won't happen, Ferrantina," was her mother's reply. "Not all girls are that unlucky."

When she went to bed, in the room next door to Ferrantina's, or while Ferrantina slept and her breath was like the sea in the night-time, Sasà would often lie for hours with open eyes, staring at the little oil-lamp on the dilapidated chest-of-drawers, burning before the picture of the Souls in Purgatory (who were supposed to protect the house), or else at the door ajar onto a dark landing.

Anyway, through that door, which would often creak in the wind, as also through the half-open window overlooking the moonlit garden, *anything* could enter! The Linnet above all, but also a dwarf with a hen's tail-feather for a headdress, whom Sasà loathed with all her little heart, and Ferrantina told her that he stole children. Elmina, on the other hand, never saw him. Sasà was ever more convinced that Elmina was an elf, or else an angel. She had compassion for all and sundry, but for her daughter never. So Sasà, like her brother before her, was afraid only of her mother, although she never never scolded her. It was as if she were somebody else's mother, and as for Sasà, well, she simply put up with her.

This then was the anxiety (or the dormant thought, or say even the dream, and also the calm though incessant terror) that with its small claws wrung the heart of that luckless child. Someone at any moment might come and snatch her up and take her . . . where? Hence that restless gaze, and the appeal, spellbound and static, that she directed at the apparently carefree visitor of the evening.

And having said this, let us return to the table ill-lit by one dripping candle, this time approaching the derelict Nodier, who sat there with one elbow propped in unmannerly fashion beside his plate, like a punished child, and truly looked on the verge of tears.

No sooner had Donna Elmina had come out with "she hears everything", than he burst forth with this exclamation, somewhat wide of the mark if he meant to refer to the insensitivity of a certain small girl:

"But blessèd are the little children, dear Donna Elmina! They at least are innocent of Linnets!"

"Explain yourself, Nodier," replied Donna Elmina, laying down her fork, with a shred of onion on it, on the edge of her metal plate. "Don't allow your imagination to run away with you."

"These are things which even a little girl may hear," complained Nodier with some warmth. "There is neither fear nor scandal in what I say, any more than there is in the sunlight."

"Meaning?" queried Elmina, slightly huffily, though not without a smile.

"Meaning . . . that the Linnet loves you, Donna Elmina," said the unfortunate, not a little wistfully, lowering his head with its honest, foolish face (foolish, we should say, simply as the world sees such things, because in business, there in Naples, Alphonse had shown himself a man of genius, able to offer a bride the most wonderful life a woman can dream of, but he was no genius in conversation); and having said the above words he seemed on the point of rushing off and hiding somewhere.

Donna Elmina, on hearing that the Linnet had declared himself, closed her eyes, and this was interpreted by Sasà as a sudden languor caused by her terror of that Personage. And we add, without comment, that the same interpretation had occurred to the acute and penetrating intellect of the prince; who, gazing at the young widow in a very particular manner, as if it were a thing that only he had perceived, promptly added, in tones of undeniable affection:

"Yes, let us leave dreams and fears aside, dearest Elmina, and the past as well . . . The fact is that the two of us are here to help you to return to life, to escape from sadness and solitude, to escape from grief . . . We are here to make you a proposal, one which you will wish to think over in your own time, in the kindliness of your heart. It would be much appreciated . . ."

"In my own time . . . in kindliness of heart!" repeated Donna Elmina in a daze. "Do you mean that it is some good work?"

"Yes . . . no doubt about it . . . a good thing, though by no means an act of charity . . ." replied de Neville, uneasy and hesitant. "It is an offer of marriage! Alphonse Nodier is offering you his hand and his life, dearest Elmina!"

The young widow did not reply at once. She too, perhaps from an instinct of self-control and dominion over her private griefs, or else from a kind of pride she shared with the prince, was afraid of her own emotions, and made it a rule never to respond immediately (unlike the prince when he was stirred to indignation) to questions or even simple observations, whatever they might be, but the more so when they were serious questions and not-so-simple observations; this to gain time for any fluster to subside, and enable her to answer as if she had heard only commonplaces, with a smile. But on this occasion it was different, or partly so; for, after sitting half a minute staring at her napkin and folding it, giving the impression that for her the supper, and indeed her life, was ended (and this suggested that she wished to hear no more on this unpleasant subject), she rose to her feet to fetch something from the sideboard and, resuming her seat, she at last replied in tones of calm and composure:

"So, gentlemen, you were saying . . ." Pause. "Sasà isn't touching her food this evening . . . fancy that! You were saying . . . You broke off in the middle of a sentence."

"No, the sentence was complete . . . And you heard well," muttered Nodier, again on the verge of tears.

"I do not deny it. I both heard and understood. But here there's a pair of ears that have grown so long they will soon be touching the ground. Sasà, my child, go off and see Ferrantina, if she is not asleep, or if she is, without making a sound, look in the next-door room for another candle. We can scarcely see each other in here."

At which Sasà did indeed climb down from her high chair, but she did not go, or move a step. She knew that in that room – less a room than an empty and derelict larder – was the bird which had just been mentioned. She had heard it. And this must be the reason why her mother was so upset. She therefore went up to her and laid her head, in a gesture at once of submission, blind faith and desperation, in the crook of her arm.

"Off you go then," said her mother after due pause. "Lillot" (this was the dwarf with the hen's feather, the cause, Elmina thought, of Sasà's fear) "has gone away." But a moment later she forgot all about her daughter, and turning to Nodier, in a level voice in which none the less a harsh note came and went, like an overmastering fury more against life itself than anyone in particular, she added slowly, forcing a far from happy smile:

"Monsieur Nodier, we meet very often. Why has this come into your mind only this evening?" For one instant, with a kind of deathly weariness, she looked at the prince, then turned her eyes away at once and added:

"I do not say no. I never say it, on principle. Marchesa Durante will certainly have told you that, Monsieur Nodier. A widow with a daughter to look after always gives thought to any offer: this one seems to me advantageous to *both* sides . . . What I would beg of you is a little time. A few matters – nothing special, in any case – to be taken care of in view of this change . . ."

"All the time you wish. Even a year!" cried poor Nodier.

At this very moment de Neville knew beyond a doubt that she hated him, he felt he had offended her by presenting and supporting this second proposal of marriage, but he understood not why. Or rather, he did understand, and the reason was this: she considered him the cause of all her woes. Only the awareness of their different positions, and how much he, de Neville, had lavished upon the Glover's family and she, Elmina, had haughtily taken possession of and distributed in works which, though doubtless good works, none the less opposed, or negated, the purpose he had had in mind, which was to make her happy (and this with a view to separating their destinies); only her awareness of this hindered or prevented the cruel Elmina from replying in a more open and cutting manner. But for this very reason the prince was certain that sooner or later she would accept Nodier: simply to pay her debt to him, de Neville, seeing that nothing was closer to her heart than to owe him gratitude for nothing. And the thought of her hatred that (now it was clear to him, and appeared inevitable as the response to every stirring of his heart) could not but increase, was petrifying to him. All the same, he still hoped he might be mistaken, and all unknowingly cast beseeching looks, now at the widow, now at her little daughter.

Sasà had at last accepted the fact that her mother was ignoring her, but she too, like the guests, seemed frozen in an emotional state that was, in her case, chiefly fear of the Spirits and aversion towards the hidden dwarf.

"Go on then . . . go to bed. Off you go to Ferrantina," said her mother in a flurry of irritation, removing her arm from under her child's head (and de Neville got the impression of a stone-hewn Chimaera fluttering a wing in her sleep), so that Sasà stumbled back and almost toppled over. Then with uncertain steps she made her way towards the dark doorway of the little room; but on reaching the threshold she halted again with an imploring look.

"Open it then!" her mother almost yelled at her, although in a voice of utter calm.

De Neville realized, turning suddenly at that serene but by no means loving command, that in all that time, from their meeting on the steps in the rain, and during supper (if such it could be called), till the moment Elmina had ordered her to go and search for a candle, Albert's daughter had not spoken a single word. And at the same instant in which he was struck by the thought of Alessandrina's absolute muteness, a more profound emotion overcame him: for the child, in the very act of turning the doorknob, had backed away, and while not retracing her steps completely, out of terror of her mother, did not succeed in concealing that superhuman suffering that sometimes afflicts unloved children when confronted with a duty they dare not face, and yet they *must*, and which therefore paralyses them. In this case, to the dark larder, which had to be crossed after all those references to the terrible Linnet, had been added the sudden emergence from the larder door, which stood slightly ajar, of a large *black* moth, which had obviously been in ambush on the other side simply to assault Alessandrina. With a rapid flutter, starting low down right in front of Sasà's nose, and then rising, the swarthy creature had dashed itself silently against the opposite wall, up near the ceiling, and it was a miracle that it had not struck Donna Elmina full in the face. Unluckily it was clear to Sasà that it was one of the Beings waiting beyond the door, and no other than *He* whose ears were so long they reached the ground. So that the face she turned to Elmina's impassioned friend, and then to her suitor, was (you would have said) one of total panic and dismay, and she put her hands to her mouth to smother – in which she succeeded – an Aaah! Aaah! of heart-rending terror, which would certainly have affected her mother, since the cause, now beyond doubt, was the Creature with the Ears, the atrocious Linnet, or its companion with the feather, coming to snatch her away. Then she could bear it no longer, but pitifully doubled up, uttering a mere whisper; and this was a grievous:

Dalinnet! Dalinnet! Dalinnet!

Which was followed by a terrible murmur, so faint as to be all but inaudible:

Aaah! Aaah! Aaah!
Aaah! Aaah! Aaah!

Was it a deceitful childish impromptu, or a sad truth?

Her mother's gaze, irate and distressed, albeit covertly so, turned a fraction to one side and, meeting that of Nodier, expressed an affectionate irony which elated her Suitor, as being an irrefutable proof of faith, and which was followed by a sort of exhortation, or command, equally affectionate though lifeless:

"Don Alphonse," she said (and this was the first time she had ever so expressed herself), "please see what is wrong with my daughter. She never listens to what I say."

"She is frightened, she has seen the Linnet, though there are no Linnets here," said the aspiring father at once, rising to his feet and hastening over to Sasà. He gathered her into his arms, while she continued piteously to moan her deceitful, "Aaah! Aaah! Aaah!". As Nodier, with the little girl in his arms, approached the table at Donna Elmina's side, as if to beg a compassionate word for the child, her mother began to laugh; which was of some small comfort to Nodier, whereas it saddened de Neville, who said gently, as he regarded that ridiculous little hand with the ring on its finger:

"Signorina Dupré, do not be afraid. It is nothing but a *palummella*."

He knew and remembered many Neapolitan expressions, and this word for dove therefore achieved a truly consolatory effect.

"Pa . . . ummella?" repeated the little girl in a voice still swollen with grief.

"Yes, paummella," replied Ingmar cheerfully. "This evening it was all in black, but tomorrow morning, my child, you'll see it all dressed in pink."

"Pa . . . ummella! Pink paummella!" Sasà repeated, softly and wearily; and having plucked up the courage to raise her tearstained face to seek out the dread apparition high on the wall, and finding only that tiny blotch, she heaved a deep sigh, as is the wont of small people oppressed with thoughts of Spirits hidden in cupboards, and looked back at de Neville with that dreamy expression which he had already noted in her – as if she herself, Alessandrina Dupré, dwelt in a cupboard or a dream – and for the first time (though he was uncertain whether it was a real smile, rather than a vague, involuntary reflection of his own) formed the corners of her mouth into what is commonly held to be a smile. Maybe it was a mere acceptance of things, maybe she was hearkening to far-off sounds, and peace.

The supper is concluded and the agreement also.
"In my heart there is but a single name." (But whose?)

The prince was touched; but as he switched his gaze to follow the child, whose head was now dangling on Alphonse's shoulder, as an hour earlier on that of her mother, his sympathy was not reserved entirely for her: it also embraced the awesome Elmina and her spirit of mortification, the cause of all that ice within her, that inner self so void and empty, yet at the same time so crowded with almost superhuman severities. He realized that even there, beneath so much self-control and indifference, lay sorrow and loneliness, and he would have liked to help . . . to succour.

"There you sit . . ." and here he was roused by the voice of his former Flame, now fresh and tender, though not without an undertone of detestable mockery, "there you sit all upset and commiserating, as if you yourself were the child's father. But her father is going to be Nodier," she concluded coolly.

"*Vous l'avez donc accepté, Madame?*" exclaimed de Neville involuntarily, grasping only that one point, and at the peak of incredulity and *despondent* joy. Though why he was despondent he could not have said.

"Yes, at this very moment . . . seeing him there . . . For Sasà's sake I have accepted him." Elmina regarded him smilingly and added:

"The arrangement suits me."

For all his confusion and agitation de Neville miraculously prevented himself from saying, "*Je vous en remercie beaucoup, Madame.*" Instead, he rose to his feet with all the affectionate nobility of a man well versed in joy, but also in compassion, in the secrets of living, and said on impulse: "Yes, Nodier . . . you are now Madame Nodier. But in my heart your name, dearest Elmina, will always remain one and *one only*, believe me." And thinking that he rightly interpreted her secret mourning for Albert, and what he believed to be the ill-fated passion of her life, that for Albert, in short, the name he had in mind was *Dupré*. But once again, by good luck or by instinct, he said nothing of what he was thinking about either himself or her; he did not say *Elmina Dupré*. She was therefore free to understand what in fact was the case: "In my heart your name (*Elmina*) will never be followed by any other" – or something of the sort; and this with a feeling of surprise and dejection that rendered her even more solemn than she actually was.

She bestowed on him the same slow, inextricable gaze as her daughter's, but with less grief in it, and replied serenely:

"In my heart also, believe me, there is but a single name."

And this, for the prince, was above everything, above the more than modest, almost childlike opinion he had of his place in the world and, indeed, of himself, if not perhaps of the hearts of others.

IV

The Sad Tale of Sasà
(The Paummella)

An informative visit to the gallery of statues.
Faint traces of a certain Hieronymus.
Nodier rejoices whilst the prince is strangely saddened

When they awoke, the day, or at least the morning, was quite a different matter from what the two friends – Nodier in a triumphant daze and de Neville a good deal less so – had been expecting. For, rising shortly before ten, they found that Donna Elmina had gone down to Naples two hours earlier, in answer to a summons from the Marchesa Durante. The reason for this was a dancing costume for her grandson, young Geronte, who had been invited to Court that evening for a children's party. This costume had turned out to be in shreds, and on leaving the house Elmina had left a note for Nodier (perhaps considering herself already engaged). The marchesa's message had been brought by Teresa, at that time living in a convent next door to Palazzo Durante, and to her Elmina had entrusted her own message, extremely brief and a complete scrawl, addressed to the two gentlemen and to Nodier in particular. In this note the young widow stated that for reasons of work and friendship she was forced to absent herself for the whole day, but that her sister Teresa would do the honours in her place. Regarding their conversation on the previous evening, she had no doubt it would be continued in a manner satisfactory to *both* parties and, even if not at once, be brought to a satisfactory conclusion.

The great jubilation of Nodier, the feverish joy of the previous evening, immediately quashed by the presence of Elmina, a joy in every respect identical (though not so wondrous and angelic) to that of the artist ten years earlier, had kept him from falling asleep until a late hour, besieging the prince with all his enthusiasms and projects. It was as if our poor merchant felt himself to be loved! Without realizing that in the eyes and in the life of the widow Dupré he counted, emotionally speaking, for no more than a good fat roll of fabric, and even then not silk or velvet for fine apparel, but linsey-woolsey for everyday wear, and therefore of no more interest than any other item in the ledger-book. He didn't realize! Not for one moment thinking of discouraging him, as he had done years ago in the case of poor Albert, partly because on this occasion the business had been managed by none other than himself, the prince was extremely pensive; nor did all the smiles, the courtesies and the down-to-earthness of Teresina avail to rid him of his state of frozen stupor, if not of downright melancholy, on account of something heartless and monstrous, not to say gross, which he felt in the whole business, though he would have been hard put to it to tell quite where it lay. Unless it be in some atrocious blindness and dullness of his own powers of discernment.

In such a state of mind (the two of them had passed the night in a room next-door to Ferrantina's, with a strange sensation, all night long, of little footsteps in the rafters, and childlike voices and laughter, and sighs and soughings, but it was the wind arising after the rainstorm, sweeping clear the lovely skies of Naples), Nodier and de Neville, having read the message, took a turn around the house, which now showed a very different face from the one it had worn the night before — and infinitely more pleasant.

It was, as we have said, already ten o'clock, and the studio, as for the sake of convenience the whole house was still called, after the rain and the wind that had plagued it seemed literally drenched in sunlight, immersed in a miniature Eden of pink and green, with all the windows open upon the garden and the sills laden with pots and window-boxes full of carnations and sweet-scented verbena, while bunches of tomatoes were hung up from nails in the wall to dry in the sun. Everything was clean, meticulously clean and neat: it could not be said that Donna Elmina was a slovenly housewife. But what a lack of furnishings within, what bare-ness everywhere! There was not a spare ornament to be seen, not a fine dress or piece of fabric, no flowers on a shelf, not an embroidered curtain. It was not a want of things, not real genuine poverty, at the root of such starkness, whatever signs there were of straitened circumstances, and a strict selectivity due to shortage of money; no, it was not this, but rather a discipline, a practically nunnish and extremely demanding Rule that Donna Elmina had imposed on herself, which deprived not only her but the other inmates of the house of every least pleasure or relish for life. One would have guessed that, for her, living was a woeful, sinful and unlawful thing. And the silence of the prince's mind was revisited by the old, old question: *why*? And the only reasonable answer to this question was that in her life there lay some guilt, or even something graver still, for which she was voluntarily atoning, perhaps to deliver herself (or someone else) from some more fearful castigation still.

In a wardrobe half concealed in a cubbyhole off the kitchen they found a great number of really beautiful little girl's dresses, which Donna Elmina had clearly been given for her daughter by the Marchesa Durante. These were all in good condition, hanging on coat-hangers and protected by old newspapers, while others, more drab and everyday, though carefully washed and ironed, were plainly visible on shelves and within easy reach, as befitted their continual use. Then there were black woollen stockings and black petticoats for the little girl (compulsory for the period of mourning, which was to last another eight years) hanging up to dry, after the drenching they had received, on a line in the garden, amid certain roses quite unusual for that month of the year.

In the gallery of the statues, still inaccurately called the studio (though this it had not been for years, but merely a depository of *finished* things – finished in the sense of being forever lost to time, since no one would ever come back and work on them), our two gentlemen, immersed in this vague bewilderment, rapturous for the one, saddening and astonishing for the other, and bringing both a perception of the passage of time and passing of all things, lingered for rather longer, finding there all the statues and busts, but above all the famous heads which had been the ecstasy and the agony of the artist before the onset (or had it in fact begun with that ecstasy and agony?) of his malady. And all of them brought to mind poor little Ali Baba. Scattered here and there, moreover, they spotted well-remembered objects such as the golden birdcage, but without its linnet, which lay headless in a half-open drawer. Who can tell where the head had flown to! Other small treasures (at least they retained some material value) such as lockets, little enamelled boxes, silver paper-weights and paper-knives, little bronze clocks and pens (also bronze), survivors of the glorious past – the time, you understand, of Jib-Sail House, the house of the month of May, which saw the birth of the mystery and the love born of that mystery – lay abandoned on chairs and chests, covered with half an inch of dust, a sure sign that Donna Elmina had never touched them, or allowed Ferrantina or Teresa to lay a finger on them; all of which made the prince's mood the graver. De Neville thereafter discovered, beneath a marble table the top of which was split in two, perhaps by Albert in a moment of frenzy, a gilded French mantel-clock, and his hands quivered with the strain of trying to wind it. Impossible. The key had been wrenched half out, and the hands seemed to be stuck at two golden numerals, and at an hour that reminded him of another time: that of the departure from this earth of Ali Baba: ten minutes to ten in the morning. It occurred to him that the garden must then have worn the same face as today, and he realized why it now lay so totally abandoned in all its guileless jubilation, though also delicately veiled by a sense of sadness.

What he did not understand – or, to put it better, he understood perfectly, but could not bring himself to accept – was why Donna Elmina had remained in that house rather than choosing to live with the Marchesa Durante in Chiaia. Her love for Albert, and her grief at his death, seemed the only reason that could have kept her there. He could think of no other answer.

Then he remembered something that was forever slipping his mind, as if it had been gently lulled into quiescence: that it had been her, Donna Elmina herself, who had alienated all the capital wealth of her husband and her son in "works of charity", as Alphonse Nodier had explained to him many times over, with complete approbation. But this charity, this altruism, always lacking any least minimal spiritual motivation, to de Neville (though not very reflective when in dreaming mood, and where Elmina was concerned he was dreaming all the time) now seemed, as he considered the situation in which the family was placed, entirely and utterly inexplicable. To give away everything, *everything*. Why so, why so?

Nodier called to him from the sunlit embrasure of a little window beneath the sill of which were a number of bookshelves – though containing no books, but only packets of yellowed papers, letters and documents tied together with string – and there drew his attention to a document in German (as an aside we here record the embarrassing coolness of the two friends as they dealt so indiscreetly with Donna Elmina's property, but that morning they were, alas, neither of them in a mood to realize the gravity of this indiscretion).

The document was very old, and Nodier imagined it must refer to Elmina, whose place of birth had always been stated by Colonel Helm's family to be the university city of Cologne. But it was not concerned with Elmina. The Town Hall of Cologne, in 1779 – therefore twenty-six years before – had registered the (presumed) date of birth of a certain Hieronymus Käppchen, whom at the suggestion of benefactors at

Court a certain wealthy Neapolitan merchant had asked to adopt. It certified that the "child" had no parents, that its features were human (we quote the very words), and that it had been found in the hollow of a tree in the neighbouring forest (rescued, therefore, from the wolves) one November night.

De Neville felt a shudder of disgust (or perhaps only of irritation at the sight of that old rubbish?), and for the first time it came into his head that the world was old, very old indeed, and he blessed the wind of change, chill as it was, that came from France. That poor Don Mariano, through his liaison with Donna Helm, had fallen into the trap of some fantasticating bureaucrat (and even Germany at that time teemed with such people) did not surprise our prince, in view of the old man's ignorance and simplicity of heart. And recalling for a moment his visit to the main cemetery in Naples ten years before, and seeing as in a lightning-flash those inscriptions on the stone, which vanished on the instant, Ingmar felt justified in assuming that the business had worked out well for the Glover and the unfortunate infant: that is, with an official adoption. That thereafter the above-mentioned Käppchen, or *Caplet*, must have died at the dawn of the French Revolution of some visceral fever, very widespread in Naples, could not but gladden the prince, because of the great moral burden this had removed from that unfortunate Neapolitan family. How well he remembered the old man's desolation, his reluctance (as the prince had been told) to leave Jib-Sail House on account of some painful memory or recollection. And this memory, it may be, was of *that* boy, and not of the gentle Floridia.

Of this, however, he spoke not a word to young Nodier. He handed the document back to the latter, who carefully returned it to the shelf, and continuing to rummage around the studio they came across the famous cardboard box tied round with string, supposed in the past to have housed the "letters", but which may have contained no more than the poor child's toys. The "letters", indeed, were not in the box, but instead there were metal plates and dishes, and jumbled up with them several pairs of the old man's shoes, almost unworn. This box, even more than the document from Cologne, opened in the prince's mind another window onto the lively and at the same time despondent life the old man had lived, and his love of young children; and this time, also, on Elmina's hardness of heart. So the plates and dishes of the beloved infant had finished up here, along with the old man's shoes and other bits and pieces; and a silver-gilt bell, broken, which maybe his grandfather had tinkled for him, to keep him amused, now also lay among that bric-à-brac. And no hand on earth would ever again awaken its silver-noted heart.

In another box, a cardboard shoe-box bearing the naïve superscription *Letters from my beloved Brigitta*, there was indeed a letter, but one only. It reminded Don Mariano, somewhat bluntly, that the Little House was not yet paid for. The instalments met by him had stopped in 1784: ". . . the illness of your son, so to speak! (*sic*) has addled your brains", the letter ended, "but for the sake of *my* children I am not forgetting the sum, in solid gold ducats, that you still owe me! Yours, Brigitta. (So get a move on)."

This shed a most terrible light upon the whole story. Donna Helm had never loved the poor Glover (at least not in the way he wished), and his children, so to speak, had certainly not made up for it; neither Floridia nor the boy adopted in Cologne; and as for Elmina, in that neglect and contempt for her father's possessions it was plain to what extent even she had forgotten him. (But who was in the long run not excluded from the heart of our dear Elmina?)

In a word, the more he saw, the more the prince felt sick at heart, in that he perceived the connection between banal things such as the old man's lack of education, and other grandiose things, such as love; and he caught a glimpse of the strange and total absence of humanity that was Elmina. And he then understood how the lives of others, with all the harshness and barrenness that they displayed – poor parched patches of earth! – are not, harsh and barren as they may be, anything but a pathetic, though terrifying, *otherness*.

Discussion of Elmina's future as wife and as seamstress.
We observe her betrothed in braggartly mood.
Further perplexities for the prince

The two friends left that room, which might well be called the Hall of Memories, and returned to the humble chamber known as the kitchen, where an odd sort of engagement supper had taken place the previous evening.

Here Teresa, in a lovely pink frock that had been Elmina's in girlhood, smiling and in the best of moods, served them coffee. She was on top of the world, she explained at once, because she had become engaged to a lad in the police force, and would therefore soon be married, and thanks be to God soon be leaving the convent where she had been living until then. A brief reference to the doll, the *pupata* as she called it, which the prince had given her when she was still a little girl, brought a smile to the lips of both of them, while Ingmar, albeit somewhat vaguely, wondered why the two sisters, following the death of Albert, had not agreed to live together again, as at Jib-Sail House. And he imagined, perhaps none too benevolently, a certain conflict of character between the two women, due to Elmina's extraordinary austerity, that would have made it hard for her to share her life with a lass of more cheerful temperament. At this point a passing reference from Teresa to "their" letters, written together to make up for Elmina's rudimentary education, at the time when they had but lately moved into the Little House, caused de Neville to smile. But not so Teresa, who seemed perplexed by that smile, as if to her the unlettered condition of her sister was not the true explanation of that "four-handed" correspondence, and she expected the prince to grasp this point himself.

And the prince did in fact grasp something, but not very much. It appeared to him, certainly, that every time the good Teresa mentioned Elmina's name there arose an obstacle, a stumbling block, a prohibition that he could not fathom, and that in fact she was teetering on a forbidden threshold, as if she knew she could not step over it; nor was it part of the prince's good nature to force her to do so. Reader, you might have likened her to a child flying a kite in a green garden, looking up, running after it, until pulled up short by a wall and a door *through which it was forbidden to pass*. O how many things, though he dared not, would the prince have wished to ask outright of the good-hearted Teresa! But one of them was this:

"Your sister," he said at a certain point, turning his gaze, full of a kind of melancholy sweetness, this way and that and every so often fixing it upon the young person in question, "your sister . . . I imagine . . . I think . . . I don't say I am right but I'm inclined to think (and I hope you will forgive me for saying so) that she ought to pay more attention to the ways of this world, which prompt us to make room also for joy . . . for gladness . . . There is no joy or gladness in your sister, dear Teresa."

He had no worries about talking in this way in front of Nodier, whose broad beaming face continued to express the most absolute satisfaction, faith and happiness. (And if we wish to go even further, a very evident liking, completely understandable, for this sister of Elmina's.)

"No joy or gladness, you are right," replied the girl, becoming thoughtful as she toyed with the string of worthless blue stones from which hung a small gold cross that matched her blond curls. "She's always working these days, in other houses, alas, what with cutting and sewing and decorating, and very often even patches" (she meant mending) "for other people's clothes, it's her one passion. And she's devoted to the marchesa! But her favourite at the moment is Don Gerontino Durante-Watteau, the only grandson of Donna Violante who, as you know" (the prince did not know it) "was a close friend of our father's. Gerontino – or Emilio – though as handsome as an angel, is a naughty lad; and I am sorry to say that even Sasà is mad about him, although he mistreats her . . ."

"Sasà? . . . So young and she already has . . . an attachment?" asked Ingmar, with bemused good humour.

"I'm afraid so!" answered Teresa, bursting into laughter like the open-hearted girl she was. "In any case, Monsieur de Neville, children often have their heart-throbs, just like grown-ups. But we were speaking of my sister. Apart from Don Gerontino Durante she has only one real passion in life, and that is to set up a big workshop, making shirts with at least seven girls to help her and the best people in Chiaia for her clientele. And she would not be displeased if Sasà, when she grows up, took over the running of it. However," and there came another laugh, though less hearty, "I think that Sasà will marry Gerontino . . . if such predictions are not too risky."

"Not always . . . Not always!" the affectionate Nodier in his optimism hastened to comment, totally enthusiastic that morning about Albert's family. De Neville, on the other hand, at the very notion that Sasà might marry Gerontino Durante when she grew up had withdrawn into his thoughts. How quickly children grow! How swift life is to pass, in Posillipo as in Liège!

"It may surprise you," began Teresa, addressing de Neville, "but other people's doings, their lives and fortunes, are my sister Elmina's passion . . . And this is because she hates her own life, she can't bear it, as if it were a punishment . . . or the Lord knows what . . ." she added, apparently to clear up some doubts which she seemed to perceive in the prince's mind.

"The result of a nunnish education," blurted out the plump Nodier with the air of a modern man who knows all about women.

"Do you think so? My sister is not very religious . . . she never goes to church, partly because she can't spare the time, but it's also that she doesn't care. Heaven doesn't interest her in the least. Work is everything to her."

These words, like others pronounced by the simple lass, the only really practical person whom de Neville had met in the mysterious family of Don Mariano, had for some little while been putting into his mind certain echoes, elusive lights, subtle threads of perplexity. Even that young marquis Geronte! He could not by any stretch of imagination be *her* son, or Teresa would not have been taken by the idea of his possible future marriage to Alessandrina, but he was dear to her; probably because at one time protected by Don Mariano, who was not related to her in any way, but whom Elmina had loved like a real father.

They returned to the subject of the workshop.

"That is not impossible . . . Indeed it is anything but impossible," declared Nodier.

"A workshop in Naples, at Chiaia . . . not impossible, you say?" burst out Teresa. "But, Monsieur Nodier, that needs money, which Donna Elmina has not got!" And so saying she bit her lip, because she too was aware of Elmina's pitiless largesse to the detriment of the whole family and herself, otherwise the money would have been there. She was also embarrassed by the fact that the well-nigh incredible dispenser of that lost fortune was right there, present at the discussion; and it was reasonable to suppose that he considered himself somewhat wronged and made a fool of by Elmina's conduct – and so he was, in a sense, but then at once he was saddened by the following thought: that Donna Elmina had refused the gift simply so as not to be indebted to the donor. This thought had not previously occurred to him in such a clear light, but he did not now thrust it from him: he accepted it as a part of his new sadness.

"But don't let us speak of such things now," concluded the kind-hearted girl, lowering her golden head before the stricken de Neville.

"On the contrary, *let* us speak of them!" laughed the merchant taking one of Teresa's hands and kissing it. "Let us speak of them, my dear Teresina. I can call you thus because from today on I am your brother-in-law. Donna Elmina has accepted me for a husband. This was the purpose of yesterday evening's visit by His Highness and myself. She has accepted me, and in so doing has become rich again, very rich indeed. This is not vanity, seeing that everyone already knows how vast is the fortune of Don Alphonse Nodier, the new king of glovers in Naples." Carried away by happiness, he was becoming bombastic. "Nodier, if I may say so, is one of the most prosperous businessmen in Naples, and owner of much-envied emporiums in Via Calabritto and at Ponte di Chiaia. He can offer a woman anything she wants. Therefore from today on – or rather since yesterday evening – we can deduce that Donna Elmina, having accepted me as a father to Sasà, can have everything her heart desires. I don't mean an ordinary shirt-factory. Good Heavens no! From now on she can throw money out of the window, let it flow in rivers all the way to Vesuvius ... a thing that some people" – and with a touch of spite he was referring to the prince – "might consider exaggerated ... But that's why I have it. Money (at least that of Alphonse Nodier) is meant for that very purpose."

He was expecting to arouse enthusiasm in Teresina, to see her surprised and moved, but the girl's expression did not change, as if he had been talking to himself.

"Is that the case? Has she accepted you?" she enquired after a while, casting a glance without any apparent reason at de Neville, and adding in subdued tones: "I am glad. But as regards my sister's financial troubles, and also her peace of mind, the matter is none the less difficult, Monsieur Nodier, because my sister never wants other people's money, ever. No loans are accepted, and presents she gives away. That is the way she is."

"There *must* be a reason," cried de Neville vehemently, but he was at once embarrassed at his indiscretion. He was beginning to feel his intelligence unavailing when confronted by the mysteries of the widow's personality (and therefore the reason for her continuous ruin). "Or something of the sort . . ." he concluded lamely, while Nodier, with childish but good-natured petulance, and paying no attention to the prince's remark, corrected Teresa: "*Other* people's money, there you are right, Miss Teresa, but the betrothed and the husband that I shall shortly be is not *other people!*"

He was a little irked by Teresa's lack of enthusiasm, but her reply was unexpected:

"You are mistaken, Monsieur Nodier, because even her fiancé or her husband, when it comes to money, are *others* to her. I tell you that my sister does not regard anything as hers but what she earns by working. Therefore she accepts nothing from anyone, because acceptance, for her, is being supported, and being supported, in her view, is servitude. She prefers real genuine servitude – washing dishes, for instance – to placing her heart under an obligation to others. That is the way she is."

"So it's freedom that she sacrifices herself for!" cried de Neville in astonishment, who was swift to draw the conclusion:

"This freedom is so dear to her that she cuts herself off from the world, renounces the entire world. Certainly she has for a long time made a gift of it to someone, and still does!" His sadness – although his fine face remained as gladsome and radiant as in the happiest moments of his life – had reached the very depths, and was now attempting to cast its shadow over the kitchen, humble though cheerful in the morning light, and over the landscape glimpsed through the open doorway, a landscape drenched in sunshine.

Now the prince (seeing that the matter affected his whole life) could think of nothing but this "someone". While very different, and not without a suggestion of arrogance, was the feeling (or mere reaction?) of the new fiancé, who understandably raised his voice somewhat, exclaiming laughingly to Teresina:

"Being supported . . . servitude! Ridiculous words to use of an adored spouse such as, I assure you, Signorina Teresa, from today on your sister is for me. She won't know what to do with freedom when she has her new slave by her side, and the whole world at her feet, believe me, Signorina!"

As foolish as could be! But the prince did not hear him. He looked outside, and felt a strong desire to enter that radiant and silent countryside. He therefore rose to his feet and (the french window being open, the steps warm in the sun) set off for the garden.

The other two followed him.

*The happy garden. We witness the flight
of the Paummella above the hedge-tops, thanks to the
intelligent use of the* Journal de Paris

There was simply no comparison between this and the garden which
de Neville remembered from that morning when he had secretly
made his way up to Sant'Antonio while the beloved Elmina was in
church, clad in white satin, for her marriage to the flaxen-headed Albert.
No comparison at all. This garden now was another place entirely, an
innocent sweet paradise.

The morning sun shone down upon a world so tranquil, so teeming
with the smiles of Nature herself, as to console even so benumbed a heart
as that of the prince. He had never really seen it that time ten years before,
let alone the previous night in all that rain. No resemblance, now, to the
unruly garden of Albert's day. Yet it was evident at once that Elmina
had never added a thing to it, or trimmed one branch, or removed one
leaf; her disregard for Nature – or rather, her constant, unyielding under-
estimation of it, her wilful blindness in the face of its glory – had led her
to neglect the garden. She had added nothing, she had simply forgotten
it; and free from Elmina the garden had breathed, had grown, and now
was a jubilation of herbs and roses (all out of season!), gladdened by
marigolds and certain mysterious blue flowers and velvety violets and pale
blue campanulas. Abandoned! Forgotten! Thanks be to God! Its saving
Grace! Some cords strung between two small trees betokened a washing-
line. On all sides thriving shrubs still dripped and sparkled from the
rain. Two or three lively birds fluttered around a low pinkish wall, where
maybe they had built a nest. This Eden was no larger than three or four
of the rooms of the house put together end to end, like a balcony running
along the south and east sides of the building; there it received the full
strength of the sun and, in the midst of the sunshine, also an indescribable sense of mystery. And everything whispered, or seemed to whisper
in the prince's ear:

"Elmina has gone away! She has gone out! Thank goodness Elmina isn't here. So rouse yourselves, O flowers, for the dance. O doves, abandon yourselves to joy!"

While thinking thus, with a pang of grief but also of bewilderment, the desolated lord of Liège, the unquiet haunter of solitudes and the long and narrow stairways of the heart, observed, passing slowly above a low blackthorn hedge, what might have been a magic object, or simply a pink sunshade, or a rag or a sheet of paper, with pink and white stripes. It rose but slowly, a few inches above the hedge, then sank again. It vanished and reappeared further on. And not a sound, a footstep, a giggle: nothing but a joyous silence.

Quite suddenly, while both de Neville and Nodier (Teresina, we imagine, must have turned away) were holding their breath, the mystery was solved and the phenomenon reduced to the everlasting fantasies that children have whenever they are delivered from some anxiety or fear. Beyond the hedge, in fact, the little girl was passing, playing a game that had come into her head like an inspiration. Sasà had risen in flight, or at least was attempting to do so, balancing herself, as if holding the ropes of a tiller, with a cloth (which turned out to be an apron of Elmina's) held high above her head in both tiny hands. Emerging from behind the hedge she passed in front of the two gentlemen without noticing them, and several centimetres clear of the ground. Wonder of wonders, she was singing to herself! She uttered a faint, low, monotonous

Aaah! Aaah! Aaah!

more akin to the lament of a creature of the wild than a real song (and indeed, she had no singing voice).

"Sasà, what on earth are you doing?" cried de Neville with a laugh. "So the Paummella can sing as well! Left to herself she sings and takes wing!"

If Sasà had heard him she made no answer.

"But Sasà, you're barefoot!" cried her young aunt in less affectionate tones. "Go and put on your shoes at once, you little scamp! You were coughing all night."

This was true, as could be vouched for by the sleepless de Neville. But he was deep in another and more complex feeling, half astonishment and half misgiving in the face of his own astonishment. He had seen the little girl rise from the ground, and this was at variance with all the notions he had of physics. He did not at that moment think of his own experiences (purely visual, if the truth be told) in the company of the Duke. In the innocent, and perhaps the very first, flight of the little maiden, he seemed to perceive some vestige of guilt, or at least the result of the indifference, not to say unlovingness, of Donna Elmina for her daughter.

At Teresella's reproving "Go and put on your shoes at once, you little scamp", he first noticed that the girl, although dressed, was in fact barefoot.

And dressed she was, but in what fashion! In the hasty, rough-and-ready manner of enterprising children to whom no one has lent a hand (and maybe never has), in a large ragged piece of flowered fabric that had been one of her mother's dresses in her youth, and which she had knotted round her tiny waist. From beneath emerged her long, bulgy black knickers, while over her shoulder she carried a yellow sunshade which had perhaps been responsible for the "flight". But was it really a sunshade? As the child rose once more beyond the hedge, before the eyes of the two gentlemen, they observed that it was simply a French newspaper, *Le Journal de Paris*, dating from before the Revolution; and how it had got to Posillipo was anybody's guess. Sasà had wrapped it round her head, twisting the two ends so as to resemble two great ears (or perhaps two wings attached to her temples?) which certainly, as they wobbled slightly, assisted the droll phenomenon.

When she saw the two men and her young aunt watching her, without a word, but at once, with a soundless little chuckle, totally unconcerned, the child shrank to the ground, leaving go of the newspaper, and seated behind the hedge continued her chant, that monotonous

Aaah! Aaah! Aaah!

as if to display her indifference: an attitude typical of children caught doing something they ought not to. But this time her tuneless voice had a different note to it: dark, weary, discouraged.

Thereupon de Neville realized that unlike Elmina, who was all of a piece (so ungenerous was he towards her!), her daughter had *two* souls, the one full of fear and the other of joy. And the fear was caused, it seemed to him, by the gloom of Elmina. (But why, why was Elmina so gloomy?)

Sasà was led away by her aunt to be clad in her darksome garments of mourning and mortification, while the two men stayed pacing up and down the garden, much cheered by the sun but perhaps somewhat stunned by memories as well as by fresh thoughts.

In real fact the prince had one sole thought: that the house, even in the sunshine, was not to his liking, any more than it had been on that day long ago when he had visited it to devise any improvements that might render it more agreeable to the newlyweds, and he was none too sanguine about the prospects of the mother and daughter, and the marriage that had been decided on to alleviate the former's situation. While he was speaking about this with Nodier, dwelling on all that concerned the widow Dupré and her new life and situation with him, his thoughts went off at a tangent following a train of small surmises that were not communicable. It seemed to him that Elmina had accepted Nodier in an act of capitulation, merely to save herself from *another* misfortune, the cause of utter desperation over which, though she kept control of herself, the poor thing no longer managed to prevail. Perhaps some disaster was imminent, and Alphonse Nodier's good fortune and peace of mind, which had always gone hand in hand with his good nature, now, faced with his decision, were covering their faces in desolation.

A disaster! A disaster was threatening the house, and the widow's actions, proud and contradictory and ultimately desperate, were intended to keep it at bay, at least for the time being. Everything de Neville had seen and heard was none to the good, even the sudden and scarcely justified absence of Elmina at eight in the morning, leaving her newly-betrothed asleep in the house. And not even our cheerful Ingmar could be satisfied with his own part in the matter. He knew that he was not loved – perhaps only "remembered", as we remember our youth – and with tears in his eyes he asked why it was that she so constantly repulsed him. He did not, on the other hand, enquire as to why, and by what right, he asked himself this question.

Things happen helter-skelter. The Porter-Boy.
Sasà gets scratched

There was an unexpected turn of events in the course of a morning which should have ended before midday in all tranquillity, with Nodier's return home and an agreement between the two friends to pay their respects to the widow Dupré in the evening, *chez* the marchesa. And the turn of events was as follows: that before midday Donna Elmina unexpectedly came home, bringing with her (so she muttered as she crossed the room) a certain Geronte, or Gerontino, laden with voluminous packages. Not Donna Violante's grandson, however, but a serving-boy in her household. They had come on foot, with Donna Elmina for the second time in a few hours climbing the entire length of the Scalinatella rather than the carriage road running parallel, in order to bring those packages up; packages, explained Donna Elmina, containing small garments in need of mending. And two things immediately struck the alert de Neville as he set eyes on that pair: firstly, the frowning, anxious look of Elmina, unusual for her, as if during those few hours she had received terrible news, or had simply wept and thought things over; and secondly the singularly fragile beauty of this second Gerontino, a child of about seven, though small for his age and in noticeably poor health. He was also shoddily dressed in old cast-offs too big for him, something inconceivable if he were the real Gerontino, the heir of an aristocratic family such as that of the Durante-Watteaux. It was therefore obvious that this was another Gerontino.

In addition the lad, who seemed not only very shy but daft with it, and wore a striped grey kerchief round his head, had stuck among his unwashed curls the tail-feather of a bird, perhaps a hen: an act of aggressive bravado to which the sons of gentlemen are seldom subject. All the same the prince was immediately struck by another thought, which was that Elmina, suddenly faced with her guests, whom she thought had already departed, had lied about the identity of the wretched child. And furthermore that this arrival with the boy overburdened with packages might have a more serious motive behind it: that Elmina, perhaps in disagreement with the marchesa about the new marriage, which her mistress may have disapproved of, had quarrelled with her and decided to withdraw all her current work to finish it in her own time and her own home.

Not to mention the fact that at this point, while the widow, after brief and almost incoherent explanations to the two guests, hurriedly shoved the lad upstairs, old Ferrantina appeared in the kitchen doorway, making no secret of her chagrin at her mistress's return home at that moment. With very sturdy hands, for her age, she held on to sad little Sasà, and hugged her to her.

Now, the little girl could scarcely be in love with the Porter-Boy (who could therefore not be the young marquis) because now, with a grim set face, glaring at the lad with loathing and without so much as a word, she was all set to attack him. The whole thing escaped Nodier, intent as he was on kissing the hand of his adored Elmina, greeting her effusively, bowing and placing his feet in third position. But it was otherwise for de Neville, who looked on in fraught amazement, and for the good Teresina who plainly saw his embarrassment.

Whispering quickly into his ear Teresa explained that the two "little ones" detested each other, and for this reason Elmina, obliged every so often to make use of the lad's services – he being the son of *a maidservant* in the Durante household, and therefore not a Durante himself – always avoided an encounter between him and Sasà. For he was a "sick" child.

As to what his sickness was, and realizing that out of respect for her sister even Teresa was fibbing, Ingmar did not attempt to enquire. What he understood without a doubt was that the lad was also called Geronte, and that Elmina was bringing him into the house, perhaps not for the first time, by stealth. It was also clear that Sasà's supposed infatuation for "Geronte" did not extend to this second Geronte (or *was* this the heir, though far from loved, of the Durante family?).

Once the children had left the room with the two women (Ferrantina had pushed Sasà before her into the passage behind the kitchen) Teresa gave the two friends the following explanation. The small boy, known as Little Geronte, had been adopted by the Durante family following the birth of the real Geronte, the heir. The poor thing was totally dumb, and practically a half-wit. He was given to continual tomfooleries and indiscipline, but Donna Violante, on account of a vow – made, it would seem, to Don Mariano – and a great sympathy for orphans, was always very indulgent towards him. Teresa could not say how old he was, maybe five, maybe seven, but for quite some time he had *stopped growing*. Donna Violante would never have thought of abandoning him, but her daughter Carlina (the wife of Major Watteau of the Horse Guards) was not of the same opinion. In fact she couldn't stand the sight of him; and so it came about that every so often the lad was dispatched to the seamstress's house. Meanwhile, between one of Carlina's tantrums and the next, the "child" was employed to perform small chores. He was not ashamed of this because he understood little or nothing.

"So won't he even go to school?" asked the prince, with a sudden pang of compassion. And once again, apt as he was to extract from every least event a theory (however much against the grain) in favour of Elmina, he assayed a few words of praise of her great Christian sense of pity, saying that she must certainly be upset by such neglect.

"But . . . could he not have medical treatment?" seconded Nodier, who had noticed that the lad, as well as being dumb, was slightly lame in the left leg, which was much thinner than the other, and also more bandy, so that he hobbled as he walked.

"No, monsieur," replied Teresa, lowering her eyes a fraction; then she added: "Besides, here in Naples there are many children in this condition, as you will have noticed" (which Nodier had not). "Either dumb, or blind, or lame. Often very nasty too. It's the result of the vile living conditions of the poor, in this city which has suffered so much . . ."

And with that Teresa, as if she thought she had said too much, dried up.

A small (or maybe not so small) secret of the Durante family lay behind the adoption of the dumb boy Little Geronte, and this was perhaps the real cause of suffering to Donna Elmina who – argued Ingmar – would have liked to be rid of him, bring him to the house no more, and avoid upsetting Sasà; but perhaps it was less her supposed devotion to the marchesa that prevented her, than some ineluctable obligation. And one and the same thought occurred to both the friends, a tacit exchange fostered by the silence then reigning in the house, and it was this: that the widow's unexpected departure early that morning had had but one purpose, namely, to fetch Little Geronte from the family palace where he had grown up and smuggle him into the Little House; and this on account of some event which prevented the Durantes from keeping him any longer, and possibly even forced them to hide him elsewhere. But what could this event have been?

There remained the other theory, that Donna Elmina was no longer *persona grata* with the Durantes, probably because of the announcement of the second marriage; and in this case the little boy became the direct responsibility of the impoverished family at the Little House. And an awful thought, or maybe no more than a depressing idea, crossed the prince's mind: that the boy was a "secret" son of Albert's, the fruit, perhaps, of an illicit relationship between the artist and the Durante daughter before her marriage. That would explain the turbulent passions which little Sasà felt towards him. Jealousy! A family malady, on account of which Elmina's present home was witnessing a repetition of the scandal of Jib-Sail House, which in the opinion of many had forced Donna Helm to withdraw to the country. This would be a clear explanation of Elmina's infinite sadness and her meek acceptance of the second marriage. It was to provide a new and better situation for the two poor orphans.

Our good Ingmar had not yet finished letting his imagination run riot concerning this unique and baffling state of affairs, and was simply standing beside the table waiting until Elmina came downstairs, alone or with Little Geronte in tow, when an almost inhuman shriek rang through the whole house, a child's voice, and so heart-rending that all the marble statues in Naples put together could not have rivalled the pallor of those two men, especially that of the oversensitive Ingmar, nor could the sudden blackness of night descending on the Gulf of Naples have caused their eyes to widen in greater terror. They scarcely knew where they were, and when they saw Teresa rush from the room muttering: "This is it!", then shouting out: "Don't worry, Elmina, I'm coming at once!", they were gripped by fearful anguish, one shattering question which could be compressed into a single name: where, at that moment, was Alessandrina Dupré? Had the shriek been hers?

They had small time to wonder before Donna Elmina reappeared, her face bloodless, holding by the hand an Alessandrina trembling and in a state of shock. And re-tying the ribbon of her bonnet beneath her chin the former revealed to the gentlemen present, who were still quite demolished by that shriek (though the house no longer rang with it, and the previous uncanny silence had returned), her sublime strength of character. It was the lad, she said, who in spite of being dumb had uttered that cry as the result of a sudden attack of the falling sickness. Climbing the Scalinatella had worn him out, that was all there was to it.

At this point, as if with the matter-of-factness of her statement she had exhausted the strength, the courage, the almost transcendental fortitude she had summoned up to carry her through that intolerable scene, and stifle the shame of it in the presence of her visitors (a shame that might even put her marriage at risk), and also, presumably, to encourage her daughter, she was overcome by a sudden access of emotion; and this found no other outlet than an unlooked-for, but none the less painful, tantrum at the expense of the little girl.

She, Elmina, pushed her daughter from her, not brutally but irritably, as if the child had been the real cause of all her distress, precisely as she had the previous evening; and it was far from impossible for the two friends to draw the conclusion that there must be no small connection between the stifled life of the widow Dupré and the presence in this world of the small person Sasà. And what in the tumult of emotions had escaped the two of them did not for long escape at least the more down-to-earth of them, the simple Nodier, who at a certain point discerned on the little orphan's face a long red scratch, a series of vivid red dots. As her father-to-be he was practically beside himself.

"Look there, Ingmar!" he cried. And then: "And what is the meaning of *this*, Donna Elmina?"

"She fell over and scratched herself . . . I don't know how . . ." replied the unhappy mother.

And seeing that Sasà, scarcely knowing where to go, what to do, to whom to address her woes, had begun to gaze at the prince with those dream-brimming eyes of hers, those of an infinitesimal mote, and yet a presence in this great, dark world, the prince felt a very strange pang at heart – for the mother, however, and not the little one. Elmina appeared to him now as one captive to some magic spell or inescapable fate – a lost soul. And when to Alessandrina (by this time trembling all over and weeping silent tears) the prince, remembering her prank with the *paummella*, began to hum the most popular song of the moment, we may state that the song, and its impassioned *ritornello*, were addressed not so much to the girl herself as to another being equally inscrutable.

"*Palummella*," ran the song* , "hop and flutter/ in the arms of my little

---

* A song far more ancient than historians suppose. Back in the eighteenth century, before the Revolution, it was sung by political prisoners in the carefree Kingdom of Naples.

girl-child/ go now and tell her that I am dying,/ *Palomma mia*, tell you her that!" And it was evident whom this melancholy thought referred to.

He had gone down on one knee before Sasà.

"Pa-ummella *good*?" asked Alessandrina Dupré, with a sidelong glance at her mother.

"That no longer makes any difference, child," replied Donna Elmina with the utmost listlessness. And to Nodier: "Forgive me, Alphonse, but this creature is reducing me to rags. She can no longer set eyes on that lad. She is consumed with jealousy. It's like this every time."

This superficial explanation, reducing the entire scene to the level of absurdity, none the less appeared, at least to one of the two friends, to have something far more serious behind it.

Donna Elmina had in fact forgotten, perhaps for the first time, the rules of good conduct which she had always observed. In the present case such rules would have required her to furnish an adequate explanation of the distressing events which had taken place before their eyes, and of the most mysterious thing of all: the presence (and also the ill-health) of the little boy. Perhaps even the shriek, not to speak of the deformity, were as nothing compared with two questions at least: why the widow had brought him to the house, presumably in the belief that her guests had already left; and what was the real relationship between those two, the seamstress and Gerontino, such as to justify the obvious preference she gave to the latter, who was after all the adoptive son of her employer, and certainly not a Dupré. And this totally to the detriment of her daughter there in the house to whom, if only on account of the name Dupré, every attention, not to say loving gesture (of which this mother seemed incapable), should have been due. And the more the two friends pondered on this secret, which with varying degrees of probability may not have been a secret at all, but simply one of life's little ironies – the love-lack and indifference of a woman, in other ways a good woman, towards ties of blood – the more it disturbed them. Not to mention the fact that they felt in themselves a wavering, or even a weakening, however slight, in their original immense trust in the Christian virtues of Donna Elmina. Well, perhaps not Christian, but virtues anyway. It occurred to Alphonse for the first time, and his heart sank at the thought, that she "didn't even love her own daughter" (as, come to that, neither had she loved Baba), and so how on earth could she love *him*? De Neville, for his part, was frankly appalled, if not enraged. His gentle and generous nature was disquieted by mysteries, and here they were coming from all sides, as if the roof of life had collapsed; they were falling like snowflakes in winter, or cherries from the cherry-tree in summer.

Furthermore, he had no liking for Little Geronte. He realized that he was not to be held responsible for his malady, but it was during the fit which had suddenly overcome him that he had scratched Sasà on the neck (for so the prince now envisaged the scratch on her face). And if he had bitten her? He shuddered to think of it. Never, never, knowing how dangerous the boy was, should Donna Elmina have allowed the two to meet. Yet she had brought him with her, on the pretext of the packages, almost certain that she would have found no strangers in the house to witness it. Angrily he deduced that he and Nodier, for her, were indeed strangers.

Teresina, who had left the room for a moment or two, now returned and told them that the lad had gone quietly to sleep on Ferrantina's bed, where he had been temporarily settled down. She was pale and hesitant, and looked at the two young men as if afraid of their thoughts, fearing that her credit had justifiably fallen in their esteem. She asked Donna Elmina if she would like a cup of coffee, and Donna Elmina said yes, following this up with an almost whispered request to use the grounds left over from breakfast. They were still good, she said.

"I like it weak, just water and a dash, as they say, and I am sure, Monsieur Nodier, that you and your friend will not mind it that way."

It was not the niggardliness, for which there was some reason, given the austere way of life which she had imposed on herself, but the cruelty of alluding to him, in addressing her fiancé, as "your friend", as if he had no other merit than that of being the friend of her various husbands – this it was that cut the prince to the quick. This, rather than an affront, was a soul-racking mockery, even to the stoical de Neville.

Nevertheless he thanked her, and then courteously enquired (though the matter was no longer of much interest to him, and all he expected was a reply at random) for how long the lad had been ill, and whether he was taking treatment.

The reply he received, although perfectly clear and even commonplace, at the same time implied something fleeting and elusive, corroborating the prince's worries (and to a lesser extent those of his companion).

"What does it matter, *how long*? Illness is a thing I don't believe in.

Illness comes and goes, because it comes from the heart, and when there is mercy in the heart the illness ends. I have seen with my own eyes, dear sir, a boy who was crippled from birth arise and walk. God willing, this boy of ours may be cured. It is true, however, that certain maladies ought not to be cured, for they are sent by God to reconcile souls to Him! So let destiny follow its course, and let us, dear sir, bow down before the injunctions of the Angels."

And at these wild, insensate words (or so they seemed to at least one of the two gentlemen present), a rare small tear, as if bearing witness to some inner wisdom hidden in the apparent disorder of her life, stole down the cheek, still soft and roseate, of the erstwhile maiden of Jib-Sail House, in expression of endless patience and infinite goodness of heart.

The two friends go back down the long "Scalinatella".
Deductions regarding matters in the family.
A light on the roof and the Paummella flies again

The decision of the two friends, when shortly thereafter they took their leave of the future Madame Nodier (not without having exacted a promise from Teresina that she would take good care of Sasà, keeping her with her on the ground floor, and forbidding her to go upstairs, at least until Donna Elmina had taken Little Geronte back to the marchesa's), did not at first appear to be the most judicious; indeed, our merchant considered it both hasty and imprudent. Nodier, as bride-groom-to-be, demanded explanations and reassurances about the rash and perhaps even risky job which Elmina had (according to her own state-ments) undertaken to perform in the Durante household: seamstress? serving-maid? or nothing less than the guardian of a mental deficient? This is how he bluntly expressed himself. He claimed, indeed he demanded, assurances, and these (he untruthfully asserted) above all in the interests of Sasà, whose sad little smile, in addition to the terrible scratch she had received from the scullion, was even now depressing him. Ingmar on the other hand, who had remained both pale and silent, think-ing about what the widow had said regarding the cause of sickness, now said (doing scant justice to what he really thought) that in his opinion Nodier ought to hasten along the wedding. Only in this way could he claim some measure of the necessary obedience from Donna Elmina.

"Donna Elmina," said the prince (while in his heart he replaced that common-or-garden title with Our Beloved Elmina), "Donna Elmina is living under the influence of an obligation that is a dream, in the toils of a fallacy that is harmful to her. Precisely this," – he went on to explain to his friend who had anxiously enquired "What fallacy?" – "precisely the fallacy of thinking that she is still the wife of Albert, and persisting in an obligation which she no longer has. It may be that among such obliga-tions is that of protecting that young fellow" (and indeed he said "young fellow", with undeniable ill-feeling, thereby attributing to Little Geronte more years and therefore more responsibility than in fact he had). "It has occurred to me – forgive my meddling, but the events we have witnessed fully justify such interference – that the obvious protection and defence accorded by Elmina to this lunatic are the result of some fault of Albert's which she is thus attempting to make amends for; and this is what causes her to put herself so meekly in the hands of the marchesa . . . of her and the secrets she is guarding. I tell you," he added, avoiding a suspicious and not a little irritated glance from the merchant, "that this fault might have to do with the birth of the unfortunate creature, and this would explain the aversion, and indeed hatred, which Albert's daughter bears him . . ."

The prince was already regretting his deductions, which were humiliating to Elmina, but passion is very often blind and apt to fantasticate. More and more he felt wounded by Elmina.

"Is that how you see it?" asked Nodier with a wry half-smile, after listening without paying much attention. Then he admitted: "It could be so . . . though it seems to me that the child is a good child" (this he said almost in spite of himself) "and I would not say that Sasà's desperation is due to jealousy."

"Well, what about that scratch? . . . It may have escaped your notice, or you may have forgotten it . . . I mean the scratch on our little girl's neck. Who could it have been? Her mother passed it off as nothing . . ."

"I have by no means forgotten. It has simply occurred to me (forgive me, Ingmar) that the wound (on the face, not the neck, if I remember rightly) may not have been inflicted by Geronte."

"Then who did it?"

"I don't know! There is certainly no one in the house but Donna Elmina and old Ferrantina, who has poor eyesight and is practically ninety anyway . . ." And bursting suddenly into laughter, as young people do even on the most absurd occasions (for Alphonse was at heart still young), he exclaimed:

"It must have been the Linnet!"

Ingmar, busy with his thoughts, did not hear him and therefore made no reply.

Eventually the two of them, who were slowly descending the famous Scalinatella which, in far different heart, they had climbed the previous evening, thought back on the decision they had taken (but not acted on) to pay an evening visit on the marchesa, not only to check on whether or not the Porter-Boy had returned there, but to take a first-hand look at how Elmina really and truly stood with the titled family down there in Chiaia, and whether all the reasons advanced by Teresina regarding the difficulties of opening a workshop in Chiaia were for Elmina *not* based on a state of mind (gratitude towards the marchesa and the moral impossibility of leaving her duties as seamstress in that household to which she owed everything, as well as leaving the care of Gerontino in the hands, so to speak, of strangers); these were not, I repeat, based simply on such a feeling, but at least as much on her express refusal to accept loans.

It was their intention to put it to the marchesa that Elmina was once again engaged and about to be married, and that it was essential, not least because of the tender bonds that bound her to Alessandrina Dupré, for her to devote herself entirely to the family life which until now she had neglected. And that for her work – if she had to work – she should be completely independent and self-employed. "Working at her own free will, in short, and probably for much better money!" concluded Alphonse Nodier, with a determined nod of his large head.

In the course of these discussions they glanced over their shoulders every so often at the impoverished dwelling they had left behind them, which at every step looked smaller and more isolated. And on one such occasion an oval beam of light, exactly in the manner of a *palummella* (which I should tell you now is a game children play with a mirror which flashes light around, swiftly illuminating here a wall and there a tree, here the foliage and there the cracks in the bark, catching them by surprise and making them wonderful, like the fluttering of a dove, and then with the selfsame swiftness vanishing); well, a light of this kind rested a moment on the grey turret of the Little House, revealing a small figure, evidently a girl who was there in the house, as she scampered in pursuit of a point of pinkish-violet light hovering over the rooftop.

At first sight you would have said it was Sasà, but that was out of the question. Alessandrina was too scared to have gone to play up there, at grave risk, and having to go right past the room where Geronte was resting; and it occurred simultaneously to our two friends that it was quite a different girl, perhaps a relative of the maidservant (de Neville remembered, with some perturbation, his letter from the Duke describing Ferrantina as an attractive blonde – something that at the time had staggered him). At that precise moment the child, as if raised into the air by the beam of light, and as if until now she had only *tried* to fly, levitated for a moment above and beyond the gutter, with nothing whatever beneath her feet; and de Neville, seized with terror, shut his eyes. When he reopened them the *paummella*, true or false as it may have been – or simply hallucinatory, which is most likely – had vanished, and the little girl along with it.

As for the bridegroom to be, either he had witnessed little, or he was distracted (which for us comes to the same thing). Or else he did not wish to complicate matters with further remarks about the immense, not to say bizarre, liberties which Elmina allowed to the members of her household: in this case those who ought to look after Alessandrina and failed to do so. The fact is that he might as well have noticed nothing, and as if he had been previously engaged solely with his own thoughts he confined himself to observing:

"Yes, opening up a dressmaking establishment in Chiaia (which I would prefer to a mere shirtmaker's, which seems rather on the modest side), ought not to cost too much . . . and the expenses would swiftly be covered by conspicuous earnings. People in Naples are very particular as to dress, as you will have noticed, Ingmar."

"That is true," replied the prince, but in uncertain tones, as if slightly off his head. And at once he added, as if in conclusion of some bewildering inner monologue, which presupposed an even more bewildering, though arcane, emotion: "Tell me, Alphonse, you who are a Neapolitan by this time and know everyone . . . Do you by any chance know of a good priest in this city? I mean a real man of God?"

"Why on earth?" gasped the astonished merchant.

It was some minutes before Ingmar answered, and even then in words addressed more to himself than to his friend:

"I am certain, Nodier, that at some time, I don't know when, but you may be sure it was long ago – and that the matter does not detract in any way from her Christian virtues – Elmina committed a sin, and God alone knows what it was. And that sin, and that only, is the cause of her suffering at this moment."

A significant silence

It may be that some of those who are following these pages will have noted how events of the utmost clarity, we might almost say "luminosity", not only evident but sensational, amply displayed to all and sundry – or if not truly displayed, at least engaged in making free of certain rooms, much as actors bedight as lords and ladies, during the rehearsals of a *pièce de théâtre*, saunter in and out of the wings and even descend to the stalls to adjust their wigs or repair their make-up – such events, we say, frequently pass unnoticed by the very people who ought to be the most concerned (to such a degree does habit quench awareness); and even celestial portents go unobserved by the woolly-headed; and absolute rogues (this also happens) obtain the governance of famous cities, giving themselves out as excellent ministers or perfect gentlemen. And the inevitable happens. In a word, the world is woolly-headed, and we cannot but conclude that only some few deeply instilled virtues of the soul, such as emerge in those who love in a spirit of pure love, can bring illumination to the human mind; whereas superficial love is as blind as a bat. Or could it be the other way round? The plain fact is that Alphonse Nodier never (or at least at that moment) showed any sign that he had grasped the import of the prince's question, and we cannot even say, considering the further observations he exchanged with Elmina's admirer, that he had seen the *Paumella* on the roof.

Or if he had seen it, dear Reader, he had forgotten it.

V

Prince and Elf

The house on the "Great Steps".
Another meeting with "Scribblerus".
Random guesses regarding the second Geronte

Nodier's apartments, although sumptuous, were among the least ostentatious in Naples, being situated at a point in Ponte del Chiaia where that narrow but celebrated thoroughfare at that time opened out, as it may still today, on the lovely stairway known as the Great Steps, the picturesque name used by the common people for what is now Santa Caterina (the sister, in a sense, of the dark, endless Scalinatella which climbed from Mergellina to Sant'Antonio: in short, to what in our narrative we have called the Little House).

The building, of no great beauty, but ancient and indeed almost crumbling with age, with two modest courtyards from which rose stone staircases far from well-lit, and indeed very drear, leading to three land-ings, also of bare stone flags, to which light was admitted through wide apertures, unglazed and cold, was itself by no means fitted to inspire good cheer. On these landings there was an oil-lamp in each corner, with a wick afloat in a basin of oil and, on the wall above, a picture or coloured bas-relief of a number of Souls in Purgatory, a cult at that time widely and genuinely professed in Naples. Half-length figures emerging from some anaemic flames, their poor hands joined in prayer on their breasts and eyes lofted on high, to implore of Heaven, or of God, the end of their torments; though truly they seemed in no particular hurry.

On the third and last storey were the apartments of Nodier: ten or twelve vast rooms furnished with an opulence scarcely imaginable, considering the mouldering state of the building, and decorated, follow-ing complete redecoration, with all the taste, but also with the ostentation of riches, then prevalent amongst the great foreign merchants in Naples, of whom Nodier was one.

Everywhere, therefore, were floors of precious marble, carpets, enchanting draperies of Chinese workmanship, exquisite screens in shades of pink and green depicting, for the most part, small lakes and gardens where solitude reigned supreme. A profusion of fireplaces, as in France. The ceilings, of a surpassing whiteness, bore stucco bosses in pink and green, while the doors and french windows – also white, though touched here and there with the subtlest of motifs, in pale shades of pink and blue, echoed the decorations – small lakes and gardens empty save perhaps for some sunshade or a passing white bird – which adorned the doors and wallpapers. The furniture, often half concealed by tastefully decorated screens, was also of the best: bureaux, chests, console tables, show-cases, small tables topped with rose-hued marble, sofas, gilded armchairs and footstools to match – just to mention the most obvious – very clearly evoked the erstwhile Kingdom of the Capets (or, if you wish, the kingdom about to be reborn, despite all the efforts of the Enlightenment). Nodier had not stinted on expense. As he had frankly expressed that morning to Elmina's sister (with a hint at the supposed penny-pinching of de Neville) his money – the spending power of that self-made man, heir to the virtuous reign of Don Mariano – after ten years of incessant work and above all native ability, was practically limitless, and his name could, with no offence given, be mentioned on the level of those of the First Citizen of the Palace of Caserta or of Naples, not to mention the mere princes and dukes around the place, with their estates in Calabria and where-have-you.

Returning therefore to the enchanted abode in question, we must not forget – scattered here and there among those isles of precious wood and embroideries conveyed directly from the divine Sol Levant – we must by no means forget further wonders: such as soaring mirrors of such sublime clarity they might have been made of air, invisible at first sight, but dizzy-ingly reduplicating all that richness and beauty (and putting to shame the unassuming Neapolitan windows); nor yet the exemplars of so much lavishness reflecting their images in the mirrors; which, to cite only a few, were many more small marvels of French and Oriental art, such as incense-burners, teapots, magic clocks, glass bell-jars (such as were to be found on many a chest-of-drawers in Naples, and one of which the present writer had occasion to admire in the house of a centenarian uncle at Pizzofalcone): precious domes of light to keep the air or the dust off exquisite Madonnas fashioned in bisque, Shepherds and Magi from the Christmas crib, clad in their robes of satin and gold, along with Angels and Archangels and an assortment of Saints, and bunches of roses, also in bisque, not to mention enamelled medallions in blue and gold; and we say nothing of certain green and gilt birds which, on pulling a little golden string attached to their throats, were made to *sing*, and slowly spread their wings (a precious secret hidden among their metal feathers and the great joy of the servants' children). All he had aspired to – and he, the new King of Glovemakers, so diverse from that austere person who was the father of Elmina, had indeed so aspired (we mean to pleasures and frivolities) – so much he had attained. And our description (not a little baroque) could indeed be endless, were we to refer, as we are tempted, to the stools upholstered in yellow satin, or the rose-hued curtains touched in with tiny flowerets that enhanced the windows; and then again to this show-case or that, and their mirrors inserted between one tiny gilt door and the next; and then to turn back, in some bewilderment, to the enormous celestial mirrors whose only material substance consisted in their elaborate frames in gold or bronze, and which conferred on that house in Naples all the enchantment, the expanse and brilliance of a Parisian drawing-room – and something more: the solemnity and prodigality of decoration to be found in some vast chamber in the palace of a king.

Nodier indulged himself, and thought that whoever entered those rooms had better faint on the threshold or be petrified with admiration. And this admiration and nothing more, although it may seem too modest a goal for so much power, that the plebeian Nodier – plebeian in comparison with a de Neville or a Dupré – desired more than anything on earth. And for people of his stamp the thing worked. (Not, we need hardly say, for the prince.) But before leaving the seductive picture of the charms of the merchant's heavenly dwelling, we should not like to forget a *natural* treasure inherent in the structure of the building; and this consisted of seven or eight pot-bellied balconies that adorned the reception rooms, one to each room, and all piled high, like greenhouses, with terracotta pots full or geraniums and carnations; and each vase protected by tiny cane fences, gleaming in the embrace of blue campanulas swaying in the wind; and lemon verbena, together with a modicum of basil, in many smaller pots ranged along the wrought-iron railings. All that was lacking were wickerwork cages for birds; or rather, some there were, but empty, for Nodier had recently lost a favourite parakeet and had therefore (such emotional eccentricities were not rare in that boyish soul) set free all the others. And this should suffice us to clear the cheerful image of the new Glover from any suspicion of vulgarity and stupidity that – due largely to so much wealth and preciosity – might have gathered about his figure.

No, our good Nodier was not vulgar; or not altogether so. And the immense popularity he enjoyed in Naples, which were unmatched in the least degree by either the esteem accorded to the prince (when they called him to mind) or the slightly disdainful benevolence which, in his time, surrounded the artist, well, in comparison such success was simply a sign of the times, if not indeed a justification of them: that is, a propensity for opulence, as long as deprived of *style*, and, naturally, a hostility towards any deep-felt, unspoken (and therefore truly aristocratic) mode of being. There had been the Revolution, but now Napoleon was lighting the rosy skies of the young century with a new sun. Wealth cannot die! Wealth is the only real Paradise of Mankind (and too bad for those who are stranded outside its gates, like the proud Elmina). That our Liègeois merchant was at present in request everywhere, as well as being (obviously) highly honoured and esteemed, was witnessed, apart from his lofty apartments in what was nicknamed the "Palace of the Spirits" – we forgot to mention this last detail – by the enormous stacks of visiting cards and invitations to parties and balls, long narrow strips of silk with a monogram and coat-of-arms in gold at one corner, strewn about the stylish little tables and consoles of the vestibule, or even propped up or stuck into the frames of the mirrors. Now, as he entered, the prince had hardly glanced at those cards (curious as ever, though today a little less so, for he seemed in the grip of new and disturbing thoughts), when a footman emerged like a shadow from one of the walls, or rather from an invisible door in such a wall, bowed to Nodier and told him in discreet tones that he had just had a visit from a gentleman he had never seen before, "Very handsome and sprightly, in spite of his advanced age, and with such an urgent wish to see you, Monsù, that it made a great impression on me."

"And do you remember his name, my dear Fernando?" asked Nodier, genuinely amused by that description. "I beg you to remember the name he gave you."

He had scarcely finished asking the question, to which the footman had no time to reply, than the gentle handbell on the door of storied coloured glass sounded its melodious summons, and half a minute later – just time for our friends to leave the vestibule, and for the newcomer to deposit his cloak and stick and ivory cane – Notary Liborio Apparente in person (the same as was known as Scribblerus, but how much aged!) entered the yellow drawing-room where the two gentlemen had already seated themselves.

De Neville was by no means pleased to see him, because the poor devil, all unknowingly, reminded him of the sad-happy days of his youth, and he therefore adopted a policy of silence and gravity, as if in the hope of not being recognized. But the limp yet very polite handshake which the Scribblerus exchanged with Alphonse was enough to show him that the two of them had met more than once, indeed that the Notary had probably become one of Nodier's most reassuring acquaintances. And he realized also that some secret trouble or anxiety fell between them.

When our two gentlemen and the Notary had all passed next door into the Chinese drawing-room, where Fernando and another footman were to serve them refreshments, they at once started talking about the events of '89 (the year 1799 was still too green in memory), and of the evils, or rather the frightful events – because the "evil" was still alive and present – which had infected the world with the Jacobin Revolution, to the detriment, above all, of trade and religion. There was no understanding anything any more! Having thus paid homage to the prevailing custom of the times, which was, as ever, complaining about the present day, they touched briefly on The Past which they had shared along with Albert and the old Glover; and they ended with a silence, and a sigh, *sur les beaux jours* they had all known in the times of Don Mariano and Jib-Sail House.

Then the Notary (who had not for one moment ceased to scrutinize and in his humble way to envy the prince, on account of the élan and social grace which cast an everlasting halo around that extraordinary person, and which had cruelly turned their backs on the Notary's own wretched life, to the point of reducing him to a few, a very few, grey hairs, and widely spaced out at that, as well as two or three pouches of yellow flesh under his chin), then, as I say, Notary Liborio went on to sympathize with Donna Elmina and express admiration for her strength of character. This point too, which was more or less a fixture in the kind of conversation which customarily passed between Nodier and the Notary (one particularly dear to the merchant, of course, but maybe unhappily dear also to the Notary), was brilliantly overcome, and the Notary who, as we have observed, never took his eyes off the prince, and was affected by some melancholy at the sight, took the liberty of asking the latter if he had already paid a call on the Marchesa Durante (old Violante, that is, not her daughter Carlina who was married to Watteau, and who lived in the same splendid palace in Chiaia).

"Watteau?" said the prince, somewhat vaguely, though hastening to add that he proposed to do so that very evening with Nodier. He had heard, among other things, that Donna Violante had been, and indeed still was, a very beautiful woman. He said this as a matter of social correctness, not knowing the lady personally and being unable to praise her for anything else.

"So she was in her day," remarked Notary Liborio after a slight pause. "Now, alas, her beauty is a thing of the past . . . But what does not pass, dear sir? On the other hand she is profoundly religious and sensitive to the sufferings of the people, and the oppressed. I dare say Monsieur Nodier has mentioned something of this. Wherefore," he attempted to say out loud, but in fact continued in a whisper, "she now fills her life with works of charity, and spares herself vain regrets . . ."

"Yes, I heard of her goodness towards Donna Elmina, during and after the troubles she underwent as a result of her husband's illness," replied the prince, on whom that whisper had not been lost. "All the same, to my way of thinking . . ." Here Ingmar broke off, in scorn of the practice of those who tend, by singing the praises of one person, to accentuate the errors and weaknesses of another, in this case Elmina, who had requested the former's kind assistance (and let no one say a word against Elmina!). He broke off, therefore, and resumed as follows: "I say this because Donna Elmina appears to me today – and there is no reason to doubt it – just what she has always been, that is, a person of great family virtues and rare good sense and good nature. Her friend is therefore fortunate to have such a friend. No question of charity in *that* case, I imagine. The word would be quite inappropriate, if not a downright perversion of the facts . . ."

Notary Liborio's initial fear of contradicting His Highness increased with every passing moment; yet a certain deep-seated stubbornness (which was really his most precious gift) did not fail him on the present occasion, so he added: "I would not define the position of Donna Violante over these last troubled years as that of a *friend* to the young widow, but rather that of protectress, indeed of guardian angel . . . But here, if I am to speak frankly, I must make it clear that when I said 'the oppressed' I was not referring to our divine seamstress, or to any advantages that might derive from that lofty protection; nor, when I used the word 'people', was I referring to the widow of Baron Albert (*she* is not of the people). I had in mind the real beneficiary of the House of Durante, to the *child* (so called because his mind is that of a child) who burdens the life of our gentle Elmina – a situation to which there appears to be no remedy. You will certainly have heard tell of him."

The reference to the half-wit boy was as clear as daylight, and also in some mysterious way offensive.

"What!" exclaimed de Neville in spite of himself, casting Nodier a very uneasy glance, "but is this boy, whom I think I have already glimpsed at Donna Elmina's, not a connection, a relative (as I dared to imagine) of the Durante family? Is our dear Elmina directly concerned with him? We seem to speak of an object of charity, and no more than that, but charity for whom, may I ask?"

"I understand you, sir. The fact is that this benefit – I allude to the protection aforementioned – did not a little to lighten the burdens of Donna Elmina, obliged as she was to look after the boy. At least until today," and here he in turn glanced at Nodier, "that was extremely useful to her."

"Forgive me, but I don't follow you."

"The boy," began the Notary with some embarrassment, "is now under the wing of the marchesa because he was previously under that of Donna Elmina, who could look after him no longer. She had done so – such was the situation at the outset – with the utmost care, of course, but the moment came when she was unable to continue. This boy, Geronte, could have remained at the Little House, but since the arrival of little Miss Dupré, and the decease of Albert, it was no longer possible. The two children were at each other's throats . . . I mean they disliked each other intensely," he corrected himself, lowering his eyes.

De Neville, and a moment later also Nodier, positively paled, because for the first time, although they had been talking about Donna Elmina for the last two days, and the merchant had been visiting her for years (having neglected her somewhat only during her marriage to Albert), they realized that they knew nothing about her ordinary day-to-day life, and that this, despite all their devotion, had been quite casually passed over.

De Neville was the first to speak, summoning his forces as never before to achieve that cool-headed self-control required to sustain kindly, or at least mannerly, everyday relations with persons of every sort, even when repugnant to one – relations which often appear to be among the most unavoidable.

"Do you mean to say," he asked – and Nodier, as he listened in astonishment, also hung entirely on the lips of the Scribblerus, for the very first time detesting his own great superficiality – "do you mean to say that he . . . this second Geronte (since they tell me there is another in the Watteau family) is also a Dupré, perhaps rejected by his father, or his mother, maybe on account of his abnormality, and iniquitously excluded, for obvious reasons, from the family estate?"

In so saying he was grasping at the hope that at least only the "father" was guilty, and Elmina totally innocent of the cruelty of the lad's misfortunes, being simply the victim of a foolish marriage which he – and how he regretted it! – had not at the time opposed sufficiently strongly.

The Scribblerus smiled, a brief, sad smile, and also embarrassed, while he fixed his eyes more on the toe of his shoes than on the carpet (decorated with a red Arabian archway, perhaps in Baghdad) on which these shoes were outlining something which to all appearances was devoid of meaning.

"Family estate? Words which have little significance to the poor . . . However, my dear sir, you are questioning me in vain, for I know more or less as much as you do. In certain matters, you see, there is no end to the mystery (even if sometimes the mystery is of no importance). And this is just such a matter. But I believe – or at least this is what is thought in Naples – that he could have been a Dupré, if fate had so willed. A truly unfortunate Dupré, and destined to remain so, in view of his malady, but none the less a Dupré, if only Albert had recognized him, at least formally. Alas, on account of his own malady, his continuously delirious state of mind, I fear that he never even saw him."

There in the Chinese drawing-room the conversation of the three men had disintegrated, as perhaps it was bound to do, and a weighty silence, behind a sheet of ice, had replaced the initial cordiality.

"A . . . natural son of Albert's, presumably . . ." hazarded the merchant with heavy heart.

"They say . . ." was the sibylline half-reply uttered, with lowered eyes, by the Scribblerus, who to the tormented de Neville increasingly seemed to be holding something back.

"And Elmina," began the prince, outwardly calm but suffering the tortures of the damned, though as determined as ever not to show his own feelings, "and Elmina took his responsibilities onto her own shoulders? What fidelity to Albert, if this is the case! And I who thought her cold, detached, almost inhuman! How she must have suffered from the presence of that boy! But tell me, sir, is it really true that Albert did not know, that he never suspected the existence of this . . . poor wretch?"

"He never knew a thing. Maybe Elmina did not wish it. In any case, after the death of Ali Baba other children mattered nothing to her – as Sasà matters nothing. The boy's mother, they say, called on Donna Elmina at the studio some time before Monsieur Dupré's condition worsened (though it is likely that she had first consulted the marchesa, since she feared that Elmina would not give her a kindly reception), telling her the whole story and begging her in heartbreaking terms . . ."

"She was fond of the boy, then?"

"Yes, but at that time she was unable to keep him (they say), on account (they say) of his infirmity. He was then both dumb and blind, and subject moreover to fits of convulsions. Entrusted to the care of a poor serving-wench – for such was his mother – he would have had small chance of survival. He was therefore taken on, after the unsuccessful attempt at the Little House, by Elmina's noble protectress, who was also a devoted friend (as who was not?) of Don Mariano." ("And therefore rival to Donna Brigitta," Ingmar found himself thinking with some amusement.) "You know that Madame Dupré was already working for the marchesa, acting as seamstress to the entire Durante household, including the servants, even when poor Albert was still alive."

"Yes, that is common knowledge," said the prince with a slight frown, "but . . . please continue."

"There is little to add, my dear sir. Donna Violante's mansion, over-looking the beach at Chiaia, is vast, practically endless, what with reception rooms both large and small, bedrooms, card-rooms and the servants' bedrooms. He, the invalid, was accommodated in one of the latter, though somewhat apart from the others, as was required by his shameful infirmity . . . His convulsions, you realize, his black-outs . . . In early days he was also dangerous, and very aggressive at times. But in all respects he was brought up as a child of the house, hence the name Geronte, with the simple addition of 'Little'. Donna Elmina thereafter – not at once, but gradually (it would scarcely have been human to expect otherwise) – conceived for him a truly sorrowful adoration . . . very similar to remorse, you understand, because that child might have been hers, if her relations with Monsieur Albert had been less distant; and moreover, how can I put it?, he was not only improving – this is now quite noticeable – but began to reveal, more and more with every day that passed, a nature of rare beauty, a soul full of sweetness and exemplary patience . . ."

These, thought the prince, were qualities rather of the widow than of the adoptee, whom he remembered as quite different: scruffy and daft, with that hen's feather sticking up on his head . . . A sign that people, and the Notary was no exception, in referring to facts either deform or embellish them, because in reality they do not observe them, or are not really interested. And this, he deduced, is what the world calls truth: always changeable, tongue-wagging and contradictory, always as misleading as a joke or a devil-sent dream.

"Did you not say that the brother and sister are in conflict?"

"The little girl, alas, dislikes him. That is logical. As you will have perceived, one cannot say that Donna Elmina exactly dotes on Alessandrina Dupré. That little maiden is alone in the world! She tries in vain to attract the attention, or should I say the compassion, of her mother."

"So it is jealousy!" exclaimed de Neville (or rather, he thought he exclaimed it, but in fact he did not utter, because Sasà's conduct was not as simple as that, and he had not forgotten that when on her own the Palummella behaved in such a way as not to seem too unhappy). "So, the little angel is consumed with jealousy!" he concluded out loud. "What a terrible thing!"

And, being jealous himself by nature, he understood; and his eyes lit up with a fervid sadness, a disconsolate half-smile.

"Yes, it is to be presumed. We very often underestimate children," began the Notary in philosophic vein, while – a fact which eventually struck Nodier forcibly – the toe of his shoe intensified its search for the entrance of the Red Mosque in Baghdad woven into the carpet. "And I think we do wrong, not only in the sight of God, but because terrible passions sometimes devastate those little souls. There is something tremendous – I mean to say a power – in those sparrow-like little bodies, beneath their few feathers . . . a power that oftentimes causes them to soar into flight . . . This is seldom borne in mind."

This observation struck gloom into our good prince.

"In my opinion," interjected Nodier at this point, his enthusiastic and optimistic spirit having by now overcome the worst of the crisis, the fact of finding himself, on marriage, the father of two children, not just the little girl, and the latter, above all, apparently woefully neglected, "in my opinion the situation is not irremediable. All that has to be done is to reinstate the two children in their previous, in short their original, situations."

"Meaning?" asked de Neville none too amiably.

"To return Little Geronte to his real mother (a washerwoman or scullery-maid, I imagine) with a small annual income which I myself, in my position as a new member of the family, would be more than happy to provide. But on condition that the woman gives her word that she will thenceforth never allow Elmina to meet the little invalid, and above all never allow him to meet his half-sister . . . Forgive me, I mean Donna Alessandrina. I, at least, see things this way. Everything, in this case, would be taken care of."

Notary Liborio failed to catch, or else took no notice of, that allusion to the brand-new connection between the merchant and the family at Sant'Antonio. He was either not struck by or uninterested in that authoritative pronouncement, "as a new member of the family". But while sitting there lost in thought, as if swamped by imaginings and an awareness of events beyond his comprehension, at which in those circumstances he could only hint in the vaguest manner, he simply stared at the prince – who also sat with clouded brow (though taking furtive glances at poor feckless Nodier) – and said:

"I wish to God, dear friend, that everything were as simple as that. But there is a sorrow entrenched there in the hearts of certain persons . . . a cry of despair that will not be stilled so easily . . . and believe me, perhaps never again. Therefore I tell you that to separate Donna Elmina from her sorrow is practically impossible. Do not attempt to do so. The outcome could be disastrous. Ah, even I, a man of pandects, sceptical about the goodness of human nature, am beginning to think that truly there is a Linnet hidden in this world; and that the song and the weeping of the Linnet are never silent."

*A weird procession. A little Elmina and a
spurious Don Mariano. Strategy of a baby goat*

He had scarcely finished uttering these words – the singularity of which lay in the fact that even he, the humble Scribblerus, seemed to know about the bird of this story – he had scarcely finished uttering them, therefore (and we may say that they struck straight at the heart of the astonished but ever vigilant Ingmar), when, almost as if in (certainly jesting) confirmation of them, chance had it that under the balcony, which overlooked the Steps, was heard the detonation (I find no other word for it) of sudden and disconcerting music.

Our two friends leapt to their feet and rushed out onto the balcony to see what was going on, while the Notary plodded after them; and at once, in the midday sun (the hour was somewhat later, but to all appearances it was still midday), in the sun that, breaking through the clouds and spattering of rain that had followed the radiant azure of the morning, now also looked down on the colourful Steps, dappled here and there with the red and yellow of the flower-sellers' baskets, they observed a small procession all gilded and beribboned like a royal retinue weaving its way up towards the top of the ancient Steps. It was now passing directly under Alphonse's balcony, on its way to the church door of Santa Caterina, some hundreds of yards further on. Looking down from the balcony of the Chinese sitting-room they could see, clear as daylight, ten altar-boys clad in surplice and stole (and all so flaxen-haired they might have come from Germany) who – four in front, four behind, and one on each side swinging censers with evident glee – were hefting the shafts of a wheel-less carriage adapted for use as a sedan chair, gilded and gaudy with lace and damask, and the framework also gilded and decked with flowers. Inside this carriage, viewed through the glass windows, they seemed to perceive the swaying body of a little girl.

Behind the carriage walked two priests, one tall, one titchy but with the sweetest face imaginable. As the procession passed he raised his eyes for a moment to the balcony, and looked the prince straight in the eye.

Following the priests came a number of working-class women in red skirts, and men holding their blue caps in their hands, some street urchins and several ancient bejewelled ladies, and, incredibly enough, a number of Swiss Guards in their tall helmets, and two inspectors from the Bourbon police force, one of whom kept scowling around him.

Ingmar, seeing himself observed by the smaller of the two priests, could not tear his eyes away from that withered, venerable person, as if struck by a thought, a flash of recognition, a feeling his wounded soul could not express otherwise, such was the mingled joy and melancholy that sprang up in his heart. The fact is that the old man reminded him of someone very distant in time, whom he would never be able to identify with absolute certainty, yet all the same – and this was the worst of it – he forced himself to try. He did not persist in this endeavour, indeed it only lasted a few moments, because an unexpected movement of the small crowd (due, perhaps, to a broken step) caused the bearers of the weird sedan chair to make a sudden swerve, so that the glazed portion tilted a little away from the balcony, giving an almost horizontal glimpse of the doll-like figure on the pink satin cushions within. It could have been, at first sight, a waxen figure of the Infant Christ, in a white camisole, with one foot resting upon the other, a garland of mayflowers round its head, its eyes closed, one hand open and slightly raised as if in greeting; but then, on closer inspection, they saw it was a little girl asleep . . . with the face of Donna Elmina. A Donna Elmina at five or six years old, alive and trouble-free (as at the time of her crimes, thought the prince), but with her eyes closed, as in sleep or in dream, we know not. Onto her brow there beamed a golden light, but never stationary, ever on the move: as frail as a tear it coursed up and down her guileless face . . . From time to time, beyond this scene, drifted flakes of snow, or sometimes the snow even lashed against dark treetrunks . . . This was no longer Naples but God knows where, and very far away. It was therefore a real vision, dating back to at least twenty years earlier, and the setting was both nordic and wintry.

The gilded sedan came upright again, and the red-robed youngsters set off once more up the ancient stairway. At the same time the women, old and young, who were following the gaudy vehicle, began to intone (in a slovenly wail, it must be said) the words of a hymn, heartfelt and mournful, that was chanted even then in the churches of Naples: "We

long for God/ who is our father/ We long for God/ who is our king!"
But at once, on this occasion, the chant was followed by an impetuous
refrain, indistinct at first but thereafter in a ringing, triumphant crescendo:
the refrain which ever struck sorrow into the heart of the prince:

O flutter, flutter, flutter, fly little Linnet,
Flutter, flutter, flutter, Oh! Oh! Oh!

Anyone of less staunch mental fibre than our diplomatist might well have
been moved to tears. But de Neville had luckily been brought up from
childhood, by an extremely severe Spanish governess, to repress any sort
of emotion, and above all not to show surprise at any kind of onslaught
with which the dauntless world of universal mystery (perhaps having
nothing better to do) continuously assaults this frail human world of ours.
So in this instance, being inured and as we know well-informed as to the
normality of supernatural events, the first thing he did was laugh, instantly
realizing that the "procession", and the entire scene which he had
witnessed, was not a real thing at all, but a phantom of his own mind. Of
course there was something real in the procession (though lunchtime did
not seem the most appropriate hour for such an apparition), and especially
in the gilded sedan, and needless to say there was a great deal of reality
in the two police inspectors (of Elmina herself he avoided thinking) who
came at the butt-end of the procession, guarding it and keeping an eye on
windows overlooking it. But the substance, the heart of the delectable
spectacle seemed to be elsewhere, inside Ingmar's head in fact, having as
its centrepiece his dear Elmina (with her secret) as she had certainly not
appeared for many a long year.

"She loves the Linnet!" said Ingmar to himself with the utmost
intensity, though for the moment without real grief, for the spirit of
enquiry forced him on. "However, the Linnet does not love her, or exists
solely for her torment and probable punishment. But for what crime?
Unhappy Elmina! How long has she been suffering, with this terrible
bird dominating her life! O may God help me to discover, to enable me,
in some way, to pay her debt to Heaven, and in the end to wipe out her
probable crime in the sight of God!" Then he thought of something more
down to earth: that to pass beneath that very balcony, knowing that he,
Ingmar, was visiting Nodier, the Linnet must have had some reason.
Simply a warning? Or was the Linnet intent on involving him also in that
bittersweet terror?

*   *   *

Heaving a deep sigh, the prince shook off these thoughts and fantasies, truly unbecoming and even embarrassing for a man of the world such as he, and confined himself to keeping his eyes on the procession, with the gilded sedan swaying this way and that, seeming to flutter like a butterfly wounded but still alive, as it disappeared up the steps between the ranks of flower-sellers and fishwives encamped on either side of the great stairway – a thing unusual at that time of day, for it was well past noon and a measure of silence reigned. Eventually even the sedan disappeared and the song fell silent. But the prince paid no attention (or else he took it for granted in Naples, that city of goatherds) to a grey and white kid only a few months old, or perhaps even weeks, which appeared on the steps, skipping and shuddering, when they were already empty. It was chasing after the procession, that was plain enough, bleating prayers and entreaties. Who knows if it would ever catch up.

"*There* is the instigator of it all! Wretched Käppchen, ice-bound Spirit!" were the words that issued, to the best of the prince's hearing, from the plump pale lips of the Scribblerus. This latter was renowned (as we may already have mentioned) for his skill in composing occasional verses (poems to celebrate marriages, mournful folk ballads etc.), so that the prince, knowing the man's natural propensity to gibberish, scarcely gave his words a thought.

He therefore followed the course of the tiny horned creature up as far as the church, where it vanished amongst rays of sunlight and cheerful tears of rain (such at that time was the playful climate of Naples). He thought of Don Mariano (he dared not pronounce the name of the daughter). Only then did he make a move, to ask of a Nodier practically in tears with enjoyment whether in that procession he had noticed any-one of their acquaintance. "No, not a soul," was the hesitant and (due to laughter) fitful reply; though he *had* heard the mournful chant. In his opinion the presence of the Police Inspectors was a portent of events far from reassuring. To the Bourbon Police this grief that was and had always been in Naples (said Nodier, and the Notary nodded agreement), was not acceptable. Or rather, acceptable yes, but not so blatantly manifested. His Majesty would have preferred it to be more modest, more muted, more assiduous in showing gratitude than (as seemed the case) annoyance on account of this "privilege" – the privilege being the grief, which was the gift of God rather than of the King.

While our cheery young glover thus spoke, and burst out laughing again, the Notary added (almost in a murmur between his puffy lips, as if he were merely thinking it) that in fact processions of this sort, though sanctioned and justified by long-standing tradition and very dear to the hearts of the common folk of Naples, none the less for some time past, and increasingly so day by day "since the Events we all remember" (alluding obviously to the French occupation of Naples, apart from that nation's present designs), betokened a certain effrontery, and suggested that Paris was allied to or hand in glove with the sorrows or, if you wish, the evident sufferings, of the "underground people". By which he meant a people, if not an entire country, which is the true and genuine People, or indeed the instigator of criminality and every sort of insurrection there in Naples.

*The underground people: merely gossip or embarrassing
truths concealed by historians? The amusement of Alphonse
and the Notary's seriousness. The bell is heard once more*

"Did you say *underground*, my friend?" enquired de Neville promptly, though in a low voice.

Without waiting for the "man of pandects" (always afraid of saying too much) to commit himself to an answer that might not have been clear, the merchant at once stopped laughing and broke in to regale de Neville with a completely frank account of the origin of certain Neapolitan customs and beliefs which the prince did not know about (though he had heard tell of them and, he had to admit, had been both moved and perturbed by them). Among these, for example, was the pious family cult of the Dead, based on a folk belief that was perhaps questionable, but none the less worthy of respect. This was that the souls of all the dead who had died in Naples in the last hundred years (but in some cases longer, there was some talk of the days of the House of Aragon), whether they had died a natural death or not – that these souls continued to dwell in and bustle about the beautiful city of Naples as free of disturbance as any other subject of King Ferdinand, sharing in the city's life, its holidays and so on, in its contempt and its tears, its dreams and its doings, on a par with every other inhabitant. These ancients were all but indistinguishable from the living . . . Perhaps a shade paler, usually more tolerant and inclined to turn a blind eye than the real live populace, for which they often revealed a mischievous and sorrowful affection.

The merchant at this point blew his nose, obstructed by tears of merriment. "In a word, dear prince," he concluded, "an enormous host of ghosts still inhabits these houses, these alleyways, sits at our tables, sleeps in our beds, takes its ease in our carriages – visible or otherwise, but ever at our sides. They are not the people of today, but of long since. They suffered much, and even today do they really ask for peace? Or else, more simply, do they long to come back and live in the places they loved, with their familiar furniture, their precious little trinkets, and inhabit the days they lived and loved? Or else are they not, perhaps, bent on revenge? This is what is currently suspected, and therefore (you may be sure of it) His Majesty does not look kindly on the continual recrudescence of . . ."

"Does he think that among those spirits there might be certain students . . . certain *liberals*? Perhaps even one or two French intellectuals, supporters of the uprising of '89?" And as he asked, a touch of sarcasm, a touch of vague dreaminess crossed the prince's brow.

"Even that. It is not impossible. But above all – Severed Heads. Many French noblemen knew Naples by repute, and had always intended to visit our city, so that as soon as they were free of their earthly bodies they requested, and obtained permission, to spend their period of detention here: Hell or Purgatory, whichever it might be. At least, that is the most widespread belief. Voices are heard speaking in French by night, *vous savez?*, and this is a surprising thing. The King is convinced of it. And more especially is he convinced that the Linnet is French. He has put the Police on his track, if you want to know."

"This must be a joke!" exclaimed the prince, apparently light-heartedly, but without changing his grave demeanour.

"That is also my modest opinion," put in the Scribblerus after a moment of hesitation while he overcame his shyness. "But I will tell you more. In my opinion the presence of the Linnet here in Naples – of which there is no doubt – has absolutely no political motivation, even if at times the circumstances might lead one to infer a connection between the bird's song (just a mere nothing flitting about in the air) and the sufferings or turbulences of the common people. Because this sorrow (or rejoicing? or longing? or mere longing for joy?) as expressed by this wretched bird has precious little to do, if you come to think of it, with the world of grown-ups, be they intellectuals or noblemen, but solely with the world of children, by which I refer to those who, reaching twenty, or thirty, or even a hundred years of age, still remain children at heart. There is a sorrowfulness in children," he continued, "in our world of Naples and elsewhere, even as far as distant Germany, that is both graver and greater than that of the intellectuals, the reformers, even of those who are clamouring for a Constitution – a sorrow that is *not* that of grown-ups, whom we usually refer to when we utter the magic word 'sorrow'. Because sorrow is a desert, and in this world only children (I refer, of course, only to real 'children', goblins or demons as they may be) can know this desert place."

At any other time no one would have paid any attention to him; but this was not that time.

"A desert in what sense?" asked the prince, knitting his brow, having with some difficulty followed the Notary's strange and hallucinatory discourse.

"Lacking in love and respect, of course, Monsieur. You must realize that children, unless they belong to the *bonne société*, confront this desert from the very day of their birth. And it is for this reason that here in Naples, as in Paris, London or Cologne, they disappear, they vanish, they dissolve like smoke in the air, before they have time to grow up. Therefore it is to this world of dark houses, loveless houses, that sooner or later they tirelessly return ..." Then, addressing the merchant: "You will have noted, my dear Nodier, that those who in Naples are known as '*les revenants*' are all *piccerilli*, are all children."

These words made the prince shudder.

"You mean, persons of small stature?" enquired the merchant casually.

"Yes. The *monacielli*, or *Käppchen*, or Caplets as they call them, are all of very short stature: they are never more than forty centimetres tall."

The prince had already, that morning, in some way come across the word Caplet, but he was too worried to give it much thought.

"*They*," he thought with relief, referring simply to the two youngsters of the Little House, legitimate and otherwise, "are already taller by at least five centimetres than the measure now laid down by this buffoon." But the calculation did not reassure him altogether, and who knows why it had ever entered an intelligence as sharp as his. But the world seemed full of surprises.

"Going back to what we were saying," continued the Scribblerus, "and leaving aside my own modest flights of fancy on the subject of children, from the political point of view this business of the Linnet looks pretty serious, and I would by no means neglect the hypothesis that His Majesty, having had information leaked to him by a certain Inspector Morvillo* , is thinking of *this* house, and this very balcony, as a nest of Jacobins. And that the sorrow that encircles Donna Elmina, who is our queen, the queen of all our hearts, and we cannot deny it, this grieving of the spirit (a thing forever suspect in the eyes of the authorities) appears to the mind of the

---

* A police inspector notorious at the time, unmentioned by historians, who credit his date of birth to *another* Morvillo, who when times changed joined the Reform Party, and ended up forgotten by history.

King, or what we can infer of it, since the most part of his thoughts are never made known to us, to be a possible symptom of insurrection . . ."

"*Des sottises!*" was the grumpy and somewhat contemptuous reply of our princely diplomatist, who understandably failed to grasp any connection between dear Elmina's secret sorrow and the intellectual and rather self-regarding agitations of the time.

"Logically speaking you are right," admitted the Scribblerus. "However, having observed those policemen there among the wailing women following the sedan chair, I am little inclined to speak of mere guesses . . . of imaginings if you will. The grief and the sorrow of Donna Elmina, her relationship or familiarity with the Linnet, these are already things well known here in Naples. And I can even suggest the possibility that, fearful of a highly likely scandal involving the family Dupré, the Marchesa Violante and her daughter, who is after all married to a cavalry officer in His Majesty's service, has now decided to send that crippled boy back to the Little House . . ."

"And so where do we stand?" burst out the prince indignantly. And he was indignant because this miserable Notary had made free of the private and intimate life of *his* untouchable and idolized Elmina. What an imbecile! What a schemer! However, those remarks of his were not entirely senseless, because he was reminded of the fact that even the angelic Sasà, on account of her carryings-on (and he had a very clear memory of her flying above the hedge and dancing about on the roof) could also be among those accused. His heart, his truly fatherly heart, quaked at this. "I'd like to see them do it!" he blurted out. "I'd immediately inform several royal Courts all over Europe, and I'd cast my net wide, if this is what they are *not* afraid of . . ."

And the prince, as he noted the wary, thoughtful manner in which the Scribblerus let his eyes rove over the carpet, was visited by the ghost of a suspicion, which was that the "leak" between the police and His Majesty's government was not the notorious Morvillo, but this very Notary, and that the informer stood before him. And since in such an intricate web as the tale we have the misfortune to be telling no further complications are necessary, we will say at once that the prince was quite mistaken in his suspicions regarding the Notary. He was certainly an unhappy man, but not a wicked one, and his eyes were averted, in evident distress, merely from the vast *affluence* of the prince, with which, ever since entering the house, he had been comparing his own condition.

De Neville, however, could not resist making a final crack, intended to warn the Notary, in the event of his joining the Linnet's party, so to speak. "Worse luck to him who fails to choose what side he is on in life, and in good time," he said. "I don't know that I am on the side of the Liberals, nor am I on the side of the Dead, especially if they hypocritically pretend to be children (or even goats). Unless they are really children, and frightened in their turn of other children."

It was not that this pronouncement hung together very well, but the unhappy Notary, after an understandable hesitation, felt a moral obligation to reply with a few words, which sounded equally sibylline:

"These are things, Your Excellency, which alas we will never understand."

De Neville obviously made no reply to this, but turned to Nodier while himself rising to his feet – having simultaneously heard the melodious chimes of the grandfather clock in the vestibule, chiming two o'clock, and the lusty pealing of another bell, which was that of the front door – and addressed him light-heartedly:

"But this evening, my dear Alphonse, we shall certainly learn something more, and we shall exculpate our beloved Elmina from the accusation that so many people" – and this dart was aimed at the Notary – "quite unscrupulously charge her with: that of slandering, with her secret sorrow or mere austerity of life, the fashions and customs of the Court of which we speak. But it is not so. There never was – and this you well know, who have chosen her to wife – there never was a simpler heart or one more devoid of critical sense towards either herself or others . . ."

"True, all too true," admitted Nodier cheerfully.

"So, my friend, you still agree to our visit this evening to Casa Watteau?"

"*Mais certainement*, and we shall have the time of our lives, old boy," replied the young glover in the merriest mood imaginable.

(Something that had escaped the prince, but must not escape us, was the swift and apparently anxious start which the "man of pandects" gave on hearing the former's astounding words, "you have chosen her to wife". And we can perhaps clear the latter's reaction of any facile, boring taint of jealousy, which can never be discounted. No, there was in it something *aghast* and *terrified*, on the extraordinary nature of which we shall not, for the moment, insist.)

*A surprise in the vestibule. The lovely statuette
and a message from the Duke to "Little" Ingmar.
To Caserta! To Caserta!*

The ring at the bell had not been repeated, but de Neville and Alphonse were already in the vestibule, partly to see off the Notary, who was taking his leave, when – they had turned back from the door and no manservant had appeared to explain why the bell had rung – on the elegant marble console right under the great gilded mirror they noticed a carefully sealed white envelope. So much light was playing on that envelope, quivering with such singular delight, that the other visiting cards and papers scattered about might not have been there at all.

To further justify the absent-mindedness which prevented the master of the house from wondering who on earth had delivered it, we should say that the letter, light as a feather, was propped against a round glass bell-jar under which glittered, with a thousand gilded curlicues and caprices, a large clock in the style of Louis XIV; while also leaning against the clock, but the other side of the bell, was a bisque statuette reflected, along with the clock, in the mirror behind: and this had certainly not been there a few minutes before. Alphonse's interest as he examined the statuette (he was a rare connoisseur in artistic matters) lay not so much in the perfection and indeed exquisiteness of the workmanship, but in the subject of the figure itself. It represented nothing more than a shepherdess of the previous century, but a delightful shepherdess, all in sky blue and pink, whose smiling and radiant features he seemed to have seen before; indeed he was certain of it. "Who does this young beauty remind me of?" the prince's friend was asking himself in a rapt state of mind when the former (the prince, that is) perceived his own name on the envelope, rather oddly inscribed to "Little Prince Ingmar", while the whole was written in the elaborate, florid hand of his friend at Caserta, the rash and saucy Polish duke, Benjamin Ruskaja. Since the letter was addressed to him, he at once opened it and started to read. Therefore between, two Belgians (alone in the house now, no longer disturbed by the procession) there fell the sudden silence that comes with joy. And while one of them gazed at the figurine, which posed a riddle, or else its answer (for the newly betrothed merchant), the other ran his eye rapidly over the few lines of the missive he had received. And we tactfully add that neither of them, as indeed happens in youth, that flurry of happy bewilderment, gave a thought to how those two welcome surprises came to be there, or *who* had delivered them. No, that was of no interest. Only the surprise was interesting.

And since Ingmar appears the more impatient of the two, we will deal with him first. Here is the text of the letter.

> My dear boy – began the letter, which bore the postmark of Caserta, but surmounted by a pigeon's wing in blue, a crafty clue as to which unofficial channels had ensured the swiftness of delivery – my dear boy, do not take it to heart if I have called you "little", for such you certainly are, but no fibs, thank you (though I know you are incapable of them), telling me that you refuse to see me. (I sought you without success an hour ago, *chez* Alphonse – maybe you realized.) I will take no excuses. Therefore please set off at once. I expect you this very evening at Caserta, that is at my house, for important communications, tidings of extraordinary interest to your spirit and, shall we say, your peace of mind. May you never again hear the Linnet! Such is my earnest wish and, I assure you, my hope. I therefore expect you, my boy.
>
> Yours, Ruskaja
>
> P.S. You will find me greatly aged, but no matter. Tell no one how you came by this letter, and least of all inform Donna Elmina. P.P.S. Take a sly glance at your friend while you are reading and he is gazing at the little French peasant girl (a gift from me), and try to guess, but intelligently, *who* he is in fact thinking of and whether he is really as faithful and generous as he says he is. All the best!

This last part was written in a rather shaky hand, in token of a complaisant old age, but then vigorously underlined to express, along with this sorcerer's years, his unflagging ability to butt in and gossip when it came to any sort of snag or affliction in the lives of his dearest friends. And Ingmar, only son of the friend of his childhood days (we must remember that the Duke had had several childhoods, that being his favourite time of life) and also of a thousand adventures together – we speak of the never sufficiently lamented Leopoldine – Ingmar therefore was, of all these friends, the closest to his heart.

We need hardly say that the prince, though overcome with joy at this letter, and before laying it down to read it again at leisure, had fallen in with Benjamin's roguish suggestion, casting an eye at his host; and he had observed the rapt expression – infatuated is putting it mildly – with which Alphonse Nodier, in contemplating that delicious statuette, was gazing upon the features, or something very like them – in short the charm – of his future young sister-in-law. Yes, he was in love: but *with whom*? Alas, that look, along with the Duke's warning not to mention the letter to Donna Elmina, confirmed the prince (had there been any need for it) in his unfathomable persuasion that Elmina was once more *alone*, that no salvation was possible for her. Everything she acquired, and now even this second husband, Elmina was doomed to lose. Wealth, happiness, family. Because in truth, the prince sadly thought (or thought he thought), she did not *wish* to establish relations, other than of gloomy and monotonous servitude, with those who loved her, and whom she herself perhaps loved. The picture of the baby goat running trembling and bleating after the procession enlightened him as to her situation in the world: one of punishment and everlasting flight, perhaps repentance. No use to anyone, ever, like a creature damned . . . she too a creature of the underground. The idea of some guilt, some frightful crime, returned with greater force to the mind of the prince, but did nothing to diminish his pain: far from it. And how beloved to him, at that moment, her comfortless situation rendered her! All the same the poor Nanny-Goat, felt the prince, bore less blame than the destruction and wretchedness of her dear ones, or even an ecclesiastical court (its suspicions aroused by her passion for financial independence) might have tried to lay at her door. Of her crimes – if such they were – she was totally innocent. And as for her *fall* into the bottom of the pit, where she grieved and deceived herself, nibbling at a bit of withered grass: well, she was guiltless also of that.

Elmina was paying for the (perhaps unpardonable) sins of someone else . . . someone she intended to save; perhaps, thought the prince (who always attributed the finest of motives to Elmina's defects), perhaps without even loving him – perhaps an out-and-out scoundrel. Out of a blind (and accursèd, he thought once more) obedience to her duty.

But duty towards *whom*?

As hard as stone, Elmina was, when it came to duty. To rescue her was impossible. However, perhaps because of its very impossibility, this thought fired the mind of our Belgian nobleman. Therefore to Caserta! To Caserta!

No more than half an hour later, after begging Alphonse to present his apologies to Donna Violante and Donna Carlina Watteau for his failure to come and pay his respects that evening, our Belgian diplomatist, in the dark interior of a blue carriage, was hurrying towards the mechanical city.

A Duke in fine fettle and a madcap in desperation.
Reappearance of the Cracovian spyglass
and investigations into a Neapolitan palace

He found the Duke far from aged, as is often the case with persons of great vitality, indeed not oppressed by emotions of any kind, who therefore preserve their features smooth and youthful. Being not only shrewd but also wise and careful about his health, the Duke, despite his great age, never appeared to grow old. His eyes glittered with delight amid (very occasional) small puckerings of compassion for the follies of this world; which, thanks to his gifts of magic, he sometimes permitted himself to observe, as on a stage, but without having to pay for a ticket.

"My dear Duke!"

"My dear madcap!"

This cheerful, vivid and affectionate expression, once used of him in happier days, was particularly touching to Ingmar, for it reminded him of the tenderness shown him in some measure by everyone during his boyhood, and now seemed to partake of his vague, aetherial yearning for that golden youth.

"Ah, but I am no longer a madcap."

"On the contrary, you really are, dear boy. More so, in fact, than before; because as a boy you were rather serious and fastidious, nothing satisfied you, indeed you demanded – *comme on dit* – the sun, moon and stars. Now look at you, gentle and compassionate towards everyone. And," he concluded with a smile, "if that isn't madness . . ."

"I don't think that's really true," said Ingmar, blushing at the thought of his aversion to the Notary and the boy with the feather.

"Not quite everyone, perhaps, but certainly when it comes to a certain Nanny-Goat . . ."

"Forgive me, Your Grace, but she whom you call a Nanny-Goat is a very worthy woman. Apart from being, as you well know," he added in grave tones, though without due reflection, "my poor Albert's only love . . ."

"I would scarcely say his *only* love," observed the Duke in all seriousness.

The two of them were seated on the veranda overlooking the lovely rose-garden which we admired one fine May morning on our first arrival at Caserta. At this hour the garden, save for a faint gleam which arose from behind the house and filtered through thin scattered clouds in the green-tinged east, was dark and slightly melancholy, perhaps with the intention (in the way in which so-called "inanimate" things often express some poignant sentiment) . . . with the intention, perhaps, of reminding the two friends that time had passed, taking away, as ever, part of the richness of the world and replacing it by things still unknown to them. A gentle breeze perfumed with aromatic herbs and wild flowers, along with a soft rustling among the trees, rose from the surrounding countryside, and every moment (we must not forget that we are in November) the night grew darker and more silvery, as if aware of the infelicity of the world, and the propriety of preserving a respectful silence.

"I sent for you . . . that is, I got a message to you – don't ask me how, dear boy – not only because I wished to express my condolences for the loss of your wife, Geraldine" (here Ingmar bowed his head), "and to apologize for not having done so earlier, though I imagined that it was not a great loss to you . . ."

"Probably not . . . I don't really know," said the prince in some confusion.

"It is not so important. Those who listen to the tidings of their own hearts must surely recognize their authority. And such people are rare indeed," laughed the Duke. "But let that go. For you she was a good and wise companion, a worthy wife, and she certainly now reposes in the Paradise of Wives. The person still bereft of repose is *you*, my dear Ingmar."

"That's very true . . . I am a little tired."

"Then the first thing to do is go indoors and sit by the fire. I have some news for you . . . and there's nothing better than a good fire to shed lustre on the bewitching lies of this world. For such is even the most fascinating intelligence, don't you agree?"

Ingmar gave the ghost of a smile, and the Duke, taking a sly look at his friend and observing him truly serious and rather pale, and noticing moreover that he looked taller and thinner than he had ever looked before, swore in his heart to console him without counting the cost (that is, scruples as to the truth or variations on it) in order to relieve the man of his well-intentioned doubts. And as he led him through the silent, empty hall to the study so secretive, glittering and prolific with dreams, he decided that the best course would be to keep him not too far from, but at the same time not too close to, the thoughts that were torturing him. Some news he did have, but he did not know, and had no wish to reveal, whether it was for good or bad. There are always so many possibilities! All the more reason for Ingmar not to know either.

To this end he constantly kept stealing glances at him, determined to profit from the least indication of his way of feeling, so as to step in with some remedy, perhaps absurd but none the less sovereign. And what indeed would have been closer to his heart than to bring peace, by whatever means, to that desperate soul? (*Desperate!* Exactly what the Duke now thought of Ingmar.)

As soon as they had entered the lovely green-papered room and were seated before the glowing fireplace, on either side of the low table covered with a green baize cloth and strewn with gleaming objects (amongst which Ingmar noticed, with displeasure, the famous lens), old Benjamin began:

"You do not know Naples, my lad, and I fear you might easily be misled by your entourage with false information concerning many things which in point of fact do not exist. Now don't think I am blaming this on any malice towards you on the part of others, or a deplorable tendency on your own part to believe in fairy-tales, but certainly there is a weakness of yours somewhere, a weakness which others take advantage of . . ."

Since the Duke had broken off, the despairing de Neville thought at once of the person who perhaps had deceived him most; so he stiffened, bowed his fine head and murmured: "I must ask you not to mention any names . . . You know whom I have in mind."

"No names. But I have to tell you something at least, or you will be totally lost, dear boy."

"Am I not lost already?" asked the prince glumly.

"Not altogether. In short . . . well, I'll approach the matter indirectly. First of all, two words about the little priest you saw at midday from Alphonse's balcony . . ."

"But wasn't it Don Mariano Civile?" asked the prince in a sudden flash of illumination. In fact, the resemblance which had so perplexed him (leaving aside the girl in the chaise) was that between the priest and Albert's father-in-law. At last he had put a name to it.

"It was not him, have no fear."

From among the many curious objects that lent glitter and interest to the green-topped table the Duke took up a small gilt-edged book, on the fattish side and with a cover of old ivory (it was printed in Germany in 1590). It bore, in Latin, the title *Concerning Dreams*, and even this title gave the impression of great age. The Duke leafed through the volume for a while, then read, his expression being one of amusement commingled with solemnity: "What we see is not always real, and not always does that which seems to us unreal have less power over the destiny of man than does the truth."

Ingmar said nothing, but with all the lustre and intensity of his fine eyes he questioned those of the Duke.

"Dear boy," said the Duke with a loud laugh, "I shall tell you no more . . . It is very certain that the *real* Don Mariano has for many years been far removed from us, sad gentleman that he was; but it is far less certain that our minds do not depict for us fascinating scenes, nor murmur to us what I would call warnings, exploiting the most diverse and cherished images."

A shudder is not a common occurrence, or not for everybody, especially if the shudderer is a man of vast worldly experience and proven philosophical soundness of mind, and accustomed to every kind of relationship with both the useful and the merely pleasurable, with the mystery and the banality of this world. But if a person is rather tired of all that, then a shudder is not so rare. And de Neville shuddered.

"You mean to say . . ." (forcing a smile), "you mean to say that when I looked down at the religious procession on the steps, what I saw was merely a dream or a dread existing only in my own mind?"

"Exactly that."

"In that case the same is true even of the girl in the chaise, whom at first sight I mistook for a waxen image of . . . of the King of Christianity?"

He had, by instinct, touched on the sore point.

"Do not deceive yourself."

"Woe is me," concluded de Neville, with bitterness and self-loathing, "that means that I ought to consult a doctor just as soon as possible."

"By no means. But just to think that it all stems from your pride, my son (and how little, in this regard, do I recognize your belovèd mother and my dear friend Leopoldine, so simple-hearted and alert to emotion and to the secret auroras of being!). But buck up, Ingmar! Accept your heart as it is, with all its little blemishes. Believe me, dreams sometimes bring us a sign, a message that comes from our own selves, as if something in us, or someone aware of us, but of whom we ourselves are unaware, loves us. So listen, and I will come at once to the matter which concerns us, and which you have to know of."

Ingmar had no wish to hear the name of "little" Elmina, or the widow Dupré, and was therefore sitting wrapped in secret sorrow, when the Duke's words, with their touch of good cheer, brought him up with a start. The Duke had at a certain point picked up from the table (removing it from its case, dusting it off with the corner of his silk handkerchief, although there was little need for it) the spyglass which we know of old. He held it out to our princely diplomatist.

"Don't refuse it . . . Don't try and squirm out of it. A house where you were supposed to be this evening will be the scene of our revelations. Through the windows, though avoiding the moonbeams striking the façade, we shall take a look at these apartments; or rather, one modest chamber in particular. It is not being indiscreet. Your good manners will not be called in question, nor will there be a blot upon your honour. And apart from that the object of our enquiry is nothing more than a spoilt brat."

Alert, intrigued, though nagged at by something or someone telling him (or shouting?) in his heart that this was not of advantage to his peace of mind, while to that voice he retorted bitterly that for some time now he had known no peace, Ingmar ran his eye towards the outer edge of the lens (all that was to be seen in the middle was a point of light); then he brought it back to the centre, and to his astonishment discerned there a small study, and a scene well known to him as the child of wealth and good family. But it was not Liège, it was Naples. Near the window was an elegant gilt writing-table, seated at which were a boy and his tutor. The boy, richly clad in green velvet, with a broad lace collar, was not more than ten or eleven years old. His back was turned and, his graceful gold pen-holder resting against one ear, he appeared to be listening to the words of his tutor, a very young priest. After an adjustment to the focus of the lens the latter's words came over quite clearly:

"Right then, young man, are we going to come out with this famous declension? Or is this an awkward moment for you, better suited to other subtle meditations that you have in mind?"

"*Rosa, rosae!*" laughed the child; and as he turned, delighted with himself, towards the invisible observers watching him from afar through the magic glass, Ingmar could not withhold an abrupt exclamation:

"But it's Geronte! The other one, Donna Violante's real heir! At least, to judge by his good looks he strikes me as such . . ." and immediately thereafter Benjamin heard this doleful observation:

"The very picture, if my memory deceives me not, of Albert as a child."

"Not exactly," was the Duke's comment. "I mean, less in his features (though he is a splendid youngster) than in his gaiety, his light-heartedness, his unbridled joy in life."

And, leaving Ingmar the first spyglass, he picked up another to watch the scene himself.

"In that case . . ." (here Ingmar was on the verge of the shudders again) "the other Geronte, the half-witted child with his falling sickness and his blind eyes and that repugnant hen's feather on his head, that living horror so dear to Elmina, is not a Dupré? Or am I deceiving myself again?"

"Very far from it, dear fellow!"

"Oh, what a weight off my mind!" exclaimed Ingmar joyfully, seizing the Duke by the hand. "So if there is another Dupré in the world it can only be this boy – somewhat ill-mannered, I see, but at least not sick or deformed. What joy you have brought me!"

"Do you have such an abhorrence of ugliness, sickness, bodily wretchedness?" asked the Duke in a faintly melancholy murmur.

"Oh, yes! It's something stronger than I am . . . I detest them," replied Ingmar, laughing but a little shamefaced.

"Yet this is what the world really is: horror and decay, small everyday torments and deformities; and there is not much truth in all the rest of it."

Benjamin spoke slowly, gravely, but in somewhat outmoded Polish, so that Ingmar only partly understood, and in any case paid little attention.

"Believe me, dear Duke," he resumed impetuously, "what caused me such anguish was not so much that Donna Elmina preferred another child to Alessandrina – a more joyful child, let us say, and one belonging more to our social sphere – but rather that to Alessandrina" (he was about to add "and me", but checked himself in time) "she preferred the Invalid, the Mental Deficient, the Lost Soul. This struck me as an aberration, a kind of perverseness very far from the angelic image we all know . . . That was what I didn't forgive" – all lively and cheerful, with a meaningless flourish.

"In that case regarding that poor wretch, also called Geronte or Gerontino Käpp (a name for an old man, in my opinion), I shall tell you no more," said the sorcerer meditatively. "You agree? For Elmina he has no more value than an elderly sick relative. Or even a cat stoned by nasty children. It is solely on account of her compassionate nature, always at the service of the weakest, that Elmina gives him preference over her daughter. But not over the real Geronte . . . you understand?"

"Who must be . . . or perhaps not . . . Albert's natural son?" asked the prince anxiously. "Or *in any case* his son?"

"What does it matter now," continued the Duke, once again in Polish so as not to be entirely understood, "if she has a real preference for the skivvy, the outcast, and is at present devoting her life to him? She loves the real Geronte, certainly, but as something additional . . . much as she loves the Linnet, but without being his true follower."

"So . . . what is your conclusion, then?"

For the time being the prince received no reply, and at this point we leave him, trembling and in doubt, to return to the real best-beloved of the Durante-Watteau family, to "Big" Geronte, whether or not he was a secret Dupré.

Continuation of the Duke's supposed revelation.
Prince, take care! Ingmar terror-stricken.
More talk of a certain Käppchen, unknown to all

In the faraway blue of the evening, that is in the schoolroom of Palazzo Durante as viewed through the lens, there appeared at that moment Marchesa Violante herself in a long purple gown, with a fan and a garnet necklace to conceal her neck, to which time had been unkind. Her powdered hair was piled high on her head in a little tower, like a diadem – in short à la Marie Antoinette. Through the white powder then still in fashion amongst the ladies at Court it still showed blond. She was the grandmother of the boy, not his young mother Carlina, who had in fact gone to the ball that evening. This information, delivered in an undertone, was a present from the Duke.

So then, it was Donna Carlina, not her son, who was to go to the ball, contrary to what Teresella had reported about the need to repair the lad's costume. Either it was a fib on Teresella's part, and the lens gave her the lie, or else the lie had been Elmina's. For such a lie (merely suspected, mind you!) there did not seem to Ingmar to be any real reason, and it therefore suggested either incoherence of mind resulting from some traumatic event, or else an inborn disregard for the truth on the part of Donna Elmina – which upset the prince much more. As he dwelt upon it he found himself once more at a loss.

"You are thinking," said the Duke, sympathetic as ever, "that Donna Elmina has lied to you. It does not even cross your mind that the plan to take Geronte to the ball was true, but then, for some reason, the programme had to be changed".

"O yes, yes, you are right! I didn't think of that."

"Well then, just watch."

The marchesa had in the meantime arrived right behind the boy's chair.

"My sweet Gerontino," said she, bending over him, with ineffable tenderness, to give him a kiss, "you will quite ruin your health with all this study. Whatever good it may do you! Listen, Don Sisillo," she added, addressing the tutor (for such was the young priest's laughable name), "would it not be a good thing, for one evening, to give up on all this Latin? If you have a heart, I mean," she added with a fetching smile.

"It would not be a good thing, no. But if your Excellency wishes it, for me your wish is a command."

"I wish it!" the marchesa declared with a laugh.

The exultation of the young student was more than to be expected, however loathsome.

"*Grand-mère!*" he cried, leaping to his feet with glee. "*Merci, grand-mère!* Thank you, thank you, thank you!"

And jumping onto a chair like a cricket or a ballet dancer, with all the verve of his sprightly adolescence, he threw an arm around that stately noblewoman; then, hopping down again he dragged her off for a few dance steps around the room.

"Gerò! Gerò!" she cried. "Leave me alone, I beg you! Just this evening I'm not in the mood for dancing, dear child."

This little scene was typical of those moments when studies are laid aside, at least in very wealthy and powerful families, in which the children are nearly always doted on enough to be able to get their schoolbooks closed for them at any hour of the day.

Growing suddenly serious, though no less affectionate, the boy asked:

"Dear grandmama, are you having troubles with your seamstress?"

"Over Donna Elmina? Well, yes. She was supposed to return this afternoon to bring back a piece of work, and also to speak to me . . . that is, to discuss a certain matter that she has in mind, I haven't exactly gathered what yet. And she has let me know that she cannot meet her commitment. I fancy she has troubles with her daughter."

"What? With that little fright Sasà?"

"Exactly, my child. Poor Donna Elmina is a real friend and an incomparable help to me, but what a misfortune for her is that daughter of hers. If she had to live with a monster Donna Elmina could not be unhappier than she is with that little wretch. She can't stand the sight of her."

"But she's very fond of *me*, isn't she, grandmama?"

"She is crazy about you, child — and you don't deserve it, indeed you don't."

The prince had no desire to see or hear any more. He seemed close to bursting into tears, though he was not a man to be easily touched.

He was also quite shaken by what we may call the *technical* means he had employed, which were amazing enough even for persons already initiated into the magic arts. He put down the lens, which the Duke calmly replaced in its fine case, along with the other, and poured himself out a glass of *alkermes*. His hands were trembling.

For a while neither of these two men of the world, seated gravely beside the fire (though a gay, silent laugh flashed briefly into the eyes of Benjamin), uttered a word. Eventually de Neville, plainly referring to Elmina, exclaimed with the utmost severity:

"I never imagined she was so infamous."

"That is a word you must repent of instantly, dear boy. She is not infamous – how could she be, our Elmina? – but she is sad. And she is sad, you should know, because she cannot escape from her sin. She has been expiating it with all the will in the world for years, but she cannot escape it."

With his heart hammering fit to burst, the prince found himself dwelling on the same old dolorous word, "Linnet", but he dared not utter it.

He needed to marshal his thoughts, and therefore remained for a long moment immersed in silence, his head resting on one hand while with the other he stroked the crystal rotundities of his liqueur glass. Finally he said:

"Duke, are you listening to me?"

"I have done nothing else since you arrived! Nothing but listen to your heart, I mean, with all its disagreeable questions!"

"Whether they are disagreeable I cannot say. But life has certainly been so for some time, at least for me. However, let us not speak of that. But promise me, I beg of you, to answer some other questions, and this time really tangible ones."

"I give you my word, dear prince."

"In that case . . ." Ingmar, with tears in his eyes, was unable to speak at once, then: "Here is the first, the most important: that odious stripling whom she is so fond of (and I say nothing of the other one, who came to the house with the packages – at least for the moment), is he really the natural son of Albert Dupré? Answer me at once, without beating about the bush. My whole life's peace is at stake . . . or rather, Elmina's."

"Stop there!" And the Duke, with a quizzical glance at his friend, also poured himself a tot of *alkermes*. De Neville waited, trembling. "Well, no," resumed the Duke. "Contrary to everything you have understood, or I have suggested to test your state of mind, Geronte Watteau is *not* a son of Albert's. He has no connection with the Duprés, or even with Jib-Sail House. He is a genuine Durante-Watteau: rich, handsome, healthy, capricious, bossy and inclined to look down his nose at others. Given time he will improve, and even become lovable. For the moment he is not, except to those prepared to overlook his defects."

"So much I had already gathered. A lad I'd heartily box the ears of if I were his wretched tutor," said de Neville, quaking with rage.

"You mean Don Sisillo?"

"An idiot, of course, a lackey, a squalid individual. But no more odious than his employer, this Marchesa Durante. So tell me now: *why* does Elmina hate Sasà and prefer – I have understood perfectly, there's no point in hiding it – our Alessandrina's despicable little rival? You tell me why, or I shall have to admit that everything I have understood, or thought I have understood so far in this whole business, has been a mistake, a vulgar error, a fraud and nothing less."

A light of compassion kindled in the blue, ever-untroubled eye of the Duke. He sighed and said:

"*Fraud?* Well said, but not in the sense you mean, not committed by Elmina at the expense of others, but by others at her expense. This is, at the moment, merely a suspicion, but I believe I am right. Besides, my boy, there is one point on which I wish to reassure you at once. In the love, bordering on idolatry, which our Elmina lavishes on this youth, and in the infinite devotion she harbours for his whole milieu, professing a gratitude to Donna Violante which the marchesa accepts, we must admit, sincerely and with true womanly affection, in all this there is nothing that can be traced back to an earlier attachment or love affair, perhaps with Watteau. Not in the sense that you, with your passionate nature and basically Catholic upbringing, would be led to fear. Therefore put such thoughts out of your mind. No, my son, I do not mean *sin* in the sense accepted throughout these seventeen hundred years of Christianity. That is not it. Ask yourself, rather, whether the truly dark side of this predilection for the young Watteau is not the aversion with which she regards all her *own* people, the family to which our unfortunate little girl also belongs, if you will permit me to speak thus of Ali Baba's sister."

"Yes . . . it seems to me that she didn't even love Ali Baba," said the prince with heavy heart.

"Nor Albert. She never truly loved him."

"Nor, perhaps, does she love her present fiancé, Alphonse Nodier!"

"No, it is certain she does not."

"And how do you know that?" demanded the all too kind-hearted prince, with a vehemence in which joy and rage were mysteriously mingled.

"I know it because, sad to say, she does not love anyone, my lad. Except for a certain individual, I suspect, by whom she has unfortunately been deceived. And this makes her misfortune worthy of infinite and heart-rending respect."

The good Duke bit his lip, fearing lest he had said more than he had intended, but for de Neville, totally absorbed in his own personal reveries, it was as if he had said not a word. The Linnet – be he bird or policeman – was for him the only demon in the matter. And the Duke had not yet pronounced that name.

Some little time passed, in a silence illuminated only by the old Pole's compassionate scrutiny of his pallid friend. Then the latter began:

"She, therefore, does not love anything that is good, no moral law enables her to distinguish between the good and its opposite; moreover, and worst of all, she positively prefers the latter. It is in that, I fear, that her sin resides . . ."

"It is not that she prefers it, she chooses it," said the Duke gravely. "Whatever redounds to her disadvantage (in the eyes of the world) is what she complies with. She has no liking for what is really hers, or what is pleasing – indeed she abhors it. Therefore, if we wish to follow such deductions to their logical conclusion, only what hurts, or saddens, her heart, the bitterest things, injurious to her worldly interests, can be said to be loved by her. But this, you understand, precisely because they are not."

"I understand less and less," stammered Ingmar. But he was not so much bewildered as angry and upset. "I have, however, to deduce," he replied, "that I was perfectly right when I thought we ought to have recourse to a priest. And I ventured the opinion that she should see a confessor."

Fire and flames, so to speak, were shooting from his eyes.

"Even in this respect you would be deceiving yourself, my son. No confessor has it in his power to free Elmina from the gravity of her obligation. Perhaps that could only be done by the revelation of the swindle of which she was made the victim when she was still a blameless little child. But for such a pure, faithful heart, would it not be too late?"

"Duke, you are driving me mad! Out with it!" exploded Ingmar. "*Who* (and it would seem for years) has been abusing the faith of our dear Elmina?"

"Who it was who gave rise to this abuse or deceit I do not know. Nor do I know who is at present exploiting it. Maybe at the time it was simply an accident, a mishap, with no really guilty party. But at this point I can only presume that there is a guilty party, and is such because of the deal of evil he is doing to Elmina, never desisting, never speaking, but fearing the worst for himself . . . his own ruin, in short. Therefore, to his own ruin he far prefers that of Elmina. The evil would consist, if I have well understood the secret of that wretched life, in the horrendous calculations of a being – or mere individual? – who is deeply depraved."

The desperate prince, in the tumult of his mind, scanned a thousand names, but none of them, unfortunately, seemed to have anything to do with Elmina any longer except for those of her dead, except for Donna Brigitta and the Glover in fact – and they were dead! There remained – or he could see no other – one ridiculous name, that of the housekeeper, Madame . . . He instantly remembered, or rather *saw* the name: "Madame Pecquod? Ferrantina Pecquod?" he asked, all of a tremble. "Or am I wrong?"

"Poor woman, she'll be ninety by now," said the Duke with a touch of mockery, though he blushed at once, for he also had reached such an age. "No, you are on the wrong tack. Tell me, rather, whether you remember the poor wretch who arrived this morning at the Little House with Sasà's mother? The boy with the hen feather?"

"What! The Porter-Boy? That thieving little rascal?"

"You are doing him an injustice, and this is another instance, dear Ingmar, of your talking off the top of your head as soon as anyone or anything arouses your dislike. He is not a little thief but a poor mental deficient, and if I speak of this it is because I know (don't ask me how) that he is completely innocent; at the most, with that appearance, only an unfortunate for whom Elmina can scarcely conceal her disgust. (Though Elmina's compassion is perhaps essential to the understanding of our story). Tell me rather whether you have heard, or seen written anywhere, the name of a certain Hieronymus Käppchen. My 'researches', as I prefer to call them at the moment, all revolve around this name."

"Käppchen . . . Käppchen . . . Capling . . ." cried the astonished Ingmar after a moment's thought. "Yes, Duke, you are right. I read it this morning in a very dusty document I found by chance in Albert's studio. A boy from Cologne, brought to Naples in about 1779 at the suggestion of Donna Brigitta . . . he was to have been a gift for Don Mariano . . . yes, in 1779. By now he would have been twenty-six, but he only lived for eight years."

"Bravo! And where else have you ever read this name?"

"On the stone bearing the names of Don Mariano's forebears and relatives. There was, indeed, a certain Käppchen, born in 1505. I say 1505, do you see the point?"

(The prince had not in fact seen this date at all, but simply deduced it almost automatically.)

"So he would now be three hundred years old, or about to become so."

"So it would seem. But it's obvious it must have been wrongly inscribed," hazarded Ingmar in a state of bewilderment.

"On the contrary, you saw correctly. And when he reaches that age he will vanish from this world (and any other) for ever and ever. For this reason, to avoid his own extinction, or take his revenge, he is on the verge of madness, and ready to do as much harm as possible. He does not hate Elmina, believe me, but he exploits her."

"At this point, Duke," said the stricken prince, "I no longer follow you. I refuse to. We are still, or almost, in the century of the Enlightenment. I do not mean that I have abjured my Christian faith in favour of faith in Reason, but I certainly take the latter into account, if you will allow me, and in this business," said he, weeping and trembling, "I see an insult, loud and clear, to Human Reason (though not that of the French variety, you may be sure). Contradict me if you dare."

"My poor boy," said the Duke with such gravity that, in speaking of it, even the light-hearted narrator of this tale is moved, "you speak of Human Reason (or French, as it may be), as if behind that Reason there were not another, infinitely greater and, believe me, by no means ignoble. It is that which resides in Nature! Speaking of which I would like to remind you – for I see you have forgotten – of what you heard from the poor Glover in the course of that walk through the graveyard, the day before Albert's wedding, a walk during which he confessed to his downcast state and admired your own grandeur, in speaking of Elmina. Do you recall what he said? 'No, sir, the heart of a woman is, after all, a fairly simple matter. I refer to the heart of Nature herself, monsieur.' And shortly thereafter, when you observed, 'Yes, the heart of Nature is very profound, but how very distant from us!', his rejoinder was: 'Not always, or at least not so far as we would like it to be . . . at any rate in certain circumstances.' These words, addressed to you by the old Glover, were a great lesson."

A great lesson! The prince was as staggered and taken aback as a rather spoilt child who suddenly discovers that old mother Life is in terrible earnest. He made to rise to his feet, as if to take his leave, and a pained small smile of mockery (or was it merely superciliousness?) visited the corners of his mouth.

"Now, Duke," he said, speaking slowly and with an effort at simplicity, "we are going beyond the limits of my admittedly poor imagination. Why should this, according to you, be Elmina's enemy, the one whose intention it is to destroy her, or who at any rate is deceiving her?"

"I did not say exactly that, please understand me. I attribute no malice to him. But weakness, confusion and a desperate desire to save himself and to go on living, cost what it may to his protectress; these, yes. He, you understand, was the secret sorrow of Don Mariano. To protect him, and rescue him – even after he learnt his tragic error – Don Mariano suffered, and loaded himself with debts . . ."

"Was it blackmail?"

"No, it was the blackest despair, which robbed him of all his life and strength. To rescue him (and I still speak of the same individual, whom I prefer not to name), to enable this person to get past that fatal date, which is now imminent – you will recall the pre-announced date you had a glimpse of there in the cemetery, and which falls at this very time and cannot be postponed. This and no other was Don Mariano's terrible problem which he passed on to his favourite daughter. And Elmina, like her father, lived for nothing other than this: to help him to survive the fatal day, and to frustrate the time-limit approaching that luckless Elf."

"Did I hear you say Elf?"

"Yes, my friend, and from now on you had better get used to the fact that this is the correct term."

"Very well." The prince seemed in the grip of some gentle frenzy, or perhaps simply helpless humiliation. "But, my dear Duke, I should like to know how Don Mariano's passion for orphans led him, or induced him, to adopt a demon – scoundrel or cretin as he may be."

"It did not induce him. He was tricked. It was from Donna Helm, who had heard an officer from Cologne speak of him as a luckless child, that he heard about this boy, then very beautiful and pitiful, and made a request for him at Court. He therefore accepted him as a normal child. He did not notice how small he was – no more than a little animal – or his large pointed ears, or see the pure, strange look in his eyes. Above all he paid no attention to how the creature was delivered. The Institution in Cologne, in fact, sent him in a parcel . . . a box with holes in it. Do you know why?"

"I no longer have any idea what I should or should not know."

"Well then, it was because Käppchen was even then subject to various sudden and terrible transformations – the signs of his decay. That box was his kingdom, both during his crises and throughout the long periods of sleep which succeeded them. That box, now very dusty (for the poor wretch has grown in stature, is now nearly of normal height, and no longer fits in it), lies in the attic – a box with a lot of holes in it . . ."

"I saw it this morning. It was in the studio."

"Yes, the poor thing abandoned it some time ago . . . he no longer undergoes transformations, and is utterly desperate. He comes and goes . . . he never sleeps, he bewails his lot . . . And along with him the luckless Elmina. (At least you'll remember Sasà's scratch? He did it. Her sister concealed the fact. But Elmina would sell her soul to save him.)"

"Does she know all about him?"

"I fear not . . . though I believe it would make no difference if she did. She adores him as the most unfortunate of her adoptive brothers and sisters – an invalid, in short. In him she worships a beloved heart. That he is what he is – a child of Nature, or even a delinquent goblin – is of no concern to her. He, for her, is simply her brother, nothing but her younger brother. For his sake she lost her youth, and may well be risking her immortal soul."

So greatly do things amazing and incredible form part of the absurdity of life, and are at one with it, that de Neville had almost regained the calm of mind of a child who waits in happy disbelief for the end of a fairy-story.

"I must be dreaming . . . I am afraid that in some way you must have been tricked. I hope you are not offended," said he when the Duke had finished, forcing himself to conceal his agitation.

"You may be right . . . if you look solely at the likelihood of things, which everybody takes for the truth . . ."

"No, for the moment I accept everything as the truth. In any case, I could not do otherwise. But please allow me to put another question at once. It is fundamental, Duke, and on it depends whether this game can continue, and whether you have not shown yourself to be too easily taken in. What role, at this point, does the Porter-Boy play in this story? What does this wretch really mean to Elmina? And I tell you outright: I accept no lies!"

"You must be joking! You shall have the truth, and at once. The little boy is indeed nothing other than a Porter-Boy, a merciful screen for the terrible individual from Cologne. His perfectly innocent journeys between the Little House and Palazzo Durante are intended to mask the comings and goings of the other. Which take place only by night, and on moonless nights at that."

"You are not telling me – and I take your word 'other' literally – that we are concerned with an individual – young or old, it matters less now – with a person, that is, utterly unpresentable?"

"No, no . . . as beautiful as the light of day – so they say. And malevolent only up to a point. He adores Elmina and she knows it."

This was too much for Ingmar.

"And this, if I am not deceived, in front of Sasà! And she promised Alphonse to become his wife! But all that does not surprise me much. When I came to Naples for the first time I knew something about the hellish life of this city, and the lightness of its women, the laxity of morals. With her beauty Elmina could not but be at the centre of it, so I ought not to be surprised."

"You are forgetting that Elmina is German."

"So she too was found in a hollow tree?" said our Belgian diplomatist with infinite scorn and bitterness. "But please proceed with your revelations, Duke."

"I will not proceed. I know nothing, or almost nothing, about Elmina, except for her infinite compassion, and I have no information except as to her angelic nature. Of *him*, however, fiend or goblin as he may be, I can in effect say nothing but that he is a poor wretch, cut off – by birth – from Holy Mother Church, and condemned, therefore, to total extinction, with an expiry date such as would terrify anyone . . ."

"But is it not possible," asked the prince in tones of sorrow and horror, and maybe with a trace of compassion, "to find out what sort of thing could eventually redeem this person, and renew his permit to remain in this Kingdom (and I do not mean merely the Kingdom of Naples), thereby releasing his sister – as I take it you hold her to be – from this desperate commitment of hers?"

"Nothing more than a valid act of adoption, registered in the High Court of Naples. Unfortunately such a document was never completed, on account of the opposition of Donna Helm's husband, who was then still alive. He had Christian scruples on the matter. Neither, as a widower, could Don Mariano achieve it, since the document required the counter-signature of a wife. Besides, years later even Ferrantina the nurse – for the children were still in the house – was opposed to it. Hieronymus grew up as best he could in the kitchen at Jib-Sail House, concealed now in some coal-bin, now in some box or other, the laughing-stock of the children, with the exception of Elmina. So the poor wretch grew fond of her. He was, at times, incredibly normal and handsome, a divine youth; but at the least outburst of rage he would immediately relapse into that small, deformed creature of the underworld which was always part of his inner self. As time passed, and the hopes of adoption (and therefore salvation) dwindled, the poor thing went into a decline. When Elmina began to grow up, and to understand how things were, she promised her father that she would marry for this sole reason – to put this adoption into effect. For this reason alone and with this intent (she was not attracted to men and had no calling for motherhood) Elmina married our lamented Albert. But this sacrifice, or deception – call it what you will – was all in vain. Albert, brought up to the French way of thinking, simply considered the whole thing laughable. And the reason why now she appears to accept Alphonse as a husband is exactly the same: the long-yearned-for adoption of this young man! Who now, in the world's eyes, is twenty-six years of age, though for those who know the facts – vastly more. And his end is so certain that those two cannot think straight any more. Never has there been such anguish in brother and sister. If you will allow me to say so, I know everything about them, but in particular I know this: only two or three days are left, you must realize, until that hapless destiny is wrought to its end. And then, for Donna Elmina, all will be over."

To which Ingmar, almost with indifference:

"For Donna Elmina? I fail to follow you."

"Because Donna Elmina would die of it."

It may be that our scatter-brained Ingmar was not so stunned or scandalized as the discovery of that plot woven behind the backs of two husbands might have justified, or simply that the outrageousness of the thing (or even sheer indignation) bereft him of any serious reflections; for suddenly, picking up the magic lens as if by chance, with apparent indifference he said:

"I understand how amazed you will be, and please do not think of me, on account of what I am going to say, as any better than I am. I despise Donna Elmina from the bottom of my heart, no less than her brother. But I feel it my duty to intervene – for love of our late lamented Don Mariano. I, therefore, could sign the papers . . ."

"You mean you would adopt this . . . Käppchen?"

"I would do it," replied this bizarre gentleman from Liège, "though evidently only if Elmina accepts me and on condition of divorce, because I would not have her as a wife for one single day. We would separate instantly." And in scornful tones intended to ward off further tears that vengeful gentleman added: "I would hold it to be my right, meanwhile, to claim a frank admission of the facts from Madame Dupré, and her consent to my meeting this individual in person. He has human features, for such was written in the document issued by the Municipality of Cologne. (Were that not the case, perhaps I could not do it.)"

The Duke was hesitant, as if in a reverie, as if he had until then told nothing but colossal lies. Such indeed was the momentary joyous hope of our poor Ingmar; but the hesitation was due only to a perfectly understandable emotion on the old man's part. The Duke, albeit he had vaguely imagined such an outcome, did not now believe it possible. Now, to his eyes, even that good Christian Ingmar appeared as one of the most eccentric of elfin sprites.

"They say. . ." he began, in the odious manner of the Scribblerus – and this brought another question into the prince's mind: why had the Scribblerus, although so devoted to Elmina, not put himself forward as the poor wretch's adoptive father? But at once he repented of the question, as of the vilest of thoughts, and told himself that Elmina, with that pride of hers, would never have allowed an "inferior" to know her family secrets. And to consent, what is more, to the loss of another soul. For in fact, thought the prince, whoever adopted that *individual* would certainly not save his own soul. The anathema of Mother Church would follow as the night the day. Not to mention the charge of witchcraft, if the full atrocity of the secret became known.

As if he had read his thoughts, the Duke spoke:

"What you ask me, whether you can meet the poor thing, may be a possibility, given the influence Elmina has over him and the desperation she harbours in her heart. But perhaps you have given insufficient thought to your own soul, dear prince. You would automatically be excluded from the Church, as – guiltless in her credulity – is Elmina. I am on good terms with Cardinal Alexander, the celebrated Court preacher (at present at the Baths for his gout) and I might be able to stave off the worst. But an anathema would be certain. I hope you are aware that the Church regards Nature as its worst enemy, considering her the true mother, if not grandmother, of the Devil."

"I know it, alas," returned the prince, lowering his eyes. His mind fled back to all his experiences in life, and he felt unjustly privileged in comparison with the "sins", if such they were, of the trees and plants in general. "But," he went on, "and I ask you to believe me, Duke, my soul is worth less than the grief of a woman . . . and of an individual such as Käppchen. Are they not in a state of desperation?"

"Indeed, they are," replied the Duke gravely.

"Then it is enough," said the prince, making to rise. "I consider consenting to the sufferings of others, sinners or enemies though they may be, is the worst of all sins. It will not, therefore, be mine."

In any good novel, even modern, which does not stray too far from the aesthetic canons of the eighteenth century, at this point, after the thunderbolt called "Recognition!" (the validity of which we shall verify later), the Narrator who has respect for himself and, rightly, for the expectations of his readers (who ask for nothing other than that those expectations be prolonged, and to this end have invested their modest sum), draws breath, takes a fresh sheet of paper, and in bold characters inscribes the gladsome and liberating legend: *New Chapter*.

And we shall do likewise.

The sufferings of a prince and
his latest (almost acceptable) reflections

In the sudden and unnatural silence that had opened in that abstruse conversation like a whirlpool at the bottom of the sea, the most unhappy and tumultuous thoughts once again began to flit about (or more precisely, to *dance*) in the mind of the prince. And it behoves us to make immediate mention of an extraordinary detail with regard to those thoughts: which is that to the promise just made, which by dint of the adoption of Caplet, or Käppchen, involved the loss of his own soul, he paid no attention whatever. Perhaps because he had never thought about his soul and the worth of it, or because he put no value on it, or because the fantastic, and probably mendacious, side of the Duke's story, together with the avowed fearsomeness of Käppchen, had already become blurred in his mind, and all that harrowed him now was his dislike of the Porter-Boy, and his distress at the protection accorded him by Elmina. That was the really painful thing. And he would have given almost anything to protect (or rescue?) the presumed Elf, instead of his wretched double, the boy with the feather, who forever weighed on his heart as Sasà's most odious rival, and his own. A repugnant figure, as being far more "needy" than the famous Käppchen, and in whom – seeing Elmina's compassionate nature – he now thought he discerned the "Great Enemy". Even the little goat that went bleating up the Steps at Chiaia was certainly a reverie of her, or else, in turn, a substitute for the Porter-Boy. And thinking of those two creatures, who struck his imagination as Elmina's implacable creditors, or the tax collectors of Eternity awaiting her heart, he was seized with absolute despair. To them, from different motives, Elmina had more or less dedicated her life, and so she still did. The same was true of Don Mariano: hence his sadness, and the punctured box that he took with him in the carriage, by night, from Jib-Sail House to the empty apartment in Chiaia which he was destined never really to live in. Around his loved one the prince saw nothing but little monsters, natural or otherwise, souls already lost or souls about to vanish for ever, who came to her clamouring for something, even for life itself, and unscrupulously blackmailed her. This enabled him almost to understand the poor woman's preference for the frivolous Geronte Watteau, who at least did not constantly remind her of her duty and remorse, but only of the lovely, easy-going scene of life that could have been hers. Elmina, in short, was making an *expiation*. But for what? Unless it be, indeed, the fault of others (Don Mariano's insanely rash propensity for fatherhood, Donna Brigitta's despotic harshness, and the thoughtless selfishness of Albert who had, with a mere laugh, rejected the idea of adoption?) And then, at the outset, the cruelty of whoever had burdened a son of the Germanic woodlands with a human fate and destiny, a thing manifestly impossible, for which other people now had to pay the price? It was on that account, he now saw, that Donna Helm had fled, and her children had forever deserted that fearsome Jib-Sail House. And maybe Floridia had fallen ill, and even Ali Baba had died from sheer loneliness and loathing of his mother – and that morning Albert had tried to stab her. Poor wretched Elmina! And now the only creature near her was Sasà . . . and he realized why the child took wing. Bewitched! She too bewitched! And on every side was heard the lament of the Linnet . . . Which in turn was the lament of sorrowing love, the thankless love of all who had been drawn to Elmina, and were lost in her damnation. He also understood, or seemed to understand, why Elmina as a child had slain Floridia's Linnet – because she heard that echo in her heart, and wished to hear it no longer.

But there had to be a way, he thought with sudden wrath, to capture both Sasà's "uncle" (already he thought of him as such) and the boy with the feather, and thrust them back into the abysses where they belonged. Firstly to prevent them – whichever was the true culprit – from scratching Sasà again, but above all from continuing to humiliate Elmina, stilling in her every murmur of affection – or at least of gratitude! – towards those who adored her.

Yes, the solution was this: to free Elmina from her mourning (thus could we describe her "debt" towards the ill-fortune of others) by adopting her unhappy "brother", and finally by means of a third proposal of marriage to replace that already forgotten by Nodier. Both these offers, of adoption and marriage, would bear his own signature, and should carry the two of them far from that devilish city of torturers and victims.

Not for one moment did he think of being able to leave Naples and the erstwhile Olympus, now gradually transformed into the Underground

City he well knew, except by taking with him the woman who had once been Albert's. By this time, in his way, he was just a poor Mediterranean gentleman, and he could never have abandoned those whom he considered (rightly or wrongly we cannot say) to be his kindred in the Dream.

Further apprehensions

More than once in the course of that long silent reverie the Duke had taken an anxious glance at the lens, which was producing a faint ticking sound, as if a watch or other infernal gadget were concealed in its interior, and had for some time been emitting a strange, wavering green light from the imperfectly closed case, an indication that scenes were still going on within. The impulsive de Neville had not observed this; indeed, heedless of the yellow-liveried butler who had appeared discreetly at the gilded door of the study to announce luncheon, he, entirely wrapped up in his unjust thoughts, abruptly returned once more to the obsessive subject of the imaginary figures glimpsed from Alphonse's balcony. It had occurred to him that there in the Procession he had noticed neither the Porter-Boy nor Alessandrina.

"Forgive me, Duke," he enquired, "but why is there such bad blood between these two children, the boy with the feather and our angelic Alessandrina? Simply jealousy? Or may the little girl, with the wonderful intuition of children, not have discerned in the wretched serving-lad the double or counterfeit figure of her hypothetical *uncle* ... of the scoundrel who is blackmailing her mother? Is this why she hates him? In that case" (with a tremor in his voice) "she would be capable, would she not, of a lofty concept of justice?"

A melancholy smile, not without ambiguity, crossed the old man's fine features, and his expression of serene goodwill was tinged with irony, with doubt, though also with some severity and reserve. He confined himself to saying:

"Perhaps there is also that. But the little girl in question, your adored Paummella, dislikes the boy instinctively – no, not on account of the protection afforded him by her mother, believe me, but merely because he is crippled, half-witted and above all wears a filthy old hen's feather. In that feather so pathetically flaunted she sees a real snub to her *petit bourgeois* soul, to her craving for *success* (for that is how Sasà is, for the most part, and her dreamy looks belie her); so she persecutes, or at least abhors him, for this reason alone. It is chiefly she who would like to see the poor, foolish, tender spirit that is Gerontuccio, born only to serve in some low den somewhere in this city, humiliated and chased out and finally banished by the family."

"Born!" exclaimed the prince with scarcely a thought to what he was saying. "Born, you say! If spirits *are* born, and have not – as I think – always existed and merely *appear* and *disappear* and constantly return to the places they have loved, as the stars return to shine over the landscape just where they shone in the beginning!" concluded Ingmar, much moved and powerless to help himself. For the first time he had pity for the lad: compared with the fearsome Käppchen he was an angel.

"Yes, born," replied the Duke as in a dream, still referring to the poor ragamuffin of the household, "but born dead unto life, to success, to the world, to the light of any noble city; as, for exclusively ecclesiastical or dynastic reasons, if you like, is the *other*, the child of the woods and flowers, the ancient Käppchen. But for Geronte 'the Second', fate has perhaps been even more unkind – because of his feather and his innate idiocy. For this reason Sasà – destined to be an exquisite young French noblewoman, I hope – cannot stand the sight of him. For her, who in that small birdlike heart of hers already cherishes dreams of marrying the real Geronte, Geronte Durante-Watteau, the boy represents nothingness and death. She even slanders him, believe me, and her terror of him is in no small part intended to set him and Elmina against each other. In truth it is Gerontuccio who is afraid of Sasà, and it is for that precise reason that Elmina always flies to his aid."

"Unhappy mother," said the prince without much thought, though he had been struck far more forcibly by the future which Alessandrina appeared to have in mind. He therefore resumed:

"Marry Watteau when she is grown up? As her new father I shall naturally prevent it. A good-for-nothing, a dowry-hunter!"

"You forget that he is only twelve years old."

"But can't you see what he has done to Alessandrina!" demanded Ingmar indignantly. "He has made her vain, frivolous – and always ready to argue with her mother."

The Duke observed him with a curious expression:

"Her new father, did you say? Of course, I was forgetting. Let us hope she accepts you."

The prince flushed and stammered, "For myself . . . I don't know that it matters all that much. The reason for my proposal, as you know, is purely and simply to rescue this stricken family. Elmina and I could separate immediately afterwards, as I already told you," said Ingmar, lying in his teeth. "Incidentally, who has the documents relating to the first adoption, the one challenged by Colonel Helm?"

"I believe they are in the hands of Don Liborio Apparente, or at least a copy. The day before yesterday, in her desperation, Elmina applied to him. She was not expecting Nodier's proposal, which now, alas, has been retracted. Another copy should be in the drawer at the top of the cupboard in the corridor."

They had risen to their feet, and were on their way to the doorway of the study, where the butler was still waiting, the Duke in cheerful spirits again, Ingmar still gloomy, when they were turned in their tracks by an even shriller sound, almost a whistle, proceeding from the lens case. The sheer pressure of the images had caused it to burst open of its own accord, and from it a vivid light was cast on the green tabletop, while Neapolitan voices and sounds of agitation proceeded from it.

"I expected as much!" said the Duke with some apprehension and, opening the case completely, he handed the other lens to the prince. The latter snatched it from him, while the butler withdrew, silently closing the door behind him. The prince looked into the lens . . . Let us do likewise.

Teresella enters the lens.
The Porter-Boy runs away, and the ribald jingle
of the Coppers' Nark. Elmina's distress

Visible at once (as a flicker like a candle receded into the depths of the lens) was the previous scene: the moonlit façade of the palace and the schoolroom of Geronte Watteau. But Don Sisillo was now standing some way off, near a mirror, as if scandalized; and the same was true of Donna Violante. For lo, see now the sudden entrance from the wings – if we may use the theatrical term – of Elmina's sister, in a yellow bonnet and flowered blue cape, and, if we may so speak of a girl so graceful and restrained, wringing her little hands. The manservant who had shown her into the room, where, as we have seen, Don Sisillo, his pupil and the latter's grandmother still were, lingered in the doorway unable to contain his curiosity.

"Forgive me, marchesa, for bursting in like this!" came the bold but troubled voice of Teresella. "Don Alphonse has sent me to see if . . . if your friend my dear sister is here . . . if she has come here by any chance."

"No, my child."

"Because, you see, my sister is nowhere to be found . . . Donna Elmina has disappeared."

It was not so much these words which filled de Neville with anguish, as something which had not escaped the Duke either, and struck pallor to his cheeks.

Behind the servant (for the record, a certain Geronzo the Foundling), on the threshold of young Watteau's schoolroom was standing the little Sufferer of that morning, the double, socially speaking, of Hieronymus Käppchen, uncle to Sasà. The boy, raising one indescribably dirty hand, and himself suspended between horror and astonishment, appeared to be threatening Geronte Watteau; but his little unseeing eyes (beautiful in their way, of a mysterious blue, and full of innocence and bewildered good nature) were focused much further off, and – no doubt about it – on Caserta. They were fixed on where the two gentlemen thought they were seated unobserved: they were fixed on the prince.

"He has seen us!" exclaimed the Duke, perplexed, though also touched with emotion.

"And what have you to say about it, Duke?"

"That certain phenomena – he seems to be aware of your most intimate thoughts regarding himself – do not conform to the rules, or at least the rules of paraphysics I have studied to date. He does not hate you, poor child, but he is reproving you. For the rest of it, don't worry. Donna Elmina might easily have gone down to Naples to do some shopping . . ."

"In the pitch dark?"

"I do not think she has great need of light – or of the natural world in general. She carries her own moonlight in her heart."

"I have no doubt of it. But the fact remains that I don't think she has much money on her. Indeed I am convinced that she has none at all," the prince replied in panic.

"And so?"

"I don't believe she has gone down to Naples to go shopping. I think she has rushed down the steps because someone ran away from the Little House before her. Whether it was Sasà, or her uncle, or this moron Gerontuccio I have no idea. But my heart is trembling. I feel that some grave peril is threatening Sasà, and perhaps her mother . . ."

"Or else, perchance, the poor dumb lad? Don't you spare a thought for him, my son?"

Gerontino, as seen through the lens, had raised an arm to shield his face. The fact is that our young scholar, turning round by chance, had spotted him, and with the sudden fury of haughty, pampered youth had yelled out:

"Coppers' nark! Coppers' nark!"

And the poor mute (as it were by definition) was unable to reply.

At once the young marquis, who had the manners of a guttersnipe, started up a ribald jingle then all the rage among the urchins of Naples. It ran:

> *The coppers' nark, the police toady*
> *Carries the letter to the Lady,*
> *But the Lady wants none of it*
> *So off he runs, the little squit.*

In which the word "nark" clearly stood for the Porter-Boy and the opprobrious term "police" without any doubt referred to the little boy's grim protectress, to whom he was wont to turn when in desperate straits.

Hearing those scornful tones the wizened little boy drew back with a curious sideways motion, at which point our diplomatist noticed an astonishing physical peculiarity: at least at that moment Little Geronte was completely transparent, so that beyond him could be discerned the sumptuous furnishings of a small salon, and further off, through an open window, the clouds in the sky; he drew back as far as an elegant bureau furnished with secret compartments in which our young student used to hide dirty books, and there (not seeing things close at hand, on account of the superhuman acuteness of his vision, which perceived only distant objects) he tripped and fell. Teresella had seen him, and went to his aid, but he fought free of her kindly hands, like a poor cat tormented by street urchins – or a little goat. He turned completely white, shrank to half his size, and dashed from the room, while Don Geronte Emilio Watteau burst out again with his chant of victory:

"Coppers' nark! Coppers' nark! I'll tell my granny and have your sister sacked. You deserve to die of starvation, the pair of you. As for you, they'll drag you off to the Reformatory!"

And now well in the vein he struck up with another warcry of the riff-raff of Naples, chanted whenever they saw political prisoners, suspected of favouring constitutional government, trudging in chains through the streets. This was the well-known:

> *Arraggiati, Canaglia,*
> *che stai dentro al Serraglio!**

"That is not proper, young man," came the velvety and somewhat timid voice of his grandmother.

The scene then seemed gradually to cloud over. When light returned the unhappy child was no longer there.

"He has mistaken him for Käppchen!" thought the prince with a slight shudder, suddenly realizing that he was being rather incoherent, for he was actually aware that the "student" almost certainly knew nothing of Käppchen. Not only incoherent, in fact, but still not a little unfair. But Elmina's cruelty towards all those around her, with the sole exception of the boy with the feather, was really and truly hard to take.

"Hark," said the Duke at this point, putting one lens to his eye, the other to his ear, "I think the lad is making his way home or perhaps simply

---

* Which may be rendered: "Rage away, you rabble/ who are rotting in the prisons."

wandering in the dark. It is poor Elmina calling him . . . Can you hear her, prince? It is certainly her!"

A distant murmur of water came to their ears, and then the prince heard the beloved voice. It contained a note of anguish and indecipherable lament:

"Lillot! Lillot! My little kidlet!

"Come back home, Lillot!

"Do it for your mother's sake!" (her actual words).

"She thinks of herself as a mother to that wretch!" burst out the prince, though with an ominous calm veined with mockery. "This means she really does love the worst of all, as you said before, Duke. She prefers him even to her own brother. How much lower can one sink?"

"Whether or not she prefers him I do not know. Neither do I know that he is the worst," was the Duke's cautious rejoinder. "But bear in mind, prince, that this Lillot — as she now calls Gerontuccio — is a child. And persecuted to boot. As well as turning out, as you know, to be her dependant, and therefore, if I am not mistaken, with some right to be cared for."

"The second orphan, therefore!" exclaimed Ingmar in exasperation. "With further rights again, no doubt? It would appear that everyone has a right to Elmina's aid and assistance except those who love her! Donna Elmina is truly inexhaustible in her passion for the afflicted and dependent — the very same, I now see, as Don Mariano! And now this! *Lillot*, what a sickening name she gives the little cripple. It's a bit much, I must say, even for a father-to-be, and Alphonse was right to pull out of it. Therefore it's up to me! I do not forget my promises . . . But two children is one too many."

Our diplomatist's heart was as heavy as lead and as turbulent as a volcano on the verge of eruption.

"Do not take it awry, Ingmar," said the good Duke kindly, almost in a whisper. "This *second orphan*, or adoptive relative — as I see you regard the serving-lad — does not exist, at least in the heart of Elmina. For one and one only is she throwing away her life, and that is the desperate wretch from Cologne. But 'Lillot' is the name she has always used, from girlhood on, for anyone who ravages her heart."

Envy once again gnawed at Ingmar's breast.

"Well and good! I am reminded of a certain M. Guillotin! Nodier probably did well to drop her. This name, Lillot, is a sentence of death for Elmina's real friends!"

This ghastly remark did not get a reaction from our Sorcerer. Well he knew the excesses that grief (and human jealousy) can run to, and was therefore inclined to overlook, rather than rebut, such observations.

"She loves no one but the lost soul from Cologne," he said gently, after a moment's thought. "But, resonant as a violin, her heart responds to any breath of wind that calls him to mind."

"Lost soul?" queried Ingmar, no less in sorrow than in anger.

"Yes, *lost* I said, because he is a child in spite of his many metamorphoses. He has no chance of return. He is not a citizen of this world. Do not forget that in two days he will be three hundred years old. His time is almost done. And we also know for certain that Alphonse is no longer enamoured of Elmina, indeed he has renounced her in favour of Teresella and spares not a thought for her. And in any case, in the course of a lifetime, it is only once that you hear the Linnet . . . and Alphonse, unlike you, has never heard it even that once. The adoption which might save the life of this unhappy creature is now entirely in your own hands."

"Lillot, Lillot! my darling child!" As faint as that of an ailing girl, the voice of Donna Elmina continued to reach their ears. And at last the two men at Caserta focused on her in a place in Naples. To be precise, in the midnight blue of the night, on the famous Steps where the Procession had taken place. By the hand she was leading a very downcast Sasà, and was shedding silent tears. In the other hand she clutched her shopping bag.

One rival had no sooner disappeared (Ingmar had not even noticed, and in any case no longer thought of, the Duke's last words concerning the now imminent death of the old Elf of Cologne), than the real rival seemed far more invincible than the first – this so-called Lillot, the cripple of the Little House. Yes, more invincible. Him indeed it was (adorned with the title of "Kidlet"), yes, him indeed it was whom she truly loved, thought the despairing Ingmar once again, and he went close to finding excuses for the shocking conduct of the young marquis. Coppers' nark! Well said! He remembered in time that he had made a promise, that he had to see at once to the adoption of Käppchen. Having got the old Elf out of the way, he would have the Kidlet (who he doubted not had made his own way home) shut up in the celebrated Reformatory in Naples; and at this point to take flight with Elmina and Sasà would be a matter of little difficulty, but the most important act of his life. Therefore, as if throwing off his desolation at still finding himself burdened, instead of

Sasà's much-feared uncle, with this ridiculous, best-beloved Kidlet (for by such a name this godless woman had addressed him!), the prince came to his senses completely, or so he thought, on account of the tears that were running down his cheeks.

"You must excuse me, Duke, if I decline the offer of supper, but I have to make a dash to Naples. Donna Elmina and Donna Alessandrina will shortly be back home, and Alessandrina will be too much alone in that hovel (which I have never liked), with a custodian, responsible for her safety, who is not a little infirm. I do not even know if Donna Elmina, in her folly or cynicism, has not decided to stay there on the Steps in search of that misshapen wretch. In which case, Sasà might return to the Little House on her own, and might not her uncle, deranged as he is, commit some atrocious mischief? No, please forgive me, but I am too worried . . ."

In point of fact it was not so much worry about Alessandrina that so kept him on tenterhooks, as the thought that she, Elmina, was, at that hour of night, out and about with that horrendous "Goat".

Such, dear reader, is sometimes the inattention (or blindness?) of the most acute diplomatists, or of the finest minds in general.

Once more the Duke gave him a compassionate look.

"Do not despair, dear prince," said he, casting another glance into the lens and then snapping shut the lid of the box. "The moon," he added by way of explanation, "has suddenly gone behind a cloud, so the lens no longer functions. Do not despair, I say, because in the first place I know certain things about your cherished Paummella that render excessive concern quite needless . . ."

"What do you mean by that? But then, of course, we are in my opinion already in the realms of the absurd . . ."

"I mean simply this: she is a child who knows how to defend herself, no more than that. Whereas I would not swear to the same about you, my boy, or about another person whom you dislike. Anyway, it seems to me that you are already too agitated to relish a single mouthful of your favourite soufflé that I have had Armand prepare especially for you: you will enjoy it some other time. I shall now order the carriage – or are saddle-horses swifter? Off with you . . . do not stay away from where your heart is. I will warn Alphonse to expect you. As soon as you arrive you will receive fresh instructions as regards your sublime gesture of compassion . . . Or have you forgotten it?"

"No . . . no . . ." said Ingmar in confusion, though in fact he was struggling to remember what promise he had made.

"Go therefore, blessèd boy, where your heart leads you, to the most disconsolate creature in all Naples, and the other who is stretching out her little hand to you, and bravely offer them your protection."

But to which of the two fair creatures now installed in the life of our unfortunate gentleman from Liège – the one with the ring or the other, the godless one – the Duke was particularly referring, it was, in view of his melancholy smile, really impossible to determine.

A hectic colloquy in the night-time.
A prince bewildered and the unexpected threat
of a mortgage on the Little House

We shall not follow de Neville throughout the wearisome return journey from Caserta to Naples, partly because we cannot see him. The moon, as the Duke has said, had really clouded over, and the darkness of night, aided by a silver-hued drizzle, continually concealed the luxurious carriage as it passed amidst hills and woodlands.

It was already very late when its wheels rumbled over the flagstones at Chiaia, at the corner of the Steps. Not a light, not a voice, but absolute silence; though from time to time a small white hand emerged from between the sullen edges of the clouds and brushed the rooftops, made a sign, then vanished. Nodier's residence, the Palace of the Spirits, was as we know on that very corner, and Alphonse himself, accompanied by a manservant, was waiting before the great doorway. He was already in his nightgown, over which he wore a sumptuous blue robe in the Chinese style, adorned with small rose-coloured dragons. The expression on his face was of the merriest.

"Hullo there, friend! Nothing to worry about! She's back."

He explained to the prince that he had been alerted from Caserta: "Don't ask me how, there was a letter for me in the vestibule, saying that you had been *en voyage* for several hours, and in great distress over Donna Elmina. It's a pity about your soufflé. The Duke told me everything."

Alphonse's gaiety and exceptional liveliness astonished de Neville not a little. He had expected – after all, the new engagement had not yet been officially announced – to find him downcast, or at least very upset, if not positively resentful towards Donna Elmina for all the trouble she had put him through. His cheerfulness struck the prince as rather curious, and even displeasing, in view of the danger (of which, however, the good Nodier knew nothing) which threatened the luckless Käppchen, and his sister's consequent despair. But this, as also his decision to intervene, he decided for the moment not to mention to the fiancé before him (though it was still unsure *whose* fiancé). It would have been too ostentatious.

"Come home, has she? Where has she been?"

"You could never imagine! Or perhaps you ought to have done so. To visit Don Mariano in the cemetery."

She was so terribly afflicted, thought the prince (half dead from tormenting and far from pure-minded jealousy, though he did not yet know of *whom*), as to feel impelled, rather than turning for help to her friend the marchesa, to prostrate herself before her father's tomb. She did not (of this he became increasingly certain) genuinely love his merry friend Alphonse, as in fact the Duke had realized, and she had no wish to marry him. She would have married him only to obtain the adoption of the poor creature from Cologne, just as she had married Albert for the very same reason, and now, of course, would marry him, de Neville. Perhaps not a wicked woman, but of questionable morality. But in spite of this the prince had committed himself to ask for her hand in marriage! His thoughts therefore wandered, hopelessly astray, from one abyss to another, finding no way out.

"And the Porter-Boy? The urchin who does odd jobs for her, is he back too?" ventured the prince, hoping with that vulgar word to minimize the boy's attractions.

"What urchin?" Nodier had forgotten all about him.

Nothing more came into Ingmar's mind, because it is part of human nature, when it suffers too greatly, to be on its guard, to stay a thousand miles away from the heart of things, from the truth of them; and we say this not with reference to our noble friend's impassioned heart so much as to the truth itself, which was far more subtle and shameful. We refer to his jealousy of the "coppers' nark" – *that* was the thorn in his flesh. No longer, or far less so, was the so-called "brother".

He felt depressed, bewildered, and very agitated.

"If that can put her troubles to rights," said he sardonically, referring to the visit to Don Mariano, "so much the better for her. If I were in her shoes I wouldn't think that the most effective way for a good mother to resolve the problems of her children . . ."

"But if she has only the one . . ."

"Very well. But the number is not fundamental in these matters. And then it comes to my notice that she has relatives, and thinks of them as her children . . ."

"If you are referring to the Porter-Boy" (Nodier had finally tumbled to it) "I can't help laughing."

"Heavens no, not the Porter-Boy . . . But you must admit that for her there's no distinction between those who love her and those who exploit her, between realities and phantoms, between genuine noblemen and base wearers of, for example, hen feathers," said the prince in tones of real dismay. "There's no distinction."

He realized that he was slightly beside himself, and that this state of mind was becoming too obvious to Nodier, who was in fact regarding him in some amazement.

"You've gone to all the trouble to rush back here tonight, but Alessandrina" (and he regarded him keenly) "was not in the least danger."

"That may be so – for you. Because you don't really know how things stand at the Little House."

He bit his lip, fell silent. He had no wish to say – for now he was certain of it – that the house was haunted. In old Naples, as in modern Belgium, they hastily sold off those dwellings in which the persons who entered them could not always be distinguished from dreams or airy vapours. He did not dare to add, in the total uncertainty which was becoming his habitual state, that his belovèd herself, Donna Elmina, was the haunted one. And he well knew *by whom*. The most to be feared of the haunters was certainly not the young man from Cologne, who was only trying to save his skin by pushing his sister into a third dishonest marriage (and here de Neville would staunchly keep his promise); no, the most to be feared was not him, but the "other", the miserable "Coppers' nark" as the young marchese had dubbed him: he who had not hesitated to transform himself into a little goat, a "kidlet", to scamper after his (the prince's) Nanny-Goat!

Yes, he was the real enemy!

The two friends, preceded by the servant bearing a lamp, climbed to Nodier's apartment, leaving the street even more forsaken and bizarre than ever; bizarre in the sense that down on the broad, cracked Steps for a while, as they stood on the balcony enjoying the soft night air, the two gentlemen observed, moving about in absolute silence carrying sacks and the flames of tiny torches, a number of small figures apparently collecting something. For Nodier – whose heady gaiety, together with that touch of uppishness that always accompanies the less noble moments of happiness, now seemed to have replaced the obsessive thought of his love for Elmina – those little figures were simply gatherers of any kind of refuse, bits of fruit and vegetables or even the stalkless heads of flowers left scattered on the ground after the morning market, destitute Neapolitans who lived on such pickings, just as a century and a half later, after the wars, they would devote themselves to collecting cigarette butts. But for de Neville, immersed in his sad thoughts about the supposed reality of the world, the explanation was less banal. Watching those small hump-backed figures, a light in one hand, skipping up and down that shabby abandoned thoroughfare, it came to him to say:

"My dear Alphonse, how mysterious and dreadful this city is. I no longer know if I am waking or dreaming."

Nodier cast him a humorous glance, while in the room behind them the servant, jug in hand, was preparing to pour fresh coffee into the little Sèvres cups.

"Meaning?"

"I don't know. But my heart quails at the prospect of leaving Alessandrina Dupré here when I go."

"You could take her to Liège, there is nothing to prevent you," was the calm reply, which still failed to touch on the broken engagement.

"You know that Sasà adores her mother – that prevents me," said the prince in deep distress. "She also has her little friendships in Naples." (He did not dare to add what still seemed to him the most brazen of these, that Sasà had got a bee in her bonnet about the young Marchese Watteau, and in the innocence of her heart already considered herself engaged to him. She would not leave him.)

"Yes, it's true" (this in answer to *adores her mother*). "And I must admit that Elmina is not a very tender mother to that creature."

"She was not to Ali Baba and she is not to Sasà. The worst of it is that none of the reasons you will remember we attributed to her unconcern for her daughter (I refer to the presence of a third child, also Albert's son) any longer hold water. Albert left no third child to any woman in this city. He died, sad and lonely, in his infinite fidelity to Baba. Geronte Watteau, whom we imagined as Alessandrina's rival (in Elmina's affections, that is) was a complete outsider to Albert and his family."

"All the better," said the dreamy Nodier.

"You fail to grasp the problem, Alphonse," said the prince, altogether neglecting to specify how and where he had obtained all this interesting information. And that was the least of it, since he neglected even to hint that, apart from Sasà, there were two other children whom they had imagined to be real catastrophes in the life of Elmina, one of whom, the "old" creature of Cologne, was not even thought to be of this world, while a certain inexactly specified Lillot – also known as the Kidlet or the boy with the feather – was downright notorious as a police informer or spy for the Bourbon government. (We mention this confusion of the prince's regarding his most "hated" rival because it was beginning to be one of the major causes of suffering in his thinking – if it was really thinking – about the poor Porter-Boy, or stand-in for the Elf.)

"I fail to do anything of the sort," was the merchant's somewhat vexed reply. "I realize that Donna Elmina is a woman with many problems, and baffling ones at that. Also I don't think her way of resolving them is as advisable as could be wished."

"Have you . . . have you found out something about her?" asked the Nanny-Goat's unfortunate admirer, his heart in his mouth.

"Yes – that she is extremely superstitious. All straightforward solutions are out of the question for her. In addition she is distrustful, and this does not add to her attractions. She never confides in anyone – and I mean never – and at times is in complete despair. I refer in particular to this very moment. When you left here today Notary Liborio took me into his confidence" (since the prince had departed only *after* the Notary had taken his leave this was a plain invention on Alphonse's part) ". . . and spoke more openly. I confess I was a little disconcerted. No – not the business of the children, that is nothing. It appears that there is a mortgage on the house at Posillipo, and that she can scarcely find the wherewithal to pay off the last instalment left owing by her father, Don Mariano, during his lifetime. It seems, moreover, that the creditor is a relative, and quite relentless, who is claiming this debt simply in order to gain possession of the house. If she loses the house she will have nothing left at all. The Scribblerus informed me that she has no savings put aside (this is merely a detail, believe me, and in view of my promise would certainly not worry me; but it shakes my confidence in her), so she could not, as she was said to be contemplating, open an atelier. She is not, therefore, even sincere."

Although in his mind the prince felt absolutely unable to judge anyone whatever, he was utterly taken aback by Nodier's mention of the mortgage and the atelier, in fact the widow's whole wretched financial situation, as if that situation had not, until that very morning, been one of his loved one's chief attractions for the wealthy merchant. Not to speak of the cold, detached tone in which he expressed himself, as if he were no longer in fact the fiancé of the poor shirtmaker, and cared very little about her. A conclusion which eluded all conceivable comment.

"Do you . . . Forgive me if I am being indiscreet, but the matter is serious," began Ingmar after a while. "Do you, Nodier, despite what you have just told me, still consider yourself Elmina's husband-to-be? Is she, for you, still the ideal wife?"

To the questioner it did not seem that the man at his side, standing on the balcony in the calm Neapolitan night – as ten years previously at the Hat of Gold, and now merely a little fatter – had reflected sufficiently before replying. He heard him say:

"Yes, certainly . . . No doubt about it, I think."

And at this point we should observe that perhaps for the first time in their lives, that is for at least twenty years of carefree familiarity, there was a real distance between those two: they were lying to each other, the one very sad, the other merely a little worried. De Neville, in fact, felt with genuine despair that Nodier had abandoned the idea, or rather the fixation which had burst upon him unawares, of being a father to Sasà; he had abandoned Elmina and her troubles to the shades by which she was persecuted. So Elmina was wandering helplessly, followed step by step by those two delinquents who never left her. Would she marry *him*? And was he in fact happy at the prospect? It seemed to him now that he felt nothing for Elmina, as was true also of Nodier. In his case his old friend's anxious and harassing questions had made him aware that something in his heart of hearts had really and truly changed. He too could say, though in far grosser terms than the prince, that he no longer felt anything for Elmina. The reason for this he did not wish to formulate for the moment, or even think of it, and we shall not betray him, but it was certainly not the mortgage, or the other troubles, or her own difficult character, or even the matter of the bad relations existing between the two children, the legitimate daughter and the poor outcast, or the part the latter played in Elmina's life (for Nodier the boy seen in the morning *was not* the mere image of another child present in the heart of Elmina: he was a poor, live mental deficient, about whose "dangerousness" even Teresina had for some reason lied). No, the cause of his change of mind lay rather in a new outlook on happiness offered him by life at the moment when he had set eyes on the French shepherdess leant up against the glass bell-jar. That shepherdess, with her rosy little countenance overflowing with health and happiness, was an exact portrait of someone whom Nodier had been familiar with for years at the Little House, and to whom, like an idiot, he had never paid the least attention. She it was, the ideal wife! And now, although he was not entirely aware of the fact – not, at least, in his conscience as a gentleman – of Donna Elmina he thought no more.

"No doubt about it!" exclaimed Ingmar suddenly, repeating his friend's words with stupefaction and bitterness. "So you observe her desperation with complete indifference! I cannot and do not understand it, friend. Tell me at least (and forgive my nosiness) whether you know Elmina's creditor, the one who imposed the mortgage. I take myself to be acting as Elmina's friend and yours if I propose to pay him a visit."

He seemed, as in a dream, to hear a quite lunatic word, and was so terrified that he did not ask for explanations. That word, or series of words, was as follows:

"*Le Poussin!* Friend, you must search out *Le Vieux Poussin!*"

Harrowed to the utmost degree, the prince imagined for a moment that Nodier must be alluding to yet another person, perhaps a criminal, who had long since installed himself in the life of his poor loved one, and who went by the name – obscure and ridiculous as are all nicknames in the underworld – of *Vieux Poussin*. He therefore dared ask no further question, or even breathe; and he did well, for a moment later there followed the absurd, but this time perfectly acceptable, explanation:

"You have every reason to be puzzled, dear friend," resumed the merchant unexpectedly, though to some extent reacting to the hint of suspicion which he had cleverly perceived in the prince's last words, and which answered his own need to save his face and character from the charge of skimping on probity (and if by piling up such false excuses he contradicted himself, we may easily justify him by reflecting that he was a *gentlemanly* fiancé attempting to shirk a promise that had become unendurable); "you are justified in being puzzled, but you will be less so when you have considered what I learnt this very day, and have not yet divulged to you. It is simply this. Donna Elmina is not without ties in life, above and beyond those we know of, and this would have mattered little had she been straightforward. But she kept quiet about it. I don't know whether or not you will credit it, but she has a brother or half-brother, insofar as he, like her, was "adopted" by poor Don Mariano. He is a young man from Cologne, a poor half-wit whom she adores, who has for years been living in hiding somewhere in this city with her people – the Civile family! All very civil, I *must* say!"

The prince thought that the merchant, rather than announcing a truth, had in some way read his mind and exploited it, and this swindle on his friend's part now gave him a hunted feeling. He fixed upon him the wide-eyed stare of a cheated child.

"Forgive the question, forgive me if I repeat myself," he resumed, trembling ever so little, "but a short while ago, my friend, I heard you utter the phrase '*Le Poussin!* Friend, you must search out *le Vieux Poussin!*' which is not clear to me. What did you mean by it? Could it be the name of one of her creditors, perhaps the most ruthless? The one who now intends to gain possession of the Little House? And – this surprises me – could there be any connection between him and the alleged 'brother'?"

He had let this phrase drop simply to gain time, not because he considered it humanly possible to get a reasonable answer to such a question. The answer he did get terrified him.

"Think what you like," snapped out the merchant, knitting his brows to feign the maximum of consternation and, of course, reproof. "Think what you like. I wanted to say that this individual, whom she calls brother – and to be precise that Hieronymus Käppchen of Cologne whose birth certificate, you may remember, we discovered yesterday morning among the papers in the studio – this individual at times, as a result of I don't know what work of the Devil which has to do with the sick personality (I don't want to say ignorant and superstitious, though so it is) of our dear lady; this individual, I say, transforms himself into a bird, and even into other children of Nature, and acquires talons, horns, hide, feathers . . . and in this way he hopes to defend himself. This is what happens whenever he is in a position of danger, and this is the reason for the scratches we saw on our poor Alessandrina's face. Yesterday morning, when he saw us, he was hidden in the house, and was afraid of being caught and punished. On account of this, if we get married, Teresella and I have already decided to clear the place out: Donna Elmina will leave, taking her dear brother with her, and if possible her cherished 'Lillot' as well. And Sasà will remain happily with us."

There was not a word in this whole rigmarole that contained a single grain of common sense, while the cruelty – all one, naturally, with joy and fullness of life – could not be denied. And now the poor prince no longer said "It's a slander!", as in the days of his happy and indignant youth;

he merely tried to struggle free from a vision of things that tormented him (of the already much-feared identification of the Porter-Boy with the rogue of Cologne he did not think at that moment, simply because in his troubled mind he did not know where to place the being who appeared to be known as *Vieux Poussin*, and along with him also poor Lillot).

"So then . . . when you say *Vieux Poussin* you are not, I hope, alluding to the Porter-Boy?"

"No, not to the Porter-Boy," said the merchant off-handedly (still improvising and anxious only to slander Elmina). "I am referring to the young man from Cologne. But he is no chicken, and still less an old man. He is simply a sham! He follows Donna Elmina from dawn till dusk . . ."

"So . . . so devoted to her?" was on the tip of the unfortunate prince's tongue. But he checked himself in time to hear:

"Fear, my friend, fear and fear again is all there is to that simpleton. He never learnt to do anything in his life, and he's certainly had time enough (three hundred years, they tell me!); that's why he was the thorn in Don Mariano's flesh . . . Nothing, you understand? Because he has an abject terror of the world . . . no work . . no fellowship . . . Just dreaming and mischief: that's how he sacrificed Donna Elmina! If Donna Elmina leaves him (or is happy, which comes to the same thing – you should hear him blubbering when he's alone!) he goes and hides, he dies. For him Donna Elmina has renounced all happiness (and you as well, in case you don't know it, my poor Ingmar), almost without any hope of release; and this solely because it was her father's command."

"And is she . . . does she know . . . that he is hoodwinking her?"

"Hoodwinking? How do you mean?"

"That his species is not human," returned the prince, remembering the Duke's confidences. "That he is only an elf, perhaps the last of them, a lost soul in this world ever since the declaration of the Rights of Man and of his consequent sovereignty."

Alphonse stared at him without grasping his meaning.

"I don't know whether she knows or not. To her, he's her brother. And for Donna Elmina, alas, there is no law stronger than the law of brotherhood."

He went on, speaking to himself as in a dream, while the prince simply looked at him – or more precisely looked at the darkened houses behind him.

"Yes, it seems really impossible that a creature as proud, free and joyous as Donna Elmina was as a young thing – you remember her yourself," he added with a touch of emotion, "that evening, all in pink? – has ended up this way, just to keep alive an old fowl not only useless but dangerous. All the same, confidentially, I have heard from a footman, a friend of Ferrantina's, that there is a hope. Once, under the wing of Elmina's charity, he attains thirty years of age – they say he is now twenty-seven – he might become, or re-become, a normal young man, as at certain times he was at Jib-Sail House. She, I believe, is looking forward to this date when she will be free and happy. But three more years! That is why I cannot marry her. Time passes for me as well, dear prince."

"It passes for everyone," said the prince heavily, coming back to himself (though only superficially, hence his calm). "In any case, I have heard something entirely different, but it concerns only those who are devoted to her. You, perhaps, no longer are."

"Tell me, man! Speak up!" cried Alphonse angrily.

"It is this. The 'boy' cannot even live for two more days – forgive me the word 'boy', I know that you would like to say 'fiend' – unless someone adopts him as a son. Which I am about to do, if you don't mind. Though not without the consent of Donna Elmina. It requires the consent of a legally married couple. Elmina is no longer married, and is not yet remarried. Therefore, if you back out, I will marry her myself."

Nodier was all surprise and, at bottom, indifference.

"You are getting yourself in a fine pickle," he said, "with a mad wife and a step-son expelled from the Church."

"Not expelled, with your permission, but born outside it," corrected the unhappy prince.

"If it makes no difference to you . . . you will of course be setting yourself of your own free will among those who are dead to Justice."

"Small loss, considering what Justice does in this world," replied the prince, who never forgot the occupation of Belgium and the infamous onslaught of the French Revolution.

"As you wish," said Nodier, speaking somewhat at random, because he was astounded at how the prince had taken his inventions seriously. "However, don't imagine that I will be a witness at your wedding. I it was who first set eyes on Donna Elmina" (but we know what a lying statement this was, for that evening at Jib-Sail House the three young men had all been together). "And there's another thing: if that wretch should really die, take it from me that he shall not be buried in the garden of my house – I don't wish it. The box with the holes" (Heaven knows how he knew) "you personally will take somewhere and bury it under a bush. Not at *my* house."

The prince stared at his old friend in utter bewilderment. He would have liked to shout, but a dry sob seemed to choke him. "My house . . .": so the Little House was now his. "*The box with the holes . . .*" The whole ghastly past, the fate and humiliation of Elmina, the suffering of Don Mariano, and the anguish of a poor reprobate, child of the flowers and the woods, enveloped his brow like a cloud. But he decided to behave as if the story unfolding before him were a quite different thing, were something fine and good!

The conversation concluded as follows.

Nodier (still on the balcony with his back turned):

"Not for my sake, mind, but in your own interest, dear prince, I tell you: leave her alone, have nothing to do with her. She is a woman bewitched, and not even as good and kind as she might sometimes appear. There are other things that I won't mention, because you know them anyway and I hate to repeat myself. But in a word, she is not a woman to marry: whoever approaches her and looks at her is lost. For me, the real reason for the Linnet's anger! The Chimaera of these parts! Albert and Ali Baba, in their time, simply by gazing upon her were turned to stone!" He heaved a sigh. "If you have really made up your mind, then do it. But I don't envy you, and I say it as a friend."

Ingmar was unable to reply at once to all this. He felt, indeed, turned to stone.

"In any case," he said after a while, forcing a smile, "you have already broken off your engagement, if I am not mistaken."

"Yes, obviously. It's just that I haven't spoken to her about it yet. But I think she will find the matter quite understandable. Obviously" (he repeated the banality) "there will be compensation on my part, and in this way the question of the mortgage will be arranged. But thereafter I hope and expect that the Little House will remain in the hands of my wife and myself. We shall make a different place of it, just wait and see! I have great plans."

Everything, for the prince, became once more shrouded in mystery: the name of the new object of devotion (although *one* name *had* been mentioned) and the actual feelings of Don Mariano's elder daughter, as well as what would happen to her and her "brother" in the event of Ingmar's being unable to bring off the third proposal of marriage. The merchant persisted in staring at him fixedly.

"Do you know what the real obstacle is?" he asked at this point with a snicker. "You won't even imagine! Little Hieronymus has a morbid attachment to that house. I don't know if he can be persuaded to leave it, supposing he survives. But one way or another he *has* to leave it. I am determined to apply, if need be, to the Police, and they, as you know, don't play around."

(The snicker continued.)

For Ingmar, however, there was nothing more to learn. He seemed to have entered a world of monsters, in which the vilest acts were considered most praiseworthy or perhaps directed towards some Christian logic solely if they served the purposes of the interested party. He realized in the end that his life had been changed, that the world was this way – and that no one could delude themselves that they could shake its fundamental inertia with revolutions or courts of law, or begin to understand it without first having visited its underground cities, the woeful cities of the heart, the bedrock of all great political upheavals and consequent petrifactions. There lay the evil: in the heart disposed to falsehood, and unconscious of its own ignominy. And in the hard, cold Donna Elmina, cold at heart but also in speech, in her underlying poverty and ignorance, in her eternal *No* to any of the propositions of *la Joie*, he began to perceive some kind of excuse – but for all that he did not forgive her. At the thought of the woman he loved he felt he was dying, and yet he hoped . . . but we do not know exactly what he hoped.

"Satisfy my curiosity on another point, my friend," he said, momentarily turning his face, pale and thoughtful, from the view of the darkened Steps to the welcoming radiance of the drawing-room (and incidentally to another footman who had now entered, and was standing with inscrutable features in the light of a candelabra, while Nodier turned to face him). "Satisfy my curiosity, if you please, by telling me whether there is another, a true explanation of the conduct of this . . . brother; yours does not convince me. Tell me if you know why the boy is so afraid, and what, after all, he is afraid of. I have not yet understood; but I feel that this fear of his is the cause of all his sister's misfortune."

"What can I say? In any case I think I've already told you. There is no other explanation. He is frightened! But not of anything in particular, being beaten for example, or even of prison. He's frightened of the whole of Christendom, the whole of Humanity – I don't know what he sees wrong with it, it's really so nice – and above all he's terrified of the Rights of Man, of the Constitution. This I was told by the Scribblerus. He has a real horror of the human species – all of it, you understand? – and of the whole species he would save only Don Mariano and dear Elmina, because (and this is laughable) he believes that they, like him, are two elves, or children of the flowers. Anyone Christian, or of any other religion, for him is Horror personified and confirms him in his dangerous (and I say *dangerous*) terror of the world. What do you think is the significance, in fact, of his passion for that filthy hen's feather he wears stuck on his head?" (At least for the moment the terrible import of this allusion completely escaped poor Ingmar, distrait as he was.) "That feather, very much the worse for wear, is the last token of his ancient bond, his bond with nature in the truly natural state, as the child of some creature of nature, of the woods, of a bird, of a fowl . . . With it he feels safe, and weeps for joy, whereas with us humans, what can he do but die!" And with a sudden surge of compassion, that belied all his foregoing spite, and falsehood, and slander, Alphonse Nodier added: "Poor little fellow. Better than your precious Paummella. Tell me, prince, do you still love Alessandrina Dupré?"

Ingmar replied with a vague nod.

"Beware!" cried the merchant, persisting in his sudden *volte face*, his bewildering contradiction. "I say no more. Although a child and innocent of everything, she is worse than her uncle."

"Käppchen is better?"

"It may be so. She is full of schemes. Käppchen has none. Only the breath of life . . . the peace of a garden . . . his big sister near him like the night, like the calm, fresh voice of the waters . . . that is what Elmina is to him."

Shattered by the sound of that sacred name, and as if groping to find out where he was, the prince turned back indoors.

At the other end of the room the second Footman had deposited another tray on a gilded console and, standing before the heart-shaped mirror (tarnished in the middle) which hung above it, was patting his grey hair into place with two fingers. After which he lowered onto his head a fetching white wig, a mass of ringlets with a pigtail, which he kept always about his person. In the meanwhile he was singing to himself a cheerful melody well known to Ingmar, the ancient air "Paummella, skip and fly". Then, recovering the tray, turning briskly and heading for the door, he broke off his song, while from every part of the Steps and every room in the Palace of the Spirits resounded the age-old refrain of the Linnet, the joyous lament:

O-hoh! O-hoh! O-hoh!

Whereafter, rising in volume and fleeting and swiftly fading:

Flutter, flutter, flutter, fly little Linnet!
Flutter, flutter, flutter, Oh! Oh! Oh!

Like a memory it was, or a long, unavailing plea, though whether to love or to death was not to be known.

The balmy-blue but no longer hopeful night of
a heart at grips with the recent changes of the world

A note which he found in his room when he retired for the night, the second message from the Duke to reach him by God knows what necromantic routes, left the prince indifferent. It was brief and earnest:

> Do not be discouraged by the strange things you are witnessing, my boy, *c'est la vie*, and you have courage enough. Instead, tomorrow morning at eight, a carriage bearing one of my servants will stop outside your house – *pardon*, your friend's house. Get into it and go wherever it takes you. Ask nothing during the journey, do not enquire of the servant where you are bound for, but trust in your devoted friend,
>
> Benjamin

For de Neville there was nothing to do but obey. However, he did not go to bed at once. He stayed out on the balcony, which corresponded (on the left, and divided from it only by a buttress) to that of the drawing-room, where Nodier was still standing, looking out at the Steps. And for an hour at least, as in those good old days when they had arrived at the Hat of Gold, he stood there listening to the sounds of the balmy-blue night, the cloudy but none the less blue night of Naples. Above all he was moved by the odour of sweet verbena, and then the happy voice of Nodier beyond the wall, softly singing: "*Nenna mia*, skip and fly . . ." The young man was thinking of Teresella! Ingmar, for his part, no longer dared to be critical about anything. In his new situation as a traveller both lonely and lost, he could only trust in the loyalty and kindness of his mother's old friend.

Eventually he went indoors and fell asleep, dreaming of a certain Poussin who came and asked him for a loan, and to whom he brusquely replied, "Come back later, I haven't got time just now." Flatly, like that, without remorse or fear of the Bourbon Police! But such, at times, are dreams: one loses or forgets a long precious upbringing which instils benevolence towards this world; a world which, on the contrary, is not benevolent at all, but – especially towards princes and children – somewhat persecutory and prone to play nasty jokes, or at least to mockery. As we know from the words young Watteau addressed to H.K., than which nothing could be clearer: "Rage away, you rabble / who are rotting in the prisons." A mockery, or a warning, certainly addressed by the Great Unwashed to all the political prisoners of that time; but also, and more cruelly still, to all the prisoners of that or future ages who may be called the Prisoners of The Dream. As we see them at dawn, passing before us after a sleepless night, their steps resounding in the void of the streets, their eyes fixed on the still distant Aurora . . . shackled, in fact, by The Dream.

VI

The Dead

In November. Reappearance of Donna Brigitta and Don Mariano. Voices and games among the tombs. A disappointing conversation

The following day, as often in November, or other times in late autumn, the day was clear and the air, if possible, even balmier than the day before. In truth the sky, with its gentle fleecy cloudlets ("pecorelle", as the common people call certain rarefied, silvery gossamer patches that in luminous flocks, one behind the other, seem to be grazing the pastures of the pearly air); the sky lit up the noble and to a certain extent cheerful Phlegraean city which, if glimpsed (hypothetically speaking) from the clouds by a gossipy bird of passage, would have appeared as no more than a heap of rubble, a patch of mauvish stones prickly with church towers, intersected by long coloured fissures in constant motion (human, perhaps?), and enhanced by precious zones of neoclassicism (and none the worse for that: we must remember that Vanvitelli and the eighteenth-century style was all the rage with the well-to-do of the time). Neighbourhoods that were poor and pastoral, or else gloomily Spanish, descended in scattered herds from the hills, to end up squatting wearily on the seashore, near what is now Via Marina. And the sea, that morning of a translucent sky-green – at least where the sky above it was clear – though cold, reflected everything: the castles, the piazzas, the colonnades, the gardens, the hovels, the inns, exactly as it had ten years before, when the wingèd company of Bellerophon had clattered in its noisy carriages from Porta Capuana. The House of the Hat of Gold, on the side of the piazza facing the jetty, was still standing, and there were the carriages with their roan horses, there were the flower-girls, and soon would come the great ladies to make their purchases in the smart English or French shops in Chiaia. But at that hour all was still sleeping. Visible also were the white sails of English ships. At that moment His Majesty irritably tugged aside his bed-curtains and at once called out, *"Gennariello!"* (for example, this being the name we dare to attribute to his most trusted manservant) and commanded coffee. He liked it rather sweet, though to take it without sugar would have been better for his health. But this does not concern us, and indeed our opinion in the matter is of no interest.

Here, however, is what touches us closely. It is a small figure. We recognize our downcast and ever-indignant prince – he looks pensive this morning! Yes, it is really him, seated in a purposely modest and anonymous carriage (in accordance with a later, confidential arrangement of the Duke's), a carriage which seems bent on being anonymous, and which was following another, a hackney carriage, which also made its way towards the streets, and thereafter the quiet grey-green hills, of Poggioreale, where the great Cemetery is situated. Behold poor Ingmar (or rather, behold his carriage) . . . it is not far from the gates. He looks about him, recognizing the places which one day, under the *Ancien Régime*, when he was the charming, convivial leader of the revels, witnessed his meeting there with his poor friends: with Don Mariano, in fact, and the humble Scribblerus. Ah, how much time had passed and now . . . nothing. He was on his way to visit Don Mariano in the cold house to which the Glover had retired from the splendours and disquietudes of this life, there to pass the time-without-end that followed his happy, fleeting stay at Jib-Sail House. This had been the Duke's enigmatic and peremptory injunction in a second note conveyed to him by the driver: to go to the cemetery, First Courtyard, the Old Chapel – by now the habitual dwelling of the Civile family.

For some time, then, another carriage (perhaps descended from the clouds, lowered by invisible stage machinery into the tranquil autumnal scene?) had been preceding that of the prince, and at the same slow, sombre pace. Like his, it was a shabby hackney carriage with blue upholstery, and a horse which hung its thoughtful head and swished its tail forever to and fro, either from old habit or a memory of summer when the flies used to plague it (they knew whom to get at, the little fiends, always going for the weakest). But, from one moment to the next, this carriage simply disappeared from sight. But finally we espy yet a third carriage, this time very smart, with a baronial coat of arms on the door, standing empty near the cemetery gates, in attendance on people of wealth and consequence by the look of it. The coachman, not an attractive person and averting his face as though he knew it, was standing before it in a bored, sullen slouch. On his head – a bizarre note in an altogether dubious costume, and in stark contrast to a horrendous drab frock-coat which reached to his boots – he flaunted a pointed gold cap. His cheeks were hollow and ashen. Seeing the prince's carriage approaching he promptly withdrew to a clump of trees, as if afraid to be seen. Ingmar, on arrival, scarcely gave him a glance; but he felt his presence, like a distant waft of music upon the air, and was reminded of another morning, at Sant'Antonio, when another cab-driver had subjected him to just such a glum, worried scrutiny. It entered the prince's mind, as he looked at the carriage without really taking it in, that a certain unhappy woman had recently alighted from it; but he coldly thrust the notion from him. Not only because the carriage was so stylish, but because it was certain that at this hour *she* was still up there in the ill-omened studio, sorting out Sasà's ragged garments to hang out to dry in the windy garden. And he seemed to hear Teresella's cheerful voice calling, "Elmina, what shall I do with these stockings of Sasà's, shall I bring them in?" And he saw Sasà secretly running and taking flight on the other side of the hedge. A strange little lady!

As we have already had occasion to mention on an earlier page of this story, from the central avenue (very clean and tidy) which began at the gates, two paths branched off, both of which, winding their way and hidden at times behind simple, unpretentious chapels, and even some in mediocre classical style, converged on the same place, which we have already visited: a quiet square to the north of which stretched a vast unkempt area on which the square itself seemed to border with some misgiving. At the very edge of this area rose, we will remember, the Old Chapel, or tomb of the Civile family. But Ingmar, his thoughts elsewhere, walked right past it, so that he arrived at the new chapel built by the Glover for Donna Brigitta, and still the property of the Helms, in spite of the fact that, formally registered in the name of the Baroness, it was intended to constitute a gift from her to her second husband (or at least her devoted companion for half a lifetime). On arriving Ingmar walked twice round the elegant, single-storeyed building, graced with a pediment from which winged cherubs eyed the visitor, and a façade with capitals and blind windows, the latter in turn being decorated with vases of dried flowers hooked onto the sills. Then, spying an open side-door into what in effect was a tiny church, lit through a square, unglazed opening, he entered. Therein were the tombs themselves, five or six of them, on which were repeated – gilded or blackened or totally erased by time – the inscriptions which figured on the façade outside. Here he found Donna Brigitta von Helm reposing (as the saying is, though who knows if it is true) by the side of the late Colonel Baron von Helm. Here was Floridia Helm, aged twelve. Not to be seen, on the other hand, and the reason was perfectly evident (this not being the legitimate burial place of the Glover and his family), were the respective places of repose, or play, of Albert and Ali Baba. The name of Don Mariano was inscribed – though merely as an "honorary guest" – but there was naturally no mention of Nadine and others whom the prince, while not identifying this as the place he had seen before, vaguely remembered – names that had appeared but once and then vanished: *Albert Dupré*, aged two, *Hieronymus Käppchen* (Caplet), aged three hundred. No, these he did not find, a clear sign that they had been removed elsewhere (or perhaps only momentarily removed from the memory of our illustrious diplomatist?). Better so. It was not, however, a thought that left the visitor easy in his mind.

"How come," the prince was therefore wondering (since uppermost in his thoughts were obviously the unfortunate children in the case, the heir of *La Joie* and the desperate Elf), "how come this muddle in the inscriptions, this coming and going, these names appearing and disappearing? Was there muddle even then, before the famous '89, over the respective roles of the souls of the dead?" Thus was he wondering when a sound of soft steps, a muted mutter of conversation (muted out of respect for the place), distracted him; and drawing slightly aside, to the left of the little window, he at once saw three persons approaching the Chapel. There they were! And *they* – no doubt about it – were Elmina Dupré, her daughter and the Notary. The sight of the latter, depressed and dejected as usual, made him realize that the widow – as he now called her – was on terms with the man of law such as had not previously been made by any means clear, and that the Scribblerus was in all likelihood fully aware of Elmina Dupré's bankrupt situation, that is of the details of her bankruptcy, and perhaps also of the misfortune of "Caplet". He was astonished not to have realized this earlier, and also that the matter was actually of little interest to him. The third person in the group, who in view of her stature might perhaps scarcely have deserved the name of "person", was indeed the sweet Paummella of the Little House, Albert's orphan. She was clad entirely in mourning, like the evening before last, her features pale and sorrowful, and her presence seemed to indicate that Elmina's feelings towards her had not gone entirely to wrack and ruin. She had preferred to bring her along, unwilling to leave her alone with Ferrantina in that gloomy house. Maybe Teresina had gone to do the shopping or, worse still, was to have a secret meeting with her new lover (though Ingmar no longer dared condemn her) and the little girl had successfully appealed to be allowed to accompany her mother and the Notary on a visit to her grandfather's tomb. At her age, thought the prince, there was nothing that failed to give pleasure and diversion. But he did not think of her mother's unwillingness (and we shall see how unnecessary such a worry would have been) to leave her alone with her "uncle". Ingmar therefore found himself in the state of mind between indifference and mental disturbance which seemed to have become habitual to him, the logical consequence of his emotion and the wounds inflicted on him by the merchant the previous evening; and he was just changing his position, shifting his weight from his left foot to his right, when the sound of voices, familiar and yet no longer so, caused him to make a bold move closer to the window opening. Lucky for him that a little column in pseudo-Doric style concealed him perfectly.

And here is what he heard (we are now dealing with the occupants of the third carriage, which we glimpsed standing near the gates); and what he heard, before catching sight of anyone or anything, reduced to nil his already inconsiderable grasp of what was going on. Uppermost in him at this time was we know not what shortcoming of emotion (or perhaps it was only extreme absent-mindedness).

We record the voices, therefore, in the colourless form in which they reached his ear.

> *Harsh female voice* (with heavy Casertan-German accent): You brought the little Miss, I see, Elmina dear. Clever of you! The better to touch my heart-strings.
>
> *Voice of Elmina* (grief-stricken): I assure you, *maman*, that wasn't the reason. It's just that I didn't know whom to leave her with. Madame Pecquod is ill.
>
> *Harsh voice*: Wasn't Teresella there?
>
> *Voice of Elmina* (quavering): Teresella doesn't love me any more.
>
> *Calm, affectionate man's voice* (*very* attached to Donna Elmina): Pray do not say that, dear girl. That is the beginning of bitter sinfulness. A great sin, is jealousy. Besides, I gather that Teresella has recently become engaged.
>
> *Voice of Elmina* (without inflection, dull, downcast): Yes, recently. Yesterday evening.

*

What the mystery of these voices might be – partly because he had for a long time known Naples to be an "underground" city, a place of suffering, where many epochs and human conditions frequently switched about, partly out of his natural discretion, and above all because of this new feeling of detachment from "other people's business" – the prince did not ask himself. Clearly these were the same people who had played a part in the life of the Glover, not to mention the Glover himself, and whom he (the prince) knew well, either directly, like Elmina, or indirectly, like Donna Helm. The fact that they were all there present, the living and the less so, did not worry him; he merely deduced that their intercourse (shall we call it domestic?) had never ceased. He was rather more surprised by the nature of their relationship, which was revealed at once as being strictly financial. He soon realized that they were talking about money. But the emotion involved, insofar as he could still take in emotion, was not this. What struck him, what even shook him into at least a semblance of distress, was the submissive voice – sounding for the first time in her life a tearful note – of Albert's former loved-one when she alluded to Teresina: "*She doesn't love me any more.*" To argue from this, as had the Man's Voice, that the cause of her vexation was jealousy, did not pass muster, and he found himself thinking of Elmina in terms which disarmed him, reducing her once heroic figure to more human, or more feminine, proportions. She had promised herself to Nodier and, despite her aversion to worldly things, she had believed in the man's feelings, believed that a man still loved her; and she was now forced to acknowledge that the charms that had been hers in the days of Jib-Sail House were really and truly hers no longer. She neither attracted nor enchanted any more. He saw her diminished, and in her unaccustomed, mediocre grief stripped of all the fabulous grandeur he had attributed to her; and along with himself (shame on you, de Neville!) he felt sorry also for the luckless Käppchen and the humble Porter-Boy. Over nothing but her shattered dream of bourgeois rehabilitation was the poor seamstress grieving now. "*She doesn't love me any more.*" Indeed Teresella, and no other, had stolen her fiancé from her.

Coldly referring these words of the speakers back to the depressing scene of the previous evening, the prince was therefore certain that Teresina and no other was Nodier's new flame, if not his passion (which she was not!). The engagement to Elmina was really broken off. Therefore once again there yawned the chasm, not only emotional but financial.

Perchance for this reason, to beg for help from creatures at one time dear to her, Albert's widow had come there with her daughter and the faithful Notary at that early hour of the morning. Exactly *who* had organized the meeting was less clear to the prince, who saw in it, however, some angelic answer to human prayers.

Thus for some moments our good Ingmar stood and thought. He no longer knew whether to be illuminated with joy or visited by fresh sadness. Clearly (he told himself) Elmina's real troubles no longer appeared to be either her "brother" or the Porter-Boy, the two delinquents who dogged her footsteps. The question was no longer either "moral" or emotional, but purely financial: the Little House threatened by a mortgage. That was what Donna Elmina was thinking about. Obviously, he found himself reflecting with relief (that we dare not call infinite, but which fell not far short of it), the adoption of her half-brother was no longer necessary; nor would Elmina, after the merchant's poor showing, have so much as considered another of Albert's friends.

This, at least, was what the prince chose to deduce; but deep within himself he was so uncertain whether his duty was not to keep his promise of adoption, that he found himself trembling. Anything, anything! he thought – or his desperate heart thought for him – but a family bond with the Elf! Even if it meant Elmina's ruin? "Yes," he replied, "even that! I don't want to die for her shameless affections!"

At this point he heard the voice of the Scribblerus, and compared with the everlasting dejection of the man, it was unusually precise and forceful:

"And now, ladies and gentlemen, let us not lose sight of the issue. We are here to settle a dispute lasting, if I mistake not, since 1776, the date of the donation, and which in my opinion ought to cease. Or have we forgotten this?"

There followed a brief silence during which the prince, at the peak of consternation at the sordidness of mundane and financial interests, a sordidness that even infected the dead, perceived a gentle rustle in the air, and passing on his right saw the glum and strange Paummella. He saw her flit, like a butterfly, to the top of a memorial column, where she remained. His pulses throbbed madly (in despite of his supposed resignation) as he heard the voice of the one who in all in the world caused him most heartache:

"Sasà, come down from there at once!" mildly she said.

"*Maman,* I won't hurt myself," replied the little girl imploringly.

After which none of the Voices thought of scolding her further. Therefore, grave and firm, the voice of the Scribblerus resumed:

"Ladies and gentlemen, let us not forget the matter in hand!"

And the Harsh Voice: "But do not forget, my dear Don Liborio, that money is money."

"My client is not forgetting that!" Both rueful and unyielding was the Notary's retort.

Some moments passed, and then again the voice of the Harsh Lady:

"That is not how it seems to me . . . if you don't mind."

And a moment later:

"Sasà, leave Geronte alone. Shameless hussy!"

Ingmar could not see all that much, but it was enough to cast doubt on many beliefs of the age – accepted by him until that moment – regarding the natural sincerity of children; ideas not supported, it seemed to him, by any proper notion of their even more natural bellicosity and, at the very least, their inclination to use dramatic means for bad ends. Alessandrina Dupré, the luckless little orphan bullied or (worse still) ignored by the mother and her pseudo-uncle, was at that moment suspended in mid-air, chasing and teasing the wretched Porter-Boy (he too was there, then?). And what with? A woman's hat, a crest of red feathers sprouting from a pale grey brim, which she had removed from a bench and was now tickling his neck with. Donna Brigitta's hat, for sure, for Elmina never wore such a hat. In any case the prince had seen his Paummella in the act of grabbing the hat from the bench, as a sparrow in flight will snatch up a crumb of bread and be off. But he was also astonished at the docility of *Geronte* – clearly, he realized, a metamorphosis of Little Hieronymus ("Little" because short in stature, but the diminutive was then very commonly linked with names, and even the child of the woods had been dubbed with it). The identity of the two figures did not at that moment trouble the prince.

This Geronte, with a face, in the full light of day, as round and clear as the moon, and the passive expression of a creature of the wilds, was putting up with Paummella's devilries in saintly fashion, as if he were quite another being from what the prince had been given to understand, and had grown to fear. He was dressed in rags, as on the first occasion and indeed the second, a sign that he did not enjoy particular privileges on the part of Elmina, and this refuted all our nobleman's terrible previous suppositions as to the place the boy occupied in the heart of his beloved. And anyway, he no longer seemed embittered and wrathful as he had through the Cracovian spyglass. Just a poor little boy of five or six at the most, far from being twenty-seven or three hundred, far from being a crafty young fellow of Elmina's age. (Here the impossibility of disassociating the Porter-Boy from the "crimes" of the "brother" re-entered the prince's mind, but we suppose only momentarily: he was already beginning to glimpse a single figure, a single rival, and strangely enough he settled on this idea.) Not, therefore, a brother of the widow's, nor a malicious sprite hostile to Paummella; not the one who inflicts scratches, in short, but the humble serving-lad, the errand-boy between the two families, between Chiaia and Sant'Antonio, the marchesa and the seamstress. "I've wasted so much of my time over him, I'm really furious!" thought the prince with infinite relief; and had it not been a case of a little child he would have tendered his apologies. But a diplomatist could scarcely sink to that . . .

And this Gerontuccio, or Lillot, or Kidlet, as the seamstress called him, with his pointed ears, his grey shorts covered with patches, and a mass of dead leaves wreathed round his skinny grey arms (this is how the prince saw him!), and who truly had nothing in common with Don Sisillo's horrid pupil, *who* he really was and *where* he really came from was the matter about which our noble friend, in his present rather fatigued state of mind, wondered least. But he met his eyes (somewhat impaired for lack of a good wash), or rather, their eyes met – and for that child with his gentle, vacuous gaze, a child incapable of rancour or even of memory, he felt a sort of indulgence in the depths of his soul. He understood the mildness of his nature, inscrutable in its simple-mindedness, and in consequence he understood why Elmina, sorrowfully and perhaps fortuitously, had come to love him. Subject to every torment or reprisal or violence, and the endless cruelty with which the immense Universe abounds, that Geronte – with his venerable name – was also a little spirit of goodness, a consoler, perhaps a secret emissary of the Powers that Be, though in this case the Powers of angels and of demons, who legitimately govern the Affairs of the world. Dispatched by such Powers, therefore, to Elmina's side, he watched over her peace, her sorrow. He carried her burdens, maybe obtained money – in emergencies perhaps illicit money, practically stolen – or else went to pay her taxes. A serving-lad! But, at all events, more a brother, a little brother, than a fiend or a lost soul. And certainly, in his humility, he would if necessary consent to be separated from his so-called "sister", from his beloved Elmina, to cross the threshold of the prison-house and remain there all his life. What he had heard every so often from the Duke and from Nodier about his dangerous character therefore appeared to the prince's eyes as slander. If anything it was Sasà, and her new family at the Little House, who did not want him around any more. Once Donna Elmina had left the house everything had to start on a new footing. It would take very little to throw those two out. No call for the Bourbon Police! All it needed was a puff of wind, a sign of the Cross. Enough simply to push them out at the door and slam it behind them, as servants do with poor desperate stray animals. Those two, at this point, were simply the children of nothingness.

And here, out of proper respect for the natural expectations of the reader, and the freedom that must be left to anyone who buys a cheap novelette trading in amours and murders, namely, the freedom to imagine and deduce for himself who is destined to be robbed and who will be chased with a dagger, we choose to stand aside, and not pursue the further anxieties and conjectures of the prince on this matter.

It at once emerged – and this elucidation of the question was entirely due to the worthy Don Liborio – that the kernel of the matter consisted in an enormous sum of money, or what was considered such by those Neapolitans now erased by the swift hand of time; and that this sum was owed by Donna Elmina to her father, and in the first instance by the latter to Donna Helm and her direct heirs, for the purchase of the Little House in 1776: a purchase and at the same time a gift (though only symbolic, never legalized) from Donna Helm to Don Mariano. The late Don Mariano would never in fact have claimed settlement from his favourite daughter had not Donna Brigitta been forcing him to do so. For Donna Brigitta had never forgiven little Elmina for being the person dearest to the Glover's heart. When the future couple had first met, the young maiden was not on the scene; but later on she was always there. And always, always throughout her lifetime Donna Helm had had to share Don Mariano's affections with her; and this takes no account of the scandal of the Linnet, which belonged to Floridia, and for whose sad end Elmina had never entirely managed to exculpate herself. So when the Eternal Event occurred, reuniting Donna Helm and Don Mariano, between the pair of them this problem had become venomous. Donna Brigitta, caring not a whit that he was unused to being dead, gave the poor Glover not a moment's peace. Even in the happiest and loftiest moments of a conversation, when both were recalling Jib-Sail House, and they allowed themselves to nourish tender hopes and dreams of a possible Future Reward, the question of the Little House and its uncompleted payment was, due to the obstinate and rancorous character of the Baroness, dragged up again. Moreover, by Law, the injured party could claim the entire price, even if part-paid – an evident abuse in favour of the proprietors! The debt was undeniable! The house had not been paid for! Besides, the youngest, ugliest and most cherished of Donna Brigitta's sons, a certain Pasqualino Helm, a constable in the Bourbon Police, was demanding it for himself (he had been entreating his mother with prayers and Masses for her soul . . .). He wanted to make a love-nest of it. Therefore, either Elmina paid the entire sum owing, including practically everything that had already been paid, or she vacated the premises. And what's more, that very morning!

Passing over the iniquity of such an act of blackmail, it seemed strange to the prince that she, having at least for a day had at her disposal Nodier's entire fortune (and his own, de Neville's, for a lifetime), had not immediately mentioned the problem of the house and the mortgage to her fiancé in order to disarm Pasqualino Helm. And it was stranger still that she had not thought of something within her power even now, even without Nodier behind her, which was to leave the Little House and move to the marchesa's palace in Chiaia. No sooner had the prince thought this, than he was stricken with shame: he had just remembered that she was reduced to total penury. Perhaps the busts of Ali Baba had something to do with her unwillingness to move: what on earth could she do with them? And remembering, moreover, the behaviour of the young marchese, and his contempt for Sasà, not to mention his real hatred for the Caplet, who dogged his sister everywhere, he became convinced that there was no way open to the unfortunate Nanny-Goat save, perhaps, an improbable marriage (and he could well understand her reluctance) to Notary Liborio. Unless perchance, at least to save her brother from the terrible sentence of death (which only now he remembered with a shudder), she had decided on marriage to the Duke's friend, to wit himself, Ingmar. In this, however, given her long-standing antipathy to him, he no longer even in desperation dared to hope. To what means, therefore, could he have recourse in order to save both the house and Caplet at one and the same time?

*   *   *

At this point he was distressed at two things: not seeing among those present either Albert or Ali Baba, which gave him to understand once and for all something which we shall not retract later on (as we do so often in this story, which is a continual series of statements and retractions), namely that for Elmina and the artist those days with their heads in a rosy cloud at Jib-Sail House had melted away for ever; and also that the artist, together with Baba, was headed goodness knows where in pursuit of his *Joie*. And he thought he also understood how this infinite absence both from home and from heart must turn the poor Nanny-Goat to stone, yet ever on the verge of tears, and all the more intent on the song of the Linnet, that gentle "Aaah! Aaah! Aaah!" which after all was heard all over Naples.

A further glance at the boy, who with a pale hand lightly covered in white down, like an old man's beard, was busy brushing off the widow's handbag – it had been thrown to the ground by Sasà while taking wing, and Elmina, red in the face with vexation, had not so much as stooped to retrieve it; a further sorrowing glance at the *outsider* had made him feel, with the same lucidity that had come to his aid on other occasions of doubt, that between the two of them, Elmina and the Elf – and against his will, in a sense reawakening to reality, he was reduced to calling him by his right name – there existed a bond that could nevermore be severed, an inexhaustible loyalty, never declared and indeed inexpressible, that stemmed from their common ancestry in the Germanic world of dreams; and Hieronymus, in his sickness and helplessness, was the primary cause of her sorrow, or at least of the fact that she would not abandon the old home, the sad and solitary life of widowhood. With a sense of stupor he recalled what Nodier had said, that the Elf had no intention of leaving the house. Everything was clear at this point, including Sasà's aversion to him (unless, that is, Nodier had invented the whole thing from start to finish).

Meanwhile the boy, having hung the bag back on the arm of his guardian angel, looked up at her and then (not sadly but inwardly, as in a dream) he looked at the prince, hidden as he was; and he seemed to be saying (or singing?) no other than "O-hoh! O-hoh! O-hoh!", but in such a profound silence, so far from any human claim on consolation, that Ingmar felt close to fainting.

"This wretch as well," came the stern, harsh tones of Donna Helm (of whom, it should be said, nothing was visible from the corner where the prince was hiding except for the flaming red hat which she, extremely crossly, had retrieved from Sasà): "this wretch as well! I always told Don Mariano: Don Mariano, I said, I don't want to see *this* one around the house. He's got to go! I was and I remain a Christian, even in my sin. I already saw, in 1779 when the box was delivered, that it was by no means clear where he came from."

"Poor creature, he does no one any harm," interposed the mild voice of Elmina, and never to the prince's ears had the voice of woman or innocent maiden sounded more gentle and redeemed from the sin of Adam. "Poor creature, where would he go?"

"He infects my house! The house you unlawfully occupy, I would have you remember, is still *my* house. And I want no excommunicates in it. I repeat: he must go!"

"Calm yourself, Brigitta, we are in a holy place!" came the despondent tones of Don Mariano.

"And then," put in the Scribblerus benignly, "it is by no means certain that souls that are saved are any better than those that are lost, or that Paradise is a worthier place than Purgatory. This lad, I agree, does no harm to anyone; he sweeps, he tidies up, he carries the heavy loads . . . Without him Donna Elmina would already have relieved the great ones of this world of her presence – and there would be one more orphan in Naples. Not to mention the fact, which I take the liberty of adding, that he has never received a penny for his services."

"I should think not!" retorted Donna Helm acidly. "The idea of being *paid* for all the blessings he receives! You forget that he has not been short of bread in my daughter's house, if we have to call it hers, which as far as I am concerned it is not." Then, changing her tone, though with forced restraint: "However that may be, I don't like him and I never have. Apart from the little thefts he has perpetrated! He steals, that one, and hides things, and smashes everything, just like the mental deficient he is!"

The astonished prince was inevitably reminded of the disappearance of the miniature from the mantelpiece, and its replacement by an ugly picture of a fleeing knight (a spell cast to bring bad luck to Elmina's admirer?, or simply an act of childish mischief?) which he only now grasped the meaning of. Not to mention the fact that the stolen miniature depicted the lovely Floridia . . . Enamoured as he was of Elmina, Hieronymus must always have resented the near-worship of the little Helm girl.

"If only he had repented!" thought the prince vaguely. But on the contrary: as he leant a little way out of the window and glancing towards the group of people, he got a clear view of the lad, who was covering his eyes with his hand. The wretch! Even though he knew he might be seen, he was *laughing*!

At this point the voices of the speakers retreated some way from where Ingmar was hiding, and only one speech, measured and serious, and not interrupted by the other Sufferers, led him almost immediately – more by the tone than the meaning of the words – to realize that a solution was on the horizon. And this solution was mooted by the Scribblerus:

"Ladies and gentlemen, I have this to say. Let us all meet at five o'clock tomorrow morning in front of the Cathedral. The weather is not cold, and your health will not suffer. Let us enter and make our way down the nave – on tiptoe! The money will be there, in an envelope at the foot of the altar. Ask me for no more details, for I am not authorized to divulge them. I am simply executing orders, I receive instructions and stick by them, and that is all: the initiative is not mine. You will sign a receipt. You may sign with blood or with fire, as you wish, but I imagine it will be with fire, because your blood – pray do not be offended, Don Mariano – has grown somewhat pallid of late. Purgatory has done you no good, and nor has the company of your wife. At least towards your poor relations you are very much changed, and I no longer recognize you."

"Thanks for the compliment!" The voice (and the feathers) of Donna Brigitta shook with indignation. "You're really out of the top drawer! However, I remind you, Signor Scribblerus, that it is a matter of a round five hundred ducats. That was the price then, and I don't think it has fallen. In fact, they tell me, the cost of living is always on the rise, and that of land no less so."

Thus was Donna Helm. But in view of his principles and his affections, not to mention the unassuming goodness and loyalty of his character, Don Mariano's submissiveness was truly hard to accept, or perhaps even understand. However, after all, such was the destiny of the man, at the mercy of an ill-natured woman . . .

*Madame Pecquod. The prince is unjustly mistaken
for a certain "Signor Immarino". A fierce exchange of
words and a heap of useless questions and debatable
answers concerning the Glover's adopted children*

The prince closed his eyes . . . reopened them. He felt he was flying, and saw the lovely city of Naples still sleeping there beneath him. He closed his eyes again, and on reopening them a second time he would in vain have striven even to guess at who had borne him up the long, long steps to the Little House: whether he had arrived there alone, or in a dream, or again whether he had dreamt only his visit to the family Chapel of Helm and Civile. Nor did it matter to him. He was at the end of his tether.

Yes, he was once more in the grip of his dominant thought, having excluded from the number of his possible rivals the creature H. Käppchen, in view of the pitiful condition of Orphan and Elf in which the latter found himself. And his dominant thought was that Elmina had a lover not merely "secret", but "secret" because unmentionable, not blessed with human nature, as well as forbidden by divine law, and that this might be the famous Linnet. He did not even faintly remember the episode of the evening they first met in the drawing-room at Jib-Sail House and a sweet voice sang on the floor above, a cruel proof (since that was the day a crime was committed) that she had no great liking for linnets. In the turmoil of his emotions (and real turmoil there is, even in certain emotional fantasies, and his was one of these) his only thought was that she loved a Linnet, and that under the name of *Linnet* many things could lie hidden, such as an officer in the service of His Majesty, some miserable petty nobleman of this *famous* Kingdom of Naples, or even (for at this point anything went!) some French exile, whether Jacobin or Girondist (for Europe was then crawling with exiles). He no longer thought, to tell the truth – and we mention this to the credit of what was left of his reason – of poor Don Liborio, nor suspected his devotion to Elmina. It could be that this devotion was tinged with admiration; but this sentiment was not returned except by a respectful regard for his profession.

Then, of a sudden, he felt that his deductions and suspicions as a man of passion had gone hopeless astray; he felt what with anger and infinite affliction he had felt on other occasions – that there was nothing *Christian* in Elmina, despite her virtue, and that his investigation of her, were it to be successful, could only lead to his wishing he had never been born. She, he told himself, had for some time not belonged to the real world, and to what world she *did* belong no Bourbon Police or Grand Inquisitor would ever be able to say. She was, in the best analysis, nothing but an uncouth Nanny-Goat!

He leant on the little wooden garden gate, which he had reached at last. It was ten in the morning, and the Little House stood before him all pink and cheerful. He looked round him with a sense of desolation.

An old woman had just that moment come out of the back door of the house and was hanging up stockings on a line strung between two saplings.

She was tall and skinny, with (apparently) closed eyes and a black bonnet on her head. It was Ferrantina. The prince recognized her, but made no move to greet her.

"Have we the honour of addressing Signor *Immarino?*" she asked after a while in a voice as deep as a man's, impassive, sardonic and far from pleasant. Nor was she bothered at mispronouncing the noble name of Ingmar – unless she did it on purpose. The prince looked around him to see where this Immarino might be, but his gaze met nothing but trees and the clouds above them.

"No call to look for him," remarked the sardonic voice a moment later, in even chirpier tones, if we may use such a term. "You are the very man, my young sir."

Our Belgian nobleman would have liked to ask the maid (it was indeed Ferrantina) how, in view of her near blindness, she had managed to see him, and what right she had to address him in such a manner. He was stunned with indignation. She forestalled him:

"I heard you come in."

"Where?" was the question Ingmar would have liked to ask, seeing that he had not come in, but was still standing at the garden gate. But he preferred to say nothing.

"Have you seen Lillot by any chance?" asked this person who, to our poor diplomatist, seemed more like the mistress than the maid or the housekeeper. "He should be back already," she continued, adding in that unpleasant way of hers: "There's a lot to do here in the mornings, but he's no great lover of work and as soon as he can he makes off. As for his meals, such as they are, his sister sees to that."

"Are you speaking of the boy with the feather?" asked Ingmar, rather coldly, because he was practically beside himself.

"Call him a boy if you like, but that one is at least thirty years old, if not three hundred, as the spiteful tongues have it. And if you saw him at the cemetery, as I seem to think, it's certainly not because he went there to pray, or to visit Don Mariano either, even if his sister does stick up for him. You can banish that thought from your mind, Signor Immarino."

The prince at last understood whom the woman was talking about, and that Lillot was the real (or at least the familiar) name for "Little" Hieronymus, but all the malicious part of what she said had escaped him. Hearing no more grave charges against the Porter-Boy, his reply was melancholy and distrait:

"As far as I know he is still a child, and went to the cemetery to visit Don Mariano. He accompanied Madame Dupré and carried the shopping – he was not just out on the loose, I think."

"Stick up for him if it suits you," was Ferrantina's acid reply. "One fine day you'll be sorry you made a saint of him, you'll learn who he really is. On the other hand it's not his fault. It was Don Mariano himself who brought him into the house, by mistake, alas . . . And when he realized, it was too late."

Exactly what the Duke had said.

Ingmar was now so deeply immersed in grief that he was incapable of feeling more – not the least emotion or trace of surprise. He therefore found it natural, rather than answering, to put a second question, though feigning indifference:

"And . . . this Lillot, does he live here, if I am not being indiscreet?"

"Where do you think he lives? With the Pope? He lives here all right, but it won't be for long. Donna Elmina is deceiving herself. And if you want to find out how long she has left, her and all of us, to live in this house, just take a walk around the rooms. Three hours ago, immediately after she'd gone off with Lillot and her daughter, in came the bailiffs, and they've stuck notices, with the value and all, on everything in the house, even the saucepans."

"No!" cried Ingmar without realizing it, emerging suddenly from his stupor and less surprised than enraged. "No! This cannot be! What you tell me is a downright abuse, and must be prevented. And so it shall be!"

He was waking, indeed he had truly awakened from his terrible sleepwalking state. Vastly indignant, he added:

"I repeat, it's an unlawful abuse. The authors (or the authoress!) of this outrage will be sorry for it. In no uncertain manner!"

"And to whom may you be alluding, pray?" asked the old housekeeper with a nasty smirk. "You mustn't be so free with your threats, Signor Immarino!"

(Really! this confusion of names was too much to bear.)

"De Neville!" shrieked our nobleman. "Monsieur de Neville, if you don't mind. Kindly remember it. You and I *are not acquainted*!"

"Ah, but I know *you*!"

"You are going too far, Madame Pecquod," said the prince, luckily remembering the housekeeper's rather barbarous surname, heard by chance from the lips of Donna Helm. By this time he considered her a far from reliable person, perhaps a witch, and certainly the real black shadow cast from the start over the Dupré household and the events which tormented it. "But I repeat," he continued, "I have to warn you – and you may draw your own conclusions – that I am now determined to carry forward my enquiry into this matter, and will not now give way in the face of anything or anyone. You had therefore better tell me outright: who is it who could expel Donna Elmina from this house? I am taking account of your tittle-tattle and more of the same kind, the source of which I am not at present obliged to reveal" (he was referring to the conversation of the phantom couple), "and other things I heard in that holy place, and I do not believe for a moment in the claims put forward by Pasqualino Helm."

"There!" exclaimed the old woman with a strange glitter of triumph in her eyes. "There, you've guessed it. Signor Helm is not acting of his own free will, he is being forced to act by *others*. Left to himself he wouldn't lift a finger. It's true that he was already on the ropes over his engagement, but he is not one to hold grudges. Anyway, the 'engagement' was really broken off only yesterday evening, while the legal action has been going on for quite a while."

(It was clear, at this point, whom Teresella had been officially engaged to until the previous evening.)

"For how long? And forced by *whom*?"

The prince could think only of Don Mariano's horribly grasping "wife".

They had entered the house by the kitchen door. Madame Pecquod (such, therefore, was Ferrantina's real name – she was not "Carlo's Ferrantina") appeared to be highly incensed, even abusive, as she scraped back now one chair, now another, maliciously indicating the numbered tags marking the confiscated objects. The prince looked at them too, even more surprised than horrified. The entire house was under restraint.

"Just one word," said he at a certain point, almost choked by the effort of repressing his wrath. And he sat down at one end of the ramshackle table. "Just one word, Madame Pecquod. Tell me who it is who hates Donna Dupré so bitterly. It is a certain Linnet, is it not? Or am I mistaken?"

He pronounced this name coldly, but with a shudder.

Madame Pecquod burst out laughing, this time good-humouredly.

"Linnet, did you say? No, you don't know how things stand at all. That poor creature doesn't hate anyone! All he does is sing! All he does is weep! The whole of Naples can bear me witness, the whole world even! No, the person who hates our dear lady is someone very close to her, and I'll tell you at once: it's Alessandra Dupré, daughter of Monsieur Albert, little Sasà whom you think of as the little damsel. The half-sister, so to speak, of our Gerontuccio . . ."

These words practically sent our Belgian nobleman off his head, though he forced himself to maintain a very gloomy silence. What he had heard, in any case, could scarcely be the truth. Silence might help him to find some sense in it.

Therefore, very simply, after a moment or two:

"Are we speaking of the same person, or are there two Alessandrina Duprés? And finally, the one you call 'our Gerontuccio', is he . . . is he the boy with the feather?"

"God save us!" cried the old woman. "That is no boy, as I already explained. I am speaking of the young marchese, Don Geronte Emilio Watteau. And to avoid misunderstandings, I assure you that I called him 'half-brother' to the little girl not because he really is, but because for years Sasà considered him as such. She loved him passionately, and the two of them made fun of Lillot. In the end Donna Elmina revealed to her daughter the real relationships between the three of them. Alessandrina was seized with a real passion for young Durante-Watteau, then seven years old, and conceived the idea, or intention, of marrying him when she grew up, but she had no dowry except this house. So she decided, I believe with the support of Donna Violante (though not of her daughter – Donna Carlina Watteau thinks of nothing but her own wardrobe), to appropriate it by legal means. It seems she has succeeded. With the complicity of a relative, that is to say by ensnaring Pasqualino Helm, who until yesterday – in case you don't know – used to visit this house in his capacity as a future 'uncle', and from whom she had already obtained a 'document' drawing up the terms of the 'donation'." (Here she went to the cupboard, took out a scrap of paper and held it out to the prince). "Obviously, her mother doesn't know about it. Her aim, as anyone can understand, and especially an *educated* man like you, Signor Immarino, is a double one: to give some semblance of dignity (because that's what property is) to the betrothal of her dreams, and to turn little Geronte, or Lillot, out of the house with all the power of the Law behind her! I can't really blame her on this score, but in my view to appropriate poor Monsieur Albert's house is shameful. And her mother doesn't know."

The good Ingmar looked round about him in genuine anguish, praying that something might awaken him from this new nightmare. The ages attributed to the "children", and the span of time covered by their story, did not correspond to the "historical" data in his possession. Either the woman's account was invented, or slanderous, or he himself was sinking into the dreams of his own mind. He was in the situation of a child who has listened to a fairy-tale with half an ear. Oh, if only he could wake up! But he retained a certain degree of courage. Perhaps Elmina's party and the Notary were on their way back from the cemetery, and would deliver him from this endless nightmare. For the moment he must be patient. He must act as if nothing had happened.

It cost him much to reply politely: "All the same, the sweetheart in this case is only four years old!"

The old woman gave him a mocking look.

"My dear sir! You still believe in people's ages! They are usually a complete convention. There are people who were never born – in the sense that they have no brains – or are only born this moment, which comes to the same thing, or else three hundred years ago without being able to get their ideas straight. Then there are people who think only of possessions, and those are the oldest of all. They may even be three years old, but in reality they are one thousand three hundred. That is what old age is."

"You told me the same thing about the boy, but he is not greedy for anything. Don't you think there's a contradiction here?"

"Dear sir, forgive me . . . The one you and all of us go on calling the 'boy' is . . . another matter. Only the late-lamented Don Mariano could say. Though my belief is that even Don Mariano no longer knows, and no longer loves him."

"Did he love him before?"

"When he was tiny, yes. When he found him at Jib-Sail House, on the evening of All Souls 1779, all wet and shivering by the fireplace (he had been delivered in his absence), Don Mariano lost his heart to him. Even the child conceived a love nothing short of adoration for him . . . and no less so for Donna Elmina when she was a little older. Elmina was four years old, and at that time she hated the lovely Floridia . . ."

(Here too the dates failed to check, but Ingmar, his head reeling, was impervious to shock.)

". . . Floridia who had a linnet called Dodò?" he ventured.

"I see you know everything," laughed the old woman. "However, you do not know the hidden motives. Donna Elmina was an orphan, a poor relation of Colonel Helm. He took her into his house and thought of adopting her, but at once regretted it, and for this reason, even before he fell ill, he entrusted her to Don Mariano. Don Mariano, who had emotional ties with the Baroness – which the Baron knew, but raised no objection, having the highest esteem for our Glover – accepted the little girl, and thereafter behaved towards her like a wise and loving father. But little Floridia already reigned supreme in the household and in the hearts of all, a legitimate Helm and of stupendous beauty. The orphan grew sullen with jealousy – she had never been very good, as you will have gathered. Now she became spiteful. Out of desperation she formed a bond with Lillot, who was the lost soul of the household, detested by Donna Helm, as in fact Donna Elmina was pretty heartily detested too. And the cruel end of poor Dodò, Floridia's beloved linnet, is a true story. It was the work of Lillot. Not deliberate, I have to say, but the result of thoughtlessness – you know how children are. Donna Elmina took the blame to protect the lad."

"The same who from time to time changes himself into a wretched scavenger?"

"Indeed, sir. At times, when he is unhappy, or afraid, he appears in the form of a strange, mangy cat and goes out on the prowl at night. Or else, for some reason, he is a young goat a few months old, or a chick running after its mother. The form is suited to his actions, which are for the most part stupid. Then, suddenly, he becomes the creature you have seen, with a feather stuck on his head."

"A sad fate!" exclaimed the prince, who had all at once forgotten his distrust of the narrator, and at least at that moment believed the story of the "Scavenger"; and it made his heart ache.

"A sad fate indeed," agreed the old woman pensively, "because if the boy – and it was his last chance – had shown his good side that evening so many years ago when Donna Floridia was offensive to Donna Elmina, and had not grabbed the linnet and set his teeth into it (which is why it died, and also why he was ever after outlawed in that house) he would now be a very different creature. His destiny was already nearing a miraculous solution. But the decree of mercy was annulled."

The prince was eager to hear more, but also grief-stricken, because he saw how the boy's misfortune (evident in spite of Ferrantina's confused account) had been an atrocious burden for the little Elmina. "If," continued the old woman, "he had not been guilty of that crime, tiny but terrible for all that – I mean the death of the linnet – his situation today would have been quite different."

"What would it have been?"

"You remember, do you not, Signor Ingmar, the evening of your arrival with Signor Dupré and Signor Nodier, and you were all waiting in the vestibule? And you heard, to the accompaniment of the girls, a very sweet voice? That was Lillot, Hieronymus as he is called in the birth certificate (naturally false) that was delivered with the box. In fact at certain moments, as a reward from Heaven for some kind act of his, he was (perhaps I should say 'was still'), or he returned to being, a beautiful youngster of ten or twelve (as Elmina had longed for him to be), fair-haired, dressed in velvet . . . Alas, he wore spectacles because he was short-sighted, and that defect he still has. He was destined, on the expiry of his three hundred years of innocence, to become a real man. But he failed . . . some lives never come to a close . . ."

"Just as well he failed," thought Ingmar absurdly, but not entirely so. He had no great opinion of the human race. However, he did not say that but asked impulsively:

"And Donna Elmina . . . did she love him greatly?"

"Fit to die for him . . . to die, I mean, to this world. From that moment on (I refer to the death of the linnet and the boy's crime, though this may be the wrong word, since his act was involuntary), Donna Elmina took to showing complete disregard for the world and its outward appearances – whether real disregard or otherwise I cannot say, for she was a little child. However, she made a vow to the Madonna of the Birdcage, who is venerated, I believe, in the church of Santa Maria of Constantinople, to give away all she had; a vow of poverty and silence in all things; she vowed that only when her brother – for such in her innocence did she consider the elf to be – was freed from the decree which declared him to be without soul, and had become a real, happy youngster accepted by Heaven, only then would she herself accept happiness, and re-enter the world of Don Mariano. Not until then."

"And is it because of this," asked the prince, his eyes wide with amazement, "that the Linnet is heard to sing? Has it come back to life? Is it not, perhaps, a vendetta?"

"Sir, I consider that possible, but not in the sense you attribute to the matter, due to your human malice. For tell me honestly if you are able to give a proper name to the persons and things of this world, all of them far from clear, and vanishing in the distance. This voice, born of a universal dream and yearning for good, is not that of a bird, and therefore such a bird you will never find. This voice is of like nature with the spring, the stars, the mild, clear nights of summer. It makes for weeping and it makes for goodness. And it is from this, this echo in the memory, this poignant, desperate yearning for good, that you realize that the Linnet has passed by. You feel that yours is not a good life, and that there is another, a better and a gentler, for which you long to exchange your own wretched life . . ."

As if for the boy long lost within him the prince was weeping now, shedding copious sweet tears, and he repented of the void that was his life. Oh, what would he not have given for the Linnet to appear, and tender him some remedy! All he knew for certain was that he could not leave little Elmina, as now he called her in his heart – nor would he attempt such a thing, ever. Either they all – the two of them and the boy – became "grown up" and happy together, or it was better . . . but exactly what was better who could say?

He suffered greatly at that moment, our good Ingmar, and the worst thing of all (and the strangest) was that part of him felt the whole story was untrue – a gigantic farrago of nonsense thought up by that old Madame Pecquod!

Lillot wounded. Sasà's lies. Drama in the offing.
The sun is darkened above Lillot and the long "Scalinatella"

Meanwhile a number of small figures were trudging up the last stretch of the Scalinatella: the aforesaid Elmina, looking a little smaller than usual; Alessandrina Dupré, looking perhaps a trifle larger, and the idiot Porter-Boy who followed behind them a-weeping and a-wailing.

Notary Liborio, two steps further back, was attempting to talk to him – or better, to console him.

Here is what had happened.

Not everything the old Pecquod had reeled off as the truth was so in fact – there were a few exaggerations or oversights. But the truth of the story of the house, as Sasà's dowry to offer to the young marchese and at the same time the last refuge of Hieronymus in this world, could be proved by a recent bitter quarrel between the two children on the subject; a quarrel during which Sasà had chased Lillot, not in fun as at the cemetery, but with genuine rage, scarlet in the face at the way he sniggered when Elmina gently suggested that the house belonged to "Geronte"; and she had managed to wrench the famous feather from off his head.

Now, that feather was not simply pasted on (let alone sewn!), but *natural*, and on Lillot's forehead there now appeared an ambiguous and barely perceptible line of red droplets. The desperate sobs of the little creature who (we must not forget) was unable to speak, touched but did not much frighten Elmina, while greatly troubling poor Don Liborio, who had learnt from Don Mariano how vitally important that feather was for the little boy. Let us not lay too much stress on other matters, save the distraint of goods and the hostility of old Ferrantina towards Sasà – matters which maybe the prince had dreamt up for himself. But the gravity of *this* event, the clash between the two children, was abundantly clear to everyone.

"You mustn't cry, Lillot," said the Scribblerus, very pale in the face, though (being rather stout) struggling to keep up with him, "it's only a scratch. As soon as we get home Donna Elmina will put on some ointment and a bandage and it will get better at once."

"*Maman*, I didn't do it on purpose," sobbed Alessandrina, sincerely or otherwise, "it was him who spat at me!" She was referring to the nasty habit of some quarrelsome and ignorant lower-class children of spitting at each other at the least provocation, as an ultimate defence and offence when words no longer sufficed (or, as in our case, were altogether lacking). "He told me that Geronte Watteau will never marry me, because his grandmother doesn't want him to."

"And how did he tell you that, my girl, if he can't talk? Or have you sometimes heard him talk, this little brother of yours?" In such terms Elmina occasionally saw fit to underemphasize her singular relationship to the boy, or bring it down to the level of Sasà's minuscule intelligence. "Aren't you telling lies?"

"*Maman* . . . He's not my little brother and he's not my uncle either. He's a Spirit, he's the Devil himself. Once I saw him rising up out of a saucepan in a cloud of smoke. And he went *pfff*!"

And so on and so forth, while Lillot cried his eyes out in silence.

They were now within sight of the gloomy house and the little garden; and the sky had darkened, as though the sun were repining.

Though still in the house and at some distance from this scene, the prince had heard the last exchanges, but accustomed as he now was to events that often smacked of the miraculous, he was not surprised. He at once set out to meet the party, unconcerned at the thought that Donna Elmina might wither him with a disdainful word on seeing him once more, and unin-vited, in their midst; but the chain of events, the debt, the distraint on the property, the wrath of Donna Helm, along with the incredible story of Sasà and her designs, and last but not least the quarrel between the two children and the loss of the feather, had overcome his misgivings as a man of the world. Going out into the garden he observed that a light drizzle was falling into the vast silence of the November morning, and that the widow was approaching leading a tearful daughter; but more authentic, less theatrical tears ran down the wan, slightly puffy cheeks of the serving-lad.

That the "child" had been taught a lesson was not in itself displeasing to Ingmar (still in the grip of his absurd jealousy), but at the same time he was upset, for the boy's distress was genuine: the one pride of his life, the hen's feather he had always borne on his head as the gift and token of nature, had been torn from him by the Palummella in a moment of tantrum. It was to be hoped that at least the wound did not become infected (and that there was no more tragic significance behind the event).

On noticing the Scribblerus, who had seen him without manifesting the fact, he thought to ask him what had become of the feather, but then he spotted it in the child's hands, clasped to his heart.

"There is bad news, dear sir," said the Scribblerus as he passed the prince; and with an expression of great concern he raised his eyes towards the Little House, in front of which they now stood. He was alluding to the visit of the bailiffs.

The prince would have liked to ask him what part he really played in the story, and from whom he had received instructions regarding the money to pay off the debt. Then, in a flash of enlightenment, he realized that the money that would save the day was Don Liborio's own. It was likely that for the sake of Donna Elmina he was renouncing all the security stored up for his fast-approaching old age.

Fortunately, to such a ruin there was a remedy.

"Have you already spoken to Pasqualino Helm?" he asked under his breath while the Notary and the poor wretch were still close by him.

But Donna Elmina had now spotted him.

"These, Monsieur de Neville," said the widow with calm and gravity but no trace of friendliness, "these are not matters that concern you. Debts have to be paid within the family, didn't you know?" (as if to rub in the fact that he was not a member of it). "If only out of respect for the Linnet!" she added with a smile far from pleasant, almost frightening, that reminded him of the cruel young girl of yore. However, rather than being a smile at all it was a grimace of misery.

And at once, casting a distant, expressionless glance at the Notary and the boy, she went on: "I think the child has hurt himself. He hit his head somewhere, I don't know how ... Have you by any chance seen my sister?"

"No, Teresella has not arrived yet ..." babbled the prince. "Otherwise," he added firmly, "I don't think Don Pasqualino would have got his way . . ." And at once he bit his lip.

"My sister does not care much about me," said Donna Elmina coldly. "You may have heard that she recently became engaged to Sasà's father-to-be. A good thing too: for Sasà two new parents at one stroke is a very good bargain. To my daughter I have never counted for anything."

"*Maman!*" protested Sasà, half lying, half upset.

After a pause: "I am worried about this boy," resumed Elmina in tones both distant and dejected. "He has hurt himself, as you see." She then went on in a low voice:

"He refuses to leave here. But now the house no longer belongs to us – to Elmina and her Gerontuccio. You, Monsieur de Neville, saw the name on that document in the studio yesterday morning, therefore I may speak about it ... Gerontuccio, blow your nose ... Hieronymus Käppchen – you saw rightly – is not my son or my brother, he is not related by blood either to me or to my father. Not to mention my husband. But he belongs in the heart of Donna Elmina, *there* is his place and date of birth, as I hope you have understood. And from that place no one on earth will remove him."

"Yes," said the prince (or thought he did), with a sense of mingled joy and desperation. And he thought to himself, "Perhaps death might ... He appears to be not only wounded, but moribund."

The calm and cruelty of men during and in the face of the worst crimes, from which they hope to obtain for themselves salvation and joy, is an almost superhuman thing – certainly not Christian. At these words which he himself had articulated in his thought, which were born of an atrocious hope – the exact opposite of that sublime promise he had made to himself, to adopt the Elf – the prince stood stock still, livid, turned to stone. It came home to him that he too was part of that *iniquity* of which, with the vehemence and injustice of youth, he ceaselessly accused the world. To take the place of the Porter-Boy in Elmina's heart he had already consented, in his own all-too-human heart, to the total ruin and obliteration of H. Käppchen.

As he formulated this thought he turned his mind towards God, in the hope that He – ignoring all the privileges of nobility and wealth that had distinguished him since birth, and his necromantic skills, and even his immortal love for Elmina – should assign to him the lowest place of all, the basest and the worst. Just as long as Lillot was saved.

When they entered the house Madame Pecquod had withdrawn. In the big kitchen, which seemed all the darker and gloomier in contrast with the sunlight which, even though wanly, illuminated the November day, an enormous quantity of peas, a sort of lush green hillock, rose intact on the table, waiting to be shelled.

Donna Elmina removed her cape, sat the little girl down at the table and took off her wet shoes; and all the while her face was streaming with silent tears. She had seen the tickets that meant restraint of goods even, as Madame Pecquod had said, on the few pots and pans.

Anyone who for whatever reason, though usually on account of arrears on mortgages or expiry of the lease and the owner's order to vacate the premises to accommodate a newly-wed daughter, has been forced to leave a much-loved home, and is now on the point of having to comply, will readily understand Donna Elmina. For her the loss of her home darkened her life. Not even her grief at Lillot's predicament – his physical damage and dishonour due to the loss of his feather – affected her more deeply than the grief that cut her to the heart at the thought of having to leave the Little House. Her very youth, mysterious yet so dear to her, came to an end with this.

The prince knew, or thought he knew, that it was all a dream. Elmina's desperation was not genuine, or at least there was no good reason for it. It would take but a word and floods of money would flow towards the house at Sant'Antonio, from Caserta, from Liège, from all over the world. Even the Scribblerus had thought it out. And yet . . . everything in Ingmar's heart told him that the house could not be redeemed, that in fact it ought not to be redeemed. Her life, Elmina's life – her eyes were on the Porter-Boy standing bolt upright in the open doorway, staring ahead as if he were blind, one hand clasped to his heart – was over and done with.

Sing therefore, Linnet, sing, tender and ill-omened bird, open your throat once more, and with it the tearsprings in the heart of her who is a girl no longer, and of him who even two centuries later, for those who knew him well, is still a boy – we mean Prince de Neville, lord of Brabant and Liège, and our own Ingmar!

And at the sight of these tears on the faces of two desolate human beings – nor should we forget the glum Paummella, or the adoring Scribblerus, nor yet the son of the trees and flowers – the Linnet, in the pain and disdain he felt for all mankind, as do the celestial messengers feel towards the volatile but featherless world, released his dizzying and joyous song, at the sound of which we feel inclined to stop our ears, the familiar:

> *O-hoh! O-hoh! O-hoh!*
> *Ohhh! Ohhh! Ohhh!*

which was followed, for the prince, by the merry and sprightly refrain:

> *Flutter flutter flutter, fly little Linnet!*
> *Flutter flutter flutter . . . Oh! Oh! Oh!*

Ingmar needed not one trill the more, or anything more pitiless. The prince fainted.

A family matter. Locked in! Great revelations and,
through the good offices of the Duke, the third proposal
of marriage. Elmina's declaration (or prayer?) to the Linnet
and Nodier's first measures on behalf of the Porter-Boy

Coming to his senses with the supreme indifference of the dead –
though dead he was not, only the life of the passions was
extinguished in his heart – de Neville became aware that he was still at
the table in the old kitchen, but completely forgotten by everyone. For
something to do he had started to shell peas, and he was also aware
that he was hoping, in his heart, that Donna Elmina would address him,
albeit it with a reproof: "Leave off that work, Monsieur de Neville, it's
not your job." But she, seated on the other side of the table and flushed
with anger, had turned her attention to someone who had entered a
moment before. That someone was our most excellent Polish wizard,
Benjamin Ruskaja.

He must have been there only a second or two, but many hours must
have passed since all those unfortunates had heard the Linnet singing.
It was night now, and a small yellow moon was rising in the deep blue
opening of the doorway to the garden. Now present in the room (we
say it at once to avoid confusion) were the engaged couple and the
Notary, and all of them *knew* that in the adjoining room, out of which
the black moth had fluttered two nights before, were Donna Helm and
Don Mariano, clamouring to be let out; for the door was locked on
the outside. Pasqualino Helm was at the door, whining and begging over
and over again:

"*Maman*, a moment longer and we'll let you out . . . We're talking."

"Traitor to your own flesh and blood!" Donna Brigitta abused him with
true Mediterranean fire – she was consumed with wrath at being excluded
from the negotiations, and the violence of her nature had prompted the
good Pasqualino to take the precaution of turning the key.

"*Maman*, a moment longer, then we'll open the door. We are talking.
Your interests are in good hands," repeated the policeman wearily.

But: "Traitor to your own flesh and blood!" came the voice, ever more implacable, of the Glover's wife; to which Don Pasqualino, turning a deaf ear, but with the unwavering patience of a favourite son, replied very mildly:

"A moment longer, *maman*, please allow us to talk," while he kept a keen but not malevolent eye on the Duke.

The latter, thus provoking Donna Helm's wrath, had placed on the table a small cloth sack, stuffed to bursting, through the coarse weave of which showed the glitter of gold. Genuine ducats they were, of origin unknown. Ingmar, on the other hand, though quite indifferent to the fact, knew exactly where they came from: namely, that the Duke had withdrawn them that very morning from his account at the English Bank in Naples.

"For you, Donna Elmina!" declared the Polish nobleman in imperious tones which for him, habitually mild-mannered as he was, were sufficiently remarkable. "Thus you will satisfy those ravenous beasts, Master Helm and his mother. With Sasà," he added threateningly, "we will settle accounts later. We shall most certainly not forget."

While Donna Brigitta, or the person whom, though invisible to us, we have recognized as the Harsh Voice heard in the cemetery, continued to scream, "Pasqualino, open the door! Don Mariano, I am being insulted! Don Mariano, stand up for your wife!" along with other protests, Sasà burst into floods of tears:

"Paummella is a *good* girl! Paummella is a *good* girl!" she repeated, humbly and meekly, in such a manner as to break all hearts.

"So she has repented," thought the prince, but without enthusiasm.

Almost as if she had read his thoughts, the widow Dupré snapped out, "My daughter has nothing to do with it."

"Ah, nothing to do with it, you say?" cried the Duke, close friend as, he was of the hero of this tale.

"Paummella is a *good* girl! Paummella is a *good* girl!" moaned that wretched creature.

"Except that she brought ruin on Lillot with her sweet little hands! The feather has been torn off! That's what she's done!" shouted the Duke even louder than before. And to Madame Pecquod: "Signora Ferrantina, this wound must be disinfected."

"Salt and vinegar! Vinegar and brown paper," Ferrantina pontificated without hesitation.

The Porter-Boy, realizing they were talking about him, tried to make good his escape.

"Stay where you are!" commanded the Duke, grabbing him. "And," he added, "get rid of that nasty dirty feather."

With one finger he flicked it to the ground, paying no attention to the Elf's gestures.

But Donna Elmina had seen all, and compassionately she bent down and retrieved the feather. The "invalid" stretched out his small red claw to take it from her (for now he had the claws of a little chick, and such a woeful little face as never was seen!), but again the Duke intervened, and this time it was Ferrantina who firmly replaced the feather in his little downy arms. "In any case," she muttered to herself in French, "feather or no feather the child is all but finished. God has numbered the very hours of his life!"

And it was at this point that the prince recalled the scene of so many years before, in the lonely cemetery in Naples, and the terrifying dates and inscriptions that appeared on the stone for an instant and vanished on the instant: true prophecies, jumbled though they might have been, which had come true for the Duprés, father and son, while the third, concerning Hieronymus Käppchen, even now appeared an imminent threat. It was the dawn of the new century, and now, it was foretold, the life of the luckless Elf would end.

"I see that you are superstitious, my dear Ferrantina," said the Duke with a mischievous smile.

"Of course! Things must always come to pass: they are *written*, dear sir. This is what you call superstition, but you must pardon it in a poor ignorant woman."

"Ignorant? But you know everything, my dear Ferrantina – or should I say Madame Civile? You have put heart and soul into destroying this family."

"At one time *I* was this family ... *I* am Don Mariano's real wife, the first and the real wife!" Thus spake the old servant, through her tears.

"Shut your mouth there, you!" shrieked Donna Helm, whom everyone thought to be the first Signora Civile.

Gross terms which left no echo, save for the muted sobbing of Hieronymus. The old woman (*could* she be the first Madame Civile?) rubbed salt and vinegar, the poor man's remedy in those days for scratches and bruises, on the boy's elfin brow, after which she applied a poultice of brown paper, binding it on with a kerchief. Meanwhile the Duke and Nodier attempted to soothe the orphan's disconsolate weeping, or, more accurately, chirping. Both his hands had now turned into claws, and therefore one of those metamorphoses into cat or kid or chicklet, which occurred whenever the Porter-Boy was frightened, was now taking place – and terrible it was to see. With those claws he was unable to replace the beloved feather on his head, but not for want of trying; in the end, in desperation, he clenched it between his teeth. (If the young Watteau had seen him now, what a triumph it would have been for him! thought one of the onlookers.)

And now his poor jowls were sprouting white whiskers, showing that this was a multiple metamorphosis; and now, in his stricken dumbness, he showed every one of his three hundred years.

An enormous silence weighed upon the house. It was broken by the Duke's voice, hard and mocking now:

"You, Madame Civile (Pecquod was only your maiden name), the descendant of French craftsmen, masters of the art of glovemaking who came here seeking their fortunes in 1734, when Naples became a Kingdom, you, Madame Civile, have supped full with vengeance. Your rightful and legitimate love for Don Mariano was not as legitimate as all that, if the Linnet did not wish it. And the Linnet did *not* wish it! and you will forgive me for saying so, but it was you who killed him, or thought you were killing him, that Good Friday, throwing the blame on poor Elmina and later on this luckless Hieronymus, a Germanic child of nature unable to defend himself because unable to talk. France and Germany – an enmity that never ceases to burn in your veins. It's jealousy, confess it! And for this reason you have ruined so many children and two whole families. Elmina, Floridia and even the unfortunate Ratlet (Nadine Dufour, in the Registry, whose name still appears on the memorial tablet, the daughter of a serving-maid and spitefully accused) thus died or withdrew from the world; and for this reason also our ingenuous Alessandrina has learnt your arts . . . She *flies*, the poor wretch, while Hieronymus is now a chicklet, now a little goat, and in desperation takes refuge in the body of an alley-cat: and his moral weaknesses have at this point become his real sickness – of them he is dying! Not to mention the fact that you set the two children at each other's throats, as once you did the two girls at Jib-Sail House."

"The next thing, I suppose, is that you'll accuse me of the deaths of that idiot sculptor and his son Ali Baba," said the old woman disconsolately.

"Such a revelation is up to you, but be quick about it."

"Those deaths, if you really want to know, were the work of the Linnet, whom *they* loved so dearly!" was the almost triumphant reply of the former workhand. "For the rest, I have to admit that that was the way it went. There is only one thing you must make no mistake about: I was and remain a Bourbonist, devoted for life to His Majesty (God bless him), and this alone – this same loyalty on her part – is what eventually led me to forgive Madame Dupré, who is of the Bourbonist persuasion herself."

This declaration for various reasons left those present quite indifferent – all except one.

"Do you think, then, that the Linnet hurts those who love him?" asked the prince, in his voice a dark dread that was new to him.

"You have said it. He destroys those who love him. Because you see, sir, he is our memory, our longing for those lovely impossible days we've all known at least once in our lives . . ." And the poor thing, who had been seated, now got to her feet and crossed to the kitchen stove, where she removed the lid from the pan.

"It's full of tears," she muttered to herself, "but it needs a little salt all the same."

"And I thought you were a lady . . . a good soul!" muttered Pasqualino Helm.

There followed loud thumps and raucous triumphant shouts from the locked room:

"Ah, my dear son! Now you see how you and the rest of them were hoodwinked by this woman! She seemed so unobtrusive, she kept in the background . . . Yes, but she really ruled the household! I realized from the word go who she really was, and held my tongue only for the love of peace. But it was all the fault of your so-called second 'father', great-hearted and thoughtless as he is, because he kept the whole story to himself. He never said that he had married her, that the Linnet was still against it, that he opposed his new love. In any case he never asked him . . ."

"So he and he alone," thought the prince, "the Linnet alone is the real fiend in this house, and not Hieronymus . . . I didn't know it, I paid him no respects . . . I never asked his opinion, and he has made a fool of me.

Will I ever be able to rescue *Little* Elmina" (thus he put it to himself, evidently thinking back to the apparition on the Steps) "from his remorse- less power, from his implacable commands, and avoid my own destruction? But in the end, I think everything depends on her. She it is who must stick up for herself by refusing the first of the Bird's commands, her unremitting love for this horrible little Goat . . ." (And here, as above in calling Elmina "little", he was plainly remembering the episode on the Steps beneath Nodier's balcony.) "Yes," his thoughts ran on, "it is here, in that absurd love of hers, that we find the root of the slavery of Donna Elmina, her loss to that world of the living that I am burning to offer her myself. Oh, that I could free her from this moral obligation to death!"

From the locked room, on a note of great distress and as it were of insight, came the voice of Don Mariano:

"Elmina, dearest daughter, you must forgive this poor woman here and this poor man your father. Life is over. And the ones who have paid the highest price" (he spoke with feeling) "have been that luckless son-in-law of mine and Ali Baba, and now also this Paummella who keeps flying and harbouring wicked thoughts . . . And we speak not of poor Gerontuccio Käpp and his sister . . ."

"Papa, do not worry about me, I feel no sorrow," replied the sweet voice of Elmina.

"And when, pray, did *that* one ever feel anything," growled the irascible voice of Donna Helm. "*That* one never felt anything for anybody. She watches them all die and all she thinks about is saving a bit of money . . . even on the morning coffee!"

Here broke in, very loudly, the voice of the Duke. And there was something extraordinarily cheerful in it, but at the same time snappish:

"Dear Donna Elmina, and no longer Madame Dupré," he said, "you have now heard everything and been able to judge. I therefore ask you openly, in front of all those present: do you wish to transform your life by immediately marrying the worthiest and most generous man in the world? Such, in my opinion, if you will pardon my presumption, is Ingmar de Neville, Prince of Liège, Duke of Brabant, a renowned diplomatist, and also my esteemed colleague in the study of occult science. You have known him now for ten years. He will also adopt your brother, who will thus escape his sentence of death. For him he will be an educator – of whom, if you will forgive me, he very much stands in need – and also a good father."

Elmina's reply was long in coming. Meanwhile:

"Have you learnt this from America and its blessèd Constitution, this idea that happiness exists on earth, and is in fact our first duty?" muttered Ferrantina sneeringly to herself. "But America has also been duped, dear sir, because it doesn't know . . . it doesn't know the reality of things, or where we are . . . each one of us."

"And where would that be?" came the mocking tones of Pasqualino Helm who had overhead her.

But these words too were destined to vanish in silence. A sort of obscure melancholy hovered in the room.

As for the prince, a man of such authority that people stood in awe of him, he was trembling now like a child pursued by Spirits up the staircase*, or like an explorer watched by a tiger from behind a tree. He could be rescued, albeit for a moment, only if the Duke spoke up again; but that belovèd voice did not make itself heard. Instead – firm, polite, but inexorable – came that, at one time so dulcet and musical, of the queen of this story.

We set it down as it was registered in the prince's heart for ever. The words were addressed – the ultimate cruelty – not to him but to his friend.

"To Monsieur de Neville, dear Duke, I am much beholden for his courtesies towards my husband, and for a third proposal of marriage in only ten years; but he is not a congenial man, nor is he devoted to His Majesty (who is not the King of Naples or of anywhere else in this world). His gifts I have always given away to others, and his loans (for the atelier) I do not want. I have already yielded Monsieur Nodier to my sister Teresina. Monsieur Nodier, in friendly agreement with my half-brother Pasqualino, will see to redeeming the Little House. To him I also leave Sasà, and even now give my consent to her marriage with the son of Donna Carlina Watteau, when these two have both grown up. I will take with me my adoptive brother. I speak of Gerontuccio, you realize (Hieronymus Käppchen is a difficult name). I hope to repair to Donna Violante's where she will give me a bed somewhere in the servants' quarters. As for Lillot, he will understand that this house is no longer ours, but that he will always have his sister Elmina by his side, and that I shall be his real home. Is it true, Lillot," (this to the agèd child), "is it true, my child, that you will forgive your poor Elmina? It is what the Linnet wishes, and with him all the Angels of Heaven. This we have

* An experience once undergone by the author of these pages.

understood, and this we will do. As for Monsieur de Neville," she added, looking into the distance, far beyond that anguished and incredulous face, "I know that he too will forgive me for saying no, because I hear, as I hope he also hears, the voice of the Linnet. We must forget each other as long as the King of life so wishes, because this is our rule: to obey the King. I speak also for this poor child of mine – and do not forget his name, gentlemen, and how much he suffered. But together we shall once more see the lovely golden gardens of our homeland, I am sure we shall . . . No, not Naples – that torment is over and done with. Is it not true, my child, that you have understood, and that you want no more torment? Is the wound still hurting?"

Gerontuccio (one of those present had looked his way) nodded his head as if to say, "Yes, yes."

She took him in her arms, for he seemed to have fainted, such was his pallor (like that of a certain towering nobleman at the other end of the table), while the prince also appeared on the point of collapse. But he still found the strength to keep silent, and silently to approach the pair, and on the cold forehead of the Elf – from which the useless poultice of salt and vinegar had at that moment slipped – to replace the fateful hen's feather, symbolic for the boy of the life he had loved and lost, the life which was now abandoning him for ever.

A general murmur of approval (and perplexity?) closed the scene, though still to be heard were voices – of Spirits, of Fiancés, of Princely Givers, of Insensates, of Poor Housekeepers and Useless Mothers – commenting on events; and still to be heard – while the Duke left the room in a huff – were the doleful whimpering of Paummella and the mutterings of the little creature from Cologne, who was finally speaking, the first and perhaps the last words of his tiny and terrible life, all self-contradictory it must be said: "*Nein . . . Nein . . . Nein . . .*" followed by "*Ja . . . Ja . . . Ja . . .*", as he ceaselessly nodded his head; but what, in the midst of his sobs, he was at the same refusing and accepting, it was impossible to say.

Close by the prince, who did not notice it, came the voice of Alphonse Nodier, speaking low but in tones strangely cold and resolute:

"Teresella dear, it's high time *you* did something: *Allons, vite!* In the studio is the box with the holes, the one the child arrived in from Cologne, and lived in for a long time by the fire at Jib-Sail House. Dust it off and bring it here. We'll put him back in it, he can't move about the house any more, he's lost the use of his legs. Besides, his whole appearance is unseemly."

A leaden silence, albeit distracted and inattentive, met this unfortunate exhortation.

"On the contrary, it is very angelic and worthy of God!" rang out the clear voice of Elmina an instant later. "Such as yours is certainly not, Monsieur Alphonse – nor is your Paradise. You have chosen to store up treasures on earth, and on such treasures you will live, as long as time protects you. But that is not long, you know. I commend you to Teresella . . . and to the Linnet I commend your friend. And now let us go, my darling one."

And with these words murmured to the child, to his head laid on her breast, the widow moved towards the door to the Scalinatella. But before crossing the threshold, while she held Lillot on one arm, like a great gust of wind with her free hand she swept away all the ducats heaped on the table. They flew in all directions, rolling into every corner of that dank cavern, and scattered and glittered like half-moons in every crack in the floor.

"*Your friend!*" This was what Ingmar remembered while the Duke's carriage sped along the road to Caserta – or maybe they were already over the Alps in bosky Austria. This he remembered, but he knew not the time, or even what day it was, or his location. That the carriage he was in belonged to the Duke he realized from its sumptuousness, the splendid blue of the curtains, the smooth rotation of the wheels, the regular and harmonious rhythm of the horses' hooves. After the terrible scene the Duke himself had accompanied him to the carriage, which was in attendance just outside the little garden, promising him that he would follow in another vehicle. He wished him to shed, he had told him, "all his tears". But the good prince had no tears left to shed, and he was alone.

All of them, all of them had vanished: Donna Elmina, the Duke, Sasà, the engaged couple, Ferrantina, the "voices" of Albert's in-laws, Pasqualino, the Notary, and above all the unhappy Porter-Boy. Of the last he still had rapid visionary flashes in the deep blue of the night: on the great Steps, in the young marchese's schoolroom, on the silent Scalinatella . . . and always with his small closed fist raised against him, Ingmar, and a bitter smile on his lips. Or perhaps not a smile, but a rapt and beseeching expression, until he reclined his little head and slept – or was that only the way it seemed?

"*Nein . . . Nein . . . Nein . . .*" and then "*Ja . . . Ja . . . Ja . . .*" in a faint chirrup, as he closed his little eyes.

And Elmina, his beautiful stern sister, where was she now?

Oh, what would he not have given to return to those wondrous days when he and his friends were planning their joyous excursion towards the Sun, to the mysterious and entrancing Mediterranean city; or later, when he was preparing to return to Naples and see the blonde Elmina once again, with all the sweetness and innocence of a youthful heart, youthful even if eternally full of scorn. In those days the little "brother" had not entered his life.

He closed his eyes, and when he reopened them not only had the moon over the woods of Caserta and of Austria, or shining on the windows of Chiaia or of Sant'Antonio . . . not only had the moon vanished, but *so much time* had already passed.

VII

Mutter Helma

The prince's return to Liège and his painful uncertainties
as to the facts about Donna Elmina and her brother.
Little visions in the wintertime. He bestows on his
beloved the title of "Mutter Helma"

I t is the distressing task of the narrator of subterranean tales involving subterranean cities, cruel tales of impassive girls, of desperate Elves, of sentimental Witches and deranged Princes, as well as other Phantoms – though phantoms they are not, but simply poor inhabitants of Europe and of Naples both before and after '93; it is the distressing task of such a narrator to prepare the hypothetical Reader for a gentle let-down together with a tentative hope . . . In what? Hope that the instructive excursion of Bellerophon towards the Sun may be resumed in the secret depths of Being, and that astonishing may be its happiness. But in the meantime such happiness is a long way off, the Linnet lies in wait and weeps in the royal gardens, and the phantoms thrive; postillions, maids and footmen circulate everywhere, with trays laden with coffee and hot chocolate; the waiters spread gossip; the purveyors of gloves and other refinements are rampant; betrothals are settled, marriages are arranged; the bells ring out for weddings in Santa Brigida and Santa Caterina; in short, life glories and frolics. Up and down the great Steps little lanterns move in the night-time . . . Children long crippled suddenly recover; children well-born and pampered, at a witch's touch, suddenly go lame . . . Some live, some die; some pray, some sing and talk wildly of love, in despite of the Linnet (who has his whims and moments of sullen intolerance). Was the prince condemned to pay for these for ever? Will Elmina's embittered brother ever emerge from his perforated box, and will the pitiful Donna Alessandrina, unloved as she builds her castles in the air, never cease to fly? Above all, what is there in Donna Elmina's heart? Who and what inhabits it? Or is it once again a gloomy cavern?

Where now, pray, is the silent Reader hidden in the heart of these noisy modern times? The patient Reader lacking Common Sense (the deadly Sixth Sense!) and provided instead with his private antenna to pick up the glacial "silence" of the Universe, the squabbles of the children of the subterranean world, the spittle, the tears, the *nein . . . nein . . . nein . . .* of their entreaties?

To such a Reader – there he is, that rare sweet-tempered gentleman – we commend ourselves: that he may excuse all, understand all, attenuate a little, touch up a fair amount, and add, if need be, a little salt to the cauldron of tears. And above all that he should benevolently tolerate, and eventually pardon, the frivolousness and the shortcomings of the narrator of this story, now nearing its end, and the omission of those Fashionable Sins which are so fundamental to a novel.

The prince, then, returned to his homeland, still in the Duke's carriage, which changed horses and postillion at every staging-place; and all these postillions wore blue waistcoats, pink hose, and Napoleonic hats covered with badges and fringes, a thing that not a little disturbed our enrapt de Neville ("Il Pensieroso" perhaps we should call him). Thereafter, one December evening, having entered the darkened gates of Liège, he had himself conveyed to his palace in the majestic Rue Saint-Gilles (or *de la Cathédral*) where, contrary to what one would have expected, knowing his eccentric and vindictive nature, with no fuss or complaint whatever he resumed exactly the same life as he had led before the death of Geraldine, and his wild (and disenchanted) last journey to Naples.

A diplomat never really retires, therefore he continued to busy himself not only with friends but with friendly States. It was only that his attitude towards the last few decades of European history had changed. It was no longer worldly and derisory, but learned and slightly pedantic, oddly critical, and therefore more demanding and even severe.

Of anyone who sang the praises of Progress – already famous though still in its infancy – and curiously enough even of certain States which were lauded as conservative but highly beneficial and friendly to humanity, he made a point of saying:

"Yes, very well . . . But has that man (or that State or Nation) ever risen right early in the morning? Has he heard the absolute silence of the world, the imperial gladness of dawn? Has he been touched, but a moment later, by the cry of the mother bird whose young have been stolen, or of the chicks whose mother has been wrested from them? I am speaking of the potentates of the earth, gentlemen – democratic or otherwise, worthy sovereigns or wicked dictators – and their certainty that they are 'the First', that they have a right to dispose at will of the woodlands and the children of the woodlands. Has he – this gentleman of the dawn – ever realized his iniquitous vanity, the infinite cruelty which induces him to do as he pleases with the little ones of the earth? How in that case can he ignore, or even deride, the justicer, the Linnet? Up there in the skies ever brighter and purer burns the star of the great Morning. Oh, harken gentlemen all, and honour the voice of the great Morning. Only after that concern yourselves with States and Nations."

Naturally even he, if questioned about his devotion to the Linnet, would not have been able to answer without erring on the side of presumptuousness, or coming out with a lot of nonsense. Nor would he have been able to make any coherent appeal to Rousseau, Voltaire or other eminent Masters of Change, since their thought had not brought about real Change (they held it was enough to understand the order of the stars). And he realized that what was lacking in both the old and the new ways of the world was precisely this: respect for the dawn and the weeping of the Linnet, and his command to remain faithful – like the children of the woods and their sisters – to that which is Nothing, or Little, to have pity for Nothingness, compassion for those cast out and abandoned, and supreme regard for every Hieronymus Käppchen and his hen's feather.

He also attempted to write his *Mémoires*, in three volumes as was then the practice; but he was always halted by a fear of being presumptuous, and thereby forgetting "little Elmina's" injunction of silence. Not to mention the fact that in support of what he wrote he could find not so much as a date, or the least indication that what he remembered, or had seen, was the truth rather than a dream; and this, together with the long silence from Naples, from his friends of that beloved Olympus, as if they had withdrawn into nothingness, or never emerged from it, or never even existed, inwardly terrified him.

Then, little by little, as if a strike in the Post Office of the Universe (or of the Devil) had suddenly ceased, news began to arrive, and it *seemed* true enough, intermingled as it was with political and military events in the ex-Kingdom (events of that kind always enjoy great credibility) such as the flight of the Bourbons, the entry of the General, the festivities, the condemnations, the illuminations (in honour of the new Kings of France), and at the same time the beginning of the grave and notorious outbreak of Brigandage, which still forms a rather tedious appendix to the history of the Liberation of Southern Italy.

Poor prince, and poor Naples – the Naples of the Linnet! In vain, as his woe and anxiety grew (all one with the absence of the fateful Bird), our nobleman tried to obtain some certain facts regarding "little Elmina" and the rest of them: the good Glover, Donna Helm, the luckless Elf, Sasà, quite apart from Nodier himself, and the Scribblerus, and the places where they had lived. Such news, however heartening and believable on first arrival, after a while always began to appear somewhat wan and listless, as if it had been invented, the product solely of the prince's grief-stricken mind.

However, here are the principal items, which arrived some years after the diplomat's precipitous departure, so we are therefore in the second happy period of *la Liberté*. We give them in the order (or even disorder) of their arrival, making every effort to accept them as genuine.

Teresella and Nodier had indeed got married, and according to the writer (Notary Liborio) their first thought had been to set up a dowry for Sasà that would enable her, when she reached the age appropriate to that dismal ceremony, to be joined in marriage to the son of Donna Carlina Watteau. It was mentioned, by the way, that Sasà had never entirely given up flying when she was on her own (almost as if company was prejudicial to her volatility), but had become a sensible girl who behaved well towards those beneath her station, and also those outside the clan. The prince, it was also said, would always retain the passionate devotion of Paummella.

Donna Elmina, as was clear from a letter, colourless and half-hearted we have to say, from the Duke – and who could have recognized in him the cheerful, mischievous necromancer, the prince of all the guesses and gossip of Naples? –, Donna Elmina had *not* married the Scribblerus, as certain malicious tongues had foretold she would; nor had Madame Pecquod (much declined since the flight of the Royal Family from Naples) replaced her among the Notary's emotional disappointments. The first Signora Civile (a title to which she had full rights, as emerged later from documents attached to her Will) remained at the Little House with the same duties as ever, a sure sign that no one, either living or dead, had made any scoundrelly claims to those poor walls, nor had grown-ups or children pestered her, and her complaints that day had been a farce – malicious like Ferrantina herself – within the general farce which the prince had witnessed with such horror. No, the house was still very peacefully administered by the Glover's former wife, who was very pleased and proud of the marvellous changes wrought by Alphonse (who was now dubbed "the French merchant", or even "the Frenchman from Liège").

Teresella, then, was happy.

As for the widow Dupré (the title of *Madame* was not bestowed on her), she had at first moved to Donna Violante's, but had later left the palace of her protectress and established her abode with some nuns at Santa Caterina in Chiaia, where she had stolidly continued to work as a seamstress. Thus she earned her living. In looks she appeared just as ever, roseate and tranquil, "a sign that she cared nothing about anyone": a note that caused the prince a shudder. But later on from another source, the Mother Superior of the sisters of "Santa Maria of the Linnet" (and the prince shuddered a second time), probably at the instigation of the Duke with the intention of reassuring him, he learnt that "a widow Dupré was indeed our guest in October 1806, but thereafter she accepted a proposal from a convent in Casoria, which required a trustworthy woman, healthy and hard-working, to look after a gentlewoman in Caserta, the widow of one of Ferdinand's generals."

This certainly meant that Donna Elmina was still esteemed and in demand for her qualities, and above all that she was alive: a fact that very soon, however, was no longer sufficient to satisfy her poor admirer.

From another letter of the Duke's (he had applied to him once again, not daring – he knew not why – to write about these matters to the Mother Superior) the prince obtained, it must be said, a few confirmations, but expressed so casually! As if Donna Elmina was, in reality, no longer cherished by anyone – or worse, not even remembered by anyone.

He therefore dared not take his suppositions any further (especially if he was awake at night with his thoughts), such grievous uncertainties assailed his mind and spirit in those hours which are called "the small hours" but on the contrary – for the sick, or for those who are remembering or waiting – are interminable.

Nor of Hieronymus Käppchen (whom the Reader may have forgotten) is there much to be said, in the sense that any reliable or reassuring news arrived. On the contrary, what did arrive was all ridiculous and foolish, much as the poor creature with the feather had been in life, and as he had appeared to our nobleman from Liège. Snippets of news so pointless that they could only be compared to the continuous chatter of children at play, breaking off the game every so often to say something scary or to laugh at someone. Once (from a vague note from Teresella in the margin of a brief letter from Nodier) it appeared that, cured of the wound inflicted by the loss of his feather, and having remained for a long time, as if dead, in the perforated box, entrusted entirely to the tender care of his sister, who supplied him with saucers of milk and crumbs of bread, he had suddenly recovered and run away from the house. But such a recovery, happening to an elf . . . well, who is to say if it really happened? Unless it was simply an escape, but where on earth to? Even his box had disappeared from the studio, and this had authorized the writer of a subsequent letter (once more, on this occasion, the solicitous Notary Liborio) to hypothesize that the child – an addlepate if ever there was one – had taken it with him when he fled "so as to sleep more comfortably."

The hen's feather, on the other hand, was found on the floor, in his overturned dish, by Donna Alessandrina, who attempted a short flight with it. Her mother, who was present, icily removed it from her hand, and at once sewed it up in a red woollen hood, which she now carried about with her wherever she went. (This came in a very droll but none the less respectful note from Teresella, to whom the Notary had shown his letter.)

Not very cheerful news, and above all very conflicting, as may be seen. From this the prince deduced, or (in view of his long-time rancour) wished to deduce, that poor Käppchen was really dead, his three hundred years of life having expired (a term which then held good for the rise and decline even of great States, such as France and Spain, and today one could cite others again), and that not having succeeded in getting himself adopted, if this had been his intention and not his sister's, by a legally married couple, his life had come to an end. By the simple expiry of the time limit, as happens to everyone; but, given the total innocence of Käppchen and the desperate love of his sister, it was something not a little hard to accept.

A further hypothesis afflicted the prince, regarding the most recent letter (again from the carefree and unsentimental Nodier), namely that the little creature was not really dead, but had been taken somewhere and "lost", like unwanted kittens or even sick people – a practice current among the ignorant and none too merciful poor families of Naples. And Nodier, who said he was "joking", had become completely Neapolitan, though combining this peculiarity with his cool French *raison*.

The prince, therefore, amid questionable impulses and the slow dawning of awareness in his heart (alas, only his heart was aware at all), gave himself no rest. Little by little, with absurd investigations and incalculable loss of precious time which should have been spent seeking for a solution, he had, he felt, contributed to the ruin of both Hieronymus and Elmina. Of the two of them he did not know which was the dearer to him (as at the outset of this story he did not distinguish between his love, respectively, for Albert and for Elmina), but he would have given his life to have them with him now. He furthermore understood that he had for ten years offended Elmina with all that money of his, and his pointless jealousy, when all she wanted was to save H. Käppchen. He realized that ever since girlhood she had forgone all possessions, and on that now distant morning even the ownership of the Little House, and lastly his own good graces, purely and simply to soften the heart of the Linnet, who wanted her to be stripped of everything, and desolate, if she was to save the Elf. But the Linnet had had no mercy.

He recalled Elmina's words, that even after their frugal supper at the Little House: "In my heart there is but a single name". Now he understood. That name was his, Ingmar's, but there was nothing to be done about it. To save Käppchen the Linnet had fixed a price: Elmina's youth and her eternal silence about her secret. If she paid that price she would be "rewarded". So he said: but he had not kept his promise.

He had collected the prize but not kept the promise . . . (Or maybe it was not in his power?). Oh, villainous Linnet!

And yet, though cursing him at times, by dint of silences and tears Ingmar had gradually crept into a sort of rueful familiarity with the Linnet, and often – sometimes in the morning, sometimes in the long winter evenings – he even used to pray to him:

"O Linnet, forget not Elmina and Käppchen. O Linnet, sacred Bird, be mindful, if thou may'st, of all poor Elves and their voiceless sisters. Deliver them from evil. Protect them, Angel or Demon as thou beest, noble Linnet, while the Sun suffuses the whole sky with joy and when the night draws nigh. And if thou may'st, lead them, O Linnet, to me."

And once, one wintry dusk, as snow was beginning to fall on a fashionable street in Liège, he saw, or thought he saw, the little "invalid" pass him by, still dressed in rags and laden with packages, like that mild November morning on the Scalinatella. His feather was again intact and in its place. Behind him, gilded, swaying from side to side, followed the glittering glass sedan-chair borne by four Hieronymuses – noble Elves, that is to say – clad in blue and gold. And all these little creatures, as they passed in front of him (the prince, with bloodless face, was standing beneath the portico of a church), looked at him with eyes both mute and imploring, or even severe.

Ardently the prince cried out:

"Hieronymus! My child! Do not leave me alone!"

But H. Käppchen, far from stopping, made a mad dash ahead, leaving – dark in the snow – the tiny imprints of a bird's feet. However, the glass sedan did halt for a moment, and the little Elmina, beneath her rosy lowered eyelids, wore a sweet smile . . . For Ingmar, a sweet smile!

He was beside himself with joy and always waited, in pale immutable youthfulness – the gift of the Linnet – for the prodigy to be repeated.

From that moment on he went searching for little Hieronymuses, and whenever he found them he took them home with him. He realized that the gardens of Liège, and those of other cities and even capitals, were full of them. They would sit with their knees drawn up and their little faces resting on them, while the snow fell on them. They would chew on a morsel of bread or, when they woke, would lap at a saucer of milk that some noblewoman had filled for them. But they were always listless, absent, deep in their own thoughts. They were waiting for someone, it was certain, and the prince knew that person's name: it was the "little Elmina"! *Mutter Helma!* he added gravely.

*Surprising (and slanderous) revelations by the
Scribblerus concerning the flight to Cologne of
H.K. and his sister, and their incredible degradation.
The prince yet again decides to save them. A further
letter from Naples and the testimony of a banker*

The prince now had new friends, including several merry young
fellows such as Albert had been (thus Ingmar forced himself to
keep his thoughts in check), whom he welcomed with all his former
tenderness. At a certain point he received a letter from Notary Liborio –
long-suffering Reader, do you still remember our Scribblerus?

He was enigmatical, as ever. After giving reassuring news, indeed
magnificent (as it seemed at first), about everyone in the Sant'Antonio
neighbourhood, and at the Little House itself, and having lauded the
"sweet content" of that family, he unexpectedly contradicted himself and
admitted that the Little House had been put up for sale, and was perhaps
already sold, by Nodier, who found it too gloomy (and besides, the roof
was collapsing). All the sculptures had been cleared out and lost, not one
of them sold, *"such is the fate of the artists of la Joie!"* (*sic*).

Thereafter he went on to allude, we must say without much nicety
towards the distant recipient, to the artist's widow. The old Marchesa
Violante assured him that, after many peregrinations from one convent to
another around Caserta, she had departed for her native city of Cologne.
Apparently she had accepted the offer of a second cousin of Baroness
Helm; but this – there was reason to suspect, and he had recently received
confirmation to this effect – was because she was still in search of that
infamous brother of hers, whose story (of the mortal danger he was
running) had been invented lock, stock and barrel by some scoundrel
and supported by his fanatical sister in order to obtain favours and
compassion which in reality he did not deserve. (I hope the Reader does
not take umbrage at the intrusion of everyday events into the legend: in
this world the substitution of one thing for another, the superimposition
of one supposed fact over another, is a continuous and perhaps endless

313

process.) It was with real malice, since he well knew the prince's touchiness on the subject of those two, that the Scribblerus concluded that "good blood will tell", and "if you're born a chicken you have to peck around"; and in short that Donna Alessandrina had had good reason for persecuting the Porter-Boy. But at present (this was the Great Surprise, and the information seemed not only well-founded but as certain as could be) H. Käppchen was in prison in Cologne, and his sister was washing dishes in the kitchens of a magistrate, in the desperate hope of obtaining a pardon for her wretched brother through the good offices of the magistrate's wife, a compassionate woman, pleading as extenuating circumstances the fact that he was born outside the Holy Roman Church.

To such straits Donna Elmina Dupré appeared to be reduced, and in such a manner ended her proud and resplendent youth.

At this the prince was on the point of setting forth again, although the first white hairs had begun to silver his impetuous brow; and this time for neighbouring Germany. He was determined to remain there until they were rescued, and it mattered nothing that both of them had so basely deceived him.

One windy evening in March, therefore, he was in his study, with the carriage already waiting in the courtyard, the horses pawing the moonlit snow, and was intent on finishing, before his departure, a number of letters containing last instructions to his two secretaries, when his personal valet – a certain Rudolph, with an elfin face – brought him a sealed letter on a silver salver. It came from Naples, from the hand of an official of the English Bank whom de Neville had known for years and esteemed personally. This was a certain William Heart (the name was already an augury of sensibility), and his letter enclosed another, this time from the Scribblerus, which the banker presented in the following terms:

To His Highness the Most Worthy Prince de Neville, Liège.

From Naples, February 3rd 1809

Most Worthy Monsieur de Neville,

It is my sad task to forward to you a letter from a friend and admirer of yours, and I cherish the hope that he is not forgotten by you, namely Notary Liborio Apparente, who left us a few days ago, and to be precise last Sunday. The local newspaper, from which I enclose a cutting bearing the news, will confirm this melancholy announcement.

Notary Liborio, a very worthy person, universally esteemed and whose friend I am honoured to have been, had been ill for some time, though I did not know it, for he kept the fact jealously, concealed, as if his disease were the occasion for deep shame. On January 31st he sent word for me to come to his modest dwelling, having a very delicate matter to confide to me. He was being nursed by his wife Elvira, a woman as depressing as she is prematurely aged, and whose very existence he had never disclosed. As soon as the poor woman had left the room, speaking in the ghost of a voice he passed me the letter which I here enclose. He entreated me to read it, and so I did. I express no judgements, forbidden by every rule of respect for the secret entrusted to me. He begged me to forward it to you as soon as he had reached "*that heaven which undoubtedly exists, and where in gladness reigns the Linnet* (his very words), *the Father of orphans and even of the little souls from the lower regions, like poor agèd Käppchen, who wander bewildered over the face of the earth.*" Who the latter is I do not know, but, as I have mentioned, for two years the Notary had been seriously ill, walking the streets day and night, not infrequently pelted with stones by the street-urchins, in search of someone of this name (I imagine a debtor of his).

Here, then, is the letter. Hoping this finds you in good health, please rest assured that for any arrangement, confirmation, or anything else in which I may be of assistance, you may write to me at the English Bank, in Naples.

Yours faithfully,
William Heart

The prince did not open the Notary's letter at once. His hands were shaking, as indeed was his whole body. He was forced to wait until the trembling ceased. But when he did open it, this was the text he read:

Noble lord, Prince Ingmar de Neville!

My span of life is running out and I am at a loss for the words that might enable me to write at greater length. I have, simply, to beg your forgiveness. For many things, but chiefly for my last letter. The truth is that I had received no more news of Donna Elmina, and of the unfortunate child whom she protected, since the time when the modest house at Sant'Antonio was sold, and the money appropriated by Teresina and her husband. I am speaking of the year 1807. Ferrantina was taken into a charitable institution. Donna Elmina – who had not uttered a word since Monsieur Nodier's decision to take the "boy" out, along with the cardboard box from which he had refused to emerge (the holes enabled him to breathe), intending I presume to abandon him in the countryside –, Donna Elmina never left the house, and above all the studio, on account of the threat under which the invalid lived: that they would secretly take him away. Ever since their wedding day the young couple had changed completely in their attitude towards Elmina. They had become overbearing and insensitive, saying that the boy "infected the house". The boy did not have any infectious diseases, but the truth is that he was old, and more than ever indifferent to everything. Except to his sister, who filled up his saucer with milk. He was very small indeed and his hen's feather (you will remember), at one time affixed to his forehead like a trophy and now lying on his chest, never left him for a moment. When no one was looking little Sasà would put her mouth to one of the holes in the box and poke fun at him. Ah, Monsieur de Neville, there are many reasons for accusing all Christianity of iniquity – or even the whole human race. She is not good, as are the trees and other creatures of nature, because she is not God's work, nor do we know where her origins lie. What unconcern, and often what gleefulness, at the sufferings of others! This was not a characteristic of our Hieronymus, let alone of his beautiful sister, still loved by all (with the exception of her brother-in-law and her daughter!).

In short, all my information, often so optimistic, was yet another falsehood. Intended to help both myself and you, dear prince, but maybe also the result of that sense of challenge with regard to you, which was always an element in our relationship. (It is no secret that I was envious of you.) Therefore, if you can, forgive a wretched man, as you forgave Don Mariano that day in the cemetery at Naples, when he owned up to Donna Elmina's financial predicament.

The truth is that I have had no news of those poor creatures for a long time (if you have received such from other sources, consider how unconvincing it is, before lending it credit); nor have I any reason to expect that it would be good news, if not that they, as I dare hope, no longer belong to this hellish abode we call the world (simply because we have no other word to signify a place so obscure and drear).

Madame Dupré left home (I find no better way of putting it) suddenly one morning in March, and in what condition no one could know better than I do: the life of Don Mariano's daughter had all of a sudden become something beyond endurance.

A full retraction by the Scribblerus.
Light shed on the last days of Little Hieronymus and
the faithful Elmina. Concerning a night in March
and a certain brigand Luigi del Re

The prince broke off his reading for a moment. His hope was that he was asleep, as on that day at Sant'Antonio, and that someone would wake him up. But the silence in the house, and all over Liège, was like a mountain of snow and of dreams, of a total stillness.

Then he resumed his perusal of the letter from one who, though dead, had sent him a last fiery dart from the enchanted Olympus:

> It was one night early in May (the letter continued) and I, my lord, had gone up to the Little House with the intention of asking Donna Elmina to entrust me with the box containing her brother. My wife was agreeable to the plan. We would place it by the kitchen fire until the boy recovered (the doctor assured us that there was some hope of this).
>
> Well then, I had entered the garden silently, and in the stillness of the night I could clearly hear the voices of Monsieur Nodier and Teresella, speaking in the kitchen. That of Donna Elmina, barely more than a whisper, I could only guess at, but the others were forceful and resolute, and for me, my dear sir, unforgettable. This is what I heard:
>
> *Nodier* That box must disappear from the studio, my dear sister-in-law.
> *Teresella* It stinks, you never clean it out.
> *Donna Elmina* You know that my brother cannot leave his bed yet. His legs have gone to sleep.
> *Nodier* All the more reason to remove him. In the country he'll get better, take my word for it.
> *Teresella* The air is better there.

Donna Elmina It's good here too. I beg you for the love of God, don't touch him.

Nodier (conciliatory) Very well, we won't touch him. But you know that even the Police are looking for him.

Donna Elmina He has done no harm.

Nodier Anyone who does no work and earns no money does harm. He is a burden on humanity.

Teresella My husband is right.

Donna Elmina I only ask you for a single day, then I will take him to Donna Violante. We'll go together. Until now her grandson has been there, and was against it. Now he's going on holiday for a while.

(Silence, then after a pause the voice of Nodier, once more conciliatory):

Nodier Have your way for this evening, but not a day longer. And I hope you don't forget it.

Donna Elmina's was the ghost of a voice, a mere whisper. Ah, dear prince, it was unbearable to see that beautiful queen of compassion brought so low.

I withdrew towards the garden gate, and saw the moon rising over the darkness of Posillipo, amidst white clouds in the deep blue sky of Naples, and also that my weeping be not heard. Donna Elmina must have joined her "brother" in the studio, where she always kept watch at night, because shortly thereafter (I don't quite know how) I heard, cold and clear, the voices of the two spouses (so low does God bring those who submit to the marriage contract, and therefore the Linnet cries out whenever two spouses arrive in a freshly whitewashed house). Their tones were quiet and neutral, but expressed something else as well. The merchant was reproaching his wife:

Nodier I told you we had to play this thing craftily. She will never leave *him*. Where her brother is concerned she is always ready to spout tears.

Teresella It grieves me to the heart to see my sister brought so low. Our father would be in anguish.

Nodier He was neither your father nor hers, but a poor old ignoramus. He believed in angels and devils.

Teresella Perhaps there are such things.

Nodier Now stir yourself, my girl. As soon as your sister is asleep on the floor, go into the studio, take the box and run out into the garden. I'll be waiting for you there.

Teresella Dear Alphonse, I hope God will pardon us.

Nodier (laughing) No doubt about it (if he exists).

On hearing this dialogue I was at a loss what to do. I thought of them simply as two heinous criminals. Oh, what I would have given, my lord, for you to be there!

I cannot tell you the terror I felt. Grief also – but terror was uppermost. To go for help, that was the only course. I remembered that in the vicinity of the Little House was a small hut, where sometimes a light glimmered dimly. It was said to be lived in, and I always thought it must be inhabited by some soul in Purgatory.

I approached it, trembling like a leaf (I'm not ashamed of it, for God made me that way) and in a small voice I asked for help. Someone emerged, a horrible shadow, but almost at once I realized who it was. It was no soul in Purgatory but the brigand Luigi del Re (nicknamed "the Madman"), in hiding for the last two years because he was a Bourbonist. When he saw me he took pity on me, asked me in and gave me some wine . . . I drank and wept and told him all. All about myself and those two scoundrels. Don Luigi, who had a sentence of death hanging over his head, was greatly astonished and frightened. He said that he would help me in the dead of night. He was also drinking and, both of us drunk with wine and fear, we fell asleep under the table.

When we woke it was dawn, but the moon of its mercy still shone above the iniquities of Naples. I then espied two dim figures making off with a bundle along the road which runs beside the Scalinatella. I say *I* espied them because it took but a glimpse for the Brigand to hide his face in his hands. He turned back, trembling, but I was able to go forward. Seeing a dim light burning on the ground floor of the house I persuaded myself that Donna Elmina was awake, and that therefore nothing had happened. Moreover what I had seen was a bundle, not a box. I thought the two figures must have been just common thieves.

But at that moment a faint glimmer appeared in the studio.

I crept nearer, making myself as small as possible, and peered in. What I saw was Donna Elmina standing, very pale and still and staring at the perforated box lying open on the floor.

I thought she must have taken the child in her arms (she had her back to me, so I could not see). But instead she was staring at the box. Suddenly she stooped, still without a word, and emptied it of a little straw. Then she started pacing back and forth in terrible anguish, and finally she emitted the cry of a homing dove that finds a ransacked nest. Time and again she cried out, in bafflement and desperation – or was it sheer horror?

"Gerontuccio! Gerontuccio!"

And then again: "My Gerontuccio! Ah, they have stolen my child!"

This voice seemed that of another woman whom neither you nor I, dear prince, had ever known, the voice of our own poor human race itself, when they rob and oppress and ravage its little ones, its dearest liberties, the last shadowy affections hiding in the den of the heart. Which is the normal occupation of all the potentates of the earth, even when disguised as teachers or as liberators.

In my cowardice I had now myself contributed to the endless desperation of the little ones of the world – and of all history.

Once more the prince felt his breath come short for the woe of it.

Because I ran away (continued the letter), foul swine that I was, when called upon to act instead of seeking help from a wretched Brigand, and because of that cry of *Gerontuccio!* which I bear for ever in my heart – no word of censure but a calm stupefaction which I cannot express, as if that poor woman were suffering death, which we must all suffer, but with some aid, which was denied to her –, because of all this I fled away again and subsequently, my lord, I invented things that were not true, and indeed, when matched against *that* truth which was known to me, were to the last degree iniquitous.

I was later told (by that same Brigand) that she for a long time went about searching for where they had taken him, until the day she found the feather, very much dilapidated, underneath a stone; and from that moment Donna Elmina lost her power of speech.

It appears that the spouses afterwards gave an explanation: that they had found the little creature dead in the box, and had wished to spare Elmina the shock of it. They had therefore replaced the old box with a new one full of straw (the one which I had seen), hoping that at first she did not notice the difference: this because they "were so sorry for her". It may be true, but the conversation I had heard argued against their good faith.

In any case, Elmina Dupré vanished without so much as a cry or a tear, as self-possessed and patient as ever. Until all trace of her was lost.

I was the last to search for Hieronymus Käppchen, being unable to believe in his death, until one night last year, perhaps in early May, I had a dream about him. He had recovered, and was a healthy little boy now – but bundled up in his sad rags as ever, his ears just a little bigger than normal, and *pointed* – and with his finger to his lips he signalled to me to keep silent. He was looking at a girl who had her back turned, and this was Donna Elmina. He gave her his little hand (and with what expectation in his eyes!), and they went off together into the distance.

Then I understood.

Ah, there in my dream the whole landscape was aburst with flowers!

But here in real life it will flower nevermore!

I would be unable to tell you more, Monsieur de Neville, even if I wished to, for my memory is weary unto death. I ask you to believe that I remain

　　　　　Your devoted servant
　　　　　Notary Liborio Apparente

Desolation in the palace at Liège. "Take them back to the stables, for ever!" cried the prince. His Highness receives a visit from one Monsieur Linnet, of Naples

The prince sat for a while, gazing at the woeful page, as if he too had been drained of memory.

Then, as he laid it on the table, he saw another, smaller sheet of paper which had escaped his notice. It contained but a few lines. Knowing of the late Notary's weakness for composing verses (always for births, marriages, funerals, for private or commemorative occasions), he did not smile or even feel the least curiosity. But the title struck him, and he realized that also the poor Notary had loved Elmina, and albeit far gone in drink he had fled while the going was good, thereby sullying his conscience with so-called failure to offer assistance (which may have been the reason for his death). So the prince read that insignificant little piece with some respect, while the tears flowed down his pallid cheeks. We set it down without comment, at the conclusion of this (so far) unpleasant business:

Title: *Donna Elmina's farewell to her golden city*

O city of my sorrow,
O city of my treasure,
My kidling with blue eyes so mild
I am sad, my child,
As you see.
Sweet Jesus succour me!

(signed: Don Liborio Apparente of Naples, Approved Poet).

Thus, with this narrative of the Scribblerus (now deceased) ended the strange tale of the excursion of Bellerophon and his friends to Naples, of the secret of Donna Elmina, of so many daydreams, passions and

323

pardons, and interventions of the Linnet, in a Naples besieged by the Sirens and the French.

As for Ingmar . . . to think he had believed so many liars in the heaven and hell of Naples, so many citizens of the dark depths of the soul. Only the Linnet was true, and the grief of one German orphan and her loyalty towards H. Käppchen.

He fell to thinking . . . he was carried away. A pen lay before him on the table, a massive pen of finely chased gold. He seized it, and on a sheet of bluish onionskin – we recall that he too had nursed poetic ambitions, so we must forgive him – he dashed down these lines:

Title: *Ingmar looks at Donna Elmina's city*

Green wall, white moon,
In the water weary weary.
That little pebble
Is my village,
How long the voyage
That is past.
The moon in the water moves
Towards the rim
Of the well.
Where I am I remain.
How peaceful is the moon . . . that passed.

No sooner had he laid down his pen than the butler appeared in the study doorway.

"Your Highness, the horses are waiting."

"Take them back to the stables, for ever!" cried the prince.

The astonished butler vanished. The prince, his head upon the table, wept.

A moment later the door reopened.

"A Monsieur Linnet, from Naples, is asking to be received by Your Highness."

"Show him in!" cried the prince once more, seized by an icy, wondrous chill.

The familiar refrain arose that instant from the garden illumined by the rising moon, and resounded far and wide:

O-hoh! O-hoh! O-hoh!

and then:

Ohhh! Ohhh! Ohhh!

Nothing more gentle, nothing more gladsome. And the prince blessed the moon that gleamed on the walls and that superhuman voice that, passing above his head, had made his darkened life so dear to him. He blessed the Linnet even now arriving, who at last would explain it all. Folly, sorrow, separation, and this joy that he was bringing with him now: utterly calm, and cold, and infinite.